Also by Kevin Knuckey
Hell's Mouth (Grosvenor House Publishing Ltd.) 2022

Expected 2024
The Vale

Praise for 'Hell's Mouth'

'An atmospheric and intriguing psychological thriller. Knuckey is an expert at describing the Cornish landscape and weather in its familiar melancholic state.'

'Gnarly, dark, butt-clenching and funny. The author has a fantastic way of describing our very dramatic and quite often moody vista's which all tied in well with the central characters. This is a very dark, twisted, and sometimes pretty damn naughty debut novel that made me cringe and laugh out loud at the same time!'

'A fantastic read, highly recommend this book.'

'Excellently written, enthralling read, packed with a twisted punch. Mind bending read into the mind of a teenager.'

'Intriguing and imaginative. Couldn't foresee how the story would end, or the many twists & turns along the way. Thoroughly enjoyable book.'

Devil's Arch

Devil's Arch

KEVIN KNUCKEY

Copyright

All rights reserved
Copyright © Kevin Knuckey, 2023

The book cover is copyright to Kevin Knuckey

ISBN: 9798863185279

To Nanny Biddy

Your grizzly tales of Devil's Arch always thrilled me and chilled me; and now they've inspired me to write one of my own. So, Nanny, this one's for you. I miss your storytelling, though not half as much as I miss your smile, or often that impeccably executed stare over the tops of your glasses. But alas, at the risk of you sending buckets of water cascading upon me from the heavens…

'Up yours, Nan.'
x

ONE

NEW YEAR'S DAY - 2000

They sat soundlessly for a fleeting moment, just the two of them: the speechless, and the scheming. Surveying the scene revealed to them by the illuminated headlights, their contrasting expressions remained equally indiscernible in the shadowy interior. Tendrils of ivy crawled down sheer embankments to either side teasing at the windows, the writhing arms of a kraken closing in, clawing, probing, examining the metal vessel for any signs of weakness. Mere metres ahead, the archway's stone face gave off a preternatural, jaundice glow in the dipped beam, causing the structure to appear sick with disease. Slimy globules of condensation twinkled on its jagged underbelly as they caught in the breeze, shivering feebly before plummeting into the ground mist as their swelling became too great to maintain purchase.

Tamsyn turned her head towards the driver, unimpressed. '*Really*?'

'Really!' the man next to her exclaimed. Darkness concealed the childlike grin from her eyes more effectively than it did from her ears.

It had been a good evening so far. A successful evening. The initial nerves Tamsyn had felt at the prospect of meeting Austin's parents for the first time had evaporated inside the first ten minutes, when quickly she realised the genuine warmth in their endearing personalities. She'd guessed that the couple's enthusiasm may have had something to do with how somehow, at the age of twenty-four, their son had never previously introduced a single girlfriend to them. This was a novelty, and that seemed to help Tamsyn feel a most welcome newcomer – if not a carnival tent specimen, curled up pickled in a jar, with two heads, and six digits on each hand.

But now, here, stationary with the engine purring contentedly…

'Are you going to move, or just sit there grinning?'

'Devil's Arch!' Austin stated, a schoolboy satisfaction in his giddy tone.

'I know what it is,' Tamsyn sighed. 'What I *don't* know, is why we're just sat here.'

Austin spoke in an exaggerated whisper. 'If you know what it is, then you'll know not to talk when we go under.'

'That's a new one on me,' Tamsyn argued. 'You have to hold your breath under there, or the Devil will possess your soul and drag you to Hell. I haven't heard anything about not *talking*.'

'Nah, man,' said Austin, 'if you talk, the highwayman's noose will drop over the bridge and hang you on your way out.' He spoke as if this legend could only be fact. 'Better go with my version, anyway. You won't be able to hold your breath with what I've got planned.'

He gave her leg a double tap, released the handbrake, and started to roll the car slowly forward.

'Wait!' she said.

The brakes gave a lazy squeak as the car came to another stop, the sound enhanced as the front wheels entered the mouth of the low bridge.

'What have you got planned?' Tamsyn was smiling herself now, albeit anxiously.

'We haven't shagged all year,' Austin said, aiming and failing to convey seriousness.

'It's New Year's Day,' Tamsyn chuckled.

'P.M!' he countered. 'Anyway, the first time we *do it* this year… will be under that bridge.'

'Well, that's not happening.'

'We'll see.' Austin reached for the handbrake again.

'This is ridiculous. What if someone turns up?'

Austin contemplated the possibility. 'I'll turn the interior light on. They can watch.'

Tamsyn laughed aloud. 'I'm being serious.'

'Look,' Austin let go of the brake and clutched her leg. 'Nobody's out tonight. The whole world was out getting hammered last night.'

'We're out tonight!'

'Okay,' he conceded. 'No one will venture along this godforsaken rat run tonight.'

This was met with a strained huff. Tamsyn knew that Austin could spend hours arguing his point once his mind was set. Best just to let him edge the car forward and hope he realised it was a bad idea before he got too caried away.

'At least close your window before we go in,' Tamsyn pleaded. 'I can smell the damp from here. It's like rotting cabbages.'

'Sorry, I farted.'

'Even you couldn't create that stench,' she sniggered.

'Right you are.' Austin flicked the switch up and smoky glass filled the void, sealing with a muffled *shush*.

Releasing the brake, the car rolled under. Looking up and around at the mossy roof and closed in walls produced a dizzying effect at this low speed. Handbrake raised again, he turned the key back. The engine died with a defeated whimper. Seconds later, headlights and sidelights blinked out. The quietness seemed palpable after the reassuring noise of the motor disappeared, leaving the couple stranded. To Tamsyn, the only sounds: breeze flapping against glass and over metal; the gentle ticking of the cooling engine; a chilling *tink, tink, tink* as dewdrops fell to the steel roof above their heads, echoed a foreboding warning.

Great, he is *serious.*

She looked over to the driver's seat. Austin's black features had all but vanished in the gloom, though the digital radio display gave enough illumination to light the whites of his eyes. They trained on her with intent, before flicking a gesture to the back seat.

This was undoubtedly his worst idea since they had met, yet there was an enticing excitement turning circles in the pit of her stomach.

Sod it, Tamsyn thought. *Why the hell not?*

With a total lack of elegance – like *that* mattered; she was about to have her bones jumped in the backseat under some supposedly haunted bridge on a seedy country backroad – she awkwardly clambered over the front seats. Once in the back, Tamsyn cursed herself for not spotting the damning evidence of Austin's intentions sooner; all five rear seats of the MPV were laid flat. Had she really been that apprehensive about meeting his parents that she could miss something so glaringly obvious?

Austin was right behind her as she turned to reprimand him. She opened her mouth to sound a condemnation, but immediately a forefinger was placed firmly to her lips.

No talking, it silently reminded her.

Lowering herself uncomfortably back onto her elbows, Tamsyn giggled like a teenager as Austin scaled the backs of the seats and crawled onto her. As he kissed her mouth his dark hand ran up her pale thigh, drawing up her dress as he searched for the lace of her underwear. Finding his target, he hooked his fingers through the fabric and started to tug down. Butterflies fluttering manically, Tamsyn did not protest, opting instead to raise her bottom from the hard back of the folded-down seat to make the removal mission run smoother.

Whether due to sheer excitement or an undisclosed need to finish before they were spotted, Austin's performance was way below par. Done and dusted in under five minutes.

Tamsyn wanted to ask if that was *really* it. Disappointingly quick for him, and too quick by far for her, leaving her unsatisfied and hungry for seconds. Curse this superstitious nonsense for forcing her silence.

Austin collapsed on top of her, breathing deeply into her smooth auburn hair, seemingly no longer in a hurry.

So, it was the excitement, she mused. *Great, it's taken me this long to figure out he's just one of those weirdos.*

She listened to his exerted breathing, listened to the drops of moisture falling on and around the car. Inhaling the cool air of the interior, something potent hit the back of her nose, trickling like dry ice down her throat. To hell with the devil, or the highwayman, or whatever the fuck it was supposed to be, Tamsyn had to break the silence.

'Austin,' she whispered, 'can you smell that?'

'Shhh,' came his short reply.

'Austin, I'm serious. It smells like petrol.' She tried to pull herself out from under him, but he was having none of it.

'All I can smell is your shampoo, and I love it.'

Tamsyn slapped him on the shoulder.

'Take it easy,' he said. 'It'll just be cos we had the engine running for a bit.'

'It didn't smell of that when we came back here. Now I can practically taste it.'

She lifted her head as much as she could with her shoulders pinned by his weight. A pulsing orange glow emanated from beyond the windscreen. In the split second that Tamsyn's mind comprehended what her eyes were seeing, the orange puffed like a magician's trick. Before she knew it, the previous blackness of Devil's Arch was a blazing inferno.

'*Shit!* Austin, the car's on fire.'

'Yeah, good one.' He lifted his face from the tea tree sanctuary of her hair. '*HOLY FUCK!*' he shouted, turning his head and spotting the ball of fire through the windscreen.

He scrambled to his knees, giving Tamsyn the opportunity to do the same now that she was free from his weight. As she clambered up, flames licked through from below the dashboard, igniting the carpet of both front footwells.

'*GET OUT!*' he roared.

Both grabbing a handle of the rear doors, they shoved hard. Each panicked push was met with a crunch of metal on rock, barely a six-inch opening coming to their rescue, the MPV *way* too snug a fit in the confined tunnel.

Austin shot a glance towards the boot. He had no idea whether it could be opened from inside or not, but the hot orange tentacles waving with fluidity up the rear window ruled that option as a non-starter.

'Stay here,' he breathed heavily, 'I'm gonna have to drive us out.'

Tamsyn looked to the front. The dashboard was now sagging in a demented smile as searing temperatures overcame the plastic moulding. Tiny tongues of amber poked through an array of dripping cavities, writhing like maggots in rotting flesh.

'That's crazy,' she pleaded, a cocktail of saltwater and smoke stinging her eyes.

'It's the only way we don't die in here!'

Austin pulled up his trousers, scrambled over the front seats and plunged into the driver's position.

'*FUCK!*' he bellowed. 'What the hell did I do with the keys?'

Fumbling in his pockets returned nothing. Intense heat coursed up his legs and he looked down to see hungry flames consuming the fibre of his trouser bottoms. With rational thinking still just within his grasp, he remembered that the tight country road ran at a slight decline. Gravity would have to take the reins from here. Reaching for the handbrake, the first contact forced him to withdraw instantly. The lever scorched his soft, fleshy palm, like he had clutched the metal handle of a searing pan.

Tamsyn screamed from the back of the car as she saw his clothes burning. His main priority now to get *her* out of here, Austin grabbed the handbrake once more. Gritting his teeth through the pain, he lifted slightly and thumbed the button. The lever fell. The car began to lurch forward painfully slowly. Too slowly. Simultaneously, both front seats erupted into flame, the driver's seat engulfing Austin's shirt along with it.

With softening tyres squelching along the surface of the road, a deafening bang rang out under the stone arch. Dropping rapidly, the passenger side's front end tipped to the floor as one of the melting rubbers let go.

Aided by the sudden movement of the blast, the MPV picked up the pace, pulling clear from under the bridge.

'*GET OUT,*' Austin shouted to the rear of the vehicle.

'What,' Tamsyn choked out. 'I'm not leaving you.'

'If you don't we'll *both* die.'

Still no movement in the rear of the vehicle.

'*NOW!*'

Tamsyn flung the door open as the car lurched on. The earthy hedges had widened, leaving her escape route to open unimpeded. Throwing herself from the car, she tumbled a few metres on the asphalt, coming to land belly-down. Lifting her face from the dirt, Tamsyn watched as her boyfriend, her *soulmate*, managed to follow a bend, ploughing through the pain in order to get the ticking timebomb as far away from her as possible.

Within seconds, a crumpling crash signalled that any fight left inside Austin had been stubbed out, extinguished. Coming to an abrupt stop the MPV rested its front end against a jagged bank of mud, stone, and exposed roots.

Tamsyn's screams of terror were met with Austin's screams of agony. Flames engulfed the interior. With an almighty boom, the night sky lit an apocalyptic orange as the fuel tank was breached. Dying branches caught in the trees. Tangerine embers swirled in thick clouds of anthracite-coloured smoke. All too soon, screams were silenced: Tamsyn's through state of shock, Austin's evaporating with his last pluming breath.

Unable to move as she watched the world she knew and loved come to an end, the next unearthly sound Tamsyn registered came echoing through the evil, darkened cavern of Devil's Arch like a contumacious summer's day. The sound was laughter.

PART ONE

2014

TWO

SEPTEMBER

Perched on a low wall, Talek watched streams of human traffic, the early September sunshine warm on his shaved back and sides, warmer still through the short mat of tight curls on the top.

He sat alone. Of course he did. Why would this year be any different to the years already passed?

He asked himself the usual questions – questions so repeated they had forced him to become bored of the voice inside his own head.

Was it a skin colour thing? Well, no. Granted, black people were still limited in numbers in this area, but the twins in the year above were dead popular. And then there was Nitesh. Okay, he was of Indian ethnicity, but as far as skin tone goes there wasn't much between them. But like the twins, Nitesh had friends. Yes, there was the odd *P* word slung at him, flowing like raw sewage from foul shit-pipe mouths. But that was used only by idiots who were too stupid to realise that, not only is it the incorrect term to use, but India and Pakistan are two completely separate countries, and you'd have to be a complete retard – or have a death wish – to confuse them. The fact that they were the same idiots that taunted *him* just made Talek loathe them more.

So, ruling out the *skin* thing, could it be because of his mother? Yes, she was weird. Halfway along the long and winding road to the nuthouse, probably. And yes, she avoided contact with other parents as if they carried the plague, spraying it over others as they exhaled toxic conversational words. And yes again, come the end of today – Talek's first day in year ten – the other kids will find out that *'the crazy woman'* was still refusing him the basic privilege of travelling on the school bus, like any normal kid; that after all these years the crazy old bint would insist on being the one to pick him up from school. To drive him straight home after.

Rule both options out and what are you left with? Just him. Awkward. Timorous. Quiet… a freak.

He leaned forward, rummaging through the contents of the rucksack between his feet. Pulling out his lunchbox he popped the lid. Cheese-flavoured biscuits; carrot sticks; one of those teeny pots of fromage frais that primary school kids were packed off with; a soft ball of foil, squidgy and shaped like a giant version of those *bang snaps* you used to get in the joke shop. Talek didn't need to unravel its twisted tail to know it contained cream cheese.

The boy sighed. 'Jesus, mum. What am I; five?'

'If you are, you're in the wrong place, little guy.'

Talek started at the sound of the female voice. Scrutinising his lunch so despondently, he didn't even notice the shadow that fell over him. Raising his head slowly he could see a thin pair of nylon-wrapped legs, going on for what seemed would be an infinity before his eyes finally came to a short, pleated skirt. The bottom two buttons of a sky-blue shirt were undone, revealing a slim, pale midriff. Higher up past a slight chest, long straight hair, dark and luxurious, bordered a face that the glaring sun behind the girl cast in silhouette. He didn't need to see the face to recognise the owner, however. The change in colour from black to tan high on her tights, accompanied by a thin vertical band and a skull and crossbones design on each leg told him all he needed to know.

'I guess I don't need to ask if that's free?' The shadowy head nodded to an empty patch on the wall at his side.

No invitation came, but no objection came either, so she sat down beside him.

'I've set myself a challenge,' she said. 'Some would say I'm delusional; that it can't be done.'

Talek turned to look at her, squinting in confusion.

'Three whole years you've been at this school, and apart from talking to someone who isn't here just then…'

Confusion turned to bewilderment. Flicking her eyes to the lunchbox, she gave a silent clue.

'… The only time anyone's heard a sound from you is when you answer the register.' Her smile sparked an intense whirlwind deep in his gut that the boy, a loner by his own admission, had never experienced. 'It's my mission to change that.'

Talek looked down at the floor. Other than hurling abuse, no one outside of his immediate family had had so much to say to him on one's own initiative. Feelings of embarrassment and shame pulled his mood lower as he realised he'd metaphorically left her hanging.

She lowered her voice to a mellow hum. 'Is this *really* how you want another year to start?'

Looking back, he found her eyes. Their crystal blue clearness penetrated his defences with a genuine and compelling quality. His full lips straightened, almost breaking into a smile, though apprehension quenched it before completion.

She sighed. After a moment of edgy silence, she spoke again.

'You gonna eat that?'

Talek slouched forward, taking in his untouched lunch. His answer didn't surprise her: a simple shrug of the shoulders.

The girl stood and took a carrot stick from the small pile.

'Same time same place, tomorrow?' She bit into the carrot with a crunch and a smile, turned her back in a delicate whirl, and walked briskly away.

Talek cleared his throat. At the sound she swivelled sharply. He was shielding his eyes from the glaring sun with one hand, straining to see her.

'Bye, Erin,' he said gingerly.

Smiling, she nodded a casual salute, before disappearing into the hustle and bustle of the school yard.

***

The high tempo military procession of hard soled shoes, along with the intermittent squeak of softer trainers, had stamped its way out through the exits, leaving a clinical eeriness to the long corridors. Hollow voices escaped the occasional open doorway, rebounding from the painted walls and polished cadet blue vinyl floor like the confidential mutterings of a hospital ward. The words echoed through the open space as if they would continue travelling throughout time, long outliving the mouths that had uttered them.

Beyond the reception desk's sliding window, stern eyes scrutinised Talek suspiciously. Outside the main doors was a cattle market of activity, still too frenzied for Talek's liking, though the receptionist's gaze offered a wordless dismissal.

He huffed and barged the door with a shoulder, heading out into the crowd. Taking a right, Talek skirted close to the pebbledash walls, aiming to keep a low profile, a rabbit creeping through a hedgerow with a thousand ravenous predators sniffing out sport. Rounding a ninety-degree angle, closer to the car park, the crowd had thinned out a touch. Not enough for him to feel comfortable, unwatched. If he craned his neck over the horde – easier said than done for someone with his disadvantageous height – he would see another creature he was trying to no avail to avoid.

Pretty much everyone knew whose mum was sat behind the wheel of the embarrassing beige Volvo estate. The former Viking warrior from an era where New Romantics dominated pop culture, and Michael Myers temporarily surrendered his slasher-king crown to Freddy Krueger, was now tired and weighed down by years of neglect. Rust eating away at the front edge of the bonnet and the bottoms of the doors. Chrome and black trim peeled and folded back on one front wing. Rubber window seals perished, split and hanging in places, with algae and moss spreading from the corners of the glass. And then there was the fish decal, divinely defying age on the left side of the once flat, now slightly crumpled boot. I mean, the fish alone!

Jesus Christ, Mother. Literally, *Jesus. Fucking. Christ.*

A large square plant pot constructed of concrete blocks, home to a wilted tangle of leafless limbs, offered itself as a reasonable place to duck from view.

Talek waited, the buzzing swarm of uniformed adolescents thinning as buses caried many of them away to wreak havoc on their home villages and rural communities. Other pupils headed towards the long descent into town. Puffs of cigarette smoke and aerosol from vapes issued from the small gangs as soon as they left the school premises. They're the ones who would soon point and laugh as the beige estate car coughed by in a blue cloud of exhaust waste. That was unavoidable. There is no way the woman behind the wheel would accept him taking much longer to get to the car. Soon she would spot him and begin beeping the horn, the act of hurrying him up only succeeding to draw more unwanted attention.

Failing to pick him out in the thinning crowd, she would perform the even more embarrassing act of getting out to find him. Swallowing his apprehension, Talek filed out from behind the bare branches, head hunkered down low. He scurried across the open plain to the parked car, focusing only on the ground at his feet. The nearside rear door gave an unpleasant yowl as he pulled it open, dropping half an inch on aging hinges in the process.

'Good day?' his mother asked, more going through the motions than out of genuine interest.

'Didn't do much. Never do on the first day back.' Talek lowered himself into the frayed caramel leather of the benchlike back seat, hoping to shield his face from the world outside.

'Sit up, please,' she said, catching his movement in the rear-view mirror, 'I didn't bring you up to slouch. You're not a dunkey.'

Talek exhaled an exasperated breath and pulled himself up, burning a hole through the messy back of her auburn head with his coal eyes. *You barely brought me up at all, you useless weirdo!* Guilt caused him a stab in his in his prefrontal cortex as soon as the thought entered his head.

'Why can't I sit in the front? I'm not a baby.'

'Because it's dangerous,' his mother replied, reversing sluggishly from the parking space. 'And you'll always be *my* baby.'

Her words made Talek want to throw up.

The Volvo reached the edge of the school grounds and came to a stop at the junction. Girl's laughter could be heard on the other side of the glass, but Talek would not look at them. Instead, he watched his mother flick the indicator lever up, signalling a right turn.

Braving another question, he asked, 'Why don't you ever go the other way?'

She looked in the rear-view. Talek caught her eyes above her high, pale cheekbones. Her face looked drawn and old, veins standing out blue at her temples.

'You can't get home that way,' she said.

'Yes you can.' He risked aggravating her now. He knew that, so he'd only press a little further. 'I saw it on Google Maps. It would be much quicker.'

'I don't know what *Google Maps* is,' she lied.

'It's on the internet. Everyone uses it nowadays.'

'If God intended us to use *that* technology, he would Skype us.'

Skype? But you don't know what Google Maps *is,* Talek considered. This annoyed him, though he had to admit the quip was annoyingly amusing.

The heavy vehicle lumbered onto the main road (to the right, obviously) and headed along St. Clement's Hill. Talek's attempt at a route change to avoid passing all the school kids on foot would always prove futile. Deciding to let it go, he prepared himself for the shouted verbal onslaught, ready to soak it up like a sponge and further lower his mood. It would be over soon. Soon… yet never soon enough.

THREE

Having no homework to occupy his time was truly a bummer. For the whole of the last school year, teachers were banging on about how hard they would have to work throughout years ten and eleven to achieve the grades necessary to get them into employment or onwards to college. This was consistently met with groans from the majority percentage of the class, regardless of the subject. There was a tiny percentage however (Talek a part of, but not comradely), that drank this promise in like Red Bull, buzzing at the prospect of brown-nosing their superiors and outlearning the students *they* considered their subordinates.

For Talek, the more homework he was provided with, the more he could be shut up in his bedroom, away from his mother and grandmother. Not that his gran was a problem. And she wasn't home at that moment, anyway.

At first he had hated these four walls, cursing his mother (secretly, through fear of upsetting her) for putting him in here. Then he had gotten used to them. After a greater period of time had passed, he had even come to appreciate the room, before finally coming to like it… maybe even *love*.

Hanging above the large expanse of glass was a selection of his original work artwork. Just pieces of A4 with a jumble of pale letters and numbers, their varying archaic fonts prominent in a mottled grey background: fractions of names and dates, romantic ideas of Heaven and God's loving arms. Their curled bottoms quivered in the late summer breeze as it flitted through the open sash below, tapping lightly against the rough plaster interior.

As the experimental rubbing grew into somewhat of a hobby, so too evolved the subject matter. To his right, one wall was completely covered: an assemblage of A1 and A3 pieces, brought together to form a mural of the parish's lost; some starting with *SACRED*, many including *In Memory Of*. The coloured waxes had also advanced. Browns, reds, greens, slates, charcoals. Earthy colours in respectful keeping with the subject.

Sat at his desk with nothing else in mind to pass the time, Talek looked out across to the aging, dishevelled cemetery: the same vista that had given him just reason to so hate this room when he was little. That very scene used to keep him awake for hours at night, imagining corpses turning in their graves, skeletal arms reaching up through the soft ground, clawing at the sky, using their own headstones to hoist themselves to standing. Every spine-tingling caw of a pheasant in the pre-dawn purple and gold was a chest tomb's slabbed top grating heavily open, forced by searching fingers of bone.

He'd pleaded with his mother to let him have the room at the front of the cottage, where fields and pastures rolled for miles, the Tresillian River lying low somewhere in their midst, and trees bloomed green and rich with the promise of new life. From *his* side of the cottage, only death. Trees banded closer together, creating unwelcoming shadows with their anthracite plumage, concealing broken and fallen gravestones, all hope sucked out of the place. It had felt as if his home was a portal between two conflicting worlds: light and dark, hope and fear, the living and the post-living.

His mother's baffling, bible-bashing response was always the same. *When the perishable puts on the imperishable, and the mortal puts on immortality, then shall come to pass the saying that is written: "Death is swallowed up in victory."*

Talek had no idea what that was supposed to mean, but he'd heard it so many times when he was younger he would likely never forget it. That was his mum, a cryptic argument for everything, and religious prophecies to delusionally vanquish any shadow of shite.

Anyway, against the odds, that small burial ground that had induced so many previous nightmares was now a quiet corner of solace for this lonely young man. Whatever beasts were gathered under the hallowed ground now slept soundly, coexisting in peaceful harmony with all who roamed the surface.

Soon enough, autumn would fall upon the isolated hamlet of Merther. When it did the ground would be spongy with dead and rotting leaves, lichen would smear into the headstones under the pressure of his brush, rather than peeling or flaking off in compliance, and the trees would drop moisture like Japanese water torture. Talek had to make the most of the fine weather before it too joined the band of dearly departed. Grabbing the tools of his trade from the bookcase: spray bottle and rag; wax crayons; masking tape; scrubbing brush; and sliding his larger sketchpads from behind it, he made his way downstairs.

He left the only home he'd ever know through the side door. This offered the most direct route from the cottage to the churchyard, alleviating the inconvenience of struggling with the heavy wooden gate that closed off their driveway whilst he was clutching his gear, but as an added bonus, the course also came with the benefit of avoiding having to pass his mother on the way to the cottage's main exit. Within fifteen metres lay the narrow steps up to graveyard: five uneven granite beams with low walls to either side, crawling vines – still with a healthy scattering of pinkish-red flowers – strangling every inch of stone.

Taking the steps one-at-a-time, Talek fought to maintain his balance. With no free hand to steady himself this proved awkward, but he managed, and the rewards were always worth the effort. Once at the summit he stopped momentarily, raising his face to the sun, allowing warm air to brush against his skin, listening as leaves chattered in the faint breeze. Feet sinking into the grassy tufts and pits that served as a pathway circling the ruin, Talek opted to head along the south wall. He stopped at the roofless porch and stared in. This was always the worst part. Although the dilapidated wreck was fenced off since the building was deemed hazardous, the makeshift security measures consisted only of thin horizontal and vertical crossing wires between four-feet-high rounded wooden stakes. Anyone who *wanted* to get in would get in. They'd have to be pretty stupid, but in Talek's limited life experiences he'd worked out that a lot of people made being stupid look as natural as breathing oxygen.

Beyond the slatestone entrance, with its tangled cloak of ivy and thorny branches, large fallen rocks luminous with moss lay partially sunken into the church's earthy floor. Trees and bushes grew inside, a crawling indoor oasis reaching for fresher air at the long-lost ceiling. There was no movement within the soulless, crumbling walls. Talek counted to ten, listening and looking intently. Satisfied that he was alone, he continued to the rear of the building, following the track around and into its looming shadow. The temperature plummeted once away from the sunlight and under the dense canopy of trees, but this mattered little; the boy was focused solely on his mission. Never knowing beforehand which headstone he would choose to take a rubbing from, he would let his feet do the talking, for some unknown reason each step compelling him to a certain marker. Today, Talek's size sixes told him that they would skirt the entire rear of the church and bring him into scattered sunlight at the structure's north face.

A line of four tombstones to the right of the ribbon of walkway grabbed his attention, their inscribed faces dark with shadow, the sun glowing upon their backs. They sat at conflicting angles, the centre two overlapping in a dead man's tussle for space. The furthest of the four was missing its upper two-thirds, long since broken off and consumed by nature. Its jagged remains reminded Talek of a miniature Mount Everest.

Was that the one? If so, the A3 pad would suffice.

His feet remained where they were.

A scuffle broke out to his left. Maybe just a mouse, or a shrew or something.

Please don't be a rat.

The unidentified noise drew his attention to that direction. Nearby, positioned in the shade close to the church's northern wall and snug between the wire fence and trampled, grassy track, a low square stone called to him. It stood upright, proud despite its size, below one cycloptic glassless window. Animal rusting sound forgotten, he stalked over, lowering himself to get a better look. Roman numerals. Unusual for this graveyard. How had he never noticed this one before? It was as if some unknown entity had just come in and planted it in the dead of night.

Perhaps expected for a youngster in an ever-modernising world, Talek's understanding of Roman numerals was limited. He got the gist of the basics. For instance, he could see that this unfortunate chap passed away at just sixteen years of age, *"XVI"*. Still a kid. Forevermore. *Eternal youth*, Talek thought, a heavy dose of melancholy washing through his body in an icy spate. The year of his death, however, that was far too complicated. Beyond his means, he would have to rely on good old google after returning home.

Abhorring the internet, his mother would never come around to the fact that this advance in technology was essential for modern schooling. At least his gran was *with it* enough to see that. If she too was stuck in the last millennium, Talek would have been screwed. The argument had been heated, threatening to hit the point of no return. Thankfully, with a *'my house, my rules'* dagger thrust forward with finality, his mother retreated. Gran had acted in favour, and not only had broadband installed (though even now it was painfully slow *out in the sticks*), but she also went as far as buying Talek his very own laptop.

Apologising to the occupant buried below the numerals – one of his quirks, maybe, yet out of sentimentality and respect, this courtesy became very much a part of his ritual – Talek knelt on the cold earth and got to work. Having gently scraped at the granite surface before spraying and wiping various dusts and grimes away, he taped a sheet of paper to the stone face. A3 sufficed. Next came his most-treasured task: the waxing. Scraping the long edge of the crayon over the sheet, hearing the rasping tones alter as the terrain concealed by the paper transformed, invariably produced a shiver down his spine; the kind of shiver you get when someone walks over your *own* grave.

Creating the latest masterpiece took near to ten minutes, mainly because Talek indulged in the morbid enjoyment he gained from the activity. Slowly, he peeled back the layers of tape one-by-one, careful not to rip the *frottage* (one of his favourite words). Reading about the history of his hobby, Talek came across this French term and instantly adopted it for his own use. It sounded so much more upmarket and official than the uncouth English alternative, *rubbing*.

Placing the finished piece back in the pad for protection, he stood, stretched out his back, and headed for home. Stopping at the church tower's lower window in its arched opening, a gaping hole where once decorative stained glass resided, Talek once again studied the building's forlorn interior. Shadows had grown longer as the evening sun lowered, but thankfully there were still no signs of life inside. Counting to ten again as always, as if to catch out any unseen prowler, he lifted his gaze. Overhead, the tower stood in stubborn defiance to the elements. Several feet above his small frame, a quatrefoil window watched over the boy and the listing headstones. The right pane was hidden behind dense, crawling foliage. The left was missing the lower portion of glass, with leaded shards hanging from the upper section like a crude, razor-sharp guillotine.

Above the windows, creeping ivy engulfed the tower to its extremity, as it did the entire south face of the relic from top to toe. The same destructive vegetation had enveloped large segments of the rest of the structure, penetrating its stonework and slowly razing to the ground this monumental shrine that first planted its roots over six-hundred years ago.

Talek shuddered under its emotive power. Diminishing in size himself, he cowered down and made his way back to the steps, picking up the pace to an awkward jog.

Returning home during his absence, he found his gran pottering around in the small boot room to which the side door opened.

'Ah, the wanderer returns,' she said, cupping his puffy cheeks and kissing his clammy forehead. 'Ooh,' she said, wiping her lips on the back of a hand. 'What *have* you been up to?'

'Just walking around,' he replied.

'Well, run upstairs and get scrubbed up, tea will be ready in…Tammy,' Sheila raised her voice. 'How long 'til those spuds are done?'

'Twenty minutes,' his mum's voice echoed through from the kitchen.

Perfect, Talek thought. *Enough time to check that date.*

The last time his laptop powered down it had run updates. The annoying result of this, booting up this time seemed to take forever. Talek used this delay to readjust several of the elements that constituted his tapestry, creating a space dead centre for the new frottage. Feeling a keen appreciation of the numerals, it deserved its place of prominence, on the central vertical line at eyelevel.

Finally booted and ready to go, he took his place, cross-legged on the carpeted bedroom floor. Opened an internet search window, the kid with the morbid hobby tapped the laptop's keys to form three words: *roman numeral converter*. Hitting the top link, two boxes appeared – the left for entering standard numbers, the right for entering Roman numerals. Talek guided the cursor to the right and patted the mousepad. The cursor flashed and he tapped the keys: MDCCCXIV

Translating as 1814, this final resting place was not the oldest he had worked on, but at two-hundred years old, Talek considered what the two-hundred- and sixteen-year-old boy beneath the stinking soil may look like. No more flesh. Maybe some matted, gluey hair. Eyeless sockets. Maggots and grubs fed and fattened and moving on to the next one. There was a lot to be said for cremation.

By the time his mother's shrill call beckoned from downstairs, Talek had completely lost his appetite.

FOUR

'This morning's main headline: an extensive search is underway for a missing thirteen-year-old male in Cornwall. Police have made a public appeal for any information as to the whereabouts of missing schoolboy Jowan Collins. The teenager, from Truro, failed to return home yesterday evening. He was last seen leaving Clement Grove Secondary School at three-fifteen in the afternoon, where he headed down St. Clement's Hill in the direction of the city centre.

'A spokesperson for Devon and Cornwall Police has expressed serious concerns for the missing teenager, whose estranged father, one Matthew Rundle, was released from prison on license only last week after serving a life sentence for a murder he was found guilty of committing as a juvenile. Numerous attempts have been made by Rundle's supervising officer to contact the twenty-nine-year-old, yet all of those attempts have subsequently failed.

'Mr. Rundle was tried and convicted for murder in two-thousand-and-one in accordance with the youth justice system. Police are warning that he may be a danger to the public, and not to approach the man if you see him, but instead to contact them immediately. Contact details, along with a photograph of Matthew Rundle, and the missing Jowan Collins, can be found on the Devon and Cornwall Police webs___'

FIVE

Although a glorious sun shone brightly among a flawless blanket of blue, the air had taken on a stagnant aura, becoming thick and arduous to inhale. Pupils gathered in small packs, huddling together with their languid conversations no more than an inaudible hum. The only other sound was the crass ratcheting of crows in the surrounding trees, their presence bleeding callous connotations regarding the Collins boy's fate.

Making his way over to the low slab wall where he persistently sat alone, Talek observed a slouching figure, with any luck awaiting his arrival. Her long raven hair swayed like a silky veil in the gentle currents. Looking at her legs, he could see the same skull and crossbones that she wore yesterday. Talek liked those. They set her aside from the other girls at school. He also liked the certain obscurity she had about her. He got it, but it left many others feeling uncomfortable in her presence.

A sense of unease stopped him in his tracks, pinning him to the floor. Did she really want to hang out with him, or was somebody putting her up to it? Looking around intently he tried to spot anybody who may be watching. There didn't appear to be anyone. The only person looking in his direction now was Erin. She was smiling a mournful smile as she raised one beckoning hand to in greeting.

Talek shuffled in his short, tentative strides, a cautious strut that had become his trademark over the years. Sitting next to her, the lost smile remained on her delicate lips.

'You okay?' she asked.
'Yeah,' Talek almost whispered. 'How about you?'
'Weird, isn't it?'

'Yeah.' Talek fought to look away from her clear, nowhere eyes and looked to the paving. 'Did you know him?'

'Did?' she questioned. 'Is he dead?'

'No,' Talek said. 'Sorry, I didn't mean to...'

'It's okay,' she reassured. 'I know *of* him, but we've never spoken. It just freaks me out that it's someone from our school.'

She put a finger to her mouth, clamping a long nail between her teeth before thinking twice and releasing it. She had flawless nails, painted glossy black to match her edgy personality. Talek prayed she wouldn't start biting them, mar their dark seductiveness. 'Do you think his dad took him?' Erin asked.

'Maybe,' said Talek. 'I didn't hear the full report. Mum had the volume low, then turned off the radio partway through. I told her it was about someone at school. She just said we don't need to know about it. She's...' Talek thought of how he could describe her politely, '... different.'

'Amen to that,' Erin sniggered.

A group of girls walked past gossiping. Talek and his new-found friend went quiet as they listened to snippets of the girl's wild, unfounded theories.

Once they were out of earshot Talek spoke again. 'It said his dad was done for murder. What was that about?'

'Pretty shocking from what I've heard,' Erin said, her face screwing up in distaste. 'Him and his mate burned someone alive.'

Talek looked repulsed. 'You serious?'

'Hard to believe, but yeah,' Erin went on, 'set fire to his car with him in it. Don't know where it happened; or how true it is, but...' She raised a nail to her lips again, thought better of it, and let her hand fall to her lap. 'Jowan's never met him. They didn't know at the time, but his mum was up the duff when the dad went down. Fifteen and knocked up.' Erin shook her head slowly, a ribbon of jet black falling over one eye.

Talek wanted to move it, tuck it behind her ear. Nothing should hide eyes that pure. 'Well, looks like he might have met him now,' Talek muttered. 'This is mental.'

Erin could not agree more. 'Sure is. Anyway, cheer me up. What does Talek Lean get up to when he's not in this shithole? What d'ya do last night?'

Talek thought over his evening in the company of two-century-old corpses. 'Uh, nothing, really.'

'What, *literally* nothing, or I'm-such-a-nerd-I'm-embarrassed-to-say, nothing?'

Talek laughed quietly, taking the comment as the light-hearted jest it was intended. 'You'll either laugh or walk away if I told you.'

'Try me,' she said, turning her head to look him in the eye.

'Sounds a bit crap, now I think about it,' he managed after a moment's deliberation. 'Maybe it'd be better if I showed you.'

'What you gonna do, invite me 'round to play?'

A burning sensation radiated across Talek's face. He hoped it didn't show, though he doubted it could possibly have remained under the surface, even behind his dark tones.

'Haha,' he laughed nervously. 'No. I mean in pictures. I can email you?'

'Or text?' she said, 'I can give you my number.'

'Not much chance of *that*,' he frowned, 'I haven't got a mobile. Mum says they're a device for lackies of

Lucifer, to spread hatred and elicit teen suicide – her words.'

'Oh...my...God! Seriously, what the fuck, dude?' Spotting the shame in her friend's expression, Erin decided it was time to let it slide. Nevertheless, she failed to hold back one last repartee. 'You need to turn *adult* overnight, like Tom Hanks. Then you can move out, get your own phone, and never call the spaz. The pics sound intriguing, though.' Erin took his hand, causing the burning sensation to expand like a mushroom cloud in his sweating head. 'Got a pen?'

Taking a moment, Talek worked hard to convince himself that this *really* was happening, that not only a girl, but a hot girl, was allowing him to contact her... and actually *touching* him. Tingling all over like a pressure cooker about to hit blowing point, he fished in his trouser pocket with a shaky free hand, pulling out a ballpoint pen. Passing it to her, Erin smiled and scratched her email address along the soft brown flesh of his forearm in tickling strokes. He would have to copy it onto paper and scrub it from his skin before his mum spotted it, but that was easy enough. The hardest part would be not wanting to erase the evidence that this encounter did indeed happen.

A bell rang across the school grounds. Erin let go of his hand, passed him back the pen, and stood. Disappointment tugged at his emotions, until he realised that the skull and crossbones were eye level and less than two feet in front of him, hovering like Eden's forbidden fruit. That was a welcomed pick-me-up. 'Have a good weekend doing nothing,' she smiled. 'I'll look forward to finding out exactly what that is.'

'Don't get too excited,' he said. 'It's not really... *normal*.'

'Even better,' Erin winked, poking her tongue from the corner of her curled up lips.

She walked away, leaving Talek with the impossible task of composing himself before he headed to today's penultimate period.

SIX

The dwelling's atmosphere was cold and stagnant when Erin returned home from school, as was the reception from her folks. Relieved to be away from it and up in her bedroom, she put her back against the door and closed her eyes, reducing their voices to an undecipherable mumble. They had been acting weird for the last couple of weeks – agitated voices when the two of them had a room to themselves, falling silent or promptly changing the subject whenever Erin walked in. Something was up, and getting to the bottom of it was an exercise the youngster did not want to undertake given the circumstances of this morning's disturbing news.

All couples went through patches like this, she supposed, but it seemed so out of character for her parents. Loves young dream even at their age, displays of public affection cringy enough to make even the most romantic of onlookers' vomit. Erin could not even recall one time where they'd had so much as a cross word to hurl at each other. Recently, however, some unknown entity seemed to have a chokehold on their relationship, suppressing the marital bliss and leaving their daughter constantly walking on eggshells.

Sliding slowly down the inner face of the door, Erin came to rest on the floor, pressing her fingertips into the thick carpet, groping for its reassuring comfort. She opened her eyes at the sound of a short vibration travelling through the laminated surface of her desk. Struggling lackadaisically to her feet, she reached the desk and grabbed her mobile phone. One new notification. An email from taleklean00.

Right, young man, she thought, walking to her bed and collapsing one her back, unaware of the smile forming on her own face. *Let's see what billy-no-mates does with his spare time.* Erin instantly felt bad at the nickname, but as far as that went at current, it was quite apt. Tapping a fingertip to the notification, the email opened onto the screen. There was no text, *charming*, though there was a single attachment.

Opening the link, an image appeared on the phone's six-inch screen. What looked like a mosaic of shadings - greens across the top; greens, reds and browns down the sides; charcoals and blacks in the mid and bottom centre – projected an ominous aura among the doodles. There were also what looked like extravagant texts scattered among the confusion: letters and numbers in archaic fonts. Staring for a number of seconds, Erin could not determine their meaning (assuming there was even a meaning to be found).

Placing a pinched finger and thumb to the screen, she spread the two digits outwards, enlarging the central area of the image, squeezing out the extremities and bringing the off-white text to the forefront. The confusion became more pixelated, yet names and dates became clear, strikingly light within the smoky clouds of grey. So, the boy had a thing for headstones. Not run of the mill, that's for sure, but Erin imagined that more people were into them than would let on. She certainly didn't think it was, as Talek had stated, *'crap."*

Hitting the *reply* arrow, Erin started typing.

> *Always knew there was something different about u.*
> *So when can I come round for that playdate? xx*

She waited. Still, the bitter mumbles persisted from downstairs, mostly low like a generator running somewhere in the remote distance, occasionally animated enough for Erin to pick out some variant of the *F* word. This was really unlike her father. Things must have gotten real bad, real quick. Unsettled, Erin reached for the headphones on her bedside table and plugged them into her phone. Opening her Spotify app, she went to the playlist she had created for times she needed to be taken away, drowning out the arguments from beneath the flooring and hoping only to be dragged back to this world by the ping of Talek's reply.

Hours later, she awoke in the pitch dark. There was no call from downstairs when her tea was ready, and after pulling her headphones from her ears, there appeared to be no heated discussion either. She checked her phone. It was quarter to eleven and there was no reply from Talek. With an effort, Erin pulled herself from the bed and walked to the bedroom door. More darkness filled the crack as she pulled it open. Her parent's bedroom door was closed, but a steady glow could be seen on the ceiling above the stairway. She made her way to the stairs, feet shushing quietly into the carpet as she treaded lightly, supportive fingers brushing softly along the wall.

As she made her way downwards, the television could be heard at a low volume. The stairs descended into the living room, where Erin could see the back of her dad's head over the top of the sofa, its premature greying curls unkempt as usual.

'Is that__'

Connor jumped slightly at the unexpected voice behind him. 'Jesus, Erin. Don't sneak up on people like that.' He reached for the remote and flicked to a different channel.

'Sorry,' she said diffidently. 'Can I watch that?'

'You don't need to see that,' Connor said in a tone that didn't invite a response.

Erin gave one regardless. 'But wasn't it about__'

'Looks like the dad was drunk in a shop doorway the night the kid disappeared. At least they *think* it was him. Pretty shit CCTV.'

'You think he took him?' she asked, still not willing to venture further into the room and take a seat.

'He was in the area at the time the lad went missing.'

Erin detected annoyance in her father's tone, but she couldn't help herself.

'Jowan.'

'What?' said Connor.

'His name,' Erin persisted. 'His name's Jowan.'

'Whatever.' Connor took a long drag on a bottle of beer he was clutching. 'Tea's in the kitchen. Why don't ya nuke it up and take it upstairs.' It came across as more an order than a question.

He was clearly under some unknown pressure. As easy-going as they come, Erin's father was never this cold towards her. Unnerved and upset, she headed back upstairs, leaving her tea where it sat cold and waiting for her.

SEVEN

'Firstly, to our main story in Cornwall, where police are still searching for missing teenager, Jowan Collins, and continue their appeal for any information as to the whereabouts of his father, Matthew Rundle. Jowan has not been seen since he left school last Thursday afternoon, whilst his father is believed to have been picked up by CCTV in the city centre later that evening. Footage shows a man matching Matthew Rundle's description, appearing inebriated, taking shelter in a shop doorway on Boscawen Street. The man is then seen leaving in an easterly direction at around 3AM on Friday.

'Devon and Cornwall Police are now gravely concerned for Jowan's safety, as he was not pictured with the man in the footage. Jowan's mother, a Learning Support Assistant at her son's school, was understandably too upset to talk on camera, but in an emotional plea has begged for her "beautiful boy" to "come home safe."

'We'll cross now to our Cornwall correspondent, Quint Molko, who is live in Truro. Quint, what's the latest on this developing story?'

'Well, Amy, as you can see behind me, police have cordoned off this idyllic garden park just on the edge of the city, where a man matching the description of Matthew Rundle was seen on Thursday lunchtime. A local resident was walking their dog, where they've claimed the man was sat on one of the park's benches with a bag of, uh, apparently *strong* lagers – several of which empty – however, he was pretty much keeping himself to himself. It's in the hours that followed that – if indeed it is *him* – that the man's whereabouts are unaccounted for. The next suspected sighting was from the CCTV footage you mentioned a moment ago.

'Just yesterday I spoke to residents of the street where Jowan lives with his mother. Many expressed their shock at his disappearance, one stating that it's "the sort of thing you only see on TV, you just don't expect it to happen on your own doorstep." The general consensus is that Jowan is a polite young man who always has a smile for his neighbours. When asked about a possible relationship with his father, Jowan's mother confirmed that he had never met Matthew Rundle – who was convicted of murder while she was still with child – and that she has never so much as shown her son a photograph of the man suspected of being involved in the thirteen-year-old's disappearance.

'Police are now conducting a thorough search of these gardens, which as well as having many areas of trees and shrubbery, also has access, albeit over tall security fencing, to the viaduct that towers over its lower grounds. As yet, nothing has been turned up by this latest aspect of the search, though we'll be on hand to bring you any further breaking news as and when we receive it.

'Quint Molko. Truro.'

EIGHT

Under a sky as overcast as the collective mood of the setting's inhabitants, and through air as cold as the atmosphere of the morning's assembly, Talek walked alone. With the floor his primary focus, he failed to notice the small gang of lads he was unwittingly heading for before it was too late. Feeling the intentionally heavy contact of another kid's shoulder, he raised his face to the perpetrator.

'Fuck you lookin' at? Freak.'

Talek's panic was visible. 'S..sorry, Ethan.'

Head back towards the floor, shuffling away and praying the situation wouldn't escalate, a foot was thrust between his jellied legs. Laughter erupted as Talek hit the deck, scraping his palms and his chin as he landed on the rough paving.

'Send us a postcard next time. Twat!'

'Piss off, Coby,' came a girl's voice, a hybrid blend of sternness and sweetness. 'Tal, are you alright?'

'Yeah. Fine,' he said, looking up to see Erin crouched and offering out a hand.

Talek took it and she helped him to his feet. More laughs came as they walked away together.

'Always get yer girlfriend to do your fighting for ya? Loser.' This was Ethan's voice once more.

Talek didn't mind. Why would he? He had a hot girl clinging to his arm, while Ethan just had his following of spotty halfwits. They reached the wall he now considered *theirs* and took a seat. Neither spoke for a moment. Erin shuffled closer, coming to rest against him. She felt as warm as the summer that was threatening to leave a couple weeks early.

'Sure you're okay?' she asked.

'It's nothing. Happens all the time.'

'Not what I asked,' said Erin. 'You gonna take up the offer of counselling, are you.'

'Nah,' Talek frowned. 'I barely knew him.'

'So you think he's dead then.'

Talek looked her in the face, confusion washing over his.

'You said "knew," not *know.*'

'Maybe. Dunno. I saw the news report on TV this morning. Gran had it on. She's not as weird as mum, so she left it on when she knew I was watching.' He absently scuffed a loose stone back and forth with the tip of his shoe, leaving white scratch marks on the ground. 'She reckons he's a goner; that they should bring back hanging for the dad.'

'No nonsense granny,' Erin teased. 'He may not be, but it don't look good.'

A girl walked past, phone to her ear and liquid tracks down her cheeks.

Erin lowered her voice. 'I think she needs to see them.'

Talek watched after her and nodded his head sympathetically.

'Anyway,' she said, sensing that a change of subject was the most appetising thing on the menu – a *sort of* a change, anyway. 'Cemetery boy.'

With an effort, Talek sniggered. 'You think I'm as strange as my mother, don't you?'

'Don't be daft,' Erin smiled, gently nudging his shoulder with her own. 'No one's *that* strange. Anyway, I like it.'

'You *do?*' Talek made little effort to mask his surprise.

'Uh, *hello!* Have you seen my tights? Graves are right up my street.'

'Yeah I've seen them,' Talek beamed. 'Not that I was looking,' he defended, heat blasting upwards like a geyser from his rapidly beating heart.

'Don't worry, boys will be boys,' she smiled. 'Question is though, when are we gonna hook up so you can teach me everything you know?'

Talek lowered his head back down to his feet. 'I don't really have…I don't actually know if I'm allowed friends over.'

Erin failed to withhold a laugh. 'You're joking, right?'

'Don't laugh,' Talek moaned. 'I've never had a friend before, so…'

This is tragic. Erin kept the thought to herself. 'Sorry,' she said. 'I didn't mean to upset you. But look, there's always a way around things. I'll just meet you there. No one will need to know. Where's the church? And where d'you live?'

'You've probably not heard of it,' Talek dismissed, hoping to render the suggestion void. 'Merther. It's in the middle of nowhere, on the way to St. Michael Penkivel. The church is right next to my house.'

'Ooh, staying hidden will be a challenge.' She smirked like she was getting off on the idea of running the risks.

'Yeah, but like I said__'

'No, I've heard of it.'

'Really?' Talek asked, taken aback. His mother's thinking behind moving in with his gran was surely all based on seclusion, hiding away from society to the best of her abilities.

'Yeah, I don't know it well, but I know roughly where it is. I live just across the river. I can cycle there.'

'You? Ride a bike?' It was his turn to laugh.

'What's so funny about that?' asked Erin, a little offended.

'Nothing,' he said, still sniggering. 'I just thought you might be too *cool* for that.'

'Get lost,' she smiled. 'Anyway, how else is anyone our age supposed to get 'round this shitty old backwater?'

True, his thoughts agreed.

'Friday?' Her striking blue eyes commanded his attention.

'Friday,' he mumbled, brainwashed.

'It's the first night of the week I don't have *the homework police* on my case,' Erin admitted.

'I didn't have you down as the type to take homework seriously,' said Talek.

'Too cool for cycling. Too cool for homework. I should hire you to do my PR.'

Sighing in unison, they shared a mutual disappointment as the bell sounded, signalling the end of their lunch break; the end of their time together.

'Shame you aren't in my maths group, ya little number-nerd,' she joked, standing. 'See you tomorrow.'

'Yeah. See ya.' Talek watched her walk away, still thinking that she was being put up to forming a friendship with him as a dare. His eyes dropped to her short, pleated skirt, her long, slender legs, sending his spine aquiver.

***

A peculiar rain descended over the school grounds by kicking-out time. Droplets plummeted plump and round, yet few and far between. Each heavy drop splatted home with the promise of an imminent downpour, the heavy clouds waiting impatiently for the signal to burst.

Gauging a thinning in the human traffic, Talek scurried towards the car park. Scanning the occupied spaces as he arrived, he could see no trace of the big, beige estate car. This was unlike the woman who absolutely insisted on picking him up every single day. On any other occasion she was dreadfully early, embarrassing him if ever last period was in a classroom that wielded any sort of view of the parent and visitor parking area.

'Mummy not here to pick you up?' Ethan's voice came in a sneer through gritted teeth from behind.

Talek refused to turn and meet his menacing gaze. Instead, he headed to the exit of the car park and onto the pavement that hugged the main road.

'Big man thinks he can walk away.' A different voice this time, no less contemptuous.

Oscar.

It was while he was placing the name to the voice that Talek felt hands connect with his back, forceful and unanticipated enough to instigate his second visit of the day to the cold, unforgiving ground.

'*CAR!*' This high-pitched scream could only be Ryan. How he fitted in with this crew, with his scrawny frame and feminine demeanour, a chihuahua running with the wolfpack, Talek could only a guess at.

In response to the sound of the warning cry there followed a cacophony of stampeding feet and curses. Talek had apparently escaped (or at the very least, postponed) a kick-in from the complete quartet.

The bumbling vehicle rolled heavily to a stop by his side. A suck of aging rubber gave out as the passenger door was pushed open from inside.

'Talek, honey, what are you doing down there?'

Jesus, Mum, isn't it freaking obvious?

'Just about to get beaten up,' he said, ambling to a sitting position. 'Thanks for finally turning up, by the way.'

'Don't be rude to your mother,' Tamsyn snapped. 'The last guests at Rosemary Cottage left the key in a ridiculous place. It's taken me most of the afternoon to find it, so blame them.'

Releasing a disgruntled sigh, Talek clambered to his feet and grabbed the corner of the open door.

'In the back!'

'It's things like sitting in the back that get me beaten up,' he protested. 'And *none* of it would happen if you let me get the bus. I wouldn't have to wait around. And this car as well, I mean, come on; it's as old as you.'

'Don't be disrespectful. Back in the day, this__'

'We're not "back in the day," Mum. Get with the times.'

Speaking calmly but venomously assertive, she said, 'In the back, now, young man.'

Talek considered slamming the front door. Pinging in his head, however, the lightbulb suggested he could do better than that. With the intention of maximising potential annoyance, he instead pushed it to gently until it clicked once. Leaving it only partially on the latch, he opened the rear door and slid in.

His mother stared back at him with raised eyebrows, before huffing and leaning over the passenger seat. After reopening the door, Tamsyn slammed it harder than *he* would have.

'Don't be disrespectful,' Talek mumbled sarcastically.

'Seen and not heard, please,' returned his mother, glaring at him in the mirror, her evil eyes daring him to offer up a challenge.

Talek refused to accept, slouching into the leather, a storm of hatred brewing in his mind.

NINE

Serrated teeth of bark bit into his back as the gnarly girth of an old tree trunk offered equal doses of comfort and pain. Dampness soaked into the backs of his jeans, chilling him to the bone. The cold soil gave off a pungent decaying scent, as if the dead that it kept entombed were by some supernatural phenomena rising closer to the surface. All in all, the experience so far was unpleasant, underwhelming, but this vantage point offered Talek both a decent view of the road, and the ability to duck down behind the low stone wall if his gran's Shogun came grinding past. Situated between himself and home, the ramshackle church – appearing even more foreboding under the thick melancholy clouds than usual – did its job of hiding his mother from view.

He checked his watch, convinced himself that Erin wasn't coming, that the whole friendship had just been a cruel joke – him the butt as usual – then berated himself for doubting her so gratuitously.

His doubt was confirmed as even more unfair as the sound of whooshing rubber on asphalt zipped with the breeze over the churchyard. Upon seeing the cloak of silky black hair trailing behind the rider, Talek stood and held up a hand. Erin leaned to the left and guided her bike to the gateless side entrance.

'You really should wear a helmet, you know.'
'And get helmet hair?' said Erin. 'Don't think so.'
'Well, I'd feel better if you did.'

Erin lifted one booted foot over the crossbar. Talek averted his eyes from the sight of her long legs protruding from black and white plaid mini skirt. Erin noted the gesture and smiled to herself. Resting the bike against the graveyard's bordering hedge, she walked over to him, high, chunky heels crunching into the loose stone walkway.

'And I'd feel better if you stopped letting those assholes push you around,' she said, hazarding a guess as to where his grazes came from. Sensing he had no response, she probed further. 'So, what happened *this* time?'

'Nothing, really,' he said, head hanging low. 'How can you even cycle in those?' He nodded at her knee-high leather boots, chrome buckles lined up one atop the other at their fronts.

'Simple,' she smiled. 'Don't tell me you've never tried.'

This got a laugh out of him. Erin could sense a slight discomfort in it, but it was at least a start.

'What's first then, cemetery boy?'

'Well,' Talek said turning his head from side-to-side. 'First, you just gotta pick one you kinda like the look of.'

'Ooh, they're all so tempting,' Erin smirked.

'Only, stick to this side of the church, or the back. I live 'round the other side and I don't want my mum to see us.'

'Whatever you say.' Erin looked over his shoulder at the ivy tumbledown. 'That. Looks. Awesome! Creepy.'

'Yeah, it's pretty cool,' Talek said, turning to look behind him. 'It used to scare the cack out of me at night though,' he admitted. 'My bedroom window looks out over it.'

'I'm not surprised it scared you. Anyone could be hiding away in there. Or *anything*.' She said the last with raised eyebrows and a drawn-out campfire ghost story *oooh*.

Right on cue, a sharp pheasant's call blasted into existence from the rear of the graveyard.

'*HOLY SHIT!*' Erin stumbled, laughing. 'That scared the *cack* out of me!'

Talek laughed. 'Good one. Lucky for me I'm kind of used to it now.'

Erin's attention diverted to where the harsh sound had erupted from. 'Hey, there's a cross toppled over back there,' she said, gazing across the ramshackle collection of *R.I.Ps* and *In Loving Memory* epitaphs. 'Let's give that one a whirl.'

There was no track heading down to the rear of the churchyard. The ground was lumpy and hard going, the grass thick, fresh and vibrant green. As they crossed, Erin rested a hand at the base of Talek's neck. Blushing, he convinced himself that she was most likely only aiming to steady herself, but her touch felt incredible, regardless.

They reached the fallen marker. Whether it was the sombre neglect of this particular part of the grounds, or some irrationally perceived word of warning, Erin was not certain. Whatever the reason, the grass underfoot had lost its vibrancy. Varying between darker tones of greens and browns it felt dry and brittle under the soles of her boots. No flowers (or living flowers, at least), or sentimental trinkets dressed the graves in this part of the small-scale burial ground. A couple of fractured stone beds in the very corner had dry stalks poking through tarnished chrome holders. They sprawled out like the wiry legs of some lethal, lurking spider.

Talek broke the eerie silence. 'What colour?'

'Hmm?' Erin looked to see him holding a collection of thick, coloured crayons. 'Oh. Black, of course.'

'Of course,' smiled Talek. 'Right. First you gotta scrub it with the brush. Gently though. You don't wanna damage the stone.'

'Why,' Erin smirked, 'are they gonna jump out the ground and tell me off?' She took the wooden-backed brush that was offered to her, unsure if he knew she was joking, and looked at the marker. 'There's no inscription.'

'Don't worry,' he said, 'some were on plaques that fell off at some point, some were on the bottom plinth and have sunk into the ground. Just pick another.'

'May as well go for the big one next to it,' she said, carefully stretching a long, striding leg over a spot where a human's remains lay deep.

Setting to work, Talek watched her slow, rhythmical movements.

'Done,' Erin said after a time.

'Excellent.' Talek reached into his bag and pulled out a spray bottle and a ball of cloth. 'Just need to give it a clean now.'

'Fuckin'ell. What are we, caretakers? We should be getting' paid for this,' she moaned, taking the bottle and cloth, and starting to spray. 'So, when's the fun bit?' she asked, her voice now smooth, warmer than the air around them.

'It's all fun.' He took a composing breath. 'At least, it is when you're here.'

'Talek Lean, are you chatting me up?'

'No, I…' he fumbled. Noticing her mesmerising smile, he added, 'Well. Maybe.'

'Is this clean enough for you, sir?' She drew his attention back to the headstone.

'Yeah, cool.' He tore a piece of A1 from his pad, handing it to Erin along with the roll of masking tape.

As she taped the paper in place a vehicle could be heard approaching from the lane. Talek looked up to see its dark painted roof just above the line of the hedge. Erin took in his dark eyes, nestled neat and alert in the round, brown skin of his face.

'I guess you know them,' she said. 'Hard not to around here, I s'pose.'

'My gran,' he said. 'You're good to go now.' He gestured toward the paper with a nod of his head.

'Cool.' Erin picked up the black crayon and started to rub, letters immediately materialising within the darkening background. 'Anyway, how come your mum doesn't like you having friends?'

Talek found sanctuary in the sound of wax, on paper, on granite. Relaxing, he mulled over the question. 'It's stupid,' he said, 'she thinks people are… dangerous.' He thought some more, the gentle scraping soothing some of the anxiety he'd felt in the days building up to this rendezvous. 'To be honest, I'm surprised I'm not home-schooled.'

'People *are* dangerous,' Erin said, her face suddenly solemn, 'just look at Jowan's dad.'

'Yeah, but not *everyone* is,' sighed Talek.

'No, but do you ever really know how to spot the difference?'

A contemplative silence played out before Erin spoke again. 'But she can't stop you from having any friends.'

'You don't know her.'

She continued rubbing, losing herself equally in the art and her own thoughts. Eventually she asked, 'Are you afraid of her?'

Silence temporarily stifled Talek as he fell deep into his own thoughts. Although taken aback by the unexpectedness and forwardness of the question, he realised he was quite unsure of the answer.

'Would you think less of me if I was?' he ventured.

'Don't be soft,' she said. 'I couldn't possibly think any less of you than I already do.'

He stared, hoping to crack her head open with his eyes and see her meaning tumble out like a river of Alphabetti spaghetti. The stale air cracked as the stealthy pheasant let out another ratcheting cry, unseen in the foliage but certainly making its presence heard. This time, both youths jumped out of their skin. As their nerves began to settle, the pair looked each other in the eye, before bursting simultaneously into laughter.

'You *were* joking, weren't you?' Talek said, once he'd caught his breath and recovered his composure.

'Course I was,' she said, laughing still, yet quieter now. 'And you don't need to answer. I think I already know.' Her face grew more serious, intense. 'Don't worry, it's nothing to be ashamed of.'

Talek doubted that that was true, but he had no intention of arguing out the details with her. He was having a good time in good company. There was no point in jeopardising the moment.

Erin broke the chain between their eyes and held up her paper, smiling once more. 'Finished,' she said. 'What d'ya think?'

'Perfect.'

They knelt on the snagging, scratching ground, staring silently at each other.

Erin cast a look to the darkening sky. 'Do you want to put it on your wall?'

'You keep it,' he said. 'I'll have your next one. As long as you sign it and remember me when it's on show at the Tate.'

Reading the unwritten invitation of a return visit, Erin stood, rolling the paper and sliding it down the front of her hooded top.

'See you Monday?' she asked.

'See you Monday,' he agreed. 'And if you're in town over the weekend, buy a helmet.'

'I'll buy a helmet when I see you stand up to Ethan and his dickhead mates.'

Talek smiled in the failing light under shifting, clawing trees. Erin took a step towards him, placed a kiss on the tips of her fingers, and rubbed them affectionately in his hair. Beaming, he watched her slight shoulders bounce with each stride of her knee-high boots as she walked away.

***

Rain pattered softly and rhythmically against the outer face of the bedroom window. A sharp spray caught his attention, dragging his eyes away from the laptop screen as a sudden gust wind thrashed drops against the glass. Talek strained his neck to watch as occasional droplets on the panes caught in the glow of his tall mahogany wood lamp (nothing in this cottage, it appears, other than technological items, was permitted to venture into the current century), trickling down until they were lost in the diamonds of lead trim.

A series of delicate knocks issued from the other side of the oak door.

'Yarp?'

The door opened slowly, his gran's head appearing through the gap. Though young for a grandmother to a fourteen-year-old – only mid-fifties herself, and accustomed to taking meticulous care of her appearance and her health, so much so that Talek had the embarrassing situation of younger dad's casting lustful glances at her if she ever had to collect him from school – the yellowy bulb of the lamp gave Sheila a jaundice hue, adding fifteen years of hardship to her face.

'Not too much longer, lovey,' she whispered.

Taking in the rain outside, Shelia entered the room and headed towards the far wall. Pulling the curtains closed, she turned and put her hands on her hips. Talek knew that when she took up this authoritative pose, she was gearing up to speak her mind about something that may cause offence or upset, and caring little for the ramifications.

'Don't want those open on a night like this, inviting all the night creatures in to tempt you away. Haven't you seen Salem's Lot?'

Having no clue what she was talking about, Talek shook his head.

'No, and you wouldn't want to neither,' she assured. 'Bleddy good film though, just maybe not for nice boys like you.'

Sheila tottered past her grandson and made herself comfortable on the corner of the bed, scrutinising him, her perfectly plucked brows raised.

'What?' he said, knowing that look every bit as well as the hands-on-hips pose.

'Who's your girlfriend,' she asked, grinning.

Shit. Talek was too caught off-guard to conjure up any fancy fabrications. Backed into a hole, he kept it simple.

'I haven't got a girlfriend.'

'No?' quizzed Sheila. 'Well, they sure as hell weren't the old vicarage's chickens I heard laughing with you behind the church.'

Excuses caught in Talek's throat, growing like a snowball as it rolled across the freezing, fluffy ground, until he could feel the lump of ice pressing against his windpipe.

'Don't worry,' she reassured, 'your secret's safe with me. Yer mother'll only stress about it. So, what's her name? Do you need any tips on where to take a lady? She must've felt *really* special, being treated to a date in a graveyard.'

'It wasn't a date,' Talek protested, face burning up under the pressure of the cross-examination. 'Her name's Erin. And she likes that sort of thing. She's even got skulls on her school tights.'

'Skulls on her school tights?' his gran blurted, hastily forcing a hand to her mouth and shooting a glance to the open door. Whispering harshly, she said, 'Blimey, I *definitely* won't tell your mother that. She'll 'ave a breakdown! Send a priest around to cleanse her, or exorcise her, or somethin' or other.'

Talek laughed at the suggestion, but deep down he thought that his gran may not have been too far off the mark.

'Anyway,' she said, rising sprightly from the bed. 'Sweet dreams.' She bent to where Talek was sat at his desk and kissed him on the cheek. Reaching the door she turned back, tapped a secretive finger to the side of her nose, and left the room, lowing the door latch quietly behind her.

Powering down his laptop, Talek walked to the window and peeled at the side of the curtain with one nervous finger. (He loved the old tumbledown in the daytime, and at night, most of the time. But occasionally…). Looking through the darkness to the misty outline of the decrepit church, he wondered what Erin was doing at that moment. Wondered if she was thinking of him.

That was the first time he saw it.

Or his overactive imagination told him he saw it, at least.

A dull flicker of light through the partially collapsed arched doorway. There one fleeting moment. Pulsing. And then no more. Snubbed out of existence: an unsubstantiated memory.

Not willing to gaze into the haunting darkness any longer, Talek let the curtain fall to its idle slumber and headed for the bathroom to brush his teeth.

TEN

Friday night's gentle rain had picked up the pace throughout Saturday, before damning the whole weekend a torrential right-off. By Monday morning, as Talek eased out of the back of the car with his head down, it had reduced to mizzle. Who would have thought that for a fourteen-year-old, returning to school for a new week of precious learning would be the highlight? Bar the tedious interruptions from the class dummies.

Yes, he was sure to face some abuse at some point today, it came with the territory. But at least he had one friend now, which was an infinite improvement on every previous school year that he waded lonelily through.

Tutor was uneventful. Just a cursory mention of Jowan. Today marked the eleventh day with no sight or sound of him, and according to the radio on the morning drive (before his mother managed to kill the volume, again), the police had received no new leads to go on. It was as if the kid had just disappeared into thin air, like a nightmare demon the moment your flitting eyes spring open, abruptly ending your vivid REM sleep phase.

Walking to first lesson – double science, a brutal way to start the week for any *normal* child – down through echoing soulless corridors, the mood of the place had changed dramatically since the first day back. The hustle and bustle, the optimism, the *excitement* even (most likely down to seeing the friends you didn't catch up with during the long six weeks off, rather than a penchant for study), circumstance had sucked the life out of these young people by the second morning, when friends, acquaintances, and associates had woken up to the grim news. As Talek moved along, an inconspicuous member of the mumbling horde, he wondered if any of that previous life would seep back into the bodies surrounding him.

Doubtful, he thought miserably.

A forceful nudge to the base of his spine. Had it not been for the sardine tin environment he would have been knocked off his feet. The girl who had unwittingly kept him upright turned and glared at him, scorning him with silent accusation.

'Sorry,' Talek said meekly.

Screwing her mouse-like snout up, the girl gave no reply as she returned her attention to the moving mob ahead.

'Watch where you're going, shitforbrains,' came Ethan's gruff taunt from behind.

And it starts. Talek ignored him. The door to his first class was less than twenty metres ahead. Luckily, Ethan was too thick to be in the same set as him for this one – as with all the other subjects, apart from the population-based stuff, like PE (Talek's educational nemesis, unless it was simply running). Of the four kids that had made the best part of Talek's secondary school life a living hell, Ryan was the only one with an ounce of intelligence. This subject was one of several that they'd shared for the past three-and-a-bit years, but without the rest of his crew there to back him up, Ryan carried about as much threat as a sedated sloth in a straitjacket.

Entering the safety of the room, Talek pulled a heavy wooden stool out from underneath a tall, insult-scarred, wooden desk. The stool's bare feet made the same horrendous vibrating commotion as the other thirty-odd on the hard, duck egg blue linoleum floor.

He sat and groped at his rucksack, removing a writing book, his biology textbook, and a canvas pencil case. Dumping the bag at his feet, he waited for the rest of the class to settle, taking in some of the constructive and creative inscriptions on the desk's graffitied surface.

'Mr Day's a pedo.' Talek frowned at the spelling error.

'Miss Gill takes it up the shitter.' Obviously this little gem was nonsense... *probably. Could be a paradox, maybe...* He wondered if he would ever look at her the same way again.

'Shelly sucks cock for a bag of pork scratchings,' he mumbled to himself. *Good for you, Shelly.*

Absentmindedly, and with a rebelliousness so utterly uncharacteristic it was as if some poltergeist force had seized his hand, possessed his brain, Talek plucked his pen up from the desk and pulled at the lid. Scribbling out the word *'Shelly,'* he scratched in bold capital letters above the original scrawl:

ETHAN

'Right,' came Miss Gill's raised voice from the front of the classroom. 'Now that you're all settled, today we're going to be looking at a marvellous *array* of cell types. I know, it doesn't get any better than this, but please try to contain your excitement!'

A mixture of awkward titters and groans ricocheted from the painted stone walls. Miss Gill turned to the whiteboard, where a number of diagrams were projected, along with printed titles. Talek couldn't help but look down at the petite, circular seat of her pencil skirt, trying hard to erase the crude accusation scrawled on the desk from his mind.

'These are just some of the examples,' she said, circling an arm before turning back to her congregation. 'But we can do better than textbook illustrations. I need you to buddy up. We got blood cells, muscle cells, bone cells, yada yada yada, but, as you know, this school isn't in the business of printing money. Thus, we only have enough microscopes for you to do this in pairs, but there are plenty of slides for you all to pass around.'

Talek looked at the empty seat next to him. *Hard to 'buddy up' when you have no buddies,* he thought morosely.

'Obviously most of you are already sat in pairs, so if you keep to your tables we can do this with as little faff as possible. Ryan, you look lonely. Over with Talek, please.'

Oh shit. 'I'm fine, Miss,' Talek protested.

'I'm sure you are, but I didn't ask how you are doing,' Miss Gill smiled humourlessly. 'Ryan! Ándale!'

Ryan pushed his chair back aggressively and uttered a derogatory slur under his breath.

'I heard that,' said Miss Gill, sharply. 'Stay behind after class, please. Then you can explain to me what that word means, presuming you're mature enough to know.' Addressing the class, she went on, 'Microscopes are in the two cupboards by the emergency exit, people. One from each pair may go and get one now. *In orderly fashion!* You are *not* protozoans.' She laughed at her own reference. No one laughed with her; with the exception of Talek. 'I will bring the slides around myself, anon.'

Ryan took a seat beside Talek and started drumming his fingers on the seasoned surface of the hardwood desk.

'I'll get it then, shall I?' Talek offered, to no response.

As he arrived back with the scope in his hand, arm trembling faintly through the weight of the chunky metal apparatus, and the apprehension of having to work in such close proximity to one of his tormentors, Ryan stared up at him.

Brushing his dark hair back over his head, he said, 'So, Ethan sucks dick, does he?'

'What?' Talek acted dumb.

'That's what it says.' Ryan jabbed a finger down on the carved text, clearly angered. 'I'm guessing *you* wrote it.'

'Don't be stupid, that's probably been there for ages. And it says "cock" actually, not "dick",' Talek started to breathe deeply, sparking his cognitive creativity into finding a way out of this situation, whilst mildly regretting his flippancy.

'So now Ethan sucks *cock*, and I'm stupid?'

'I wasn't calling__'

'Good,' Ryan cut in. 'Cos if I was stupid, I wouldn't notice how fresh the *"ETHAN"* bit is compared to the rest.'

Talek looked down at the written abuse in despair. Detective Ryan was right. This handywork had clearly been added recently. The blue ink stood out boldly in comparison to the rubbed and faded surrounding indentations.

Briefly postponing his agony, Miss Gill appeared with a small collection of glass slides.

'Sit down, young man,' she said, eyeing Talek over her turquoise framed glasses. 'I trust you two know how to work that thing?'

Neither answered.

'Excellent,' she said, before shuffling to the next table.

Waiting until he guessed Miss Gill was out of earshot, Ryan turned to Talek and whispered, 'Ethan's gonna be pissed. You better hope your freak of a mother ain't late again.'

Talek surveyed his unwanted partner, hoping to spot any sign of jest in the boy's comment. Swallowing hard, he soon realised there was only malice hidden in those calculating irises.

ELEVEN

Walking in a trance towards what he hoped had become a regular rendezvous point (nothing had been agreed, but Talek was optimistic that such things now went without saying), the weight of an intense morning had started to lift, relieving the pressure on his burdened shoulders. Biology with Ryan had been an emotional mountain to climb, with devious looks cast and threatening comments aplenty… This was only a temporary reprieve, of course. Come three-fifteen, if the tired and beige unlikely getaway vehicle was not in its usual spot, engine running and ready to roll, Talek was a dead man.

Rounding the corner had come with a proverbial kick in the balls. The tall, skinny-but-not-too-skinny girl with the raven hair was nowhere to be seen. Instead on the duo's spot on the wall, sat Oscar and Ryan. Ethan stood before them, kicking a stone against the brick base, waiting for the rebound, kicking it again. Talek stopped in his tracks, only slow enough for Ryan to clocked him. Looking up, the scrawny weasel uttered something to the bulky top dog, unintelligible to Talek's ears, but clear as day to the fearsome ringleader. He rotated his head to face Talek, a sardonic smile lighting up his spiteful face. Quick thinking and past experiences reminded Talek that there was only one option. For boys like him, flight would always win over fight; to run like a chickenshit was the best advice he could give himself. He turned and made to scurry away, though an unexpected broad chest instantly met his face. Obviously a part of the plan – simple, yet brilliantly executed – Coby was there to bar Talek's passage.

The victim's words came weak and without confidence. 'I don't suppose this can wait 'til after school?'

Coby let out an amused snigger. Being Ethan's wingman, he clearly thought that the slight against his friend, permanently etched on wood for all to see, needed to be avenged without delay. As powerful arms pounded on his chest, Talek's balance could not stand up to the force of Coby's shove. Toppling backwards uncontrollably, arms and legs flailing like Bambi on ice, he felt his back come to rest against yet another human buffer stop.

Ethan's stale breath trickled nicotine air into his ear. 'You're fuckin' dead, pal.'

Talek had to act faster than ever if he was to get out of this situation. If Ethan had gripped the rucksack on his back, it would all go horribly wrong. Talek had always worn the straps fairly tight – nerdy, but his way: practical, secure. Had he ever envisaged a scenario like this, he would surely have thought twice and made the bag easier to discard, enabling him to slip free and leave Ethan staring stupidly, eating the runaway's dust. Beyond Coby the school's entrance lay gaping, an invitation to some fantasy world of freedom and peace. Talek felt sick to the stomach at the thought of leaving the premises without prior permission from either a teacher or the dismissive end-of-day bell. Bunking school just wasn't his thing, but ahead could be his best, if not only, means of escape. Lunging forward, without a jarring movement whipping him back, Talek just had time to recognise that not only had Ethan *not* grabbed his bag during the shove, but he had also not expected the little pussy's plan to flee. Luckily for Talek, Ethan's brain was too slow to execute an instantaneous physical reaction, leaving Talek just one more assailant to beat.

Evidently, Coby was equally unexpectant, making a delayed and half-assed attempt to sling a clotheslining arm at the runaway. Talek had always felt mildly aggrieved about his lack of height, though being of an unconfrontational nature he had avoided the raging affliction of the Napoleon Complex. Still, it had niggled at him from time to time. Now he could finally feel smug about his lack of stature. Easily ducking under the clumsily outstretched arm, there was nothing but open space before him.

Running to the gates, he soon heard the thunderous trample of following feet. To his disappointment, the sounds were not accompanied by howling shouts. He could have done with the wild pack of pursuing hounds drawing more attention to themselves. His only hope now was to break free from the school grounds and use all the attributes of the Arctic hare to outrun, outmanoeuvre and outfox them. Reaching the gates first he had a snap decision to make: turn right towards the housing estate, where the following hunters could easily split and intercept him at separate ends of the warren's intersecting roads; or left, along a road he had only ever viewed from above on the internet. The bird's-eye perspective had painted a consistently green picture surrounding the thin, and not-always-visible, grey ribbon of road. An expansive patchwork of open fields filled either side, with small groves of trees dotted here and there; easy to lose a tailing band of savages…in theory.

Valuing his life over fear of the unknown, Talek took a punt on the left, surprised to hear the trampling feet diminishing. He knew *he* had always been quick, but these guys weren't in the school rugby team for no reason (with the exception of Ryan, whose slighter frame and greater agility left him better suited to the football team).

Maybe it's all their smoking, he thought as his feet pounded the pavement. Leaving the walkway and the institution behind him, Talek hit the back lanes. He sensed the gap growing but dared not cast a glance over his shoulder; the darting oribi that turns to check on the learning young cheetah was sure to feel the tap of a tripping paw and the warm piercing of canines through its vulnerable neck. He'd watched enough nature programmes to know *that*.

With the school diminishing unobserved in the distance, Ethan's ordering shouts rang out. Not as far behind as Talek originally thought. If he continued along this claustrophobic road it would all come down to whose legs or lungs gave first. He couldn't run forever, so that left one option. He *had* to lose them.

Tangled hedges and open fields sped by in a blur. As all hope began to feel lost, an opening offered itself in the tall hedgerow to his left, approximately twenty metres ahead. Having ran at a near sprint for what must have been at least half a mile so far, he was starting to slow. Arriving at the opening, a tubular-steel gate barred the entrance to an empty field. The terrain would be harder going on his exhausted legs, but the hunters would be subjected to the same obstacles in the life or death chase. Climbing the gate hurriedly, Talek lost his footing on the rounded metal surface, tumbling down the other side in the process. He picked himself up with no time to mope over the pain in his knee, caused by a heavy thud against metal partway down. His mind raced through the limited list of options.

The gateway was directly in the corner of a rising field of knee-high grass. To press up and along the hedge would leave him in full view of the chasing pack. The hedge itself was a seven-foot-high tangle of brambles and nettles. A sure-fire way to get scraped and sliced, but what the hell. He could scale it.

Mere seconds passed before a burning sensation paled the scrapes and slices into insignificance. Bumps and hives peppered his hands and legs, an excruciating consequence of his intimate relationship with vast armies of stinging nettles. Trying to blank out the pain, moisture welling in his eyes, he landed with a stumbling thump in the next field. Keeping low, Talek followed the hedge running parallel to the road, ignoring his own body's pleads to just give up and accept what fate had in store.

'He went over the gate,' Ethan panted as the troop came to a scuffling halt. 'Oscar, stay on the road. Don't get too far ahead. Cut the bastard off if he tries going back. Dumb and Dumber, you two come with me.'

The progress Talek had made on weary legs along the next field was notable when he eventually heard the heavy rattle of the gate. If he could extend his lead across this lumpy terrain, whilst they still had the hard surface of the road to work in their favour, then surely he was in with a chance. If Mother Nature's cruel joke involving the nettles was the most severe injury to be inflicted upon him today, then it would have to be chalked off as a *good* day in the life of Talek Lean. Looking upwards along the rising ocean of grassland, he could see a copse of trees crawling out into the high point of the field. Seventy, maybe eighty metres away. He would almost certainly be clocked crossing the open expanse, though reaching the thicket would offer the best chance of losing his tail. Certain that those dipshits weren't skilled trackers, the numerous trunks and foliage would do the rest.

'OVER THERE!' Coby's voice bellowed from somewhere in the rear distance.

Crossing a worn dirt track, leaping over tangles of knotted weeds and shrubs, Talek stopped face-to-face with the aging bark of a girthy evergreen. Chancing a look back to his tormentors, the youngster's concern built like heat in a furnace; there were only three of them. Was Lady Luck smiling on him? Had one pair of cigarette-damaged lungs forced a premature end to one feral creature's chase? Or had they combined their devious minds to figure a secondary attack… an ambush of some kind? No time to dwell upon the possibilities. The three in sight had covered a third of the distance between the far hedgerow and the trees. Not willing to tempt fate, Talek refused to assure himself that things were looking in *his* favour.

Entering the sanctuary of the trees, the poor light burdening the day became even gloomier, his way shadowed and shrouded by dense green plumage overhead. Ahead of him, trunk after dark trunk barcoded the distance. Running, weaving, he progressed deeper and deeper into the resilient protective columns. Without slowing, Talek cast another glance back. No sign of movement, but looking back proved to be an idiot move, something more suited to the numbskulls giving chase, he liked to think, than to his above-average-intelligence self. Firstly feeling a heavy knock to his right foot, he was now flying gracefully through the air, arms flapping and hands grasping at open space. Turning his face back to the onrushing floor, the squared edge of a hulk of stone came within millimetres of cracking his skull open and spilling grey matter onto the soggy vegetation.

Talek hit the spongy ground, his open mouth taking in an unhealthy helping of damp, woodland flooring. He tried to suck in a breath, having the wind knocked out of him upon landing. As he finally managed a pained inhalation, the pungent aroma of rotting leaves and sodden earth caught in the back of his throat. Composing himself, his mind flashed back to the slick wall of stone that had come hurtling towards his face, a destructive torpedo emerging from the deep blue. Rolling over, Talek saw the structure. Rising high above his fallen body, pointing like a colossal finger at the gods through an opening in the leafy canopy, stood a granite obelisk. Out of place, unexplainable, yet rising with defiant confidence and pride.

The giant, four-sided monument looming above baffled the youth to the point where all aches and pains were forgotten, wiped out as if by voodoo healing powers. Staggered rows of glistening block tapered to a point. The clouds above had a dizzying effect as the soared past, causing the impressive structure to look like it was toppling over, falling towards his helpless form. Talek's inquisitive side was captivated, his lust for learning stimulated.

What the hell is an obelisk doing here? In the middle of butt-fricking nowhere.

Distant voices snapped him out of his reverie. He would deeply love to study this thing, but that would have to wait for another time, another day, provided there were any remaining before he shuffled off this mortal coil. Finding his feet again, Talek continued in the direction he had been going before the trip. The unplanned stop had reinvigorated him, flooding his body with oxygen and providing him with a second wind. Pressing on fast, he dodged between flanks of trees like a slalom skier. Unaware of his bearings, Talek eventually came to a rutted pathway. Tight and winding, it crawled centipede-like between the trees, trees that, as before, blessed him with a good level of cover. Heading downwards, he followed the path into the shadows.

Stopping after fifty metres or so, Talek listened intently. Hounding voices that had previously surrounded him, rebounding in echoes from the bark-armoured static sentinels, had faded and died. The only sounds now were his own laboured breathing and the protesting rustle of leaves against the sighing breeze. Taking a minute to calm his erratic breaths, he kept a keen ear to the dank air. Still no other human sounds. This plight may just have swung in his favour.

Weighing his options – and deciding they were few – the boy pushed warily on down the narrow track. To go back in the direction from which he came, or to cut sideways back into the mass of trees posed a greater risk of running straight into Ethan and company. Really, the decision had made itself. To follow the path further down into unknown dimness was the only logical course of action. He had not journeyed far when he noticed what appeared to be two low stone walls a short distance ahead, one to the left of the track, and one to the right, each just two or three feet high. Cautiously, he made his way towards them, keeping a watchful eye through the trees as he went, prepared to run at the first hint of movement.

No other living thing had caught Talek's attention by the time he had reached the walls. An irregularity of wide, flat stones in browns and reds lay cemented together horizontally. The crowning layer – again a mismatch of sizes – had been placed vertically, pointing their serrated edges to the sky like a lethal warning to intruders. Batons of timber ran snugly against and slightly higher than the stone, serving as a deterrent to anyone who might want to leap from the structure, though if anything, the wooden beam would aid a person intent on hanging themselves, serving as a great place to tie the rope.

Stooping until his fingers brushed the gritty floor, he made his way to the centre of the bridge, keeping low behind the wall before gingerly lifting his head to peer over the edge. A narrow road climbed away gradually before disappearing around a sweeping bend. Concluding that this must be the road he had seen on the internet, the road he had started to follow before dashing into the field, Talek made his way back to the construction's beginning. Judging the bend in the road to be no more than twenty metres away, he made to scramble down a bank of intertwined vines and slick stone on the further side of the tiny bridge. This, at least, may offer some chance of cover if the crew came into sight. (Or so he hoped.)

He slipped down the slimy surface, feet landed heavily on hard asphalt. Eyeing the low arch in front of him gave him a chill from the small of his back to the nape of his neck. He could see the browns and reds of the stone above the arch, a clear addition that appeared to be added hundreds of years after the original build of voussoir elements as black as death. The opening was barely wider than a family car. By the time its warped wall started to vault inwards, even a medium-size van would run the risk of getting wedged in if the driver was stupid enough to attempt passing through.

Dripping with stagnated moisture, looking into its ribbed anthracite-dark inner walls and ceiling was like staring into the throat of some great, grotesque amphibian. Even the sky over this ancient monster had darkened, as if to befit the intimidating essence of the setting.

This could be in a horror film, Talek thought, stepping forward as his mind conjured a series of hideous images. That was when the smell hit him. Whatever this thing's last meal was, it freaking stank. Inhaling the cloying atmosphere was like facing the last escape of air from a decaying corpse. Pinching a thumb and finger to his nose, he braved another step forward.

One foot inside the beast. Two…

What happened next was utterly incomprehensible, a devastating assault on Talek's perception that he would later confess to Erin as a feeling worse than death itself. The black chasm of the tunnel had become brighter than spring morning sunshine. Crippling pain seared though his eyes, engulfing his brain. Unable to defend itself against such intense heat, Talek's entire body erupted into flame. Polyester and cotton fabric turned to plastic and stuck fast to his torso. Looking to his dark hands, frightened to the point of utter breakdown, their skin started to blister, bubbling pink and yellow before melting to bone at the tips of his fingers. The air had become even more unbreathable as it scorched his lungs, altering from the rotten smell of dead bodies to a miasma of intensely heated paint fumes and fuels, and liquifying plastics and rubbers.

And the screams.

Not just his. He *was* screaming, but he was not the only one. Inconceivably, he was not alone in here.

Collapsing to his hands and knees, praying for the end and petrified that it would not come at all, Talek's fingers sank into a hot and sticky substance. Tarlike rubber clung to his skeletal digits. The scalding substance gave off a putrid aroma of charring flesh, as if it vented the last traces of a human life, leaving a spectral impression of their final, macabre moments of mortality.

Looking out from the bowels of Hell, Talek could see the outside world, unaware and unaffected by what was happening under the arch. Toppling onto his side, the pain becoming so immeasurable it had surely reached its pinnacle, the boy rolled determinedly. Salvation was mere feet away. Given the choice, he would die under an open sky, *not* inside this fetid abomination.

Landing on his back with solemn clouds overhead, all pain ceased as suddenly as it had begun. All screaming had cut off abruptly, as if a soundproof steel door had slammed shut on the fiery realm. Rays of light shone through small windows in the cloud, piercing the canopy of gently shifting leaves and branches in a myriad of heavenly shafts. Burning flesh and chemical smells had been replaced by that earthy odour that exuded from the ground when rain followed a prolonged period of warmth.

The whole world seemed different – not just from inside the inferno of the archway (which, as Talek rolled his head back towards, was nothing but unextraordinary darkness once more), but also from the gloom of the day that had preceded that harrowing event.

Still lying on his back, he raised both hands from the reassuringly firm ground and hovered them over his face. Fingers the same brown they always were, paler on the soft undersides than on the backs. Sky blue cotton and polyester shirtsleeves were grubby from his misadventure, but completely intact.

'What… the… hell?' he breathlessly wheezed out.

TWELVE

The room seemed somehow unfamiliar: emptier, lonelier. Emptiness and loneliness were usually preferable for this solitary character, but after the events he had endured that afternoon he felt… What did he feel? Diminished? Subjugated to a higher power? *Changed?*

Yes, that was it. Simply, changed. The vulnerability that had always been an unwelcomed and inextirpable aspect of his character had intensified, yet at the same time he felt invigorated. The pain was real, so real; unlike anything he could draw comparisons to from his past. Could this phantom attack come again, and at its own will? Maybe that was his vulnerability – that he could do nothing about its timing. But the strength that came from *surviving* such a brutal assault as that which befell him under the imposing little bridge? Beyond measure. A demon tried to consume him that afternoon, he was as sure of that fact as he was sure that day follows night, and the moon controls the tides. And although his fear and frailty had reached near-fatal levels, he had fought. He had fought, and he had triumphed.

Sitting in the darkened room at his newly positioned desk (under the window overlooking the ancient Church of Saint Cohan and its circumambient oblique headstones), Talek opened his laptop and fired it up. An ethereal blue glow transformed his face as the bootup screen flared into life.

Mother was pissed at him, and she'd made little to no effort to conceal her anger. Not only had he skipped school that afternoon, but he had also dared to venture down a road she had not permitted him to travel on. And after finding him, slouched and suspicious-looking walking towards home only a few minutes after she had left to collect him, he had come out with the most ridiculous, godless, dark fantasy of torment and hellfire.

How could her son even dare to come up with a filthy lie like that. That is *not* how she brought him up.

After screaming at him to be silent in the car, the groaning of the vehicle's reliable workhorse engine was all that filled the void, pressing in on his auditory nerves like a vice onto soft wood. He was better off up in his bedroom, out of the crazy woman's way.

Pawing at the silky smoothness of the mousepad, Talek opened an internet window and clicked on the email link in the top corner, praying to see a familiar, friendly name appear once he tapped in his password. For the first time that day he managed a smile. Hovering the curser over the name *'Erin'*, he tapped open the most recent email:

> *Missed u today. Please tell me u r ok? It's my fault. Landed myself a detention. If I'd been there… xx*

Talek swallowed the words as if they were lumps of coal, each one causing a welling in the eyes and the swelling of a sentimental smile on his lips. It wasn't her fault; he should be capable of surviving one lunchtime without her. Attempting to collect his thoughts and rein in his emotions, he looked up from his laptop and out into the consuming darkness. The dramatic swaying of the trees informed him that once again the wind had picked up. Once upon a time he could not have summoned the strength to even glance at this scene, let alone actively watch the death dance of the trees. Seeing them swoosh and lurch under the night sky, lowering their hungry limbs to the crumbling church and the tilting tombstones, had previously caused him to believe the old, knotted wooden watchers had come to life, that they would reach down and rip the stone epitaphs from the hallowed earth and pluck the old building from its foundations before devouring the lot, whole.

The things we see as children…

Breaking his trance from the darkened obscurity of the churchyard, Talek returned his attention to the laptop's glaring screen. He tapped a few spontaneous words, echoing what was in his head. Then he depressed the delete key until his onscreen thoughts became nothing but a blank draft once more. Those feelings were his alone… for now, not Erin's, not hackers, and certainly not yours or mine. Sighing, he looked back to the outside world, its nebulous blankness a symbol of his own sentiments.

Blankness?

That was wrong; so wrong. Ascending the granite steps, a huddled figure rose. Draped from top to tail in black, it moved apparition-like towards the fencing that cordoned off the ancient ruin.

With that, Talek's newfound strength evaporated. He stood and yanked the curtains closed. Dropping back to his chair he typed one sentence before hitting send:

I think I'm losing the plot xx

THIRTEEN

The Volvo's wipers shoved at the driving rain, beating away the water in torrents and leaving clean half-arches on the screen for only fractional seconds at a time. Leaves torn prematurely from their branches sped like sailboats along flowing streams at either side of the road, accumulating at storm drains ill-equipped for the excess levels of water and debris.

'No silly ideas about bunking off today, young man.' Tamsyn gave an inarguable look in the rear-view.

'I wasn't *bunking*,' muttered Talek unproductively.

Averting his eyes from the glassy reflection of hers, he focused on the liquid tracks tracing down his side window. Every few moments their downward course was forced sideways as gusts of wind pounded at the car. As if sharing a group telepathy, each droplet coexisted perfectly in mesmeric murmuration.

'Just don't go *anywhere* until I'm there. I shouldn't be late.'

Whatever, he thought, feeling no urge to reply.

Arriving at the drop-off point Talek exited the vehicle, closing the door firmly behind him. Pulling his fur lined hood up over his dense, short curls, he sheltered his head from the hostile weather, and his embarrassed face from the even more hostile glances and titters of other children. He scuttled towards the school building, his mind running through the timetable that lay ahead, more as a useful distraction than actually planning his day.

The distraction served only to unsettle him more. Today was going to be a nightmare. Another helping of science, with Ryan; P.E. with all *four* of them, and boys and girls were split, so no Erin. Worst of all, according to the radio on the way in, this weather wasn't happy with just being crap, it was set to get worse. Wetter. Windier. Angrier. People were even being urged to stay at home, especially the elderly, for fear of a threat to life. Threats aside, this meant no outside lunch. This man was flying solo.

Reaching his desk in the tutor room, Talek placed his bag on the floor below and took a seat, resting his wrists on the table's edge and staring at its bland laminated surface. No scribbled witty insults on this plasticky surface. No chance for him to get carried away and land himself in a whole heap of shit, again.

'Again,' the voice came from his tutor, Ms Baines. Strict, long in the tooth, and well known for having the ability to speak her mind without even a cursory thought of any offence she may cause. 'The local law enforcement will be in Deputy Head Sharples' office today for any person who may have information about Jowan.' She straightened a pile of dogeared workbooks prepared for her first class, before sliding them to the side of her desk. 'Though why they've been here every day since, asking the same questions to the same people and, *surprise surprise*, getting the same fruitless answers, rather than getting out there and looking for the lad is anyone's guess.'

Tell it like it is, Bainsey, you old bat, thought Talek.

'I've got information about him.' The voice of Henry Dillinger. Class clown. Occupying a space on the back row. Most of the group looked to him with smirks on their faces, eagerly awaiting the *smart* that was sure to come next. Talek was not one of these. 'He was a nob,' Henry beamed.

The limited number of faces in Talek's camp turned in scorn at the jackass seated at the back. The majority of the class, nevertheless, erupted into fits of laughter.

'Settle down!' Ms Baines ordered. 'Thank you Henry, that's very helpful. Perhaps I can escort you to the officers and you can personally deliver that information to them.'

Silence from the dippet with the runaway mouth.

'Just as I thought,' Ms Baines said, taking her seat with a self-satisfied smile on her ugly mug.

With Baines' monotonous call reeling through the register, Talek drifted into a swirling pool of his own reflections, the names and confirming mumbles around muffling down to nothing. Henry's use of past tense vocabulary struck an emotional chord, and his tutor's failure to call him up on it only served to compound the deep sense of foreboding.

He was…

***

'How was your day?' Tamsyn asked with an apathy that hit like a physical blow to the chest. She could have been asking the steering wheel, for all the genuine interest that was in her tone.

Talek stared at the back of her scruffy auburn head, wishing the headrest would shield it completely from sight, or better still, force it into the windscreen, spreading her pointless brain like a Jackson Pollock masterpiece.

'Uneventful,' he said. 'We didn't go out all day. So that kind of messed up my plans for running away.' *Also, those bullying assholes you don't seem concerned about were very subdued, but I'll keep the important stuff to myself seeing as you don't give a toss.* He guessed they were expecting to be in a lot of trouble after yesterday. It would appear, however, that nothing had been done about the situation, thus assuring their survival to torment him another day.

'That's nice,' she said. A standard answer to confirm that she was paying no attention whatsoever.

'Do you think Jowan is dead?' He had raised his voice in an attempt to make the question impossible to evade.

'What?'

Looking in the rear-view mirror, Talek could see that his mother kept her eyes on the road. He could also see that her nostrils flared, a sure sign that she was straining to stifle her temper.

'Jowan. Do you think he's dead?'

'What sort of question is that? I don't even know who you're talking about.'

'Yeah, you do,' he said pleasantly. 'He's been all over the news. TV. Radio. You probably just blanked it out cos your precious God might've let him down.'

The Volvo rolled to a stop as the car in front waited to make a right turn across oncoming traffic. Tamsyn reached her left arm around the back of the passenger seat and turned to stare her son into submission. 'That's enough of that!' she snapped, the whites of her eyes glowing a painful pink. Her mouth was set in a switchblade scar.

'It's just that,' Talek went on, shifting uncomfortably under her damning gaze, 'Henry used the word "was" when he spoke about him, and Miss didn't correct him.'

Riding the clutch as she excessively plunged the throttle, Tamsyn took her sickly pink eyes from him and pulled away on the now unimpeded road.

'We don't talk of the dead,' she warned flatly.

Guess I got my answer.

'Which is why I like this weather.'

Cos you're miserable, Talek wanted to say. Instead, he went with, 'I don't follow?'

'It keeps you out of that wretched graveyard,' she said, flicking a glance at the mirror. 'Stops you from doing the weird things you do.'

You call me freaking weird… Jesus H. Christ, woman.

Exiting Tresillian, they rounded the right-hand bend to the bridge in silence, just the mumble of the engine and the slush of tyres through rain drenched tarmac for comfort. Hitting the bridge, the water below had risen dramatically in sound and volume. Beyond the low parapet to their right, a raging spate plumed from below the intrados, spewing up a shit-brown froth as the currents roiled and ripped at the river's silty mud bed. The low grassy scrubland that usually sat in view to the right of the narrow channel was completely submerged under the liquid copper surface. Talek had never seen Tresillian River so high or so volatile. Banking trees on the left, trees that were accustomed to let their extremities sway and gently kiss the channel's glassy surface, were being yanked and stripped of leaf, twig, and branch by the sheer power of the surging water.

Once off the bridge, Tamsyn flicked the indicator lever and cut across the oncoming lane, hitting the backroads towards home. Watching the sudden disappearance of the river and its filthy flurries behind tall, ferny country hedges was a welcomed sorcerer's trick to Talek. He longed to be in the comforting dry safety of his bedroom. More importantly, he longed to be out of this car, no longer having to look at his mother's scruffy head, or her plagued eyes in the rearview.

FOURTEEN

Fresh morning air – the cool calm after the storm – brought goosebumps to the exposed flesh of Deanna's arms, her fine blonde hairs standing to attention as she squeezed her legs into her wetsuit under the shadow of her T5's raised tail.

Kayla was already crouching on the flat grassy bank, sliding water bottles into snug compartments on each of their kayaks. Kayla was always the first to be ready, which is why she was the one leaning over now, busying herself with the morning sun warm on her black neoprene-covered back.

Sliding her arms into the wetsuit, Deanna pulled the van's tail down and headed over. The damp grass was cold on the bare soles of her feet, yet the glistening blades felt luxurious as they tickled her skin, like stepping onto a plush new carpet after tears of tiled floors.

'Can you do me up?' she said, reaching Kayla and turning her back to her.

Kayla straightened up and pulled at the zip pull extender. Giving Deanna a playful slap on the bum, she said, 'You know, the cord is there so you can do it yourself.'

Deanna laughed, 'And deprive you of the view? Right, have you got the keys? I'll grab me camera and lock Doris up.'

'Camera's already in.' Kayla raised the key fob and pressed the closed padlock symbol. Doris chirped in response. 'And the van is now locked.'

'What would I do without you?' said Deanna, placing her cold hands to the sides of Kayla's face and giving her a kiss.

'Oh, and by the way,' said Kayla, 'your deck hatch is really tight. You might wanna lube that up when we get home.'

'That's what she said!'

'Dirty bitch,' Kayla sniggered. 'Come on, let's do this.'

Taking the lead, Kayla headed to the front of the kayaks and threaded each hand through a carrying handle. Deanna made her way to the rear and did the same. Between them, they carried the two crafts to the bank and lowered them to the ground. The tide was low, the river only a narrow channel, but at this point the body of the winding sea snake ventured closest to the grassy bank. Which was good. Who would want to sink their feet into that foul, sloppy mud of the riverbed if they didn't have to?

'Ugh,' Deanna crinkled her nose up. 'It stinks!'

'Oh, soz,' Kayla smiled, 'I thought that was you.'

'Shut it!'

'Must all be from yesterday's deluge, churning up God-only-knows how many years of shit.'

Both turning their individual kayaks parallel to the flowing water, they lowered them the small drop to the surface and stepped down carefully, grasping tufts of grass on the bank as an added security measure. Taking a seat, each released their paddle from the bungee tie and pushed away from the bank.

'So,' said Deanna, 'where to?' She looked to Kayla, who was rocking gently on the craft a few feet away.

Placing her paddle across her lap, Kayla pulled her wavy ebony hair back into a ponytail, securing it in a band she'd kept around a slim wrist. 'Um, how about head towards Malpas, a cheeky Pimm's at the Heron, and then back again?'

'What?' Deanna blurted. 'That's gotta be what, three miles each way?'

'So, you would've earned your halftime tipple,' Kayla grinned. 'Unless you're not *man* enough, of course.'

'Your gob is gonna get you in trouble today, missy.'

'Promises, promises.'

Deanna pushed the front of Kayla's kayak with the tip of her paddle, rotating her girlfriend anticlockwise. Thrusting the blade into slick water and gaining a head start, she shouted over her shoulder, 'Looks like you're the one who can't handle it.'

Kayla smirked as she watched Deanna's short blonde pixie cut drifting away, its pink highlights catching in the sun like a chemical fire. *You crack on love*, she thought, letting her counterpart build up a head of steam. Deanna had never outpaced her before, and that wasn't going to change today.

Leaving the village of Tresillian behind, the surroundings turned from quaint waterfront properties to a vibrant green of trees still thick with foliage, rising tall from the ascending embankments. Wildfowl chattered quietly, hidden away in their lofty canopies. Water trickled, and the therapeutic slap, slap, slap of the bow on its clearing surface carried the couple blissfully through their day of leisure. The difference in weather conditions between the previous and present day was staggering. Dropping half a blade into the water behind her and spinning the front end to the left, Deanna fumbled with the deck hatch as Kayla eased up behind her.

'What ya seen?' Kayla asked.

'Egret. Fishing,' replied Deanna. 'I think it just caught something, so hopefully there'll be more where that came from.' She was not too worried about missing the opportunity. The egret's pure white plumage had always mesmerised her. Deanna felt that if angels existed here on Earth, then they were surely sent in the form of these majestic white birds.

'It'll be full up by the time you've opened that thing,' Kayla pointed out unhelpfully. 'Here, I'll give you a hand.'

Drawing beside the craft and reaching over, she placed her thumbs in the hatch's recessed grips. Deanna placed hers on the opposite side, and between them the black plastic disc budged with a protesting squeal.

'Thanks, muscles.'

'You're welcome,' Kayla smiled cockily.

Placing the hatch lid on the bow of the kayak, Deanna pulled out her camera bag. Removing the device and lifting the strap over her head, she got to work with her paddle once again, gently guiding it back to find the position she had drifted from. Kayla watched on with a contented smile. This was her *thing*, what Deanna came kayaking for. Kayla was the more athletic of the two, but as long as Deanna could bring her trusty Nikon, she was happy to go along with whatever her partner wanted.

Toying with the 18-140mm lens – not as large as she would like for wildlife photography, but she was limited to size due to the kayak's small built-in waterproof sack – she found the egret and adjusted the manual focus. After taking four or five shots in conjunction with the javelin jabs of the egret's bill, Deanna got the shot.

'Yes!' she whispered loudly, after hitting the *'play'* symbol and seeing a silvery fish hanging from the bird's deadly, yellow neb.

Placing the camera back in the bag, and in turn the bag into the hatch, she spun herself with the paddle and sidled up to Kayla.

'Happy?' the dark-haired young woman asked.

'Big time,' Deanna answered, 'but whereabouts do you think we are?'

Kayla had long since given up on Deanna's obsession of labelling her photographs: location; date; even the bloody time. Serious OCD issues. Right on cue she caught Deanna checking her wristwatch.

'If you look down to that far corner,' Kayla used her paddle as an extended finger, 'that's where the river bends at St. Clement. Looks to be coming on a mile away, so I reckon that just the other side of those trees,' she said as she swung the paddle towards where the bird continued its stealthy, calculated wading, 'must be, uh, Merther.'

'Merther?' repeated Deanna, her face screwing as she drew a blank. 'Never 'eard of it.'

'Why would you have? A farm, maybe three or four houses. Oh, and a *really* old church. I'm talking ancient. Creepy as fuck, falling to the ground and being eaten by weeds. You'd love it,' Kayla assured, 'we should go there with your camera one day.'

'Maybe,' said Deanna. 'Anyway, onwards. It's gotta be Pimm's o'clock, right?'

***

Sliding an SD and card reader into the corresponding port on the front of her computer tower, Deanna watched as a harlequin of thumbnails spread consecutively across the monitor. Finally, after the continual reproduction had stopped, she hit the *import* tab and looked on as the percentage bar grew.

'I'm going up for a bath,' Kayla said, placing a hand on Deanna's shoulder. 'You coming?'

Deanna caressed the back of the hand. 'Tempting, but no ta. I wanna get a few of these edited.'

'If you edit them, they're no longer genuine photos,' Kayla argued.

'It's an art form.'

'Whatever.' Kayla pulled her hand back and headed for the door. 'Your loss. But if you change your mind…'

'Okay,' said Deanna, waving a thank you to her back.

Listening to the water running upstairs, Deanna smiled. It had been a perfect day, and a long soak with the woman she loved would be a fitting end. She got up from her swivel chair and went to the kitchen. Grabbing a bottle of wine from the fridge she poured out a couple of glasses, before returning the bottle and headed back to the living room.

Ninety-two per cent.

Placing one glass on the desk, she made her way upstairs with the other.

'Change your mind?' asked Kayla, as Deanna knocked and entered the room.

Deanna looked at Kayla's slim, milky body stood in contrasting jet black lace underwear, the dark scorpion on her left abdomen, the monochrome leafy rose vine on her right thigh. Yes. Tempting, she most definitely was. 'So *very* nearly,' she whispered. 'Just thought I'd bring you a drink.'

Smiling, Kayla took the glass. 'Ooh, you do look after me. You sure you're not gonna stay? It's getting' *hot* in here!'

'Keep it warm for me. Hopefully I'll be done quick enough to join you.'

Kayla leaned forward and kissed her gently on the lips. 'Mmm, you're such a nerd, tapping up the mouse rather than tapping up *this*.'

'I know,' Deanna laughed. 'Like you say, it's *my* loss.'

Leaving the room, Deanna headed back downstairs. She shuffled into the chair, struggling to find comfort. This, Deanna put down to knowing she'd be more comfortable soaking in a luxurious heated tub. She picked up the glass and took a sip. A fair chunk of the images were *deleters* (as was always the way when snapping shots on a wobbling watercraft), though there were a few decent shots of the boats anchored offshore below the

Heron Inn. Deanna toyed with those, refining them, altering the warmth, clearing any blemishes, using her H.G. Wells magic on any unwanted heads poking out of cabins.

She was aware that she was taking too long before she even got to the first capture of the egret. *What an idiot; who edits backwards, duh.* Deciding after all that she did want to be up in the steamy bathroom, she skipped the few shots of the bird striking its bill into the water to no avail. Flicking past, the image with the glistening fish filled the screen. Eyeing the photograph, her first thought was to darken the surroundings in order to enhance the already impossibly white feathers even further, and to bolden the yellowy orange of the egret's spear of a bill, as well as the gleaming gold of its calculating iris. Looking down the sleek feathery body, her gaze fell to bird's anthracite legs, so prehistoric in their genetic structure: long, thin, and scaly skinned, double-knuckled toes leaving tiny dark pools in the sodden mud at the water's edge.

That's when she saw the gnarly branch less than a metre from the bird. An inverted replica of the hunting creature's own gangly limbs. Only bigger. Much bigger.

Deanna stared at it for a long time. Rising from the mud to the left rear of the elegant wader, it thinned as it went on, twisting at a large knot, then extending briefly at a forty-five-degree angle. From its flat, stumpy end, twiglike limbs as knuckled as the egret's scaly feet probed at the air. Only, unlike the feet, there were five digits. Not four. Four curling in claws from the tip, one smaller one sprouting from the side. Zooming in, she could see that the thin coating of mud had started to dry in the morning sun, flaking and peeling from the base material.

Deanna zoomed in further until the screen filled with just the mudflat and this protruding... *branch?* No. Time became a void. Suddenly, Deanna deeply regretted refusing Kayla's invitation of sharing a bath. She could have been up there now, secure between the raven-haired beauty's thighs, sipping at the wine whilst enjoying having hot oils massaged into her shoulders (one of Kayla's many specialities), with her masterful, dexterous fingers tracing seductively down the ridges of her spine. Instead… instead of staring at *this*.

'Didn't fancy joining me then?'

Deanna started at the unexpected sound of Kayla's voice. She turned sharply to see her partner wrapped in a towel behind her, arms folded, eyebrows raised. Kayla noticed instantly that any trace of colour had drained from her girlfriend's face. The artificial light cast from the LCD screen added an extra touch of death to her complexion.

'What's the matter? You look like you've seen a ghost.'

Deanna raised a frightened finger to the picture displayed on the screen. 'What d'you think that is?'

Bending her back, Kayla peered concentratedly. The tips of her wet hair brushed like icicles against Deanna's cheek.

After staring silently for what felt like an eternity, Kayla felt he stomach convulse. She swallowed hard. Voice barely a whisper, she said, '*Oh, my, fucking, God.*'

FIFTEEN

A chiming bell had never filled Talek with such jubilance before. Even the end-of-day bell could not have sounded so sweet as that of the lunchtime call. Yesterday was a drowned-out abomination. Today, glorious sunshine. Back to what September was all about, peachy weather now that the kids were all back at school, after a lame six weeks of patchy cloud and drizzle. Not that he minded. Being outside now meant that he could see Erin, provided she wanted to see him, of course. He had not received a reply to his emotional plea-mail, but there could be any number of reasons as to why that may be the case.

Picking up his bag from under the desk with one hand, and grabbing his workbooks in the other, he tucked them away. The lesson was history. *Literally*, History.

'For anyone who didn't bring in their homework today,' Mr Amos blurted, his annoyingly buoyant fringe bouncing with every amplified word, 'I want it *before* the next lesson.' Chairs clattered and he fought to speak over the din, fully aware that with the sound of the bell, what little attention had remained on him rung into another existence. 'I don't care if your dog *died* choking on it, I'll take it with the stench of the mutt's last living breath lingering on the pages!'

How delightful, thought Talek, racing for the door.

A ton weight lifted from his shoulders as he saw Erin waiting for him on the low slab wall. The relieved burden quickened his steps as he beelined towards her, neither knowing nor caring if any of the assholes were in close proximity.

'Hello, stranger,' she said as he took his place next to her.

'Hi.'

'Is that it?' she said. 'Is that all you've got to say? "*Hi*"? I thought you were going mad. You don't want to share your logic?'

Talek thought about it for a moment. 'Not here,' he said at last. 'People already think I'm weird, if anyone overhears, I'm a dead man walkin'.'

'Okay. Weather's good, how about I come around yours after school?'

Talek gave her a worried look.

'The graveyard, obvs,' she smiled. 'Not your house!'

A visible relief washed over his face. 'Yeah, I suppose.'

'Oh well try not to sound too chuffed about it.' She gave him a gentle elbow to the ribs.

'It's not that,' he said, lowering his head and scuffing the toe of one shoe into the ground. 'It's that I li… I don't want you to think that I concoct these weird, dark fantasies in my head.'

'I like you too,' she said, 'if that's what you were trying to say. And I'll believe anything you have to tell me. I don't think there's any reason you'd have to lie to me.'

'I wouldn't,' he said, looking up with a palpable sincerity in his eyes.

'Good,' she smiled, this time with an affectionate shoulder nudge. 'And I, you.' Erin took in a deep breath of warm, wildflower scented air. 'Plus, I've kind of got my own stuff I need to get off my chest. Stuff at home. I'm thinking you may be a good listener.'

Talek would likely never disclose this to her, for fear of being mocked, but he felt he could listen to her dulcet tones all day.

Content with chewing the fat some more – small talk, school talk – lunchtime passed in the blink of an eye. The end-of-lunch bell rang, and as if receiving a blessing from above, no sign had been seen of Talek's quartet of nemeses all lunchtime.

***

Erin's breath caught as rustling footsteps neared, deadened by the thick grassy covering. She knew it had to be Talek, but as she sat with her back to a granite slab, her mind wandered to the dead rising from their earthy prisons, and ghostly figures creeping disturbingly amidst shards of sunlight cast though ancient, twisted yew trees. Scratching leaves came as whispered conspiracies, keeping her senses on high alert.

'If you're thinking of jumping out on me,' Talek's hoarse croak drifted over, 'I can see your feet.'

Her laugh from beyond the grave (for want of a better expression), brought a smile to his face.

As Talek rounded the headstone, Erin said, 'There's room for two if I shove up a bit.'

'I think I'll just sit in the path,' he said. 'I don't think Martha would appreciate *both* of us leaning against that stone.'

'Who's Martha?' Erin asked.

'She's right behind you.'

'What the fu...' Erin snapped, springing to her feet and swirling around. 'There's no one there.' *Maybe he is going mad.*

'She's there alright. Six feet under.'

'Oh, shit.' *Or maybe I'm just an idiot.* 'Well, now that we're both on our feet, is there anywhere else to go around this redneck joint?'

Thinking about it, Talek shook his head. 'Not really.'

'Are you serious?' asked Erin. 'All this space and nowhere to go?'

'I'm just worried about getting spotted.'

'Am I that embarrassing to be seen with?'

'No, it's not that,' said Talek, looking flustered. 'You're… okay.'

'Great. What an accolade. I'm *okay*.'

'That's not what I meant,' he said sheepishly.

Erin gave him a reassuring smile. 'Don't worry. I'm only teasing.'

Letting out a nervous laugh, Talek scratched his head and looked around. 'Actually,' he said, 'we can go down to the river. If we go out the north gate___'

'Whoa, hang on there,' Erin interrupted, '*north* gate? Who do you think I am, Dora the friggin' Explorer? Point, man!'

'Oh, sorry,' said Talek. Raising his arm he pointed a finger in the direction of a long wall to the right, where Erin's bike leaned partially sunken into the bracken. 'If we go out there, to the corner and into the farm lane, we can cut into the next field. A hedge will hide us all the way down to the woods and the river.'

'Sounds like a plan. Let's get a wriggle on.'

Having hopped the hedge and descended onto muddy ground that still squelched underfoot, Talek stood to his full height. Ensuring that the irregular wall of earth, rubble and bramble concealed him from the watching windows of Scoan's Cottage, he urged Erin to follow him over the rutted field. They walked hurriedly, and after two-hundred metres or so reached a thick, wooded area. The scent of fallen, rotting leaves was palpable, serving to remind the pair that the year was further on than the day's sunshine portrayed. Making their way in over the gnarled root strewn floor, blue sky gave way to suffocating Sacramento green.

'How long do we have to be in here?' asked Erin, a sense of trepidation in her tone.

'Three or four minutes,' Talek said with an impassive insouciance, like this solitarius dreariness was precisely his kind of environment. To Erin it spoke volumes of the boy's lonely upbringing. 'It's only a hundred-and-fifty metres or so, but it's not the easiest terrain. We'll hit a private road soon, then we can follow that, cut through more trees, then we'll hit a grassy bank by the river.'

'You certainly know your way around here,' Erin said, looking around warily.

'With only here and the church for entertainment, I don't have much choice. I'd much rather be out losing myself in the wild than sat at home with my mum.'

Erin considered probing him about that particular mother-son relationship, about what made his mum so… so like she is. She decided not to force that conversation. Talek would open up on that front if and when the time felt right, and if ever he felt comfortable.

Once the traipsing along the private road and the jaunt through another thicket of trees — thankfully on a much smaller scale than the previous gloomy overhang — on the opposite side was complete, they did indeed come to the promised grassy bank. The lush carpet bubbled and frothed underfoot, yesterday's surge of heavy rains and rushing waters by no means ready to soak away fully just yet. A little further on, a convenient pair of semi-submerged granite boulders offered at least somewhere dry to park their bottoms. Before them the river flowed lazily, tickling the grass' edge with a tranquil gurgle. Thankfully the tide was high, alleviating the encompassing reek the mudflats often emitted.

Shuffling on her slender bottom and finding a miniscule degree of comfort, Erin whacked the ball into Talek's court. 'You first. Hit me with it.'

'I don't know where to start,' he said, thinking hard. 'You know when Ethan and the others chased me out of school on Monday?'

'I've heard a few rumours, but the details are sketchy. It'd sound better coming from you.'

'Well, so they tried collaring me, and somehow I managed to run past Coby. You know he's not the quickest.'

'Yeah, cos he's a chump and you're a little pocket rocket,' Erin cut in.

'Maybe, but I'll let *you* tell him that,' Talek sniggered in jest. 'Well, when I got past him, the only place to run for was for the school gate. Anyway, I pegged it down the backroads, cut into a field with a load of trees at the top end, and lost them. And that's when I ended up on this bridge.'

'Is that the old one over the backroad?' Erin asked.

'Yeah. You know it?'

'Everyone does,' she said, trying not to sound demeaning. 'That's Devil's Arch.'

'Devil's Arch?' Talek looked confused and concerned in equal measures, the colour draining from his cheeks so much he could almost pass for a white boy.

'Yeah. Why, what's the matter?'

No answer.

'Tal, what happened up there?'

'Nothing,' he said. 'At least, not *up* there.'

Noticing beads of perspiration materialise on his prominent forehead, Erin placed a comforting hand on the back of his. A slight tremor was evident under her palm, prompting her to wait while he attempted to regain some composure.

'I scrambled down the far side of it, stopping for a while to make sure they weren't gonna head back to the road and come down that way.' He stopped and picked up a piece of jagged stone. Spying the tips of a branch breaking the water's constantly moving surface like the pleading hand of a swimmer caught in a riptide, he threw the stone towards it.

'Nice shot,' said Erin, after the stone clipped the extremities with a strangely hollow *doof*.

Talek paid no heed to the compliment. 'I figured they weren't coming, that they must've gone back to school. So, I decided it was safe to do same. I went under the bridge, and…'

'Go on,' she urged, 'it's okay.'

'It's like… It's like I caught fire. The hole tunnel turned blinding bright, and I was burning alive. Literally. Not *felt* like; it *was* happening. Only, I couldn't've been, cos look at my arms.' He held them out to her. The skin was unblemished, sensuously smooth.

'But when I was under there,' he continued, 'they didn't look like this. They were bubbling up; blistering. My skin was melting. I could see the bone, and all. Shit, I could even see the flames. Smell burning fuel, burning rubber, and my own frying flesh and hair.'

'Jesus,' Erin whispered, lost for anything more productive to say.

'It was a feeling worse than death itself. I collapsed. I could hear screaming all around me: someone else's, not just my own.' A tear rolled down his puffy cheek. Erin thought of thumbing it way; decided against it.

'I could see outside the tunnel,' said Talek. 'The road, the hedge, everything was… normal. Everything that was happening to me was happening under that *fucking* bridge!'

Erin was taken aback by this mild-mannered boy's use of the *F* word. Whilst being no stranger to the use of colourful language herself, she had never heard it from *him*. The sound was so alien from his innocent lips.

'I managed to roll out. And that was it. Just like that. All over.'

He tried reading her silence as water lapped gently at the shoreline. 'So, I'm nuts, right?'

'No,' she protested. 'It's just, everyone thinks that place is haunted as it is, and I've heard a so many stories about it. But that? I mean, what the fuck?'

'You believe me?'

'As crazy as it sounds,' she said, 'yeah, I think I do.'

A cold chill ran down her spine. Moving closer to Talek she snuggled against him. The heat from his body, and his reluctance to move away were instantly reassuring. Sitting in silence for a short while, they watched as flashes of sunlight shimmered like pyrotechnics over the shifting body of water.

'Looks like a hand,' Erin eventually broke the peace, looking to where Talek had previously launched the stone. 'I must be goin' dippy after hearing what happened to you.'

'What does? That?' He gestured to the finger-like sticks breaking the surface several metres out, his face scrunched up in bafflement.

'Well, it does to me. Imagine that. How freaky would that be?'

'Now who's the nutter?'

'Shut up,' she laughed, another alien sound given the macabre topic of conversation.

'So, assuming I didn't imagine it all, what do you think the flames mean?' he asked after another silence. 'I mean, these things usually have a meaning, don't they?'

'Beats me,' she admitted, 'but if that was a genuine hallucination, I want to find out. Leave it to me. I love stuff like that.'

'Weirdo,' he chuckled. 'Anyway, what gives with you? You didn't sound too happy at lunchtime.'

Erin pulled her knees up to her chin and wrapped her arms around her shins. The light breeze played with a silky ribbon of jet black hair hanging down beside her pale-skinned cheek. Talek wanted to delicately brush it behind her ear, desperately wanted to feel its smoothness, but…

'Where to start?' she said, as if asking the question to herself.

He allowed her time to come up with her own answer. Turning his attention upriver, he cocked his nose up as sour country air from the nearby dairy herd drifted on the balmy current.

'They've been arguing a lot recently, my olds.' Erin started picking absently at a piece of dry skin on her knee through the torn fabric of her jeans. 'I always thought they were indestructible, but recently…'

'There's nothing you can think of that may have changed that?' *Stupid question, dickhead. If there was she wouldn't be so confused.*

'Not that I've noticed,' she answered. 'I only catch a few words of it before I have to stick my headphones on and drown out their trash-talk. There was one thing that struck me funny the other day though. I heard mum say, "he's due for release." I haven't got a clue who she was talking about, but just after, my dad said something about it maybe being better if we just moved away.'

'Moved away?' Talek felt a lump rise in his throat and a tightening of his chest muscles.

'That's what he said.' Erin looked into his eyes and registered the look of despair. 'Don't worry,' she said, 'I won't let that happen.'

'I wasn't worrying,' said Talek, feigning coolness, but struggling to break the intense visual lock between them.

'Thanks,' she said in jest, 'that makes me feel *real* special.'

'I didn't mean it like that,' he defended, embarrassed. 'So, no guesses who *he* might be?'

'No,' she frowned, 'but if they're that concerned, maybe he was banged up for something one of those two did, and he got nailed for it. Or maybe he did something to *them*. Either way, I've never seen them so far apart.'

Even under the heat of the day Talek noted a quiver wash over Erin.

'If,' he stumbled, 'if I was to put my arm around you?...'

'I'd like that,' she smiled invitingly.

He did. Erin snuggled harder against him, her body noticeably cooler than before. The sun lowered in the deepening blue sky. Neither wanted to move, nonetheless the world rarely complies when we're finally content in the comfort of a soulmate.

SIXTEEN

Arriving back at the churchyard the air carried a refreshing chill, the sky turning a mellowing orange sherbet as the sun made its descent below the western horizon. The pair walked quietly through an opening in the stony hedge that surrounded the grounds. Crunching grit underfoot amplified in the quietude as they strived to remain inconspicuous.

'Shit!' Erin whispered, looking down at her bike. 'Flat tyre.'

'Oh. Whoops.' Talek crouched down and lifted the bike's back end off the floor. Turning the rear wheel slowly with one hand he inspected the aging rubber closely. 'There it is,' he said, 'a thorn.'

'Great!' Erin stomped a foot down on the path and struck a dramatic hand-on-hip pose.

Talek would never tell her, but she looked damn hot when she was in a strop.

'Now what am I supposed to do?' she whined. 'My dad will kill me if I'm not back before dark. Especially with the mood he's in at the minute, and some psycho child snatcher on the loose.'

'Well, it's not like it's *your* fault,' Talek pointed out, knowing only too well that that *never* washes with parents. 'Wait up, I'll be back soon.'

Breaking into a run he disappeared around the front of the church. Standing under the watchful gaze of the ivy-strewn tower, Erin grew cold. Rustling noises from all points of the hallowed ground grabbed her attention: beneath creaking trees; creeping behind gravestones; even from beyond the glassless windows of the old, gutless cadaver.

Two minutes later Talek reappeared from the direction he had run off in. 'Come on,' he called. 'And bring your bike with you.'

Wondering what was going on, Erin pulled her bike from the foliage and rolled it along the side of the church. Her relief at his arrival was so palpable she noticed her chest was heaving, as if she had been unable to breathe whilst standing abandoned in the shadows.

'What's the plan?' she asked when they were side by side once again.

'Mum's at one of the cottages. Gran's gonna run you home.'

'Introducing me to the family, huh?'

'Don't worry,' he assured, 'she's cool. But don't ever think I'd hate you enough to introduce you to my mum.'

They laughed as they crossed in front of the ruin, a sound so defiant of the surroundings it stood out like a vuvuzela at the final of the World Snooker Championship. Rattling the bike down a series of granite steps, Erin caught a glimpse of a slim lady no more than ten years older than her own mother. Stooping, she pottered around at the rear of a four-by-four, boot open, shuffling accumulated junk about.

'Is that your *gran*?' blurted Erin. 'Flippin'eck she's in good shape!'

'Yeah,' smiled Talek, 'I dunno what happened to my mum to turn her into such a scruffy ol' codger.'

'Say that to her face, would you?'

'Not even if she was knocked out,' he laughed.

Sheila stepped out from under the jeep's boot at the sound. 'Ah, this must be the mysterious *Erin*,' she said.

'Hiya,' Erin chirped pleasantly. 'That's me. But I wouldn't say *mysterious*.'

'Rubbish,' Sheila said, moving in for a closer look, 'that gorgeous dark hair with such blue eyes. There's definitely something intriguing about you. It's little wonder my grandson fancies you so much.'

'What?' Instantaneously, Talek felt the burn hit his face like the shock front of a nuclear explosion. 'I don't___'

'Zip it, matey,' interrupted Sheila, shooting him a side-on glance. 'There's no point denying it. Come on then, lovey,' she said, turning back to Erin, 'let's 'ave that bike. I'll stick it in the back.'

'Thanks very much,' said Erin, 'you're a lifesaver.'

'I know, girl. So long as ya don't tell 'is mum 'e 'ad a girl around. Blasted woman would 'ave a fit. Right, the pair of you, jump in.'

'Your gran's ace,' Erin whispered to Talek as he held the back door open for her.

'Only reason I stay,' he said, tensing up again as he slid in next to her.

***

Connor paced up and down the front drive, mobile phone clamped tightly in his hand. Of course, Jessie was going to blame him for Erin not being home. That was a given. His wife was so high strung at the moment, and so frosty towards him, she probably even blamed him for the sinking of the Titanic, the Boxing Day tsunami, Jemini scoring a staggering *nil pois*, and the disappearance of Malaysia Airlines' Flight 370 six months ago. Not a scrap had been heard from that ill-fated Boeing 777-200ER flight since it lost contact with air traffic control roughly thirty-eight minutes after take-off. Deviating westwards from its planned flightpath somewhere over the South China Sea, the passenger plane vanished from military radar almost two-hundred-and-thirty miles from Penang Island. Hell, Connor didn't even know where Penang fucking Island was, but still it was bound to be his fault.

And Erin, leaving her phone in her room. That would be *his* oversight, for sure. He should have checked with her as she was darting out the front door. Not that she gave him much of a chance, springing like a greyhound from its trap when the barred doors flipped open. *But who's the mechanical lure?*

Simultaneously with the knobbly scrunching of chunky all terrain tyres drawing near, two parallel yellow beams rounded the corner. Starting at his feet they tracked up his legs, until his entire being was bathing in light. Forced to raise a defending arm, Connor squinted through the crook of an elbow, attempting to determine who the unknown vehicle may belong to.

'Mr Samways,' a female's voice sounded confidently over the running engine.

The window started to rise as the door opened. Vanquishing into a series of gentle ticks, the engine's powerful hum proceeded to cool.

'Yeah,' he said, still shading his eyes, 'and you are?'

As the back door swung open, Connor could make out the unmistakeable frame of his daughter exiting the Chelsea tractor.

'Really sorry I'm late, Dad.' Erin's voice lacked its usual confidence. 'I had a puncture.'

'A puncture?' her dad sighed doubtfully. 'Really?'

'It's true. I've gott'un in the back,' the woman interjected, taking in Connor's roguish good looks as he uncovered his face. 'I hope you're good at filling holes,' she smirked coyly.

Connor couldn't help but notice the woman's playful smile in the glow of streetlights. 'And you are?' he said, his voice brusque.

'I'm Sheila, this young man's gran.' She gestured to Talek as he climbed out. 'And I give her a much warmer welcome than you've given me. Manners cost nothing, my good sir.'

Taken aback by the woman's ruthless candour, Connor calmed, saying with a hint of embarrassment, 'Shit. Sorry, I've, uh, I got a lot on my mind.' He held out a hand. 'Connor. And I *do* appreciate you bringing Erin home.'

'No problem,' said Sheila, taking his hand and holding the shake for a prolonged moment, 'she's a delight. And she's welcome around ours anytime. As long as my daughter's not home, that is.'

'Okay,' Connor said, curious, but not curious enough to probe. 'And where is home? Just so's I know where to find her if I need to.'

'I'm afraid my daughter doesn't like people to know *that*,' Sheila smiled pleasantly. 'Your lass must be very influential to get it out of my Talek, here.'

Striking Connor as very odd, he had to ask, rather accusingly, 'Isn't that a bit, uh, fucked up?'

'She has her reasons.' Sheila kept the smile on her face, though the amiable sentiment behind it had started to ebb with the deliverance of the last statement.

Creeping a few strides away, Talek and Erin had drifted into their own quiet conspiracies.

'I tell you what I'll do,' Sheila said, turning to the open driver's door of the Shogun and rummaging in the internal pocket. Retrieving a pen and scrap paper, she tore off whatever was written on its crinkled surface and scribbled a message on the blank half. 'Here's my mobile number. Feel free to give me a buzz *anytime* you want to. To check on Erin… or whatever.'

Handing the paper to Connor, the smile had resumed transmission of the playful front from a few moments before.

'Anyway,' Sheila continued, 'let's get you Erin's wheels and we'll be out of your hair. Tal, make yourself useful and fetch the bike.'

The boy scarpered around the back, praying he could make light work of the lifting, and in turn not appear the weakling in front of girl.

SEVENTEEN

Body Found in Tresillian River: Search for Missing Teen
By TATUM BLAKE
Content Editor

A body has been found off the banks of a river in Cornwall, near to where the search for a missing 13-year-old was taking place. Jowan Collins has not been seen since leaving Clement Grove School on the afternoon of September 4th.

Devon and Cornwall Police have stated that the body of a teenaged male was found by local kayakers Deanna Hoskins and Kayla Moyle, where it lay partially submerged in the mudflats of the Tresillian River near Merther, St. Michael Penkivel.

Searches have been taking place in and around Truro for two weeks, though it's purely by chance while editing photographs from their trip along the stretch of river that Deanna Hoskins made the grim discovery. It is believed that the body had been fully submerged in the mudbank until torrents of water rushed through the area during a recent storm, shifting the top layer of silt and revealing the human remains.

Although formal identification has yet to take place, police have said that the victim is of an approximate age with the missing Jowan, and that the boy's family have been informed.

"Your thoughts, prayers and unshakable dedication"

A spokesperson for the Collins family has expressed that they are in deep shock and suffering, and wish to be given privacy at this profoundly distressing time. The spokesperson went on to thank everybody involved with every aspect of the search for Jowan on behalf of the family, quoting "Your thoughts, prayers and unshakable dedication have helped us immeasurably through these inconceivable and traumatic times".

EIGHTEEN

'Crazy, huh?' said Erin, taking an empty chair next to Talek.

The noise from over a thousand spindly chair legs dragging on the wooden floorboards was unbearable as three-hundred pupils filed in for the unscheduled assembly. Talek felt as if he had stuck his head in a giant, stuttering jet engine.

'Do you think it was him we saw?' she asked, pulling her jacket tight around her front, even though the stuffiness of the hall had already hit stifling levels.

'I'm trying not to think about it,' Talek whispered.

'It was, wasn't it?' No answer. 'Oh god, you think it was, don't you.' This follow-up was not a question.

'How did *you* hear about it?' Talek said, breaking an uncomfortable pause.

'TV. You?'

'It was on Gran's iPad this morning.'

'Your gran's got an iPad?' blurted Erin, sounding almost excited in the harrowing chasm of the charmless space. 'You sure she's actually your gran at all?'

'I hope so,' he mumbled, 'I gotta be related to *someone* normal.'

'Settle down, please, everyone.' No response. '*QUIET!*'

This was a rare appearance from the Headteacher, who at the age of sixty-four years and two-hundred and eighty-one days, preferred to hide out in his office, avoiding the detestable children whilst desperately counting down the seconds to his retirement. His deputy was itching to jump into his grave, to peel the gold-fronted *Mr Bridges - Headteacher* plaque from his office door and replace it with *Mrs Sharples*. She was more than capable of doing his job, and she was welcomed to it, too (if she was happy to pay him off until the end of the current school year, of course). Mr Bridges had more than done his time. Yet after forty-two years in education, this was a first. A dead pupil. Worse, a dead pupil whose mother was in the school's employ – not that Bridge's knew her that well. He vaguely remembered her as a student, but several years had passed since he felt obliged to know each of his subordinates by more than just putting a face to the name. Surname, at that.

He thought back to the boy's father, a lifetime ago now – literally, a life sentence ago – rueing the possible missed opportunities. Had Bridges had the chance to act? Were there any signs of what the two youths had done all those years ago? Or even what they were capable of? If so, he could have acted sooner, then maybe the Collins boy would not have even come into existence. *Born to die. What a tragic waste.*

He took in the shifting mass of students, his fingers tightening on the sides of an ornate beechwood lectern, centre stage, face set in a grimace. His congregation: some sat fidgeting, some stood doddering. Many were murmuring meaningless bleatings like politicians in the House of Commons, a cattle market hum to the proceedings. They had all heard the news from some source. Whether authentic or fantasized, that shit didn't matter… the conclusion was the same either way. These kids didn't need him to stand here and tell them about it. But – thanks to the new nanny state that was so blissfully missing when Bridges had assumed the coveted position of top-of-the-food-chain – pastoral care was now one of the essential parasites feasting on his grey matter and sure to make his relationship with retirement a very brief affair.

'When you're quite ready,' he said in a sombre tone, 'if ever, boy!'

Attention turned to a gangly, scruffy-haired, zit-splattered boy standing in the centre isle near the back.

'Just find a seat, for the love of God!' Bridges stared at the startled boy, who scrambled into one of the row's harbouring a lone empty chair, tripping over a seated girl… *Sadie Frost? Sarah? Fucked if I know...* in the process.

'Don't touch me, minger!' she groaned in disgust as his bony fingers scored a touchdown on her leg.

Give me strength, Mr Bridges pleaded in the private sanctum of his thoughts. 'I'm sure you've all heard by now,' he spoke softly, 'that the body found yesterday is likely that of our friend and fellow schoolmate, Jowan Collins.'

Talek felt a tickle on the back of his hand. Looking down, he saw Erin's delicate fingers – her ghostly pale skin in stark contrast to his own coloration – wrap tentatively around his. Squeezing gently in compliance, he sensed a freshening cleanse sweep through the toxic air.

'Our aim over the coming days,' the Head continued, 'is to provide the care and support needed to help you all come to terms with this tragic loss. My door is always open, as is Mrs Sharples', though we will also be receiving the services of a chaplain for those who require a more personal and specialised level of support.'

Looking around at the sea of faces in front of him, Bridges pondered over how he would have taken this news as a child. It was hard to believe that in the swirling ocean of emotions presented before him, such differing island states could rise from the waters and coexist in apparent harmony: the plainly distraught and tearful; the listless indifferent; and even the schadenfreude smiles that twitched askew on the faces of a few.

'Compassionate leave will also be offered to those who may benefit from a little time at home with their families.'

A whispered chorus of *yesses* and *awesomes* circulated the restless crowd.

Little bastards, Bridges mused bitterly. 'DO NOT ABUSE IT! Student welfare is of the highest priority, but if I suspect any of you of taking advantage of this devastating situation… using it for your own sickly gain…' He didn't need to elaborate on the threat.

Silence descended upon the entire student body, regardless of which camp they sizzled their sausages in.

'Right, let's wrap this up. Back to your tutors,' Bridges instructed. 'You can discuss your personal preferences moving forward there.'

He turned and exited stage left, considering the bottle of single malt locked away in his desk's lower drawer.

As a commotion of sliding chairs and thuggish yells broke out in the hall, Erin looked to Talek. 'So, what are you gonna do?' she said, her body language and tone downcast.

'Well,' he frowned, 'I don't wanna go home. Knowing he was lying dead just a field's width away from me the whole time. Freaks me out. What about you?'

'I saw him,' she said, with tears welling over the dark liner of her eyes. 'At least I'm pretty sure I did, so I was gonna go home. I can see why you wouldn't want to, though.' She let go of his hand, forgetting that some time ago she was desperate to feel its tender touch. 'You could come back to mine if they're putting on busses? Mum and Dad will both be at work.'

Talek mulled over the prospect, as nervous as an infant wildebeest at the murky edge of a crocodile infested crossing, yet simultaneously as excited as a puppy at the park.

'I'd better be here when mum comes to pick me up,' he said regrettably. 'She flipped out last time, so…'

'I'll stay then,' she said, 'so you're not on your own at lunchtime.'

'Don't worry about me,' he gave her what he hoped to project as a comforting smile, 'I'll be okay. You're right. We *saw* him, so you go home and chill out. Take as long as you need. But email me to let me know you're alright.'

Both standing, Erin threw her arms around Talek. Holding him in the embrace she whispered in his ear, 'Stay safe, little man.'

Hesitantly, they broke the hold, tearing apart with the stubbornness virgin Velcro. Following their own paths, they exited the assembly hall into their own solitary world.

Meandering slowly into a long corridor, Talek allowed himself to be dropped by the peloton, accepting that even in a crowd he would feel so alone. It was great to finally have a friend (amazing, in fact), but she was still his *only* friend. In his eleventh year of schooling, that was a pathetic accomplishment. Had it been him that was murdered and dumped in the mud, what legacy would he leave? In years to come would a new tenant at Scoan's Cottage, of a similar age with his current self and suffering with a similar social awkwardness, and similar quirks and foibles, go wondering into the graveyard at the Church of Saint Cohan and take a frottage? What would they find if they did? Closing his eyes, Talek could read the waxy scrawl like it had been tattooed on the insides of his eyelids:

SACRED
To The Memory Of
TALEK LEAN
Who departed this life
leaving his mother, grandmother
and JUST ONE friend
Rest alone, sad little man

Little man. Opening his eyes again he saw that the horde of living dead had increased their lead over him. To his right was the boy's toilet. Deciding he needed a moment, he opened the door and entered. Immediately after the door closed behind him, Talek was hit by the strong odour of cigarette smoke. A blue-grey plume rose through the opening above the end cubicle. Fearing he already knew the stall's occupants, he turned to take his leave.

Too late. The veneered MDF door gave its high-pitched warning screech as it swung open. It hit the solid wall with a loud clash.

'It's that fucking little queer,' laughed Coby.

'Awesome, grab the little twat!' came Ethan's voice, echoing from within its panelled surround.

The force at which Talek's bag was grabbed from behind was impossible to fend off. Spinning around uncontrollably, he found himself launched into the hard, painted plaster surface of the toilet's wall. It was his face that made first contact, his nose cracking and erupting in a rush of blood. Feeling another heavy contact deaden the muscle high on the back of his right leg – a piston-like blow from a knee – Talek's lower limbs failed him. As he slid helplessly down the wall, a vertical red streak left in his wake like a scene from some ultraviolent gory horror, a pair of hands clutched at the straps on his shoulders. Forcibly, Talek was flung backwards across to the pissy floor under the urinals.

Ethan stood over him, a psychotic smile painted crudely on his face. 'Just cos some prick's got himself killed, doesn't mean you get a free pass.'

Swinging a foot forwards, the hulking ringleader's trainer connected hard with the soft flesh of Talek's side, barely missing and consequently sparing Talek from a run of broken ribs.

'We should've done this the other day,' hissed Ethan, spittle now forming around his curling lips.

The foot came in again, followed by another from Coby on his opposite flank.

'Pick 'im up!' Ethan ordered.

Grabbing at the front of Talek's shirt (the cheap fabric that started the day sky blue, now turned a deep maroon down the middle), Coby pulled hard, yanking the boy to his feet, ripping the top few buttons from their threads in the process. Hurling him around, the bag on his back was grabbed again. Somehow managing to avoid tripping over a series of feet, Talek found himself forced face-to-face with his blonde-haired torturer. His vision was blurring. The smoky scent in the air had turned to cloying iron. Claret creeping in though his parted lips left an unsavoury copper taste in his mouth, teasing the back of his throat.

Ethan smiled, winding back his evil head. As if spring-loaded, the slab of a brow surged forward. With a fresh blast of searing pain to his already broken nose, accompanied by a brilliant flash of dazzling light, Talek's consciousness expired, the brilliant light becoming an all-consuming black hole.

NINETEEN

Nothing moved in the low light cast by a crescent moon. The intricate labyrinth of shadows that spread around the church grounds could have hidden any number of skulking entities. As Talek watched the unchanging scene through the window, his bedroom door opened with a subtle creak behind him.

'What's that?' his mother's voice broke the thick silence as she focused her attention on the illuminated screen in front of her son.

'Just an email with my homework,' Talek answered, clicking the *Minimize* tab to clear the screen of Erin's name in the sender address box. His voice was muffled through the crooked nose and fat lip.

Sensing the woman wasn't finished, he waited, swinging slowly from left to right and back again on his chair.

'Draw those curtains,' she said, giving her son no chance to do so before she slouched over and completed the action herself. 'You don't know who might be watching.'

'There's no one out there, Mum,' he wheezed.

'You don't know that. Not for sure.'

'There *never* is,' he argued. 'Who would ever want to come out to this lifeless dump?'

She ignored the contemptuous remark, though the boy could see from the darkening of her expression that he had hit a nerve.

'So,' she said changing the subject, 'what did you do to end up in this mess?'

She had barely said a word to him while they were at the hospital. Now she seemed by all accounts to be blaming him for the incident.

'I went into the toilets,' he snapped. 'Sorry, is that not allowed?'

'Don't be flippant. Who, did this to you?'

Talek let out a long rasping breath. 'Ethan and Coby,' he said, 'but Ethan, mainly.'

'Who's Ethan?' There was no hint in her voice that the question was open to skirting around.

'You've seen him hangin' around after school. Blonde hair. Big, love himself dickhead.'

'That doesn't help,' she said sharply.

'I can show you his picture,' said Talek, right clicking on the Chrome icon, aiming to open a new window without Erin's email flashing up on the display. Tapping the *F* key, he clicked the first option listed among the dropdown web addresses.

'You're not old enough to have that,' she barked.

'Actually, Mother,' he said, 'you can have an account at thirteen.'

She cast a mistrustful look at him.

'Anyway,' he carried on, 'as I have zero friends, *I* don't have an account. But you can still look people up on here.'

Typing the name *Ethan Scales*, a handful of profile pictures appeared. After tapping the curser on the appropriate image, the screen filled with information about the boy in question, along with a horribly clear picture of his menacing face. Even the smile reeked from the enjoyment of the latest kick-in he had dealt.

'Oh yes,' said Tamsyn, moving in for a closer inspection, 'I've seen that face.'

'Well,' Talek said, turning to look his mother in the eye, 'I hope you're not planning on getting involved.'

Giving him a vulpine smile – a smile that could not have looked more out of place – she said, 'Somebody has to take action. I'll talk to the school.'

Kissing him on the forehead – a sign of affection even more incongruous to her usual mannerisms than the accompanying smile – she turned and left the room.

'And make things worse,' he whispered to the empty chasm behind him, 'thanks a bunch.'

Allowing a moment for the disturbingly pleasant look in his mother's eyes to wash from his memory, he reacquainted himself with the laptop. Shutting down Ethan Scales' mugshot was a relief. He didn't know why, exactly; it wasn't like he was going to crawl from the screen and inflict more pain and misery upon him, like some digitalised poltergeist. But still, just viewing that disturbing smirk was painful enough. Shutting it down came with a satisfaction that could only be topped by wiping the face of the *flesh and bone* Ethan off the planet.

Opening the email window, Talek read:

Hey u,

How was school? Hope u missed me. And if u did, tough luck.

Should've come with!

Possible breakthrough with Devil's A-hole. What I said about Jowan's dad, that's only where he frigging did it!

This bloke was parked under DA when they torched the guy's car. Shagging his beeatch, apparently. Dirty buggers! Anyway, the woman got out alive but the bloke wasn't so lucky.

Imagine if it was him u heard screaming? (Halloween theme tune playing in my head!)… but you probs don't know what that is. Nerd!

So what do u make of that?

Much love little man xx

Digesting this info was like trying to eat a bowl of shredded cardboard with Play-Doh for milk. The story was harrowing enough. But to think that there were *other* screams in that hellish, supernatural place, screams that were as authentic and absolute as the deadly silence that followed after he'd rolled back out into the natural world.

Talek felt an insurmountable urge to puke. Forcing himself from his chair, he flung the curtains open again. Flicking back the brass latch, he slid the lower sash upwards, suddenly desperate for oxygen. If any air had attempted to enter, it was no more than a cursory clawing of listless fingers over the ledge. Sucking in the stagnant, vaporous atmosphere, its oppressive taste forcing him to relive his first experience of that damp and dripping tunnel, Talek held onto it temporarily, only exhaling once his lungs had begun to ache and burn. Tiring of the still nothing beyond the windowpane, and taking his leave, he headed down for a glass of water.

Downstairs, he found his mother seated at the kitchen table, his gran slumped opposite with her arms crossed on the oak top. Their mumbling voices fell mute as he entered the room and took a glass from the draining board.

'Don't let *me* stop you,' he said, rinsing and then filling the glass from the mixer tap.

'It's nothing that concerns you, little man' Sheila said cheerily. 'Your big ears can save their flappin' for another time.'

Enough with the little man *shit?* he thought, irked.

'Whatevs,' he muttered, 'I'm goin' bed soon so I'll say night now.' He headed back to the kitchen door, keen to be alone again, his unsettled mind struggling to find amenity with either setting or company.

'Ahem, not so fast!' Sheila teased, raising an elegant cheekbone in his direction.

Returning with his shoulders slack, he gave her smooth skin a gentle peck.

'That wasn't so bad, was it?' she said. 'Nighty night then.'

His mother requested no such show of affection. Leaving them to their conversation that had *zero* chance of not concerning him, Talek reached the secluded sanctum of his room. Latching the slatted wood door behind him he began to feel more at ease. The warning jitters of an impending barf-fest had eased, and he was able once again to sit at his laptop in comfort. To say he was relieved not to have thrown up was as unnecessary as confirming that grass is green, the sea is blue, or the pope doesn't shit in the woods. His entire left side hurt like a bitch, and any amount of strenuous heaving would have left him a crippled mess.

Keeping the conversation simple in the hope that Erin was eagerly awaiting his reply, he speedily typed:

> *Got my head kicked in today. Broken nose. Bruised ribs. Guess I should've gone with you.*
>
> *Good work Inspector. The 2 in the car, do you know their names? xx*

He had no idea what possessed him to ask that particular question. In his mind, what happened in there – sound, sight, smell – all were authentic. So, either he was going mad, or he had some kind of sixth sense, like that weird kid in the film with Bruce Willis. The names of the car's occupants were irrelevant.

Just as Talek had hoped, Erin appeared to be eagerly awaiting his response.

> *WTF? What happened? Was it Ethan? Are u ok? The guy who fried (is that insensitive?) was called Austin*

Michaels. The girl's name remained anonymous. Why? xx

Why? Good question, and one that Talek could probably not invent the answer for in his current state. He stared out of the window, as if this would help. It didn't. Outside, the rutted ground, with its concealed granite steps and its flat slabs rising like neglected teeth, had fallen into total darkness. In a relatively cloudless sky, the slit of a moon had somehow found shelter, briefly depriving planet Earth the security of its guiding illumination.

Fighting its way through the numb air, a rustling sound mutedly filled his bedroom like the quiet sliding of a used bedsheet from a mattress. Looking intently into the blackened world outside, Talek tried to define its source. Nothing moved. The anthracite canvas hid its secrets like a padlocked diary. Eyes playing tricks on him, he attempted to blink away the deep purples and blues that proceeded to swirl in his vision, as these imposter colours often do when your focus is so intense upon a single object.

Squinting hard, springing his lids open like a bear trap with a split personality, he finally saw it. That familiar tinge of yellow, dancing on the crumbling, weed-choked stone walls of Saint Cohan's collapsing entrance. This time around the light persisted. Talek started pounding the keys of his laptop with a heavy index finger, one at a time and eyes flitting between the letters and the old ruin as the phantasmagoria played upon the dying tissue of its gutless belly.

Yes, it was Ethan. No I'm not. Him and Coby jumped me in the toilet. Not in a gay way. And who gives a shit about sensitivity?

I want to go in the church. You up for it? xx

A two-word exclamative pinged up instantaneously, followed by the two letters that had become a standard signoff between him and a girl for the first time in his lonely life:

Hell yeah! xx

PART TWO

2000

TWENTY

JANUARY

Opening only fractionally, an unseen force brought the front door to a scrunching stop. The air that wheezed through the gap came with an undertone of festering food. With a persuasive shove of the shoulder, Kieran could just about squeeze his emaciated frame through to the small, darkened entryway. He flicked on the light, the customary blue spark and sizzle of electricity a warning not to linger a finger on the switch. At his feet, the obstruction sat black and stinking. One of them had managed to get the rubbish bags to the door, but no further. Nevertheless, even removing them from the pantry-come-waste-tip was an achievement for either his mother or her fella.

Neglected cries rattled down the stairs with a high-pitched animal quality, a vixen screaming gratingly in the night, only hungry for milk rather than a mate. Kieran balled his grubby white T-shirt up to his nose, gauging its level of toxicity. Not too bad. Intent on fun earlier, he really didn't care whether he was sloppy or not. But now it was time to grow up and act responsibly; soon he would be left literally holding the baby. And although it might be fun to get the little cherub high on fumes, he'd probably best refrain from doing so.

Stepping over the rotting garbage from who-knows-how-may weeks ago, Kieran reached the door to the living room. It was shut. Naturally it was. Why would the doting mother want to listen to the desperate, loathsome cries of her second born? dragging the harried woman away from her narcotic necessities. Reaching for the handle – past experiences informing him there was no need to keep the volume down to avoid causing any disturbance – Kieran clutched and lowered the spindly aluminium bar. Immediately, the overpowering stench of vomit hit him like butyric cones of Parmesan cheese being stuffed into his nostrils.

With the door fully open, the odour's source was indisputable. *She* – his mother: the mother who was destined to fail (if not destroy) his baby sister, as she had failed him – lay elongated on the sofa, her pale and vein-mapped arms spilling over one arm of the couch behind her head. One foot was raised over the other end, the scaley sole of the other foot on the floor. She looked dead, and maybe that would have been a good thing, but Kieran feared she wasn't. He thought for a moment that her pale skin looked whiter than the porcelain of the toilet. Of course it did. Even if you could class her skin as sallow, it would still appear purer than the throne that sat in grim, unclean state upstairs.

Where the boyfriend was, who cared? Probably at a pub, paraplegic and hopefully unable to stagger home. Bellicose by nature and able to back it up with brute strength, Kieran could do with a night off from being the big man's punchbag.

He headed to the kitchen, turning his head in disgust as he noticed drying puke forming a crust on his mother's chin. Did he owe it to her to check that she was still breathing? that the stupid bitch hadn't choked on her own vomit? Probably not. But she *was* his mother. And that was his little sister bellowing for attention upstairs. Could he let the woman dwindle away as if she was a mere lonely leaf blowing along the roadside, only itself to talk to, only its own ear to hear its lonely scratch and scrape? Surely it would be better for everyone if she could just slip away.

A sharp rise of her bony chest and a snotty sniff delivered the bad news: she wasn't slipping anywhere.

Through in the kitchen a phantasm of shadows haunted every space, cast by the decaying yellow light of the open fridge. He powered up the main ceiling light, exorcising the demons before heading to the grime-smeared appliance and closing the door with an exasperated flick of the wrist. Looking to the chaotic worktop, Kieran saw in amongst the plastered foil Chinese takeaway containers a tub of formula milk. Putting a pan of water on the burner to boil, he found a bottle and cleaned it as best he could. This was not the way he had envisaged his life turning out, but if he didn't shut his little sister up quickly, the neighbours would be phoning the police. Or, worse, baby Billie would scream throughout her mother's comatose state, only silencing her pleas when her tiny, deprived body declared itself expired.

Entering his mother's bedroom, he was pleased to see that Zane was indeed out for the evening. Billie turned towards Kieran at the sound of his reassuring sigh. Her face was red and puffy. How long she had been left, screaming and alone, he could not hazard a guess at. Plucking her out of the cot, he put his back against the wall and slid to the floor. The baby girl cradled in his arms accepted the bottle's rubbery teat greedily, making soft cooing sounds as she took in the vital liquid, her sobs petering out with occasional snuffles.

Kieran closed his eyes and smiled at the dramatically contrasting qualities of his character: playing hero to the infant held safe and secure in his grasp, providing temporary immunity from the actions of that *car crash* of a woman downstairs; and being the tyrannical villain who had very possibly just taken the lives of two innocent lovers.

TWENTY-ONE

'Where the bloody hell have you been?' The shrill call from the living room as Matt clicked the door quietly closed. 'I've been going out of my wits.'

Shit. He was hoping that she had just gone to bed and not heard him creeping in at two minutes to midnight.

'Sorry, Mu,' he said entering the room, 'I was playing football with Kieran. A group of girls from school came along and we lost track of time.'

'Well, as long as you wore a coat,' she said, lifting herself from the sofa and wrapping a woolly dressing gown tight around herself. 'You be stupid, and I'll be a granny far too young.'

'Ugh, you're gross!'

'Give over,' she said in a *don't-come-that-with-me* tone. 'I was fifteen once, you know.'

'I don't *wanna* know. Anyway, I'm home now, so just go to bed.'

'Okay,' she said, placing a kiss on his cheek. 'Crikey! You reek of smoke.'

'Yeah,' he said, forced into thinking on his feet, 'some dickheads at the park set fire to a bin.'

'Prats. Anyway, I'm knackered so I'll say nighty night.'

'Night,' he said, relieved that an interrogative line of questioning did not ensue.

He made his way to the kitchen, flicking on the lights and filling the kettle. It would interrupt his sleep, though he felt that that would be hard to come across tonight anyway, regardless of how much coffee he poured down his gullet.

Making his way back into the living room, Matt fired up the television and scanned the channels for anything that may take his mind off the evening's events.

Truth is, he would rather have been with a group of girls, doing sensible *or* stupid things… it really didn't matter which. Nonetheless, he had followed Kieran like a loyal canine, acting on all his idiotic ideas even though Kieran was a year younger than himself. In his head, his own interrogation proceeded. Why? Was he afraid of Kieran? the lad both younger and smaller than himself… Or was he just bored of the other kids in school, of the way they happily conformed to a governed existence? Was that why his desire to impress the other boy so intense?

Try as he might, Matthew Rundle didn't have a single answer. The reasonings were nebulous.

He killed the telly and thought back to the couple in the car. Yes, it was fun at the time, but not at all what was intended. Just a tiny trail of fuel leading under the arch; that was all. A car would come along; Kieran would drop a match, a lit rag, or a fag or whatever he'd had up his sleeve, from up in the camouflage of the hedge. The car would drive along the chain of flames, just like on a Scalextric track, only *so* much cooler. They had plenty of woodland to run off into if the driver decided to get out and come looking for them.

But this car…

Why did it have to stop right underneath the two youths in hiding? As it resumed its journey, creeping under the bridge at a dawdle, Kieran's smile was black and cunning in the darkness of the night. Fully submerged under Devil's Arch, the car stopped again.

The boys waited. Nothing happened.

When muffled giggling noises drifted up the tangled face of the overgrown hedgerow, Kieran slid down to the surface of the road. Matt tried to grab at his mate's shoulder to no avail. Following his master – as is the doting lap dog's way – he landed on the blacktop as quietly as he could manage. Crouching below the level of the vehicle's windows, the giggling from inside continued, accompanied by a gentle rocking. The boy's looked at each other through the gloom, hands over mouths to contain their amusement, a live sex show something they had never witnessed before.

That was when Kieran decided to step things up a notch... when it all started to go disturbingly wrong. Raising himself to standing, the boy peered through the blackened glass of the rear window. Moving back to the hedge, he reached up and grabbed the jerrycan. He looked at Rundle. Rundle shook his head, his complexion frightful enough to glow like the moon. The disapproving gesture had no effect. Before Matt knew it, fuel was forming a multitude of glistening streams down the car's glass and bodywork. The pair took a backwards step. Kieran fired up a match. Flicked.

Rundle laughed as they ran away. Amusement? Shock? Incredulous to the situation? Christ knows. But now, in the cold and forsaken realm of his own haunting thoughts, he sensed a cataclysmic shitstorm brewing on the horizon.

Matt had dared a look back as they gaily fled the scene. A ball of flames met his eyes, though the ball was rolling, edging out from under Devil's Arch. So, the pair were at least functioning enough to get the car moving, which would suggest they also had enough life left in them to get the fuck out of it once they were free from their stony confinements. Even so, they could easily have been killed, and if anyone had spotted Kieran and himself in the area, they were screwed.

He downed the remainder of his coffee – the heat burning the roof of his mouth, his throat – and made another before heading to his room.

Reaching the landing, his mother's childish chuckles could be heard through her bedroom door, as his dad did things Rundle didn't want to know about to her. *Knackered, my ass*, he thought, entering his hideaway, hoping to shut out the giggles and groans of pleasure.

He threw himself onto the bed, firing up his MP3 player and pressing the earphones firmly into his lugholes for good measure. With the coffee left to go cold, sleep swallowed him faster than he would have thought possible, though his slumber was plagued by fire and blood-curdling screams.

TWENTY-TWO

Tarmac, cracked and pitted, glowed orange under the watchful gaze of giraffe-necked streetlamps. Worn road markings of white and yellow paint lurked barely visible beneath the heavy coating of surface water, whilst a dense, dreary mist hung stubbornly in the air. Nobody was out walking, save for the very occasional dog owner, their faces down, raincoat soaked and glistening, hounds seemingly impervious to the weather, skittering along before them and stopping every few metres to sniff or leak – or often both. Morons prowling the streets in debadged Kev cars with oversized body kits passed in groups of three or four vehicles at a time. Those same vehicles reappeared every few minutes as they completed another lap of the city centre's limited circuit. Clouds of spray swooshed red at their tails, while menacing big bore exhaust warbles rebounded noisily from the varied facades of aligning terraced houses.

Emerging from the hazy entrance of Truro's long stay coach park situated just his side of the Morlaix Avenue roundabout, the awkward gait of a cowering teenaged boy turned his way. From up in his bedroom window overlooking the street, Kieran recognised the figure instantly.

Great! What the fuck is he *doing here?*

Stupid question. Fact is, Kieran was expecting his cohort to turn up, and sooner rather than later. Why wouldn't he? The damning facts of how their little stunt on Saturday night turned out had reached the inhabitants of every backstreet and byroad in the county. Hell, the country even, gaining main story status with both ITV and the BBC's national news coverage. Seldom did such a dead-end county at the ass-end of nowhere offer up such delightfully gruesome fodder.

Opening his small top window Kieran hissed down, 'Rundle, what the fuck? I told you never to come 'ere!'

Matt looked up with an exaggerated shrug of the shoulders – *what the hell was I supposed to do?*

'You ain't comin' in,' Kieran continued in a forced whisper. 'Round by the funeral parlour. Hop the wall. Keep jumpin' fences 'til ya get to mine.'

'How will I know which is yours?' Matt whispered back a dumb look on his shadowed face.

'Other than being able to count in single fucking figures, you'll see me out there!' Kieran pulled the window hard, putting an end to any possibility of a response.

Leaving the room, he passed his mum's door. It hung ajar, with little Billie's sorrowful sobs creeping through.

Sorry, missus, you're on your own this time.

Downstairs in the living room, Melissa sat sprawled on the sofa with half aware eyes like a pair of piss holes in the snow, just visible through a dingy plume of smoke. A long, crumpled reefer smouldered between a leathery thumb and forefinger.

'Your baby's crying,' Kieran said bluntly as he passed.

'She'll 'ave to wait,' his mother mumbled without looking up or attempting to even move.

Heading through the kitchen whilst pitying the doomed sprog upstairs, he left by the back door and headed into the overgrown, ramshackle garden. On hearing the struggling sound of an intruder a property or two away, Kieran pushed his way through the jungle of vegetation, making for the rear. With a clamber of knees against wooden panelling, Rundle heaved himself over the final hurdle, landing in a heap at Kieran's feet in a series of exhausted sighs.

'Get up ya prick.'

'Have you heard?' Rundle asked, flustered and patting himself down.

'Who fucking hasn't?'

Fair point. 'Kier, what the fuck do we do?'

'Just act normal, you spaz. What else can we do?'

'*WE KILLED SOMEONE!*' Rundle blurted.

'Shut your fuckin' mouth,' Kieran hissed. 'D'ya want the whole friggin' world to know?'

'What if the woman saw us?'

'Saw us? Are you mental? That dude was nailing her like a squeaky floorboard. All she could see was fuckin' fireworks.'

Matt took a moment, breathing in the crisp January air, trying hard to gain some control of his emotions, emotions that had until now been spiralling like a helter-skelter tipped on its cone-shaped head.

'Are you going school on Thursday?' he finally managed to ask.

'No way,' answered Kieran.

'So much for *acting normal*,' Matt said before thinking the bold move through.

'Me not turning up *is* normal. And if you want to keep me on side, you might wanna stop that hole in your face from pissing me off.'

Matt cast his gaze to the dark and tangled floor. Kieran had made a valid point.

'What about you?' Kieran asked. 'You going?'

Rundle looked back up. 'Am I fuck. I don't know what to do. I may just leave home with a bag of food and hide in the trees behind the duck pond.'

'Great plan. Is that all day, or forever?'

'Not sure.'

Kieran laughed – a strange sound in this ungodly situation. 'You're such a member.'

'We need a plan,' Rundle suggested.

'Fucking plan, what are you on? We don't need a plan, we just need you to get your dick out of your ass and back in yer mouth so you can shut the fuck up.' Kieran pulled a pack of cigarettes from the pocket of his jeans. Sparking one up, he passed it to his partner in crime before readying another for himself. 'Maybe we both need to go back. Looks suspicious if we're off at the same time.'

Rundle agreed with a wordless nod of the head, before craning his neck and blowing a puff of blue smoke to the heavens.

'When you've finished your fag you need to disappear,' Kieran went on after a moment of silence. 'Don't come back 'ere again. You know I don't want anyone seeing this shithole.'

The moist air had started to flatten Kieran's fine hair. His face glowed a warning orange as he took a drag on his cigarette. Heeding the warning, Matt took his final drag and flicked the dogend over the rear fence. 'Give us a bunk-up and I'm outta here.'

Eager to get the boy gone, Kieran discarded his own glowing butt and obliged. Lacing his fingers and forming a scoop with his palms, he waited for Rundle to stick a foot in, and hoisted him up. The sound of the boy landing in a heap once again, only this time on the other side of the fence, caused Kieran to smirk. *Dingus.*

Turning back to head down the garden, his amusement expired as suddenly as the life of a swatted fly. Standing black in the kitchen doorway's rectangle of light was the intimidating silhouette of his mother's boyfriend. Kieran swallowed hard and made his way towards the bulk of a man, thinking he may not be back to school on Thursday after all.

'Zane.'

'Nancy boy.'

'Been there long?' Kieran asked in a faltering voice.

'Yep,' said Zane, flatly.

'Hear any of that?'

Zane stepped down from the doorway and lowered his sweaty forehead to Kieran's, a menacing grin transforming his face. 'I own you, dickhole!'

TWENTY-THREE

This morning was no better than the previous few days, as far as the weather was concerned. With no money for the public bus, and no offer of a lift from the man who *'owned'* him, Kieran arrived outside the school gates wetter than a fly fisherman's waders. He strolled onto the walkway with his head hung low, aiming to attract little to no attention. To have a fringe would be great. To have one that covered half his face would be perfect, the hefty price of looking like a drongo a price worth paying.

There were stares from some of the kids in tutor. Whispered mutterings. The odd sardonic snigger. No sign of suspicion from the teacher, however. At the sound of a bell, Kieran stood and made his way for more of the same treatment in English class. If this went on into the fourth period, he had already made up his mind to scarper at lunchtime.

'Right,' Miss Casey called as chair legs rubbed along thin biscuit carpet tiles, and pupils huffed and puffed as they settled down. '"Lord of the Flies."' A communal yawn broke out from every corner of the cold and clinical classroom. 'Chapter twelve, *"Cry of the Hunters."* I'm sure you won't have forgotten what just happened to Piggy... You've only had one sleep since, so a gory recap is quite unnecessary. Once you all have your copies ready, as you're sat with your face glued to the desk, Kieran Jose, you can start us off.'

Kieran looked up in alarm. Slightly miffed at his failure to respond (though in all honesty, not in the least bit surprised), Charlotte Casey trained her gaze through the bustle of fidgeting youngsters and studied her target's face.

'On second thoughts, Jarred, you take up the reins, please.'

'Yes Miss,' said Jarred, timidly. He cleared his throat, quietly bricking it at the thought of reading out loud to the rest of the class. '"Ralph lay in covert, wondering about his wounds."'

Laughter erupted throughout the entire classroom, Jarred's amusing mispronunciation relieving the pressure building like a pressure cooker in Kieran's mind.

'*What?*' asked Jarred, perplexed.

'Settle down, people,' Miss Casey sighed. 'It's 'wounds', ooo, as in injuries, Jarred, not 'wounds' as in what you might do to your grandad's watch. Please, carry on. And whoever laughs next will have to read the rest of the chapter, which I must warn you is almost twenty pages and will take us to the end of the book!'

The sea of deep and sky blue uniforms fell silent.

'"The bruised flesh was inches in dia…diameter over…"' Jarred went on, his voice trailing off and fading from Charlotte's consciousness like the steadily decreasing mumble of a passing aircraft. She looked at the young boy whom she had intended to read the passage first. Targeting him was meant as a mild form of punishment for missing yesterday's class, to embarrass the boy who appeared so uncomfortable when forced to speak publicly. Also, as a bonus, it would have been further payback for all the shit he'd given her since she inherited this particular form back in September. Miss Casey originally had little doubt that he was just playing truant yesterday. He was just one of those kids who earned themselves *that* label faster than they would ever earn themselves any merit. Upon seeing the greenish-brown swelling on his face however, darkening to purple at its epicentre fractionally below one eye, deep regret and shame constricted her chest, hampering the natural rhythm of her heart. His poor attendance level, his lack of energy and work ethic, the low standards of his schoolwork and his total disdain for homework, his struggles fitting in with his peers. All those attributing factors combined had flashed up a red warning flag to the upper echelons at the school: a warning duly noted by the school heads, though as yet with a failure to embark on a single attempt at further investigation. He now sat with his head down, shielding hands tightly linked and at a right angle to his brow.

The lesson wore on. After twenty minutes of reading, the class dissected certain passages, extracting the metaphors and similes, pitching in with their views of the connotations. Kieran remained with his face hidden, undisturbed and allowed to withdraw himself from any participation, no matter how large or small.

As the bell rang for break and the students started to file out of the room, Miss Casey waited for the boy to near her desk.

'Kieran, can you stay behind, please? Just for a moment.'

He sighed, his shoulders slumping as he stopped before her desk. 'What? I haven't done anything.'

'Please, sit down.' She gestured to the nearest empty chair.

'What's this about?' he asked apathetically. 'I've got better things to do than be sat here with you.'

'And what would they be?' Casey raised her eyebrows, expectant.

Nothing.

'Do you want to tell me what happened?'

'Not really,' Kieran muttered, placing his elbows on his knees and looking at the floor.

'Well, how about you at least try?'

'It was just some kid in town,' he offered, still without bringing himself to look her in the eye. 'It was nothing.'

'I've never seen *nothing* look like that before.'

'I don't give a flying fu… what you've seen.'

The door squeaked open and the blonde head of a girl in the year below craned in.

'Not now, Sam,' Miss Casey said. 'Can you come back at lunch?'

'Oh, okay,' came the surprised response.

Casey turned back to the boy. 'I've also not seen a child leave a bruise that severe before. Did they use a weapon?'

'Did he fu… Uh, no. He didn't. Just got a lucky blow in.'

'You know, you can tell me anything in complete confidence.'

'Like what?' Kieran blurted, making eye contact for the first time in the exchange.

'Like what *really* happened.'

Kieran sprang up, tipping his chair backwards onto the floor in the process. 'So you don't believe me? Thanks a lot!'

'I'm merely pointing out, if you're worried about any repercussions, you needn't be. I can help.'

'I don't need your help.' Kieran stared at her for a few seconds, face set and lips tight in a pale scar. Finally breaking the intense gaze, he turned and left the room.

So, there is something there, she pondered to herself.

Opening the top draw of her desk, Charlotte removed an A5 notepad. She fanned the pages until the first set of clean lines revealed themselves, and set about writing the conversation as precisely as she could remember it: date, time, dialogue, body language. Once the details were in print, rather than just in the incident book of her brain, she picked up her desk phone and keyed the three-digit extension for the designated safeguarding lead.

***

Outside in a thick, clinging mist, Rundle waited at the exit with the twitchiness of a condemned killer spending their last mortal moments on death row.

Relieved to see the figure rocking up at his side, he blurted, 'Where've you been, man? You were supposed to be back yesterday! And what happened to your face?'

'Jesus,' Kieran tried to keep his voice low, though the annoyance he felt at being bombarded first by Miss Casey's line of questioning, and now by this dinlo, made it a hard task. 'Give me a chance to get out the fuckin' door.'

Rundle backed away a pace, momentarily keeping his mouth shut, waiting for the younger kid to speak next.

'Seriously, man, you've gotta chill the fuck out.'

Rundle lowered his head, frowning like a toddler who had been told off for asking for sweets one time too many.

'Come on,' Kieran urged, 'I'm goin' down to the courts for a smoke.'

'Have we got time?' Rundle asked, not wanting to invite a ticking off from his next teacher.

'There's always time,' Kieran assured.

Once at the far end of the courts, they opened a mesh gate and headed into the group of bordering sycamore trees. Underneath the covering branches, the stagnated air was rich with the smell of rotting leaves and sodden earth. Kieran removed a pack of Marlboros from his bag, slid out a butterscotch and white stick and clamped it between front teeth. Passing the pack to Rundle, he lit the cigarette and took a long, smouldering drag.

'So,' Matt said, cupping his hands and pulling them away in a cloud of smoke, 'spill.'

'Zane.'

'What the fuck?' asked Matt in surprise. 'As in, your mum's boyfriend?'

'D'ya know any other wankers called Zane around here?'

Fair point. As far as names went, that one was far from common in his experience.

'Why the hell did he do that? Have you told anyone?'

'Yeah, I just told you.'

'You know what I mean, Kier.'

Kieran gave a flippant shrug of the shoulders.

'You *have* to tell someone.'

'I can't,' said Kieran, exhaling another plume of dirty grey breath. 'He knows.'

Rundle showed no immediate signs of recognition. Finally, the realisation hit home. *He knows…* That could mean only one thing. The grey branches of the sycamores began to twist and turn around him. His breathing became erratic. His head began to spin sickeningly. Guts churning, he lurched over, this morning's breakfast coming up and hitting the floor with a gruesome splat. Placing a grasping hand on the nearest trunk was all he could do not to collapse in a distressed heap.

'Dude, don't fucking yak on me shoes!'

There was nothing in return, only a cursory wipe of the mouth with the back of his free hand, and a vacant stare from eyes that had grown to saucers in a face drained of blood. Kieran grabbed him by the scruff of his shirt and thrust him one handed against the gnarly old tree trunk.

'No more pissin' about,' Kieran demanded. 'You're gonna sort your shit out or I'm gonna cut yer fuckin' throat right now. Leave you for dead in this shithole.'

That was too much for Matt. Turning to the side, he projected more vomit in one long, lumpy stream. Kieran let him go, patting him forcefully on the back as the boy hunched over, hands on knees.

Somewhere in the distance a bell rang out. Shouting voices of pupils on the tennis courts diminished. Soon there was only the sound of birdsong, cheerfully defiant over Rundle's wheezy breaths and the miserable patters of water dropping from the trees.

'Better?' Kieran said as his friend straightened up, an unusually sympathetic air to his voice.

Matt managed an unconvincing smile. 'Fucking perfect.'

TWENTY-FOUR

Bridges sat behind his desk, leaning back thoughtfully, legs crossed, and hands clasped together one his lap. His hawk-like eyes studied the boy's etiolated bruising over the top of his smeared glasses in contemplative silence. The frown he wore drew his eyebrows towards the top of his nose, raising their wiry hairs like the keratin quills of a threatened porcupine.

To Kieran's left, Miss Casey adopted a similarly ponderous posture. Kieran couldn't help but like the woman. She was alright – as far as teachers went, anyway. She had his back, though that could in time come with some pretty devastating consequences of its own. And she certainly had looks on her side, so that helped. But this interference into his personal life had left a sour taste in his mouth. Sour like the odour in the Head's office. Freshly watered soil supporting the potted plants in the window gave a musty stench. Mr Bridges just smelt old, like he should be stowed away in a shed watching a trainset performing its repetitive oval circuits, or perhaps better still, sat in a puddle of his own piss and faeces in an old fart's home. Blending with the aroma of age and earth, there was also a distinct tinge of alcoholic spirits polluting the atmosphere.

Casey uncrossed her legs, shuffling from one slight cheek to the other, and recrossing her legs in the opposite direction to rebalance the numbing tingles. Kieran watched Bridges as the dirty old bastard's eyes dropped in the direction of the knee length skirt, riding up a few more inches and giving him a little extra luxurious nylon thigh for the wank bank. Yes, Bridges was thankful that *that* still worked, even though his sex life was beat (pardon the pun) into extinction years ago. Small mercies, and all that bollocks.

The wall clock ticked loudly, its heavy clack, clack, clack echoing out an impending doom from the painted walls and dark-stained furniture.

Miss Casey broke the uncomfortable stalemate. 'Mr Bridges... did you want me to start?'

Bridges leaned forward and placed his chin on his knuckles like a statue Kieran had seen pictures of: The Thinker, or something like that. More like, *the Winker!* Thankfully, however, Bridges was fully clothed, unlike the famous bronze man; neither person opposite wanted to see that wrinkly old ballbag hanging down, like a rotting pear with separation anxiety. 'No,' Bridges spoke flatly, 'thank you. I assume you gave me all the facts previously, so if you could just take notes, perhaps?'

The condescending tone of the Head's voice made it clear that this was not up for discussion; Casey, although the only truly concerned party, was no more than a tiny cog in a vast, sedentary machine.

Pompous prick. 'Well, maybe you should just *start*, then,' she fired back, with a little venom of her own.

Bridges shot her down with a stern glare.

'How are you, boy?' he asked, looking back to Kieran.

'Um, okay, I spose.'

'Well, I'm glad to see the bruising has abated.'

Kieran turned to Miss Casey, a lack of understanding clearly displayed in his expression.

'He means *gone down*,' she said kindly.

'Oh.'

'Now,' Bridges took the lead again, 'do you want to tell me how you got them in the first place?'

'I already told Miss,' Kieran said, shifting his glance nervously down and pinching at the fine blonde hairs on the back of a finger. 'It was some kid in town.'

'Well, Miss Casey was not entirely convinced by your story.'

Kieran shot another look to the young English teacher.

'It's okay,' she said gently, 'we're on *your* side.'

'Would you care to change your version of events?' Bridges offered, leaning back into the psychiatrists' pose he started the meeting in.

'Not really,' Kieran mumbled.

'Speak up, lad.'

'*NOT REALLY!*'

'That was a little unnecessary,' Bridges complained, 'we are sharing the same airspace.'

Miss Casey scribbled a note in her pad. Once she had finished, the deep clacking of the clock's second hand refilled the void, booming as if it originated from within the depths of Kieran's own mind.

Finally Bridges spoke again, voice just as calm as it had been before. 'How are things at home?'

Here we go, thought Kieran. 'Fine. Why wouldn't they be?'

'Your attendance leaves a lot to be desired, young man,' he said. 'I think we may need to speak with your… parents? *Guardians*?' *Well done for knowing your students*, thought Kieran. Mr Bridges carried on without waiting for confirmation, 'Try to get to the bottom of things.'

'Good luck with that,' said Kieran.

'Meaning?'

'Mum's busy with the baby, ain't she,' he pointed out confidently. 'She won't have time to see you.'

'And what about your father?' Bridges persisted.

'Ain't seen him since he walked out on us three years ago.'

The Head sighed, bored of the lack of cooperation. 'Is there any other responsible adult at home?'

'Only mum's boyfriend. But he works away. Ain't seen him for weeks, either.' The deceit came easily, as it often does when one wills something to be true.

Bridges shot Casey an exasperated glance. Looking back to the waste-of-space kid, he said, 'Well this is futile. You're free to go. For now! Miss Casey, could you please grace me with your presence for a little longer?'

Eyeing Kieran with disappointment written all over her face, she nodded for him to leave the office. Feeling guilty and relieved concurrently, Kieran lifted himself from the chair, gave her an apologetic frown and strolled out. Passing the opportunity to listen at the door, he set his face to the floor and headed away at a brisk pace, desperate for the main exit, destination: home, with every intention of barricading himself in his bedroom, baby sobs or no baby sobs.

***

Taking a shortcut through the coach park, Kieran weaved his agile way through the constant flow of headlights on the busy street beyond, and fumbled in his pocket for the door key. As he entered the house, the hallway was in darkness. No crying baby. Just the sound of shagging noises from the television drifting through from the lounge.

Opening the living room door, he was surprised and disheartened to see Zane spreadeagled on the sofa, fag in one hand and a can of super strength lager hanging from the other. His jeans were unbuttoned, and some slut was riding this balding fat guy on the screen – some home-shot amateur crap, by the looks of it. A close-up shot from between the bloke's doughy knees confirmed that his meaty phallus was stuffed in the brunette's ringpiece.

'*How 2*'s changed a bit,' Kieran snarked.

Zane made no attempts to shut down the image on the screen. Or tidy his crotch area up, for that matter.

'I'm guessing mum's not here. Or is she upstairs *lubin'* up for you?'

'She's up the hospital.' Zane rolled his head towards the boy stood in the doorway. 'Which is exactly where you'll be if this gets back to her. Unless you want a ride on this?' he said, clutching his groin.

'You wanna explain to the ol' bill why a fourteen-year-old boy clawed his own throat out while you had yer li'l tallywhacker up his ass?'

Just a soundless stare for an answer.

'Didn't think so. Why's she in hospital?' The question was uttered with more than just a hint of indifference. Then he remembered how no baby sounds were heard when he'd returned home.

'Stupid fuckin' sprog of hers broke her wrist.' He lifted his can and took a lengthy glug, before belching vehemently.

'What? How can a three-month-old do that, exactly?'

'Fell out her cot,' replied Zane, the lack of emotion causing Kieran to clench his fist at his side.

'The cot's got sides,' he pointed out. Sucking in the fumes of Dutch courage floating in the air, he said, 'And how d'ya know its broken? You're not a doctor.'

'Cos although we've all got two elbows,' Zain muttered through gritted teeth, 'we don't usually have them both on one arm. And they don't usually break through the skin,' he added with a crooked smirk on his face.

'Excellent,' Kieran quipped, 'we'll expect a visit from social services then. That'll go great, cos this place is like a palace.'

In a display of speed that the boy would think impossible from the lazy fucker on the sofa, Zane was up with his rough fingers clamped around Kieran's neck, compressing his windpipe while forcing him back against the wall.

'Breathe a word to anyone,' he snarled, stale lager invading Kieran's young nostrils, 'and I swear to God, if social services do come 'round, they'll be finding your corpse under the fucking floorboards.'

As Kieran's face transitioned from red to purple, the man released his grip. Kieran turned and headed to his room before his lip could dig him an even deeper pit.

TWENTY-FIVE

Cautiously placed footsteps creaked their way up the stairs, the sound creeping into the pitch-black room through a gap under the door. Looking at the dim yellow light under the wooden slats, two shadows shifted slowly from side to side. Left foot, right foot, stopping as the paired. Tamsyn ignored the short series of timid taps, yet the visitor failed to get the message. The iron latch gave its metal-on-metal grind, and pale light awoke a congregation of shadows within the room.

'I brought you a cup of tea,' Sheila's voice soothed.

'I don't want it,' Tamsyn mumbled in response.

'Nonsense,' her mother argued, 'a cup of tea makes everything better.'

'Can it raise the dead?'

An uncomfortable silence darkened the room once again. Sheila carried the tea over to her distraught daughter's bedside table, careful not to spill any of the steaming liquid as she placed it on a laced doily. Seating herself on the edge of the bed she lovingly smoothed Tamsyn's hair away from her eyes.

Tamsyn broke the temporary silence. 'Do you think there's a God?'

Sheila wrinkled her brow at what she thought was an odd question. 'Of course there is. The evidence is everywhere you look.'

'*Where?*'

'Just look out the window. That church was built hundreds of years ago. With the tools available, a feat like that wouldn't even have been attempted if it was only for a fantastical Being. And life. Every living thing is the result of His work. Or Hers. I mean, no one comes face to face with their maker until the Great One deems it fit.'

Tamsyn looked to the window. Nothing could be seen of the rundown place of worship beyond the black panes.

'So,' Tamsyn said, 'the Devil has to be real, too. I mean, if God is.'

'Yes,' Sheila smiled, 'Satan *is* real. But never fear, Tammy, the All-Powerful Lord reigns triumphant.'

'Yet Austin's still dead. Killed in flames under the Devil's own arch. Where was your *All-Powerful* God then?'

'He can't be everywhere,' Sheila defended, 'especially in a damnable place like that.'

'Yet the Bible preaches an omnipresent God.'

'You're just bitter at the moment, and you'll feel you have reason to be,' Sheila said with an acrid sharpness. 'But you'll see the light eventually, if you look hard enough. "Seek and ye shall find." The Gospel of Matthew. The only reason that His House is hidden from you right now is because you're blinded by anger. But that will pass. He'll see to that. Just give it time.'

Tamsyn took another look at the night-blackened windowpanes, more to break away from her mother's deluded eyes than the expectation of a divine intervention. Sheila trained her own eyes in the same direction. Blinking hard, astonishment and disbelief flooded Tamsyn's brain like a narcotic lake. Before her, whether through an act of divinity or sheer coincidence, the heavy covering of clouds parted above the small hamlet of Merther, allowing a heavenly burst of moonlight to bathe the ruined church beyond the glass in a divine lunar embrace. It's falling, crumbling entry porch shone as welcoming as the Pearly Gates. Leaves of ivy fluttered like angel wings on its commanding, rejuvenated tower.

Sheila turned back, smiling at a speechless Tamsyn. 'There. You see it now.'

Having made its biblical statement, the parted clouds rewrapped their camouflage cloak around the moon. The Church of Saint Cohan reversed through its stages of metamorphosis. White, through to grey, evanescing to black. Leaning forward and picking up the cup of tea, Sheila motioned for her daughter to sit up. Once Tamsyn had done so, Sheila handed her the beverage, remaining quiet for a couple of minutes and allowing the apparition to sink in.

Finally, she placed a warm palm on the back of Tamsyn's free hand. 'It was Austin that I came to talk to you about, lovey.'

Tamsyn studied her mother's face, still unable to attain a verbal transaction herself.

'They're releasing his body tomorrow.'

Shocked into a response, Tamsyn flustered, 'But… It's too soon. They still don't know who did it.'

'Whichever demons carried this out, they had no physical contact with Austin. The coroner will have nothing more to gain by holding onto him.'

Tears welled at the bottoms of Tamsyn's eyes, thinking back to the word *body*, how it threw up such brutal certainty. He was dead. Austin. And that was that. No second chance at life. No going back. No miraculous resurrection.

'At least now his parents can start planning the funeral,' Sheila spoke on, gently. 'He can be put to rest.'

Removing the cup from Tamsyn's grasp, Sheila stood. She leaned forward, placing her lips momentarily to the young woman's forehead.

'My door will be open all night if you don't want to be alone,' she smiled. As Sheila left the room, the clank of the latch confirmed Tamsyn's solitary confinement.

Rubbing her watery eyes and cheeks, Tamsyn clambered lacklustre from the bed. She walked to the window, kneeling on the floor in front of it as if before an altar. The Church of Saint Cohan sat still and secretive in the gloom. Its call was gentle, no more than a whispered temptation in a lover's ear. But it beckoned all the same.

TWENTY-SIX

First period: maths. A wonderful start to the day, if you're not Matthew Rundle. But unfortunately for Matt, he was. He headed to his usual spot. Front row, far right. The front row thing was not his choice. In fact, it was antithetical to his desires. The seating plan was purely because Mr Copeland deemed it necessary to keep an eye on the Rundle boy '*at all times*'.

Face to the floor, Matt passed Copeland's desk, his rucksack dangling lazily from one hand. Lifting the bag and dropping it forcibly on his own desk, he noticed something very out of place. A pair of polished black shoes poked out from underneath. This was unusual, as he always had the luxury of not having to share his workspace with anyone in this particular lesson.

Lifting his gaze to take in the owner of the shoes, Matt's eyes were met with a shy smile, black-framed glasses (giving a slightly geeky but not unappealing look), and alluring green eyes through the glass lenses. And her hair: luxuriously smooth and as orange as marmalade, pulled back and tied in a neat ponytail.

'Oright?' he said.

'Hi.'

'Newbie?'

'How'd you guess?' she asked, still smiling.

'Haven't seen you before,' Rundle offered matter-of-factly, deaf to the wave of sarcasm her words came surfing in on.

'I'm Amber.'

'That's an understatement,' he said, transfixed by her shock of red hair. 'Not that I'm takin' the piss,' he explained, flustered. 'You know, I mean, I'm not calling you a *ging* or anything.'

'It's okay,' she smirked, still with that innocent shyness shining through.

'Rundle, for God's sake, sit down, lad!'

Matt turned to see Copeland brandishing a death stare in his direction. Rounding the desk, he took his seat next to the new girl.

'So, I guess you're *Rundle* then,' Amber whispered.

'Matt,' he said, tipping her an intrigued smile.

The lesson ground on, Matt and the newbie working together through the tedious tasks handed out by Copeland with monotonous persistence. Drifting off into boredom as the challenges became excessively mentally draining, the bell signalling breaktime came as a reviving electrical kick from a defibrillator to Matt's comatose state.

'Got any plans for break?' he asked, stuffing workbooks into his rucksack.

'I was gonna do some shopping, maybe catch a film,' Amber smirked.

'Gobby shit, ain't ya?'

She laughed. 'Just winding you up. I literally don't know *anyone* here, and nobody was very forthcoming in tutor.' Amber nervously ran a finger above one eye, tucking straying strands of fiery hair behind her ear. 'How about you? Don't suppose you fancy keeping a sad loner company?'

Having decided within a matter of minutes that he liked the little redhead, Matt said, 'Come on, then. Can't say you'll enjoy hangin' around with me, but you're not exactly spoilt for choice.'

Making their way out of a side entrance, they passed a treelined, grassy recreational area. Eventually they arrived at the outdoor sports courts and took a seat on a low, slabbed wall. The sun was shining in a clear sky, yet the cold fangs of late January bit into bare flesh. Kids scurried here, there, and everywhere, some kicking a ball around, some playfully grappling, some leaning against the mesh fence just trying to look cool and carefree.

Every now and then a figure would slink through the fencing to the rear of the court and skulk under the surrounding trees: the smokers, Amber cottoned on straight away. It was a wonder there were no breaktime supervisors loitering around, what with how blatant Amber thought the motives of these shifty individuals were.

'So,' she said turning to the boy at her side, 'what sort of things are you in to?'

'Me?' He sounded surprised by the question. 'Uh, normal stuff.'

'Well that narrows it down. Normal stuff like?'

'Like, football. And music. Indie, mainly. Guitars and stuff.'

'Are you a musician?'

'No. But I can kick a ball okay.'

'Well, that's good,' she sniggered. 'And *that* lot going into the trees? You smoke?'

'No. Yeah. Well, sometimes. I can take it or leave it.'

'It's cool if you do,' she said, 'I'm not a complete nerd. Just don't breathe over me if you do. That's all I ask.'

May have to quit, thought Rundle. *Think I wanna do more than just breathe on you.* 'What about you? What's your bag?'

'People watching, mainly,' said Amber, smiling as she took in the confusion on his face. He puckered up like she was speaking in some foreign tongue. 'Amongst other things. Music one of them, but if you're into *guitar* music you'll probably say what I listen to is shit. Or *gay*.'

'Sorry, can we just rewind a bit?' he smirked. 'People watching. WTF?'

'It's fun,' Amber tied to sound serious, 'you can learn *so* much about a person just by watching them. You should try it.'

'I wouldn't know where to start,' Matt said doubtfully.

'Try her,' she said pointing. 'With the mousy brown hair and the purple jacket. Just say what you see, like Catchphrase'

'Well,' said Matt, studying the specimen, 'she's a girl, innit. And she's got weird hair, like messy fucked-up blonde.'

Amber burst into laughter, a sound that Matt felt warmed the air around him rather than mocked his pathetic attempt at character analysing.

'Well go on then, Miss Marple. Whatcha got?' he laughed along with her.

'Okay,' Amber accepted the challenge, looking back to the girl. 'She's socially awkward, you can tell that by how her shoulders are slightly drawn in, and the way she keeps flicking her eyes from side-to-side but not turning her head. I say *drawn in*, but she's practically cowering. That's a big giveaway.'

Rundle looked on, an inward admiration of the redhead at his side swelling in his chest.

Amber continued with, 'And she really fancies one of those two kicking the ball to around her. The lanky one.'

'Get to fuck,' Rundle blurted. 'She's a rug muncher. Gotta be.'

'I think your gaydar needs servicing,' Amber said with a cocky smile. 'Every time he goes near her she drops her head to the floor and clutches her bag tight. It's a defence mechanism, kind of like a comfort blanket. You watch.'

As if scripted, the lanky kid went to retrieve a ball that rolled towards the fucked-up blonde. Her head dropped. Her arms clutched.

'She probably thinks he's gonna nick it,' Matt argued, referring to her bag. 'Those two have got a bit of a rep.'

'Nope. She doesn't do it when the other lad's near her.'

'And you've seen this?' Rundle watched on.

Amber remained silent. It took a moment, but without keeping them in suspense for too long the other kid ran towards the nervous looking girl, stopping only a foot or so away. Her face remained away from the ground, the bag free from a strangle hold. The socially awkward eyes still flicked from left to right.

'*Holy shit*,' whispered Rundle.

He stared in awe at the girl sat next to him, marvelling at this supposed superpower that she somehow possessed. Matt had never looked at people the way she did. Gazing into their soul in an attempt to fathom *the real them*. In fact, the only people his eyes lingered on were what he considered *punani*. Possibly the very reason he had given this redhead the time of day in the first place.

No. That was not fair. Yes, he thought she was hot, in a *geek chic* kind of way. And that fiery red hair burning his retinas… Christ on a bike! But she was more than just his perception of eye candy. An ethereal awakening seared the comprehension into his brain that this was the first time he'd seen beyond the milky flesh, the small-but-neatly-rounded chest, the slender curve of her adolescent hips. Amber intrigued him. It was the strangest, yet the best feeling.

Looking down the length of the playing court, Matt observed a familiar form entering through the back of the mesh fencing. He stretched out an arm and extended his forefinger.

'Okay,' he said, 'do him.'

Amber leaned her head in and scoped along the arm, ironically oblivious to Matt's body language as minor tremors ran though his every nerve as she narrowed the gap between them.

'Fuzzy blondie-brown hair and tie pulled loose?'

'Yep.'

'Okey dokey.'

'*Okey dokey?*' Matt laughed. 'Who the hell says "okey dokey" anymore? Other than my gran, I mean.'

'I do. Now shush, I need to concentrate.'

Amber watched as the subject sauntered down the court, able to maintain a straight line on account of other students stepping out of his thoroughfare.

The breeze played with her clementine ribbons. Rundle's gaze fixated as loose tendrils twirled and waltzed on the currents.

'Right,' she said, only partially drawing Matt from his trance. 'Bit of a chip on his shoulder, and most people know it. Kids are making an effort to get out his way and no one is talking to him. So, socially, he's more a reject than awkward.' She looked to Rundle, making sure she still had his attention, rather than asking for confirmation.

'He won't have many friends,' she went on, 'if any. He's looking at everyone with contempt, so if he does have friends there'll only be one or two. And he probably treats *them* like dirt. Uses them purely as entertainment, or as a scapegoat if his idiotic plans backfire.'

Fucking spot on, Matt thought. A silence ensued, expanding between them like overheated liquid as he drifted deeper into deliberation.

'Look out,' Amber said after what felt like an eternity. 'He's eyeing you up.'

'Yeah,' Rundle sighed. 'I'm that *one* friend.'

'Oh. Sorry,' she offered sympathetically.

The boy approached.

'Oo's she?'

'Oright,' said Rundle. 'This is Amber. Amber, Kieran.'

'Nice to meet you,' she smiled up at him.

'Whatever, carrot-top.'

There's that chip, thought Rundle, as usual unable to stand up to his so-called friend and defend a fellow pupil's honour. He looked to Amber, who just frowned and lowered her head to the ground like this kind of treatment was quite ordinary and came with the territory, though it was wearing a little thin.

'A word,' Kieran turned back to Rundle. 'In private!'

Matt eyed Amber in appeal. She gave a nod of consent, even if only a slight one.

'What you got next?' Matt asked Amber as he stood.

'Geography, with… I think is it Russell?'

'Excellent!' Matt beamed. 'That's mine, too. I'll save you a seat if I get there first.'

'Ditto,' Amber smiled. *If I can even find the place on my own.*

The two boys turned away and headed off to one of the court's side entrances. Amber listened to the dying embers of Kieran's bullying slurs.

'What the fuck, "*I'll save you a seat*,"' he said in a mocking voice. 'You got yer tampon in? Fuckin' bender!'

'How does that make me bent? She's a gir…'

TWENTY-SEVEN

Tamsyn stood inside of the funeral home's lavish foyer, after listening to the tiresome expressed sympathies – and not so sympathetically, the rules of the house – watching closely as the director made his suspicious, arachnid retreat to his office. Once the door had clicked shut, a sound amplified by the flat, plastered walls, she turned to her mother.

'I still don't get why he couldn't be buried here.'

Sheila frowned, 'We've been through this, hon. It's just their custom. They could have flown the whole family over here, but they couldn't face saying goodbye to them again. And they can't bear the thought of living here without their only son.' She placed a tender hand to her daughter's cold face. With as much care as she could muster, Sheila said, 'He belongs in Nagua, with the rest of his family.'

'What the hell will they do in *Nagua*?' Tamsyn argued. 'It's ridiculous.'

'Well,' Sheila thought for a moment, 'farming, I suppose. I don't mean to stereotype, but that's what most of them do over there, I think.'

'I can't believe they're making me miss the funeral. He needs me there.'

'It's going to be fabulous, either way,' Sheila assured. 'Trust me, I've looked into it. There'll be singing at the service. A dazzling rainbow of flowers everywhere you look. Jazz music accompanying him down the street. A celebration of his life, good and proper. Not that morbid, moping tripe *we're* used to.' Sheila gave a shifty look around, hoping no one was in earshot who may take offense. Offending people didn't usually bother her; they could take her as they found her, no secrets, no camouflaging paint job. But this was not the right time, and certainly not the right place. 'He would love it.' She placed a gentle kiss on Tamsyn's cheek. 'Gedda wriggle on, treasure. It's time.'

Tamsyn turned to a pair of glossy walnut doors and stared, anchored to the spot as if her feet had taken root in the plush maroon carpet.

'I can go in with you,' Sheila offered from behind, her voice a soothing whisper.

'No,' said Tamsyn. 'Thanks. I was the only one there for Austin that night. And I failed him. I want to be the only one with him now.'

Reaching for the gold-finish knob on the right-hand door, she gave it a twist. It opened onto a long, cavernous room, its centre isle a sweeping continuation of the maroon carpet. Inhaling deeply, Tamsyn took a tentative step forward before turning and closing the door slowly behind, unable to cast a glance at the woman on the opposite side of the threshold. Once the deep echo of the doorlatch had abated, a silence that seemed impossibly solid entered the chapel of rest. Listening hard, only the sound of her own breathing broke through the eternal peace. Convincing herself that she was alone seemed completely irrational. Though she knew she wasn't. If the dead spoke, her boyfriend had nothing to say. His determined silence was taken as an accusation.

Steeling herself away from such odious thoughts, Tamsyn braved herself to turn around. Standing with her straw-like hair in an unkempt fashion, shoulders slumped and cardigan hanging limply from her increasingly frail frame, she studied the eerily serene space. To either side of the carpeted walkway, rows of beechwood chairs, upholstered in smooth lavender fabric, sat on impeccably polished walnut flooring. The walls were ivory, adorned with intermittent lavender-shaded wall lamps, and small, dark wooden crosses, spaced approximately six feet apart. At the farther end of the chapel a wall of jagged, finely cut sandstone reached upwards to a vaulted ceiling, presented in a randomly staggered brick effect. Rising towards its zenith, another dark wooden cross hung projected from the sandstone masonry, only this one on a much more imposing scale than its counterparts on the adjoining walls. Looking up, strong beams arched and came together at the ceiling's central apex, an impounding, impenetrable fortress. For a fleeting moment Tamsyn thought that this was how Mr Geppetto must have felt, doomed in the confinement of Monstro the whale's great belly.

Below the cross, atop a catafalque of rich oak, lay the long wooden box that contained the last remains of the man Tamsyn had unequivocally fallen in love with.

In life, Austin was tall and broad, athletically built with a physique more suited to rugby than to sprinting. The coffin, however, seemed unsuitably small. Tamsyn's experience with death was limited. You could count the number of funerals she had been to on one depleted hand, though they each shared one characteristic: the coffins had *all* appeared too small to accommodate the lifeless vessel entombed within.

Edging step after wary step closer, the cuts of sandstone enlarged, the vaulted ceiling towered ever higher, an unscalable mountain range where the option of turning back was inhumanly removed from the equation. The dark cross hung dominant, expanding as though it were absorbing incorporeal liquid. Austin's coffin stayed as it was. Small. Unexceptional. Consumed by the magnitude of its overbearing surroundings.

No flowers, Tamsyn noted of the near-bare lid: a seeming affront to the Dominican Republic's celebratory customs. Had her mind been able to function adequately, and not roam lost in a labyrinth of despair, the wretched young woman might have considered the implications a four-thousand mile flight may have on a delicate bouquet's already limited life expectancy.

Beneath the spongy carpet, the wooden floorboards gave an ominous creak as she stepped up to the catafalque. Tamsyn felt a tightening in her chest. Breathing suddenly became an unnatural bodily function, the carbon dioxide a possessive spirit needing to be exorcised forcefully. Maintaining a regular pattern became even more unattainable as she lifted a hand and hovered it palm-down over the lacquered finish of the coffin lid. Her lungs filled with a sharp intake of air and held it there, momentarily ballooned. Finally, as her hand lowered and lay flat out on the cold, hard surface, Tamsyn's lungs deflated with a slow, serpentine hiss. Chest receding, the young woman felt smaller, akin to the cadaver in the wooden box that lay horizontal at waist-height, both inferior under the considerable cross and the vast ligneous ribcage.

She smoothed the immaculate surface. Its coolness under her soft, padded flesh gave the wood the feel of polished marble. Lifting the hand at her side to join its counterpart on the lid, Tamsyn spread her arms until both baby fingers came to rest against a small, brass cross. There were six of these in all, protruding from the lid of the coffin like rococo headstones on a scale model desert cemetery: two at the corners of the head end, two at the obtuse angles designed to contour the shoulders, and two at the corners by each foot.

Tracing the outline of the cross to her right the vertices scratched gently at her skin, stimulating the senses, soothing an eternal itch. She ran her fingers over the top of the brass form, clasping it between thumb and forefinger and giving it a gentle, yet persuasive, twist anticlockwise. There was a slight giving movement, partnered with a shrill squeak of metal pulling through fibre. A shiver ran through Tamsyn's spine at the sound.

Adjudging the noise of the screw to be too quiet to carry though the solid walnut doors, she twisted again, commanding her left hand to do the same. Working her way around the wooden top, she soon stood with six glistening crosses laid out in her palm. Spiralling metal threads, like a rattlesnake's warning tail, jutted menacingly from the base of each. Crouching, she lowered them to the soft carpet, desperate to be relieved of their sudden, scorching weight.

Facing up to the coffin once more, she let out a faltering breath, unaware at that moment how she would soon wish she'd kept the pure air in her lungs. Turning her hands over, Tamsyn placed the tips of her fingers under the lid's shallow overhang, applying a gentle upwards pressure. The lid gave with a vacuumlike sucking sound, the pure air of the chapel of rest filling the internal space of the coffin, expelling Austin's decomposition gasses and banishing them to the open void of the chamber.

The stench was intoxicating, and to Tamsyn's dismay, vomit inducing. Letting the lid fall back into place – another burst of cloying decay rolling in a ghostly tsunami as it did so – she ran to the only suitable place for such an event: a small round table in the corner of the room, its covering white cloth balling at the floor. On hands and knees, she lifted the tablecloth, shoved her head underneath, and retched. Nothing but spit and catarrh. Fortunately, she had not been in the mood for breakfast.

Composing herself against the decomposing reek as best she could, she regained her feet, letting the cloth drop to the floor, covering the mucousy mess she had left. She dusted herself down, ready to reembark on the mission she had without thought assigned to herself. Arriving back at the small box, as she placed a hand either side of the lid and lifted for a second time, a newfound confidence rendered her near unshakeable. Tamsyn turned to the side and placed the lid (a slab of inexpensive wood so much lighter than she had expected) flat onto the floor.

The nature of Austin's fate had seen to it that no amount of embalming fluid could disguise his demise. Though the pungent pickle-smell of formaldehyde was present, creeping into her nose like some brain-seeking parasite, scent paled into insignificance in comparison to the omnipresent odour of charred flesh and scorched hair. The rich, sickly-sweet tang of overcooked pork crackling, as if the inebriated chef had passed out at the spit and left the meat to cremate over an undying flame, trickled down Tamsyn's throat, turning her stomach yet again.

This time she held defiant, composing herself before the next stage.

Finally ready to act, she peered into the coffin. Austin's corpse was covered in its entirety in a white sheet. Blooming rosettes of grimy reds, browns, mustards and juniper greens decorated the material here and there, as drops of bodily fluid broke through the thin remains of flesh and muscle tissue, absorbing into the fabric in a tie-dye fashion.

'This isn't really him.' Her own voice startled her as she tried to convince herself, compelling herself to follow the speedily devised plan through. Shutting her mouth, she continued the pep talk in her head. *This is just something he used to walk around in. Nothing more. Just complex clothing that can be easily discarded. Landfill.*

Taking another deep breath, odious atmosphere all but forgotten in the intensity of the moment, Tamsyn reached for the sheet. Sliding it slowly down, she unveiled the remains concealed beneath. The thing that vaguely resembled a human head was a monstrous mess. Austin's strong, thick dark hair was gone. His ears: melted away leaving tiny, twisted holes at either side of his skull. His nose had taken on an unrecognisable pointed feature, the cartilage bright red and painful looking. The mouth hung wide open (having not been set closed, as this body was most certainly not meant for public viewing). Lips burned and shrunken back to nothing, exposed a set of inconceivably long, yellow-black teeth. His eyes were closed, though the marginally concaved appearance of the melted lids gave every impression that the beautiful brown globes that once lay behind had suffered a fate paralleled with that of the nose and ears.

Unveiling further, a scrawny, gloopy neck appeared, sized more appropriately to an adolescent than the big, sporty hulk that she remembered. Gleaming like a beacon of hope, a silvery item shone within the deep, sunken tissue of the neck just above Austin's manubrium bone. Placing her face as close to the barbequed corpse as she could bear, Tamsyn read the inscription: SAINT CHRISTOPHER PROTECT US. At the pendant's centre, a man with a walking cane struggled on, with the burden of a child on his shoulder.

Tamsyn let go of the sheet, watching as it fell weightlessly and settled over the vaguely human form. Slipping a hand either side of the neck, she curled her fingers around and sunk them into the depleting flesh. Its chilled temperature was the very antithesis of its flame-grilled appearance. What meat that remained was tacky and oily, with who-knows-what liquids filtering through the permeable membrane. Convincing herself that she was merely kneading raw lamb into a marinade, she was able to lift the neck. With the head rocking back as though it could detach at any given moment, Austin's mouth closed partially as the slack jaw rolled on its axis. Tamsyn stopped to listen, the movement giving the impression that the deceased was contemplating what to say.

No words were necessary.

Working her fingers delicately around the chain, she located the lobster clasp. After one sickening moment where the scorched fragments of Austin's skin pinched between her fingertips, the tiny lever eased back. Tamsyn worked the clasp free. Lowering the neck back to the upholstered bed of the coffin, she grabbed at the pendant and pulled. The chain gave a long and unsettling sludgy dredging sound as it cut into the soft tissue, coming away from the body with morsels of the man caught in its delicate links.

Lowering it like a coiling serpent into her hand, Tamsyn placed the chain secretively into the pocket of her jeans.

'*Safe travelling*,' she whispered, pleading with the huge wooden cross above not to let her removal of the patron saint of travellers have a negative impact on the soulless shells' next journey.

After replacing the soiled sheet over Austin's face, she bent and lifted the coffin lid from the floor. Slotting it gently onto the open-topped box, she methodically inserted the six brass crosses, twisting calmly with fluid motion until each cruciform was tightly in place.

As if dealt a physical blow from an unseen hand, the magnitude of the events that had just transpired hit home. On frail, uncertain, and unsteady legs, Tamsyn staggered her way to the front row of lavender-cushioned chairs.

She slumped heavily into a seat, trying to find some equilibrium, awaiting a rap on the door she thought would have already disturbed her. The rap that said, *time's up*.

TWENTY-EIGHT

Mist, murky and grim, rolled across the playing field like a chemical fire smoke cloud. Clawing its way silently from the listlessly lapping river it consumed all in its path, driving before it a dampening edge to the late January chill. The crowd gathered by the rear of the ugly, single-story City Council's Parks department building were too raucous to indulge in the therapeutic and mindful harmonies of murmuring water, and the light tinkering of halyard ropes from a run of nearby boats, being carried across the open space by the soft breeze.

Empty play equipment bathed silently in a white-blue glow from tall lamps within the parameters of the adjoining tennis courts. Its usual infestation of children, a crawling skin infection to which the only miracle cure was that of night cover, were all either waiting to board the plane to the land of nod, or had their passports checked and stamped and were already soaring though dreamy skies.

Beneath the shadow of the conifers and spilling onto the football and cricket pitches however, the small congregation of binge drinking and pot smoking teenagers had to rely on the faint light of the quarter moon, and their own measly fires to see by. Luckily for these adolescent tearaways, the woodsmoke odour and the strong scent of marijuana rebutted the eggy hydrogen sulphide stench emitted by the many millions of microbes in the mudflats, currently exposed in all their noxious glory by the low tide.

Prying his back from the somehow enticing discomfort of the cold wall, Kieran reached for the ludicrously oversized, hangover-assured plastic bottle of cider that lay between his trackie-bottomed legs. Unscrewing the cap he took a long swig, face screwing up at the apple's bitterness, before handing the bottle over to Rundle. Matt took the beverage greedily, scouring the area for his much-needed gingersnaps fix. She said she was coming, but that may have just been talk. Who knows?

'What the fuck are you so twitchy for?' Kieran asked, noticing the boy's darting glances. 'Ain't no coppers around.'

He was right. He usually was. Not even the tinny, rattling racket disseminating from a small pair of low-cost MP3 speakers being thrashed so hard they would soon become *estinto,* would motivate the local law enforcement out to disperse a gathering of stupid kids.

'I'm not looking for the pigs,' Rundle protested.

'*Oh*, I think you are,' Kieran smirked. 'You're lookin' for that ginger pig, ain't ya?'

'She's not a pig!'

'Ginger pig, ginger pig, let me in...'

'Fuck off!'

'Alright, chill out.' Kieran's smirk turned to a menacing leer. 'Bit touchy about your pigs.'

Ignoring the scornful remarks of the boy he was *so* lucky to call his best bud, Rundle sprang to his feet with a beaming smile and ran at a trot towards the conifers shielding the playing fields from the garden area. Spotting the source of the dopey, doting dog's suddenly joyous behaviour – stood casting nervous glances from one direction to the next, arms crossed at her chest and caressing her own shoulders, looking ever the loner – Kieran shouted after him, 'If she likes her men to be desperate and have tiny todgers, you're well in there!'

Matt didn't hear. Every sense in his body was preoccupied with the girl ahead.

'You made it,' he said, a little out of breath upon reaching her.

'Kinda looks that way,' she replied, her tone lightly mocking but her smile wide and genuine. Stretching upwards to look over Matt's shoulder in the direction he had come from, her face altered in the most miniscule of transformations, offering a hint of discouragement. 'So, you brought your pet ape, then.'

Rundle knew it wasn't a question. 'Kieran? He's no ape; he's a friggin' caveman. But don't worry about him. Put up with him for long enough and you'll get to like him.'

'No,' Amber said flatly, 'I won't.'

Feeling the moment slipping away down the slopes of Amber's disdain for Kieran, Matt prepared himself to commit his second crime in a matter of weeks. Only this one was the unwritten and much pettier crime of *Muff Before Mates*. Matt suspected that correctional time would be well worth serving for that one.

'Tell ya what,' he said, 'I'll go back and get me bag. It's got drink in it. Then we can wander around everyone else for a bit.'

'If you like. Or maybe,' she smiled conspiratorially, 'we can wander off, just the two of us for a bit. As long as your boyfriend doesn't mind?'

'I'm not bent!' Matt protested.

'Good,' she laughed at his horrified countenance. 'Neither am I, so we should get along peachy.'

Matt shrugged off the embarrassed feeling at being the subject of Amber's teasing. 'Don't go anywhere,' he said, before turning away and walking as coolly as he could, back to fetch his gear.

'What ya playin' at?' Kieran asked as Rundle returned and grabbed his bag.

'Won't be too long,' he answered. 'We're just goin' for a walk.'

'Fuck off! You're ditching me? For a fuckin' walk… with a ging! Well don't expect me to be sat here when you get back.'

'Don't worry,' Matt answered, too elated to pick up on the true meaning of the statement, 'I'll come find you.'

With that he was gone, trotting his was back along the dewy grass, fine spray puffing in clouds with every heavily landing foot.

'Where were you thinking?' he asked as he got back to Amber.

'You tell me,' she said, 'you're the one who knows where everything is.'

'Course,' Matt laughed a little foolishly. 'Sorry, my bad.'

Staring into the expanse of mist, an idea struck him. 'We'll go that way,' he said pointing into the dingy distance. 'That gets you to the river walk. Seems a good place to start.'

Amber shrugged her shoulders in agreement, and the pair set off into the doleful darkness. Reaching the end of the playing field, they headed through a small wooden gate. Mudbanks opened up before them, with a narrow ribbon of glistening black water running through a deep, weaving channel at the tidal river's far side. The temperature plummeted as the air became even more moist than it was over the field. Amber gave a shiver under the sudden atmospheric change. Matt had no *real* experience with girls: no proper girlfriends, or anything even closely resembling such a thing, though he guessed that this was as close as he had ever come such luxury… even though he hadn't officially *asked her out*, or whatever. But that shiver brought back memories of a couple corny films that he'd seen. Mimicking what was perceived to be the male's role in such situations, he pulled off his hoodie and handed it to her.

'Are you sure?' Amber asked.
'Yeah, course.'

'Thanks.' She smiled and slipped the garment over her head, instantly basking in the transferred warmth of his body.

Waiting for her to ruffle the fabric straight, Matt said, 'Let's head down this way.'

Amber looked back to the lights of the city centre as they grew smaller, the glowing yellow cathedral s appearing impossibly dominant, as ever, towering over rooftops and refusing to diminish against the impenetrable black sky. Conversation was kept to a minimum as their persistent feet guided them onwards, shoes scraping along the fine gravel of the riverside path. Neither really knew what to say, but the silence felt in no way uncomfortable. There seemed no real need to say anything; it was a stage of perfect tranquil balance in a relationship that some couples could try forevermore to reach, ending in total failure, yet other couples find in a matter of moments.

Leaves tittered overhead in hushed voices, as if offering a mark of respect to the opted silence between the young humans passing under their watchful shadow. As Matt gazed up at their secretive shifting, a light tickle on the outer pad of his hand stole his attention. He looked to his side, where Amber's nervous smile was just visible in the low light of the fractional moon. He took the gentle hint, along with her cold hand. Her skin felt pure and smooth, the most precious thing he had ever been privileged enough to embrace.

'What's over there?' Amber's silky voice whispered, her breath flowing visibly, like molten silver.

Matt followed her line of sight across another hazy field, to a building with rows of seats ascending on its left side. 'That's the cricket pavilion.'

'Looks like a nice, quiet place to chill.'

Matt considered this. No lights shone from within the clubhouse. The small triangle of car park was devoid of vehicles.

'You okay with jumping fences?' he said.

'If you help me.'

He could, and did. After helping hoist Amber over, she grabbed his hand, steadying him as he climbed the swaying mesh chain-link. Setting off across the flat, well-kept grass, they walked in the direction of the stand, fingers still intertwined.

Amber embarked upon the concrete steps first. 'Back row?'

'Sounds good,' Matt grinned.

Taking their seats, viewing the empty cricket pitch, Matt dropped his bag to the floor and fished around. 'Vino?' he said, sitting up with a slim gleaming glass bottle in his hand.

'Whoa, where did you get that?'

'Nicked it off me mum. She's got boxes full, so I doubt she'll miss it.'

'And if she does?' Amber giggled. The sound was enticing in its mischievousness.

'As far as she's concerned, I hate the stuff. It wouldn't have anything to do with me. There's just one thing,' he said, sounding disappointed with himself for a glaring oversight, 'I didn't bring any glasses.'

'Just crack it open.' Amber leaned into him. 'I'm sure we'll manage.'

Time passed in keeping with the bottle between them. The pair talked the small talk, huddling close, the warmth kindled by their touching bodies driving away all coldness from the misty gloom. With the wine now all but finished, Matt offered Amber the final dregs. He eyed the immaculate flesh of her porcelain neck as she tilted the bottle and drained the last of the liquid. Placing the cast-off on the floor, her eyes met his. Head dizzied, as much by the uncharted occasion as from the alcohol, she leaned forward and placed her sweet wine lips to his. Parting her mouth slowly, Amber instigated an oral exploration, as their hands – as if with built-in minds of their own – began to anxiously explore other regions.

TWENTY-NINE

With nauseating degrees of apprehension, Tamsyn opened the bedroom door, focusing on the rectangle of light at the mouth of the stairs. She stepped cautiously onto the landing's soft pile carpet. The glow from downstairs radiated yellow up the walls and a large proportion of steps, failing only to bathe the top two, and in turn keeping her bare feet in stealthy shadow.

Echoing across the tiled floor of the kitchen, the irregular clang and clatter of pots and pans reassured her that her mother was busy preparing their evening meal. Predictable scents of roasting meat – a smell that now invoked much less homely and much more macabre connotations for her after her recent horrific experience – and steaming vegetables rode on the crest of every sound. Her mother, forever obsessed with roast dinners; herself, ready to vomit at the thought of another huge plateful of essential, homecooked motherly love.

With the coast clear, Tamsyn inched tentatively to the bathroom. Dropping the cast iron latch, she stood consumed in the blackness' protective grip, the sound of her own breathing now louder than any other. Today had been the first day she'd been out since… She couldn't bear to think about *that* since; after endless scrubbing, the stink of charred, festering flesh still lay embedded in her skin. The anxiety that came with such a simple deed as stepping out of the house had taken its toll, yet today's venture was absolutely necessary.

Steeling herself to search blindly for the cord, she wrapped her fingers around it and pulled. The room filled with jaundiced light. The extractor fan hummed into life, drowning out her exhalations. Moving to the mirror, Tamsyn placed a hand on either side of the basin. The cold bite of glazed porcelain penetrated the thinning flesh of her palms, edging upwards through her wrists like an inexorable caress from the grave.

Studying her likeness in the glass, the young woman took in the undeniable evidence that the traumas of the last month had left behind. Those traumas had done little to hide their impact, her gaunt façade deteriorating at an unfathomable rate. Hazel eyes receded deeper into their sockets, sockets that now lay in shadow, like the gaping entrances of a pair of mineshafts in a rugged landscape. The whites had lost their purity, and along with it any sense of hope. Her cheekbones had developed into harsh wedges under tightening skin; the cheeks themselves becoming shallow, dried out ponds. Fine cracks had begun to charter reddening lips, as if the dried bed of the ponds fissured by intense savannah sun had contaminated the banks with their deathly disease.

Unable to look upon the face any longer, Tamsyn straightened her back and traipsed, feet dragging, to the toilet. Turning her back to the bowl, she lifted the front of her baggy T-shirt and slid a slim box from the waistband of her fleece bottoms. Placing the package between her teeth, with two hands she lowered her bottoms, letting them fall around her ankles before she sat on the wooden seat.

Plucking the box from between her teeth, Tamsyn looked with distaste at the backs of the lightly trembling hands that now clutched it. Metacarpals prominent, a furrowed field drained of its rich earthy colour. Veins slithered over strands of straw-like bone, like blue serpents under a colourless topsoil. The sight of her own body repelled her. Post-death decomposition, it seemed, had started its devouring procedure antemortem.

She opened the packaging and pulled a white stick from inside. Sliding a plastic cap from the stick, Tamsyn guided it between her legs and into the bowl.

Performing the necessary, she waited.

And waited.

Each passing second felt like a fully served life sentence, each delicate tick of her wristwatch a condemning pound of the judge's gavel.

Suppressing her fear enough to view the result, a pale blue cross confirmed the disheartening, daunting news her repulsive body had already insinuated.

THIRTY

Kieran slotted his key into the front door. Taking a moment, he conversed in his own head. Did he really want to enter the house? Home had never felt so unlike home. In fact, he had spent the whole day so far trying to avoid the place. Hanging around town, wandering aimlessly, ducking into a doorway at the first sight of any familiar face. Not that the wearers of those faces would make any attempt to communicate with the likes of him. Rundle would be the only one who would, but he was nowhere to be seen. Probably hiding out in private, sticking it to his new girlfriend.

Stupid ginger bitch, worming her way in, a bitter voice in his head spoke.

Another voice in his head informed him of the lack of noise from beyond the white plastic door.

Wrong. It wasn't merely a lack of noise. The void within those secretive, concealing walls – walls where what happened within, stayed within – was completely devoid of sound.

No wailing baby.

No boyfriend hurling abuse at whomever rattled his cage *this* time.

No television for his stoned, drunken mother to slouch in front of with vacant, faraway eyes; eyes that stared wide yet relayed nothing to the addled brain behind.

Turning the key, Kieran nudged the door sluggishly with the tips of his fingers. Still not a whisper, a blank page disclosing nothing. Stepping through the darkened opening, the thud of the closing door was a welcomed break in the silence. Nonetheless, the break was all too brief. Everything was once again hushed, the soundless quality so complete and enveloping that it reminded Kieran of the green boxlike room at the hospital he'd once upon-a-lifetime-ago had a hearing test in. For reasons unbeknown to himself, he could never quite forget the fuzzy dizzying pressure the silence of that room forced upon his senses, squeezing his brain like an overripe plum.

To his left, the living room door stood fractionally ajar, a baleful invitation to explore further, to lift the concealing flap of the freakshow tent. What lay beyond? Had his mother grown a beard? Or his baby sister a second head? Maybe the boyfriend had simply left a bloody massacre worthy of a scene in a True Crimes episode; two dismembered bodies lying in a splatter paint of claret. Prodding at the flimsy plywood surface with the toe of a trainer, the door soundlessly opened. Nothing out of the ordinary (if he ignored the fact that his mother was not sprawled out wasted on the old two-seater settee, and that the television screen for once had nothing to declare). The blanket she hid from the world, and the demands of a hungry or discomforted infant under, was piled in an untidy heap at the sofa's base. Rubbish made sporadic appearances across the floor, though that was a given.

The door to the condemnable kitchen was wide open, an illuminated ceiling light the only clue that anyone had been there. Its sickly glow crept along the living room carpet like a toxic chemical leak. As Kieran stepped into the room, a wet slap on the grubby lino flooring prompted him to look down. Spreading away from the spot he stood, a circular pool of clear liquid edged into the middle of the room. He was undoubtedly wrong about the glowing lightbulb being the only sign of human inhabitation.

A few feet away at the further edge of the spillage, an empty pan lay upended on the floor. A tangle of limp noodles lay intertwined like an evisceration of intestines from some strange, chromium beast. To the side of the once boiling lake, a babies dummy foretold that this latest incident was unlikely without its casualties.

Kieran turned and headed back through the living room at a canter. Hitting the staircase, his urgent footsteps, in tandem with his rapidly beating heart and accelerated breathing, reinforced what he already knew, yet no one else would believe – that he truly did give a shit about his little sister, an innocent child who (like himself) had not asked for any of this. Had not asked to be born. Had not asked to be dragged through life by an alcoholic, drug-dependent mother, and hated by her fist-throwing asshole of a potential stepfather. No matter how much Billie's constant crying had worn Kieran down, they were in the same boat; akin, adrift, and facing the same adversaries.

Arriving at the entrance to the bedroom Billie and his mother shared – along with that scumbag, if he saw fit to return from his boozy nights out – Kieran gazed through the open doorway. Just enough light penetrated the curtained window to show the youngster's cot was empty. This was always going to be the case, as he knew all along. Seeing it in reality nonetheless, as undeniable as day and night before his very eyes, filled him with a choking fear.

He stepped into the room, placing his hands on the smooth, wooden cot railing. Once again he found himself weighing up his options. If he was to go to the hospital – which is possibly where they were (but, Lord only knows, they may be capable of killing the sprog, dumping the tiny, battered body, and doing a runner) – how would he get there? Too young to drive, no money for a bus, and hitching a lift could take forever. And then, maybe some perv would pick him up and expect a down payment of a blowjob, or something even worse. It happens.

Had the sack-of-shit boyfriend gone with them? Highly unlikely. There was a better chance of monkeys flying from the guy's ass than there was for *him* to do the honourably thing. Kieran laughed at the thought, unable to help himself despite the desperation the current situation carried. Seeing the prick scream as those vicious winged primates, the ones that scared him so much in that Wizard of Oz film when he was young, came tearing out of the jerk's sphincter one after another. No. He was far more likely to be in one of the nearby pubs. And if Kieran found him in one, half pissed and riding the inebriation express, who's to say he wouldn't give Kieran a good kick-in for daring to interrupt his session?

Blowie? Kick-in? Blowie? Kick-in?

***

When push came to shove, the decision was easy. No more than ten minutes later, propping up the first bar that Kieran had ventured into, slouched the intimidating figure. An unsavoury looking jakey sat to each side, both laughing noisily at some quip unheard by Kieran. Both tipped back heads displayed teeth that suggested neither of the gaping mouths they squatted in could even pronounce the word *dentistry*.

Kieran approached from behind, tapping the guy in the middle on the shoulder, nervously. With drowsy eyes, Zane turned. His teeth, initially bared through laughing, disappeared as his amused expression turned to a grimace, the stage curtain dropping and bringing an end to the happy scene. 'What the fuck are you doing here?'

Kieran swallowed a lump of angst. 'Billie. Where is she?'

'Who the...' Acknowledgement dawned on Zane's stubbly face. 'Oh, the brat.' He turned to face the bar, grabbing his half-empty pint glass and sinking the last of the golden liquid in two seconds flat.

'Another,' he shouted to the barman, who was in an alcove at the rear of the bar, piling glasses into a dishwasher.

'Just tell me where my sister is.' The teenager's voice behind him was imbued with spurious confidence.

Laughable. 'Relax, Rambo.' This time Zane didn't bother to turn around. ' She's at the hospital with your useless cunt of a mother.'

'Thought as much!' Kieran couldn't help his tone coming across as accusatory.

'Listen 'ere you little shit,' Zane sneered, him and his drinking partners spinning on their barstools and exacting hateful looks on the newcomer. 'If that silly cow's too fuckin' useless to look after that fuckin' thing, it's not *my* problem. You ask me, that slag should've been sterilised at birth. Then there wouldn't have been any dumbass kids to worry about.'

There followed a moment of tense silence, Kieran's young eyes darting from one grotesque figure to the next.

Zane broke the stalemate. 'Fuck off outta here, little boy. Playtime's over.'

THIRTY-ONE

The knock, amplified by a solid oak surface, was a determined one.

'I hope you're decent,' her mother's voice muffled through, 'I'm coming in.'

With no time to protest, the iron latch clunked upwards. Tamsyn pulled the bedclothes around her as the door swung inwards.

'Gawd, it's like a bleddy cave in 'ere,' Sheila said, marching across the room purposefully and ripping the curtains apart. 'Know what time it is, do you?'

'No,' mumbled Tamsyn through the quilt, 'and I don't care.'

Sheila gave an exaggerated countenance and raised her wristwatch to her eyes. 'Oh, would you look at that? It's time to get out of bed, stop feeling sorry for yourself, and realise the world evunt stopped bleddy turning. That's what time it is.'

'Do you even *realise* what I've been through?' Tamsyn's tone was meant to come across as flabbergasted, though Sheila only heard a lame whine of self-pity.

'I know exactly what you've been through, sweetheart.' She sat on the edge of the bed and ran her fingers through her daughter's hair. 'And now you need to understand that you can't go through it forever.'

'How can I be expected to get over it?' Tamsyn's voice was little more than a whisper as she sat up and pulled her knees to her chest.

The room grew brighter as fast-moving clouds cleared a path for the morning sun. Dust particles danced in its rays like a thousand microscopic fairies performing aerobatics.

'The sun'll 'elp,' Sheila smiled. 'That's what it's there for. Cheer folk up. Snuff out the darkness.' She leaned forward and kissed her daughter's forehead through wispy tangles of fringe. Standing, she said, 'Get dressed, brush your teeth. Sort that godawful bird's nest out; anyone would think you were one of those tree-huggin' protesters. I'll put the kettle on, and when you come down I've got a surprise for you.'

She left the room and Tamsyn listened as her footsteps grew quieter and more distant, descending the stairs at their usual spritely pace.

Walking into the kitchen ten minutes later, Tamsyn found her mother swirling the teapot in rhythmical circles. Satisfied that the perfect cuppa was ready to go, Sheila poured the steaming liquid into two cups. Immediately the strength of the brew made itself clear, its rich scent drifting spectrally across the open space.

'Here you go, love,' said Sheila, placing the pot on a cooling stand, and handing Tamsyn one of the full cups.

'Thanks.'

Tamsyn took the mug with both hands and lowered it carefully onto a coaster on the large family table. The farmhouse table had been underoccupied since her father had passed away, after losing his short battle against pancreatic cancer at just thirty-eight years of age. Tamsyn had not yet told her mum that there may, in the not-too-distant future, be three seats taken once again. In fact, she was not even certain herself. What hope did *she* have of raising a child who was without a father? Given the mental trauma her mind was wrestling through each and every day, she could barely look after herself. And sleep was difficult enough to attain: the burning horrors of that freezing January night playing on a loop whenever the lights went out; the piercing cries of wind through leaves in the churchyard a constant echo of Austin's and her own screams. Add throwing a whining child with no respect for regular sleep patterns into the mix? Well, that would surely scream her into insanity.

'So,' said Tamsyn, attempting to drive away the thoughts plaguing her mind, 'what's this surprise, then? A psychiatric assessment? A box of wacko-pills. A time machine?'

'Very funny,' Sheila replied, without even a hint of humour in her voice. 'It's outside. Come on.'

Grabbing her daughter by the hand, Sheila led her to the door with the conviction of a teacher marching a disobedient child to the Head's office, an uncompromising telling-off the prize. She opened the door onto a bright and serene morning, the kind of morning that could have you believe there was absolutely no evil in this world, that life was all happy endings, shit didn't stink, and every sinner was a saint. As they stepped out into the pure country air, Tamsyn turned her gaze to the right. The irregular supporting boundary of the cemetery teemed with wild flowers, not as colourful as they would be on a summer's day, yet making a decent effort, nonetheless. Yet the worst winter of Tamsyn's life wore on, the sun and the approaching spring doing little to remedy the plight of the survivor. The hedge-come-wall stood as a testament to the rugged hands that built it many lifetimes ago. How it hadn't fallen with the weight of earth behind it yet, spilling the lichen-covered, fractured tombstones towering crookedly above onto the roadside, dragging a myriad of underlying old bones with it, was anyone's guess.

Turning her head to the left, Tamsyn took in an unexpected sight in front of the garage. Stood before the deep brown metal door, a car she didn't recognise took up a large proportion of the drive. She wondered how she could possibly have missed it through the kitchen window that hovered at its side. It was big. It was beige. It was boxy. The things we miss when our eyes refuse to see.

'Who's is that?' she asked, the smirk on her mother's face telling her what Tamsyn prayed not to be true.

'Who's is what?' The smirk widened to a Cheshire Cat grin. 'Oh, that? That's your new car, lovey.'

'My new…' Tamsyn was mystified. 'Isn't… Isn't it a bit, *big*? And what do I need a car for anyway?'

'Aw, you ungrateful bugger!'

'I don't go anywhere!' Tamsyn protested, striving to contain her annoyance.

'Well, that's gonna change, isn't it,' Sheila cheerfully insisted. 'Starting now.' She took a step towards the car and turned back to face her daughter. 'And that's not all. It's unlocked. Go ahead and pop the boot.'

'I don't need to *pop* it,' Tamsyn sighed, 'the window's bigger than my bedroom's.'

Stepping up and looking through the large rectangular sheet of glass, she turned back to her mum. Confused. Insulted. 'Cleaning stuff!'

'No flies on you.'

'Great. Thanks.' Tamsyn placed her hands firmly to her hips. 'No, seriously. That's brilliant. But if you're dropping a hint about my personal hygiene, that stuff can't be used on skin.'

Sheila mimicked the hands-on-hips pose. 'Har, bloody har! It'll be novel to you, but I was thinking you could use it on other things, maybe.'

'Industrial quantities of it?' Tamsyn was struggling to grasp her mother's point.

'Well,' Sheila smiled back, 'there's a lot of surfaces, and they ain't gonna clean themselves.'

This was greeted by a shrug of the shoulders.

'Look,' sighed Sheila, 'you need to get out more. God knows you can't spend your whole life mopin' behind those walls. I won't have it.'

Tamsyn opened her mouth, preparing to object.

'Uh-uh!' Sheila waggled a forbidding finger. 'I need help with those cottages. We've got too many of them for me to handle on my tod, 'specially now I'm gettin' on a bit. We'll split everything down the middle, fifty-fifty. The dunkey work, the paperwork...' she smiled at her daughter again. '... And the profits.'

'So, your ambition for me is to be a cleaner?'

'*And*, the *profits*,' Sheila reiterated. 'You'll be co-owner of a business! And besides, cleaning's never done me any 'arm, and that's only a part of it anyway.'

'And you want to split the profits *and* the workload?'

'Well, *yeah*. The two kinda go hand in hand. Come on, you ole grimalkin, what d'ya say?'

'It's helping you with the donkey work I'm worried about,' Tamsyn admitted, scraping the toe of her deck shoe into nothing on the drive.

'Come on, ole girl,' Sheila said quietly. 'Not shy of a bit o' graft, are ya, flower?'

The words Tamsyn uttered next, voice muffled and face to the floor, were possibly the first words to ever shut her mother up. 'I'm pregnant.'

THIRTY-TWO

A shifting tide of schoolkids streamed noisily along the corridor, forcing their way past one another like conflicting waves intruding upon and vacating an ever-changing shoreline. The bright morning sun glared through a long bank of classroom windows, scything warming shards of yellow from the repetitive run of open doorways lining the walls.

Contrary to the conditions beaming in from the world outside, Kieran's mood was dark, his stride determined and menacing. Target acquired, eyes locked and boring holes in the back of its head some twenty metres further along. The target moved with all the nonchalance of one who had never done wrong; no skeletons in the wardrobe – or perhaps more accurately, no char-grilled carcass fused with vehicle upholstery in the wardrobe.

Fucker got over that *quick*.

Quickening his pace to match the urgency required, Kieran made a last-minute lunge, dropping a heavy hand onto Rundle's shoulder before the boy could disappear into his tutor room.

He turned to look at the bearer of the forceful hand. 'Kier! What's up, mate?'

'What's up?' Kieran repeated. 'You, fuckin' ditchin' me on Friday. That's *what's up*!'

'Yeah, uh, sorry about that,' Matt said, looking suddenly sheepish, 'me and Amber, uh, you know.'

'Okay, enough already,' Kieran screwed his face up in distaste. 'I don't need *that* image in my head. What about the rest of the weekend? With that ging again, I suppose?'

'No,' Rundle admitted. 'It's a bit weird, that one. I'll catch you at break.'

Kieran watched as Rundle turned and headed into the classroom, his carefree swagger enduring.

Finally, first period came to an end. Time had crawled painfully slowly, Kieran sitting restlessly with gritted teeth as he mulled over the *'It's a bit weird...'* comment. Rundle had seemed unconcerned about the possible reasons why he may not have seen Amber, but then again, that lad was as thick as pig shit. Now, loitering in the shade of trees at the end of the tennis courts, Kieran spotted Rundle making his way over, strutting through the crowds, that vacant grin still etched upon his face, like an excited puppy.

'So, you shagged her.' Kieran pulled a packet of cigarettes out of his pocket, jammed one between his lips and handed another to Rundle. 'Whoopty fucking do,' he mumbled around the butt, cupping his hand and sparking up.

Rundle waited for the lighter to be offered, lit his own, and exhaled the smoke through the immovable grin.

'Sparing the details, you gonna tell me what was so weird? Was it her pubes?'

'Piss off! You're just jealous.' For the first time today the clown's smile painted on Matt's face began to dissipate. 'Well, anyway, after we... you know... we got talking.' He placed his back against a tree trunk and slowly slid to a seating position, wrists on knees, his gaze shifting between the soft needle-strewn ground and his cohort's stern expression. The fixed glare that greeted him insisted that he continue.

'Anyways,' Rundle took up the non-negotiable invitation, 'we were getting on awesome... or at least *I* thought so. We chatted for ages. I've never been able to just talk with a girl like that.' He took a drag, returned his wrist to his knee, and discarded the excess ash with a flick of the thumb. All the while Kieran watched, silent, waiting.

'I told her things I thought I'd never tell anyone. And she seemed fine with it. She barely reacted at all, just let me carry on, and___'

'*What* things?' Kieran bluntly interrupted.

'And I arranged to meet her on Saturday, but she never showed up.'

'*WHAT*… things?'

Rundle's lost eyes stared at the floor, words choked by the thick ball of smoke in his throat.

Finally, he managed to speak, low and barely audible. 'She's cool. She won't say anything.'

'What the fuck have you done?' Kieran hissed.

Nothing. Not a word. Even the noise from the playground had drifted off to another time, another galaxy.

'Fuckin' answer me, dipshit!'

The boy on the floor looked up, helpless and shaking his head gently. 'Sorry, man. I'd been drinking, and___'

Rundle's sentence was cut off as the glowing cigarette end left his best friend's hand at speed and hit him just below the eye. The contact was too brief to cause any pain, though the same could not be said for the foot that was driven forcefully between his parted legs. Propelled by agony, Rundle arched forward and clutched both hands over his groin. The same piledriving foot that had caused such discomfort came hurtling in again, this time fracturing his nose. Blood streamed as the skin over its bridge split like a launched water balloon.

Matt had lost count of how many times the shoe returned, dishing out more and more excruciating consequences for his stupid, big mouth. When the kicks stopped coming, Matt's brief reprieve lasted only seconds, before his blurred vision caught sight of an arm being raised, the fist at its end bearing down like a piston at his head.

THIRTY-THREE

Baby Billie lay content in her mother's arms. A babbling brook of gurgling noises ensued as she drew from the bottle. If God existed, he was one twisted entity, and he had the infant playing ball: happy baby, happy family, doting mother, the boyfriend at work earning an honest crust. Everything was rosy.

What these self-righteous intruders don't know won't hurt them, Melissa thought, smugly.

'She's certainly rare.' It was the woman in the power suit that had spoken this term that was older than her years. Deep red trousers, matching fitted jacket pinned at the middle by a single button. Highlighted blonde hair shining like liquid nectar, pulled into a ponytail so tight it looked fit to shed the skin from her skull. Her made-up face sported a thick pair of lips wearing a prosthetic smile, the same deep red of her outfit. 'Such a lovely thing.'

Melissa smiled back, fighting hard to keep the contempt she felt for the young woman from breaking through the façade.

Sharp-suit's associate closed the folder that had lain open on his lap for the entirety of the meeting. The notes he'd jotted after each and every invasive question remained secret – for now at least – entombed within the foreboding black covers. He reached forward and plucked up the mug intended for him from the table, noticing a concerned glance from his colleague. *I know we're not everyone's cup of tea*, he thought, *but I've never been poisoned before*. Besides, she had emptied her own, and she wasn't choking or throwing up… yet.

He took a sip. The brew was now cold, and there was that slightly sour tang of milk that had started to turn. Gross enough for the warning glance of his co-worker. He smiled a *cheers*, looking her up and down, a habit he could not manage to shake. Some twenty years younger than himself, he spent much of the day fantasising about banging her hot little ass. She'd give him a heart attack one day, but shit happens. Some things are worth the ultimate sacrifice.

'Well,' he said, forcing his mind back to the task at hand, 'I'm satisfied we have everything we need. Lauren, is there anything you'd like to add?'

'Nope,' she smiled at him, springing to her feet, eager to be out of the place.

'Well, in that case,' he rose, holding out a staying hand to Melissa as she was readying herself to follow his lead, 'no, no. You just carry on doing what you're doing. We'll show ourselves out.'

Lauren looked back to Melissa, her deep red smile superficial, immovable. 'It was nice to meet you… both of you.'

Whatever, slut. 'Likewise,' Melissa managed through pursed lips.

'We'll get the report written up,' the man said – Melissa failed to listen when he announced his name on arrival – adjusting his shirt as his gut fought to burst free, 'and there'll need to be another visit, of course.' He noticed the mother's eyes sharpen on him, a falcon sizing up its lunch.

'Nothing to worry about,' he hastened, chortling nervously, 'just a formality. We'll, uh, we'll be in touch in due course.'

The pair left the room, the front door clicking shut behind them and freeing Melissa from her BAFTA-worthy performance. With the windows open in an attempt to at least sap the intensity of years' worth of cigarette smoke, amongst other polluting fragrances, she waited until the voices of the two Children's Services officials disappeared up the road. Satisfied that the interrogation was over – for now at least – she withdrew the bottle from the baby's hungry mouth. Lowering the bundle to the floor kicked off a series of whines and sobs. But that was a tough show. Let the little bundle sob. Let her scream the house down. Right now, a spliff was the most important thing. To calm the nerves. Get her mind back to its preferred state of numb equilibrium.

Reaching for the cushion at her back, Melissa pulled the concealing fabric forward. She looked down at Billie. Small. Insignificant. Vexatious. Bitching. Screaming. A burden. Hovering the cushion above the distressed infant's face, a storm brewed in her mind; a cauldron of bitter thoughts boiling with *what ifs?* She envisaged what life could have looked like without the arrival of such financial and emotional drains. The freedom that awaited her if she could just erase those mistakes from existence and memory.

Billy stared back, face reddening and eyes pooling with salty liquid.

Melissa turned the cushion over in her hands, contemplating. Finally, she found the zip on its cover, ran it back, and slipped her hand inside. Feeling for the scrunched foil pouch, she withdrew the weed and exhaled with relief. Before she had time to open the package and prepare her joint, she heard the gentle grating of a key sliding into the lock of the front door. Zane must have been scoping the house out from nearby, waiting for the unwanted, uninvited visitors to leave.

'Oh. It's you,' she moaned as the new arrival entered. 'What're you doing home this early?'

'Got suspended,' Kieran replied, his lack of emotion bordering on sociopathic.

'Oh, well done. That's brilliant, absolutely *fucking* brilliant!' his mother exclaimed. 'Way to go to draw more attention to us. What the *hell* did you do this time?'

'Who were the suits I saw leaving?'

'Keep your nose out. I ask the questions.'

Billic continued to fuss on the floor, her agitated legs kicking helplessly at the air. Kieran noticed the unfinished bottle next to her. Moving across the room he lifted his little sister from the tacky carpet. Picking up the bottle once he had her held securely, he placed it to her searching lips. The crying stopped immediately, replaced by a course of contented coos, mixing in with sporadic sobs as her tiny lungs slowly reassumed a natural rhythm.

'I kicked Rundle's head in,' he said matter-of-factly. 'Who were they?'

'Right. And why did you do that?' Melissa sunk back into the sofa and commenced skinning up.

'Cos he's a mouthy cunt. Who the fuck were they?'

'You're the mouthy one, ya filthy little gobshite.' She tucked the paper in, rolled, and ran her tongue across the gummy strip. 'Social Services if you must know.'

'Fuckin' told you that would happen?'

'Watch your mouth!' Melissa snapped. Placing the cone-shaped spliff between her dry lips, she flicked at the lighter. Her eyes sparkled with an evil dancing glint of orange behind its taunting flame.

'They'll be taking her away soon, with the shit job you and that prick are doing. God knows, I wish they'd taken me away years ago.'

'You ungrateful little bastard,' Melissa hissed.

Kieran never had time to react as his mother launched the cigarette lighter at him. Though it was only light plastic, the throw had enough determination, venom, and accuracy to split the skin as it connected with the bony ridge of his upper left eye socket. Feeling warm blood trickling around the hollow of his eye, he swallowed the lump of anger rising menacingly in his throat. Retribution could wait until he wasn't left holding the baby. He locked onto the woman's gaze just long enough to see concern loom up on her face.

'You'll pay for that,' he said calmly.

Turning his back, he headed for the exit, taking his kid sister with him, away from their repugnant mother as she trembled with worry.

THIRTY-FOUR

AUGUST

Dragging torturously on, summer trudged by, an endless passage of heat and exhaustion. The tourism industry was booming, as was always the case in this bucolic county. Surrounded by some four hundred plus miles of Celtic Sea and English Channel coastline, with an abundance of sandy beaches, lazily flowing creeks, and waterfront holiday retreats, good old Kernow was a must for those seeking clean air and a laid back way of life.

Early august sun came beating through the glass as Tamsyn leaned on the sill of an upper window of one such property. She watched on in a daze as an ensemble of twinkling bubbles glided listlessly across the brown-green surface of Tresillian River. Having just changed the third set of bedclothes that formed only a fraction of the between-guests ritual, she had to stop to pull herself together before tackling the vacuuming. To Tamsyn, it seemed that her belly was swelling noticeably more with each passing day, and her fussing mother had seen to it that each of her properties with two floors now contained a vacuum cleaner on each level. *'We can't very well 'ave someone in* your *condition lugging those bleedin' things up and down the stairs all day!'* she'd stressed.

Without exception, on every occasion that her mum uttered the phrase *in your condition*, Sheila would smile fondly and give her daughter's tummy an affectionate rub, where the little bump was snuggling as it prepared itself for the outside world.

'Not so little anymore,' Tamsyn sighed, looking down at an unfamiliar body.

She raised a hand, wiping a light coating of sweat from her forehead with the back of the wrist. Although it was still before eleven in the morning, the sun through the glazing felt as intense as at its afternoon peak. Couple that with the exertion endured and her *'condition'*, the excess perspiration was justifiable. Studying the slow-moving water once more, Tamsyn's head began to thrum. A gentle buzzing behind her ears came and went in steady rhythmic pulses as oxygenated blood was pushed to her brain, carrying a wave of self-doubt through her arteries.

How on earth was she going to cope with a child?

She didn't know the first thing about parenthood. *That* had not been part of her long-term plan. And with no Austin to embark on this journey with her…

Another thrum, as if brought on by the mere recollection of his name. This latest surge proved more dizzying and more vigorous than any of its predecessors.

Other than being forced to share in the company of her mother through their living arrangements, Tamsyn all but went into a breakdown at the thought of being face-to-face with another human being. What was supposed to get easier – which Tamsyn was beginning to understand was just a load of horse crap that people shat out of their drivelling mouths, through a lack of knowing what to *really* say, though feeling they have to respond somehow – only increased in difficulty with every passing breath. What started off as truly devastating, just kept on evolving into something far more unbearable. Time was not *The Great Healer*, and she would never be capable of bringing a small, helpless life into this world. Her pain was hers exclusively, and for no other soul to intrude upon or share in.

And in a world where one person could take the life of another in the most heinous and diabolical of circumstances, getting away with it seemingly scot-free, then surly the greatest sin of all would be subjecting another soul to it.

Finding the slow stirring of the water suddenly disturbing and melancholic, Tamsyn straightened her aching back and drifted away from the window. Splitting like a log under the razor-sharp steel blade of an axe, excruciating pain ripped through her skull. She had painkillers, though they were in her handbag, and that was downstairs. Feeling that the short trip was still more than she could manage, she backed up unsteadily until the backs of her legs rested against the bed. She turned, the freshly laid sheets the last thing on her mind, and let herself fall face first. Squeezing her head violently between trembling hands, Tamsyn clamped her eyes tight, cancelling the world and all its traumas out. The upstairs carpets would have to wait.

***

After an hour of respite, Tamsyn saw to the vacuuming in the three bedrooms and the small landing, cleaned the family bathroom, and proceeded to make her way to the top of the staircase. Once the first few steps had been cautiously navigated, the dizziness she had experienced at the window returned with renewed vehemence. She groped desperately for the smooth, rounded wood of the banister, her feeble fingers merely brushing at the polished surface. Buckling underneath her weight, her knees folded like a house of cards in a gust of wind. Heading into a tumble, her first instinct was to wrap her arms securely around the bloated dome that harboured her unborn baby: the baby she had so recently thought that giving life to would be a serious act of cruelty.

As her tumbling body came to a thunderous stop at the foot of the stairs, Tamsyn's vision blurred red as a gash on her forehead spilled claret into one eye. A stabbing pain struck the pit of her stomach. Shaking wildly, she forced a hand down beyond the aching swell. Inspecting between her legs she felt a sticky, wet warmness. In complete contrast to the harrowing, blood-soaked scene, a relieved smile brightened the woman's face. God, it seemed, had atoned for her impending act of cruelty with His own almighty act of mercy.

THIRTY-FIVE

Amber's calf muscles strained mildly, enhanced by the weight of her thoughts as much as the steady rise of the paving slabs ahead. Covering her mouth with one hand, she slid the other around her stomach, empty of food yet unsettled through familiar seismic vibrations.

Her mother soothed her as best she could, running the flat of her palm in gentle up down strokes along her daughter's ridged spine. As for Amber's father, his huff was perfectly audible, his attempts to hide his true feelings of disapproval half-assed to non-existent. Mandy shot her husband a sharp stare of condemnation, potent enough to make a hunting grizzly bear back up a step; a knack mothers had mastered over the years whenever somebody threatened to unsettle or upset one of their own.

'Come on, love,' Mandy spoke softly to the youngster, 'you know we have to do this.'

Amber looked upwards, eyes scaling the face of the grotesque cuboid structure. Four stories of glass and cheap plastic panelling, bordered by columns of depressing grey brick, glared down at her in accusation. Passing clouds reflected in the multitude of watchful windows, shimmering with a sickening effect. Unable to face the foreboding gaze of the monstrous hulk any longer, Amber shot her eyes to her left, across the car park. Marked police cars aligned the boundary wall, whilst over its crest vehicles streamed in constant supply along the busy A390.

Life goes on, I guess...for some.

The information she was about to disclose to the authorities inside the building would have immeasurable ramifications on the lives of certain peers. She needed to obtain at least some measure of fortitude. From withing herself, from outer elements; anywhere would suffice.

Every meagre ounce of encouragement would be treasured. Blanking the ceaseless flow of vehicles, and the odd *jam sandwich* amid the idle row of blue and yellow cheques, one soaring behemoth rose like a phoenix from the city sprawl, whisking her back to *that* night. Its Gothic Revival façade impossibly imposing, even from this impeded vantage point, the cathedral diminished each and every building that plagued the surrounding streets. Granite spires glowed with divinity in the afternoon sun, the copper of the bell tower a beacon of enchanted green. God may or may not exist, she didn't know for sure, or really care. The evidence she had witnessed through her life hadn't convinced her either way, though in recent times the odds were stacked in favour of a fictitious Being – just a fairy tale for those seeking assurances and comfort through life, with the added benefit of a belief that better still was to come after leaving this mortal coil. He or She also acted as a convenient figure to blame for some whose lives had befallen darker paths… Not to mention an excuse to exact war for many, where *our God is holier than thine*.

Yet the superstructure's awe-inspiring magnificence ignited a strength in Amber that she had not felt before, one she desperately needed to indulge in now, to open herself like a floodgate and rejoice in its deluge of divinity.

Straightening her posture, she gave her mum a reassuring nod. The trio restarted their journey up the solemn stone incline, their steps slow yet purposeful. Reaching a full-glass door, they stopped under a blocky concrete entryway. Before her dad could reach for the handle, a man in uniform – looking much like he had only just gotten out of short trousers – appeared at its inner face.

'Hello,' the young PC said informally.

The three new arrivals cast uncertain glances between one another.

'Carl…' Mandy prompted her husband, whose mouth hung soundlessly open.

'Uh, hey,' Carl answered. 'Sorry, not done this before, don't quite know the drill.'

'No problem, Mr?'

'Collins… Carl Collins.'

'Okay, Mr Collins,' the PC smiled, 'just let me know the purpose of your visit and I'll point you in the right direction.'

'Right. We're here because our daughter here needs to report something. A crime.'

PC Beckinsale looked down at the slight roundness of the young girl's midriff. He raised his eyes, focussing now on the face, its skin immaculate and as smooth as new porcelain. This girl was clearly under the age of consent.

'Excellent. Well, that's normally the case.' He sniggered at his own pun. 'Then I guess you'd better follow me.'

Carl gestured to his wife and daughter to enter first, contemplating the apparently inexperienced PC's inconsiderate turn of phrase. *Excellent? Glad you think so, nob'ead.*

***

Shivani Chhabra leaned back in her swivel chair, arms folded across her chest and an expression of incredulity on her mug. When Beckinsale had brought the three civilians to her, she too had jumped the gun with her assumptions, just as her colleague had done. Acceptable maybe for the young constable, but an embarrassing rookie mistake for someone with her years of experience in the service. The two Bath Stars on her shoulder weren't easy for Chhabra to earn, especially given the fact that not only was she female, but she was a female from a minority ethnic background. Though the winds of change were slowly clearing the Bullingdon mentality from the force, Shivani had had to work harder, act smarter, and be forever clinical with the results she delivered to fight for recognition within a sea of white male co-workers.

But this? Inspector Chhabra had let herself down, and the fact that nobody else knew of her misjudgement did little to quell the frustration that gnarled away at her now. Everything from here onwards had to be exactly on point before she could redeem herself on an internal level.

When the Inspector was initially called into the room, she saw a timid young girl, flanked (presumably) by her parents. On one side the sorrowful-looking mother, head down, weighed by a frown; and on the other, a father appearing both ashamed and angered, mouth set tight, nostrils flaring agitatedly. As for the girl herself, she was clearly under sixteen years of age. Too young to be sporting the small but not unnoticeable growth under her folded hands. With that indirect evidence, and with a crime to report…

Rape. Rape with damning, life changing consequences.

Either that, or another – and far less common – case of girl meets boy; girl likes boy; boy likes girl; boy gives some old chat, turning on the charm; girl opens legs; quick in and out in some sordid setting. The result: girl gets pregnant, regrets the fornication, and the boy finds himself facing a rape charge.

How wrong both Chhabra and Beckinsale had been.

After seven months investigating a fatal arson attack on a vehicle containing two lovers, not a shred of useful evidence had been unearthed. Hour after ceaseless hour of interviews: known felons; civilians linked to the victims; residents from hundreds, if not, thousands of properties within a three-mile radius of the crime scene. Even the city's homeless community. Nothing. Not so much as a fresh fart to sniff at.

And then right off the street, in walks this young redhead, as if delivered by Brahma Himself. A scratchcard with a win to reveal behind every UV ink panel. Scratch once, you match the *where*. Scratch twice, the *when*. Okay, neither of those were unknown to the police, but scratch at window number three… and there's the *how*. Still mostly known to Shivani and her comrades, though not a hundred percent.

Windows four, five, and six, those were the real treasures. Multiple jackpots. Names. Addresses. Motives.

Chhabra's strictly business face was an uncrackable forcefield, keeping a secret lid on the butterflies that partied in the lepidopterarium of her gut.

'We will of course arrange for your immediate protection.' Inspector Chhabra eyed all three in turn. Centring on the young girl, she spoke in earnest. 'What you've done is an incredibly brave thing. *Incredibly* brave. It was also the right thing to do. By leading us to these youths you could have helped protect an untold number of civilians in the future.' Shivani stood. 'Someone will be here soon to make arrangements for the three of you. Beckinsale, ready the conference room. Assemble everyone available. It's imperative this goes without a hitch *first time*!'

Beckinsale didn't need the ramifications of a botched mission spelled out to him.

***

Looking from his bedroom window at a tangerine skyline, Matt squinted hard repeatedly, striving to adjust his dry eyes to the natural light conditions. For the best part of the day – the best part of the summer holidays, in fact – they had been fixated on the pixelated, fast moving graphics of the television screen.

The blossoming romance he'd shared with Amber had been extinguished soon after it ignited, the memory of her flame-red hair sliding over his fingers greying to embers. At the time it felt like true love; standard practice, maybe, for any fifteen-year-old lad who got their willy wet. Now it felt like none of it was ever real, like he had concocted her through sheer desire, and all he was left with were fragments of fantastical memories, kicked up and circulating like dust clouds on old floorboards as his mind sporadically opened the door onto better times.

As for Kieran, he may as well have been dead. Cuts and bruises heal faster than a fractured friendship.

Beyond his lonely window, the smooth waters of Truro River mirrored the tangerine sky, only interpreting the tone a more intense, rusting shade. Fluffy gold and grey clouds in the sky skimmed bronze and graphite across the glassy surface of the watery world below.

Breathless conversation, mingled with the soft trample of trainer-clad feet, drifted upwards from the passing road. Looking towards the sound, Matt spotted two women jogging along the pavement running between the currently desolate carriageway and the gently rocking run of small sailboats and runabouts at the river's edge. Laughter broke out between the pair as they plodded in the direction of Boscawen Park (some private joke that the void between them and himself would not allow the boy to share in).

He heard no sirens, but as the reflective strips of the runner's Hi-Vis jackets burst into life, pulsing intermittently from silver to electric blue, he felt his world implode around him. Swallowing a substantial lump of sour panic, Matt gazed north-east along the river, towards the main cluster of Truro's varied buildings. Yet more blue lights danced away beyond the supermarket car park. They were with a quarter of a mile of a terraced house door he knew they'd be aggressively knocking at in a matter of moments. Not so close as this line of three vehicles – one black and inconspicuous, two quite the opposite with their blue and yellow checks, bold lettering, and pulsing beacons – that came to a stop at the base of the grassy bank below his own ill-equipped hideaway.

***

Dragged from her vegetative slumber by some unknown commotion breaking out nearby, Melissa propped herself up on one elbow and rubbed her blurry eyes. Perplexed by phantom thumping and thudding, she laboriously swung her legs from the sofa, spilling the ashtray that had lain on her stomach when she passed out, and kicking over the half-spent bottle of cheap voddy that had stood uncapped on the floor.

Billie, for once not screaming for attention, began to fuss and fidget on the grime-stained carpet as the disturbance continued.

Melissa's first thought was that Zane had returned home drunk. Kieran had probably gobbed off at him for no reason – the ungrateful, shit-stirring little bastard that he is – and was now receiving the pummelling he so duly deserved.

Rubbing at her throbbing forehead, two things occurred to her, blowing her theory out of the water. One, the thumping seemed to be issuing from the other side of the front door; and two, her son had just come bursting into the living room like his ass was on fire. That would not have been possible if Zane was laying into him. The brute would not have been so sloppy as to let the kid get away.

Noticing the writhing bundle on the floor with barely a second to spare, Kieran leapt over his little sister, his trailing foot mere millimetres from fatally stoving in the baby's exposed temple. He shot through the kitchen and into the tangle of a rear garden without so much as a parting glance over his shoulder. The thought briefly entered his consciousness that he may never see this house again (no bother), nor his sister. Little Billie would have to make it through life without him there to protect her from her own dysfunctional family. In a perfect world, he would have grabbed her up and pulled her free from whatever living hell lay eager to blight her future path. However, this world was not perfect, and neither was he. The sprog would undoubtedly slow him down, and life had critically and instantly informed him that it was every man for himself.

Dog eat dog.

Cutting left as he reached the end of the garden, Kieran was greeted by flimsy fencing that separated their scrubby patch of land from the neighbours'. The old and rotting wood creaked and groaned as it swayed under his weight. Smashing through it would have likely been easier, though the clamour it created would attract all manner of unwanted attention. Dropping down on the other side, there was just a bare block wall to scale before he would land in the rear lockup of the funeral parlour that completed the terrace. Taking a run-up, the fugitive planted one foot high up the wall and launched himself.

Clambering over, his belly flat against the wall's top surface, he lowered himself nimbly down the stony face, crouching low when he felt hard tarmac underfoot. He looked around to find himself shielded between two stationary hearses. The setting sun lighting the sky ablaze transformed the elongated windows of the two vehicles from crystal clear to a jack-o'-lantern orange. The contrasting darkness of their black painted metalwork and engulfed glass screamed echoes of a fateful night in his recent past, a night that undoubtedly led to this moment, with the aid of his so-called mate's fucking big mouth.

It had to be that bitch, he thought, as he strived to gain some composure. Looking out from his bedroom window less than five minutes previously, Kieran had seen several sets of blue lights. They had simultaneously skirted along either side of the river. No prizes for guessing their intended destinations, or their damning purpose.

Other than traffic noise bypassing the city beyond the parlour grounds, nothing else could be heard. No shouting; no police radio's static-strained voices; no trampling of hard-soled shoes. That was something very much in the runaway's favour.

Two large wooden gates in the opposite wall kept Kieran concealed in the funeral home's rear enclosure. Safely out of sight, though far from out of mind, precious moments were provided to consider his next move. To stay here much longer would be madness. As soon as the old bill established he had left by the back door, this would be one of the first places they reached if they were able to track his footsteps. The walls to either side of the double gates were as high as the gates themselves, though there was a handy shallow step running horizontally along its length, approximately halfway up the white rendered stonework.

Result, Kieran mused, *put there just for me. The twisted hand of God.*

Straightening to a standing position, the kid who siphoned a jerrycan of petrol a prankster and emptied it a murderer, made his way across the deserted yard, eluding to a life on the run. An impossible existence with endless possibilities. Reaching the boundary wall, he looked up. As Kieran curled his fingers over the uppermost surface, a deafening clap of steel on wood sent the gloss-black gates crashing inwards.

THIRTY-SIX

Sheila studied her daughter as the subdued young woman plunged her hands in and out of a bowl of steaming froth. Tamsyn had uttered few words in the days since the unthinkable happened. The swelling in her belly remained stubbornly, a callous reminder to Sheila of the little grandchild she would never have the privilege to nurture.

'I don't expect you to do the dishes, you know. Especially when you left a full plate.'

'I've got to do something,' Tamsyn murmured.

'Well, you're gonna 'ave to eat something at some point, too.'

'Says who?'

Sheila balled the tea towel, plonking it down onto the worktop with a heavy hand. Leaning back and sighing deeply, she moaned under her breath, 'Give me strength.'

'Seriously,' barked Tamsyn, 'look at the size of me! Hardly look like I'm starving, do I?'

'That's just the ba___' Sheila took a blade to her words, her foot only toe-deep in her mouth.

'Baby weight?' Tamsyn laughed dryly. 'Yeah, good one, Mother.'

'Well it's bound to stick around for a bit,' Sheila defended. 'Took me weeks to shake yours off.'

'At least you had something to show for it.'

'Yes, and I intend to keep it that way, so forgive me for giving a *stuff* about you.'

The conversation was killed momentarily, the only sound the slam of each clean item of crockery onto the drainer. Sheila stepped behind her daughter, running her hands through the girl's hair, and pulling it backwards over her shoulders.

'Don't wreck me plates, lovey. They evvunt done anythin' wrong.'

Tamsyn snivelled.

'Look,' Sheila said, 'don't fly off the 'andle at me, but are you sure you even… you know?'

Sheila had had her doubts about the miscarriage, doubts caused mainly by the bump's unremitting determination to stick around. Truth be told, she wasn't entirely convinced that it hadn't even grown a touch.

Tamsyn shot an angered glance, scowling a silent *do I look like a frigging idiot?*

'I'm only saying!' Sheila tried to reconcile. 'Lots of women lose a bit o' blood during pregnancy.'

'*"A bit"* is a *massive* understatement! I fell down the stairs, smashed it up, and now it's dead. There was plenty of evidence.'

A wrecking ball of culpability struck a blow to Sheila's gut. Why the hell didn't she insist they worked together? Her upstairs, Tamsyn down. *She* was the guilty party here. She inflicted no deliberate harm upon her unborn grandchild, but the blame lay at her door all the same.

'You haven't left the house in days,' she said changing the subject. She knew the statement not to be true. She had spotted her daughter leaving the grounds of their cottage on foot in the dead of night, disappearing into the dark a couple of evenings past. It was obvious where Tamsyn had gone; Sheila had seen her muddied knees through a crack in the bedroom door when the girl had returned. 'You had the radio on at all? Or the telly?'

'Nope.' Tamsyn snivelled again. 'Why?'

'I'll finish the washin' up, love. You go on through to the front room. I'll get us a tipple when I'm done.'

Tamsyn clutched the brush harder, taking her time, yet vehemently scrubbing each dish and pan to within an inch of its life. She sensed her mother had something to say, and the need to hear it failed to overpower the desire *not* to. 'Get us a drink all you want, but I'm more than capable of finishing the dishes.'

'Suit yerself.' *Teasy sod!* Sheila left the room, giving her daughter the space she so craved.

Finishing up, Tamsyn reached forward and flicked at a sash lock with each hand, before struggling to slide the lower panes upwards. The evening air trickled through like treacle, sticky, dense and oppressive.

Outside in the grey haze her Volvo sat silently on the drive. Her mother had scrubbed at the driver's seat until late on the night of the miscarriage, ridding the caramel leather of its chilling smears of blood, left by her sullied clothing. Tamsyn had watched secretly through an upstairs window. She believed the remnants of her torment were cleaned as much by her mother's tears as they were by steaming, soapy water. Looking at the motor, sat obscured by the dying light of a muggy evening, Tamsyn felt only contempt for the boxy vehicle. Contempt for the car that, had she not been gifted by her mother, she would in turn *not* have been upstairs in that riverside holiday let. She would effectively have nothing whatsoever to do with the woman's cottages, or that staircase. A chain of events that she had not asked for had taken from her the child that she did not want, yet looking at the four-wheeled monster that spun the chain into gear, a raging bitterness brewed in her empty womb.

Unable to look at the dormant fiend any longer, Tamsyn turned and stalked morosely to the living room. Sheila was leaning forward at one side of the three-seater sofa. On the coffee table before her were two crystal tumblers, each containing a measure of golden-brown liquid.

'Any reason mine's got half the amount of yours?'
'Just playing safe,' Sheila smiled sympathetically.
'Right. Whatever. Just get over it, Mum. Please.'

Nothing more than a dissatisfied raise of the eyebrows from the older woman.

Partially satisfied at the result herself, Tamsyn asked, 'So, what's all this about?'

Sheila patted the vacant cushion at her side. 'Sit down, love.'

Tamsyn did as bid, a sudden ominous nervousness swimming through her bloodstream.

'I don't know how best to tell you this.' Sheila cupped Tamsyn's hands in her own. 'So I'm just gonna come right out with it. We had a visit this afternoon, while you were napping. I thought it best not to disturb you. It was from the police. You remember Inspector Chhabra?' Sheila's words were met with a vacant, yet somehow affirming stare. 'Well... they've arrested someone. Two, actually. Kids, by all accounts.'

Tamsyn's breath froze, her eyes widening as the embers of her darkest memory reignited in an overwhelming flashback. 'You mean... for...' The final word trailed off, escaping as nothing more than an inaudible whimper. The man's name was just too upsetting to voice clearly after her mother's declaration.

'Yes,' said Sheila, tightening her grip on her daughter's hands, the warmth from the dishwater draining in a sudden chill. 'For Austin.'

The pair gaped at each other in contemplative silence. Freeing her grip, Sheila reached for the lesser-filled tumbler and handed it to Tamsyn, before plucking up her own with a slender forefinger and thumb, and knocking back the generous helping in one urgent mouthful. Tamsyn gaped down at hers anxiously, as if she had been handed a deadly tonic rather than a fragrant brandy. Her parted lips barely moved, nonetheless the words that fell from them were distinct.

'But... how can kids...'

'We may find out. One day,' Sheila attempted to sound soothing. 'Or we may never know. What we *do* know is they've been caught, and the little buggers won't be able to put anyone else through what you've been through. Now drink up, sweetie. May not be sensible as you've no grub in you to soak it up, but I think you need it.'

Before managing a single sip, a low stirring pain in Tamsyn's midsection began to twist and groan. Within seconds of the start, the feeling intensified, spiralling rapidly out of control. Reminiscent of the pain that painted the floor at the bottom of the staircase a deep claret, the excruciating ache caused her hands to tremble violently. The scent of rich liqueur magnified as golden liquid sloshed turbulently over the sides of the glass. Fingers suddenly too weak to hold the vessel, the tumbler plummeted onto her lap, bouncing off and hitting the carpet with a heavy *thunk*. As her stomach began to cramp, Tamsyn wrapped her arms tightly around herself, as if strangling her body would suffocate the throbs.

Flustered and panicked, Sheila grabbed the stricken girl, cradling her and kissing her dishevelled tumbleweed of hair.

'*MUM,*' Tamsyn screamed, '*WHAT'S… HAPPENING TO ME? FEELS LIKE… AARGH! I THINK I'M DYING!*'

'Quite the opposite, my flower,' Sheila reassured, flustered, ecstatic, tearful. Sheila's doubts over the miscarriage were apparently vindicated. 'Let's get you on the floor; get you comfortable. I think the little'un's comin' after all, and a tad earlier than expected.'

THIRTY-SEVEN

In a brisk, whipping wind, Eliza stood on the pavement outside of the neighbour's rundown, terraced townhouse, the hem of her long sleeved tee all but chewed through in a fit of anxiety. The distressing sound of young, desperate cries from next door was no stranger to her ears. The harsh reality was that it was a grating ruckus that seldom ceased. That relentless crying, nevertheless, had been growing steadily quieter as the day wore on, ebbing in strength as weather's hostility grew. And in the last twenty minutes, it had not been audible at all. This development may have been due to traffic noise winning over, or the poorer conditions creeping in, or maybe because... Well, *because* didn't bear thinking about.

In the aftermath of the spectacle a week previously: crack team swarming in like plague of locusts; teenaged boy being apprehended and lowered into the back of a marked car, shocked and sheepish with a shepherding hand protecting his crown; a mother who couldn't even be bothered to bring herself to the front door in a woeful, blubbering protest, imploring her son's innocence. A mum herself, although younger and relatively less experienced, there was nothing Eliza would not do to protect her own flesh and blood; be it from the serpent under the bed, the monster in the closet, or even the state empowered law enforcement. Come hell or high water, she would die for her young. Her own moral code aside, however, in the case of the family next door, both the mother and her boyfriend had been hidden away in shamed seclusion ever since the boy was carted off by the bacon.

Or so Eliza had presumed. And in all honesty, with the baby girl's endless screams coming as standard even through the thick walls between the two properties, how could she have possibly known any different? Who could blame her for jumping to *that* conclusion? As her sense of unease and discomfort reached its crescendo, Eliza had plucked up the courage to knock on the door and check on the couple she found so loathsome.

There had been no answer.

She'd knocked again, hard enough to hurt and redden her knuckles. Still there was nothing. Not unless you counted the crying sounds that had persevered involuntarily beyond the upstairs window at the time.

Eliza had tried the door to no avail. It was (perhaps predictably) locked. That was the trigger for her to finally make the call. What service do you even ask for in that circumstance? Eliza had no idea. Given that the crying continued whilst she ran back into her house and spun the three numbers on the dial, she opted for the police. Now that the only sound sucked from the upper window was a deathly silence, she was pleased that the fuzz must have had the sense to request medical assistance. Frantically waving the ambulance down – suddenly fearful that she had wrongly assumed its destination, inadvertently killing some other hapless soul off with the delay – the paramedic pulled the motor to a stop at the edge of the road to her side. Further sirens could be heard approaching the roundabout. Seconds later, a chequered meat wagon slowed to a halt several metres from the rear of the ambulance.

Five officers alighted the van, padded and helmeted. It was evident that they were not willing to take any chances whilst one of the property's residents was in custody, suspected of committing a most heinous murder. Of course, the service hadn't named him during their press conferences and statement issues on account of the boy's *minor* status, but you didn't need to be Einstein to work it out. Plus, in any small city, as in any small town, village or hamlet, word worked its way around as vehemently as water fills a sinking ship.

Grabbing large holdalls and backpacks, the two paramedics stood at the ready as Eliza nodded to the correct property. Filing in line, the officer at the front rapped on the door, bellowing commands for any would-be tenants to open up. Giving only moments for a response that would never come, he then gave the all-clear to his crew.

A hulking muscular giant of a bloke with a five o'clock shadow covering his square jaw like felt, and a nose as crooked as a question mark strode forward. In each of his gloved hands was a metal handle, both fixed to a weighty red metal cylinder. After offering a warning call to stand clear, he rolled his gigantic shoulders, thrusting the hardened steel ram forward. The door gave little opposition, the frame splintering as both latch and deadbolt tore through the cheap uPVC.

Ploughing through the opening, three of the officers broke left into the living room. The remaining two headed upstairs, beckoning the paramedics to follow. Eliza was left staring through the entrance, unwittingly and aggressively chomping on her fingernails.

***

The first bedroom revealed nothing of any significance, unaltered from the night of the arrest when the police had made their futile search for evidence. Empty crisp packets and crushed coke cans on the bed and the small chest of drawers; television still on, though now displaying a snow-filled screen. The drawers and wardrobe were empty of clothes, with the previous occupant's now sat in some lab for forensic testing.

Beth followed the officers with trepidation as they headed for the second door, her colleague, Steve, close at her heals. The leading officer edged the door slowly open, baton in hand ready for confrontation. Just a small, family bathroom: grime on the sanitaryware; mould on a shower curtain that hung clinging to the outer panel of the bath; damp spreading like a virus on the walls and ceiling. No human life.

Moving on, they reached the third and final door. As the officer pushed at the glossy white panelling, Beth got the 'in here' call that, as a recently qualified paramedic, she'd been equally hoping for and dreading.

Stepping over the threshold she took in the scene. At the opposite wall, a partially opened pair of net curtains, soiled and stained, swayed agitatedly in the breeze from the narrowly open window. The very air seemed to take on the nicotine-mustard hue that oozed from the walls. Stood against the left-hand wall a cheap MDF wardrobe had one door hanging forlornly askew. Clothes spilled from its bottom shelf, into and over two lower drawers that lay crookedly pulled out. It gave Beth the impression that the stench of the garments was so vile the wardrobe was spewing them up.

To her right was an unmade double bed. The dark sheet was covered in stains; many of them white and crispy looking, implying that the bed had seen a lot of action since the last laundry day. Empty vodka bottles and an overflowing ashtray decorated a single bedside table.

Tracey Emin, eat your heart out, she thought to herself, sensing the inappropriateness of voicing her opinion and gaining a few nervous titters.

Finally, at the foot of the bed rose the scratched wooden framework of a baby's cot.

'Excuse me,' Beth said, squeezing past the big lad who'd busted the front door open.

Arriving at the side of the cot, she forced herself to look down. Crochet blankets had been kicked into a pile at one end. Further up, pale, motionless hands protruded from the stained, off-white sleeves of a babygrow. Below a headful of dark hair, a bloated face loomed, every bit as pale and motionless as the hands. Hanging grotesquely open, the mouth produced no sound. Fighting back tears, Beth slowly reached down to the baby lying so much like a discarded doll at the rubbish tip. Taking a steadying, strengthening breath, nauseated by the rank tasting air, she pressed two trembling fingertips at the side of the infant's neck.

As out of place as an armadillo in the Arctic, Beth's sobbing chuckles defied the solemnity of the setting.

'Holy Shit, Stevie-boy!' she grinned. 'It's weak, but there's definitely something there.'

PART THREE

2014

THIRTY-EIGHT

OCTOBER

Rearing its cold, grey head, October broke with a solemn mizzle impeding the air, clinging with a luxurious chill to the exposed skin of his face and hands. Nevertheless, any feelings of sobriety brought by the cleansing moisture was extinguished as the hefty blue doors clapped closed with unnerving finality at his back. The grating of heavy iron bolts sounded out an undeniable confirmation. Emotions battled for dominance within his skull: the elation of standing unchaperoned outside the fortress walls, and the anxiety that came with realising the last time he had done this, he was still just a kid. Fourteen years. The world couldn't have changed massively, but that boy was now a man. Could he fit in when freedom came as a different concept to him now?

Looking beyond a low redbrick wall, an imposing block of flats eyed him with suspicion. A mixture of yet more redbrick, with cream plaster and dark panelling attempting to add a contemporary aspect to the façade. At its centre a vertical run of double balconies rose from the first floor to its fifth and final level; the pinnacle… *welcome to the penthouse. As you can see, the balcony boasts a wonderful vista of Devon's County Jail, a charming Grade two listed Victorian building, dating back to the mid eighteen-hundreds…* The array of potted plants and rectangular boxes of flowers dotted on their grey railings tried, and failed, to brighten the place up under a slate sky.

Kieran fished through his pocket. A travel warrant and a pitiful forty-six quid discharge grant. In a bag over one shoulder he carried a skimpy offering of personal possessions. Not much for a man of twenty-eight, but some of high importance, nonetheless. Newspaper cuttings: his trial; a mother that disappeared like she had been beamed up by fucking extra-terrestrials or something, leaving her own baby girl for dead in the process, screaming and writhing in her cot. *I hope the aliens used a spike mace to probe the junky piece of shite!*; and the miracle baby's survival, days on end starved of food and human contact.

Breathing in a dizzying gulp of dank city air, acrid petrol and diesel odours filled his mouth and caught in his throat. Although the rush hour was over, a slow, continuous stream of traffic trickled along the street beyond the prison ramp. After a few moments basking in his new-found freedom, Kieran would take that ramp and leave the premises – along with its endless cream tunnels, metal fencing, and steel doors – behind him. Forever? Who knows? Forever is such a small word for a thing that keeps on going, and we all have so many plans in life that it's only natural we leave ourselves open to constant disappointment and tragedy.

Turning to give the building one final *fare-thee-well* glance, the pale, decorative masonry of the entrance towered with a degree of elegance. You could almost be fooled into thinking the place offered a certain grandeur. The fact was that this was the third establishment Kieran had been lucky enough to call home, since he was so unceremoniously hauled from the funeral parlour carpark, fourteen years ago. The reality was that this abode was by far the biggest shithole of the three. Inside these walls lurked a diseased, defunct, crumbling establishment, desperately in need of demolishing rather than renovating. The cells housed a catalogue of vile, violent vermin; the screws too few in number to do fuck all about the wretches infecting each space.

Here on account of being (or at least attempting to be) a model inmate, Kieran had been transferred to the Category B prison to see out the remaining six months of his sentence, closer to *home* and in preparation for being reintroduced into society. He never envisaged that this would be the hardest place of the three to keep your nose clean; you would have more chance scaling the walls with your bare hands and skipping off into the sunset than you would staying out of the odd punch-up. Luckily for Kieran however, he was in most instances the victim. (Funny how luck can be on your side when serving you a beating.) And on the odd occasion where *he* was the perpetrator, he had the good sense to keep the act witness-free... not that there was really anyone willing to grass in there.

Juvie had first come as a rude awakening, acclimatising Kieran to institutionalisation, discipline, and structure. That transition from being practically a phantom on the outside, to having every movement monitored on the inside, was a tough one. Once adapted to the correctional way of living, the time became a breeze. Knowing the easy time would come to an end, nonetheless, he had at least hoped to enjoy the facilities until the age of twenty-one. The devastating news was delivered a week before his eighteenth birthday: Category A awaited in the form of HMP Long Lartin; he was deemed *"appropriate"* for incarceration with some of the most despicable men this fine country had to offer.

Despite the initial apprehension over a stretch breathing the same putrid air as a selection of notorious murderers and sex offenders – including at various points Vincent Tabak; the nurse, Ben Green, with an apparent thirst for injecting patients with potentially lethal drugs; 'Cabbie Killer' Christopher Halliwell; and perhaps most infamously 'The Suffolk Strangler' – Kieran slotted into life at Lartin like fingers in a comfy glove, wearing its fortifying walls as comfortably as a nun goes commando. For the large part he kept to himself as best he could, played the game, doing what he was told, when he was told to. As with all of his fellow inmates at this CAT A,

Kieran had his own cell, though through the Incentive and Earned Privileges system, and his ability to avoid negative interactions with the wardens and with the sickos and psychopaths around him, he'd ended up with his own television *and* access to cooking facilities.

Life could have been worse on the outside. Sometimes, it was easy to forget he was locked away. Of course, you got the odd reminder of how fragile the glass you treaded on was, of how razor-keen the line between staying below the radar and drawing unwanted attention to yourself could be. Take this guy Subhan Somethin'-or-other, a child killer; even people who have committed diabolical crimes of their own, it seems, cannot abide convicts who involve children in their malfeasances. Although the motive was never confirmed, a year before Kieran was transferred to HMP Exeter, the child killer met his demise in a prison cell, strangled to death and turning from predator to prey.

At the Devon lockup, life was different. Having shared cells came with its own problems. Confrontation became harder to avoid. Violence was rife. Kieran's own cellmate, Tyler, took more than his share of hammerings. Yeah, he had a fuck-off big mouth, much bigger than the bodily apparatus the Good Lord gave him to back it up. His slight frame and pallid complexion made him a good source for the medium-sized fish in the pond to feed on, enhancing their own reputation and currying favour with the circling sharks. Even knowing this, one petty jibe was enough to activate the sarcastic retaliatory dribble that constantly hung from the tip of Tyler's whip of a tongue. Kieran helped him out on the very odd occasion, though staying under the radar and getting the hell out of HMP Cesspit was always top of his list of priorities. Yet with or without help it invariably ended with fresh cuts, fresh bruises, or freshly fractured ribs for the skinny little gobshite. That big mouth was hanging open, silent, and breathless on the morning Kieran slipped in the sticky pool of Tyler's blood, after jumping down from the top bunk. Tyler's pale and fissured wrist dangled motionless from the lower bed.

Kieran guessed he'd just grown tired of paying the penance for his own runaway lip.

Smiling sadly at the memory of one of the only mates he'd made since his school days, Kieran turned and began his descent of the ramp to civilisation.

Reaching the end, he looked left. Past the block of flats, the road continued on with no indication of what lay waiting in that direction. On the opposite pavement, three youths were walking along, talking loudly, each with a can of cider in their hands even though the day was still young. Seeing the exit that Kieran stood at, and Kieran's obvious *inmate chic* attire, they put the two together; simple maths, though they looked the sort to even struggle getting one plus one to equal two. The front lout raised his can and jeered, his servile followers following suit. Kieran gave the universal five-knuckle-shuffle symbol, and looking to the right he saw his destination signposted: St. Davids Station. Unfortunately for him, that was the direction the dickheads across the road were heading. Hoping that they would soon hang a left into the city centre, he set off, keeping pace with them on the opposite pavement.

As he strode, a niggling feeling of wrongdoing treaded with him. You get so used to the absence of freedom that when it's finally granted upon you, the very act of freedom seems a crime in itself.

Shuffling slowly towards him some thirty yards on, an elderly woman with a flimsy canvas shopping trolley in tow eyed him suspiciously. Assuming her to be local, Kieran guessed she knew the inmate's trackie bottoms and jumper – the only clothes he had to fit – all too well. She slowed, torn between two evils: the con, or the louts across the road. Contemplating, the old dear saw the group of drinking teens cut across a walkway towards the town. Breathing a sigh of relief, she made her way to the curb. Like Moses parting the Red Sea, the slow-moving vehicles on both sides of the trafficway came to a stop for her to pass, on to relative safety.

Fifteen minutes later, after barely tolerating the smirks and mutterings from what seemed an endless supply of students hanging around close to the college campus, Kieran arrived before the long (and institutional-like, itself), exterior of Exeter St. Davids Station. Next stop, sunny Cornwall, where a new chapter, one involving kid sister Billie, would begin.

THIRTY-NINE

Exploding like Mexican free-tailed bats pre-San Antonio sundown, the uniformed, rucksack-wearing masses spiralled in a spectacular fanfare from the double doors. Many headed to the tailback of awaiting busses, others heading for the park for a kick about or to doss around, whilst a number beelined for the city centre. Erin's destination was the bike shelter, having decided that the usual school bus with the usual colony of jackasses was no longer the transportation for her. Talek walked with her, the late September sun low and warming.

'Your shiner looks good in this light,' Erin jested.

'Thanks,' Talek frowned. 'I'm thinking of getting the other one done. I could pass it off as eye make-up.'

'Bad outlook,' she said, seriously. 'Be proud of your bruises? They show what you're strong enough to put up with.'

'Next you'll be telling me that my twisted nose suits me.'

'It kinda does. Shame it'll probably straighten out.'

'Yeah,' he smiled at her as they rounded a corner to the bikes, 'I won't hold my breath.'

Erin stopped, grinning, and stooping to place a delicate kiss on his cheek. 'So what if it doesn't; it adds character. My little man with a big attitude.'

Talek blushed at the reference. 'You still coming over?'

'Wouldn't miss it,' she said. 'What other man could treat me to so many romantic dates surrounded by corpses? I got some stuff to do at home first. I'll see ya dreckly.'

'Cheers,' Talek smiled awkwardly.

Doubling back, he made his way towards the carpark. The crowd had thinned to a small number of stragglers, though spotting the boxy estate sat like a doomed invitation, a formless Scandinavian alternative to the Griswold's family station wagon, there were two things standing in his way.

'Nice face,' Ethan teased, Coby loyally sniggering without the need for being prompted.

'Well, as much as I know you like looking at it,' Talek braved in response, 'I need to get past, so if you wouldn't mind.'

'You callin' me queer?' Ethan hissed, as Coby sidled behind Talek, denying any chance a retreat. 'Gettin' a bit of a habit, that.'

'I'm really not bothered what you are.' Talek aimed to convey calmness, a slight twitch of the mouth and a flaring of the nostrils letting him down.

'I reckon that's exactly what he's saying,' Coby chipped in from behind.

Ethan gave a subtle nod, spotted by Talek, though he had no time to react. Talek sprung forward, the air being driven from his lungs through the sheer force of Coby's open palms on his back. Ethan caught him, hurling him back into the Coby's constricting arms. Standing with his right fist clenching into a demolition ball, Ethan readied his swing, before Talek's one good eye directed the young thug's attention to the Volvo, parked and staring keenly as a lurking crocodile.

Another nod from the blonde-haired boy, and the grip from behind slackened, before releasing the relieved prey completely.

The barricade shifted, leaving Talek to pass by on unsteady legs. The distance to the parked car was only a short one, yet the sensation of eyes burning into the back of his head tunnelled it to a gruelling and insurmountable expedition, each motion forward appearing to draw the vehicle's safe interior further away.

'What was all that about?' came his mother's voice as Talek finally pulled the back door open. Disinterest seeped in stale exhalations through her cracked lips.

'You know exactly what that was about,' he mumbled, the smell of old leather clagging his nostrils as he sunk into the worn material.

'Are you going to stand for that?' His gran's voice came as a surprise; so used to heading straight for the backseat, until then Talek hadn't even realised she was riding shotgun.

'No sense in making things worse,' Tamsyn said calmly. 'I'm sure karma will find a way of dealing with them eventually, if the school won't.'

Without another word, Tamsyn fired up the engine, reversed from the parking space, and steadily crawled off the school grounds.

After a tense drive home, lacking even the most mundane time-filling chit-chat, Talek left the cottage, his artist's tube hooked under one arm huntsman's rifle style, and a bag on his back for effect. Heading purposefully towards the church steps, the orange sky to his rear offered no comfort in the chill of the setting sun. Becoming more biting with every step, a teasing breeze flicked at each scrap of nature, turning leaves and grasses a deep grey as shadows elongated under the watchful windows of the old relic.

He found Erin sat on the ground, back resting against a gnarly, aging tree trunk. Tall, listing headstones left her body partially obscured. A brown-orange scattering of fallen leaves skittered around her bare feet.

'Why've you taken your shoes off?' asked Talek.

'Don't you ever enjoy the freedom of soft ground on the soles of your feet?' She looked up at him earnestly, tucking her long dark hair behind one ear, with slender, painted fingertips.

'Yeah, when I'm on a beach, maybe. Not in a graveyard, when I'm only six feet over the six feet under.'

Erin laughed quietly and hauled herself up. 'There's nought under this patch but roots.' Eyeing up the hobbyist's disguise she said, 'You're gonna have to tell your mum at some stage. I'll get a complex, think you're embarrassed by me.'

'Embarrassed? You know that's not true. If anything, it's you who should be embarrassed by me. You're so far out of my league you may as well be on a different planet.'

This brought a coy smile to the girl's pale face. 'So, are we doing this or what?'

'Yeah,' said Talek, doubtfully, 'just got to stay low. You can see the entrance from my place.'

'I know the drill,' she smirked, threading an arm through the crook of his free elbow. 'Lead the way, little man!'

Peering through a run of tall sycamores along the burial ground's western border, Talek checked the reflectionless windows of Scoan's Cottage for signs of life. Coast clear, he motioned his confidante towards a wooden gate situated among the meagre security fencing. Bolted and padlocked though it was, the gate's apex at no more than four feet from the floor acted merely as a token deterrent.

'Gentlemen first,' Erin whispered.

'That was never a thing,' he said, launching his drawing tube over the gate. He raised a foot to the first rail, braced the top, and proceeded with his second foot to the next rail. The structure wobbled slightly, the steel clatter of the latch striving to burst its confinements causing concern. Talek held still momentarily, allowing the wobbliness to abate, and the confidence-breaking rattling to cease, whilst scrutinising the grounds of his home.

Felling a helping hand on his backside, he breathed harshly, 'That'd be sexual assault if I did it to you.'

'Don't tell me you're not enjoying it.' Erin's jesting manner could be heard through her airy response.

'I should've said "ladies first", see how the shoe would feel on the other foot.'

'You mean the hand on the other ass.'

His nervous system streamed tingling impulses at the thought. Cocking a leg over, he scaled the summit and dropped to the other side. The lesser-trodden brush was spongy and thick. Holding out a hand, Talek felt Erin's warm clutch as she mounted the wooden frame herself. Once over, they huddled close together in the small space, eyeing the dismal and forlorn entrance to the old church.

'Maybe we should have done this in full daylight,' sighed Talek.

'And risk being easier to spot? Come on little man, don't be a pussy,' she said affectionately, 'I need you to protect me.'

'Thanks,' he frowned. 'From what though?'

'Only one way to find out.'

Crouching, the pair stepped forward into the collapsing porch, waving their arms high to fend off teasing tendrils of ivy and spiders' webs. They stopped short of the final entryway. Before them, the bed of the church was nothing but fallen granite stones, deep emerald green with moss, and scores of spinelike, twisted trees that had burst through the floor decades before. Not a scrap of original flooring from the structure's heyday could be discerned. The vines and leaves from within scratched and groaned in the soft through-draught, a long-dead congregation repeating murmured conversations and private consultations with the Almighty.

'Can you hear that?' Talek said, voice scarcely more than a whisper. 'It's like it's talking to us.'

'Yeah,' Erin couldn't help vocalising louder than her counterpart, 'it's awesome.'

'It's terrifying. And you're messed up.'

A scurrying noise broke out, short and sharp. Whether from within or through the glassless windows from another area of the grounds they could not guess.

'Probably rats,' said Erin.

'Rats? Great!'

'There's nothing wrong with rats,' she soothed. 'Is there anything you're not afraid of?'

'No,' he answered bluntly.

'Not even me?'

'Particularly you,' sniggered Talek. 'Just gimme a few more seconds.'

A din of silence buzzed in their ears. In his head, Talek resorted to counting for composure.

One, two, th…

A booming roar filled the roofless porch, repeating again and again. Talek whirled around, his jeans snagging and tangling amid a brambly clumps. Unable to keep his balance, they dragged him to the floor, his head narrowly avoiding a large, uprooted slab. Erin stood over him, hand pressed against her heart, complexion an even more deathly hue than its usual pure pallor. At the gate the massive brown-black head of a German Shepherd jerked in rhythm with the thunderous barks. Teeth flashed vampiric and bright in its dark muzzle as jaws sprang, fearsome eyes menacing.

'Get out of there!' a man's voice shouted from behind the hound. 'What the hell do you think you're doing? Bloody kids.'

'We were just___' Erin tried free the words, before the man cut her off brusquely.

'*GET OUT,*' he yelled.

'If you didn't want me to answer, you shouldn't have asked,' Erin challenged, cockily.

By now Talek had scrambled to his feet, heart thumping like oil derrick. 'Come on,' he wheezed, 'let's just go.'

The dog owner stared as they navigated the gate once more. Talek struggled as deep fear prohibited his limbs from functioning adequately.

'Hurry up,' the man snapped.

'We're going, ya teasy old fart,' Erin smarted.

'Enough of your lip, young lady.'

'Call your fucking mutt off and this will be a lot easier,' she said, taking a degree of pleasure from the reddening anger washing over the man's face.

Talek hit the ground, grabbed Erin's arm as she made the descent, and led her away. She turned back to see the guy still staring obsessively after them. Raising her free arm she extended her middle finger, before blowing him a sarcastic kiss.

'You're off your friggin' head,' Talek said to her when they were safely around the corner and out of sight.

'Maybe I am,' she said as they stopped to catch their breath, 'and maybe that's why you love me so much; opposites attract and that.'

Talek looked her earnestly in eyes. 'Maybe it is,' he said.

After staring intensely into each other's souls for an imperceptible period of time, Erin raised her hands to either side of his face. Her icy fingertips felt like droplets of crisp winter lake water on his cheeks in the twilight air. Leaning forward, she placed her lips softly to his. Inexperience left him doubtful that he was doing it right, but for Talek it was the most amazing moment of his entire life.

'Right, madam…'

For the second time in as many minutes, their hearts leapt into their mouths. Searching for the voice among the sycamores, they spotted Sheila's head poking up above the rocky wall.

'…There's no way I'm letting you ride home in this light,' she went on, 'so put him down and I'll give you a lift.'

'I'll come, too,' said Talek.

'Not on yer mother's watch,' Sheila answered. 'She's just checked your homework diary. Get your ass in hass and your beak in the books.'

The youngsters smiled at each other, shoulders shrugging in silent agreement, and headed to Erin's bike, shyly rubbing shoulders.

FORTY

Sheila eased off the throttle, slowing the Shogun and watching the hulk of a man trek purposefully onward. Pulling up alongside, she hit a button on the door panel, lowering the passenger window.

'Thought I recognised that frame,' she called out from inside the jeep. 'Where you headed, stranger?'

Connor crouched down, straining to see the driver through the dark void, dashboard lights adding a miniscule glow to the features behind the voice.

'Oh, it's you,' he grinned, resting his wrists on the door frame and peering in. 'You following me or something?'

'Don't flatter yerself. And even if I was, you got a problem with that?'

'Not particularly. I'm just off to the Wheel for a pint; you up for it?'

'Up for what?' Sheila smirked playfully.

'For a pint, of course,' he said, picking up on the hint, nonetheless.

'Na,' she said. A look of what was hopefully disappointed dulled Connor's countenance. 'I'm something of a traditional ol' bird I'll have you know; I don't drink pints. Do they serve wine?'

'Yeah,' answered Connor, a sly, enthusiastic expression forming, 'red *and* white as far as I know.'

'Very sophisticated,' said Sheila. 'Saddle up, cowboy.'

Connor opened the door, jumping in keenly as if the invitation had a fast-approaching expiry date.

In the homely cosiness of the pub an open fire radiated and cracked next to their old, bleached oak table. Sheila was not one to advocate drink-driving, yet with Connor already on his third Doom Bar, she felt it only fair to make a token effort; and besides, no five-O (or anyone else, for that matter) patrolled the Merther back lanes after dark. Her second pinot was sliding down nicely. That, and the company of this fine-looking younger male, revitalised her and induced a youthful giddiness through her bloodstream.

'So,' Sheila raised the glass to her lips, customary baby finger extended aristocratically, and took a dainty sip, 'what brings you out on yer own? Make a habit of leaving the wife at home to look after that young maid of yours?'

'Not usually, but lately, things are just… I dunno.' He lifted his pint, taking a large gulp of the amber draught and placing the glass back down. Heaving his chest, Connor sighed, not allowing the drinking vessel to leave his firm grasp. 'Anyway, Erin's not home yet.'

'Shows what you know,' Sheila said. 'I just dropped her off. That's why I was out this way.'

'Oh,' said Connor, looking down at his drink.

'What, you didn't *really* think I was just out stalking you, did ya?'

'Well, I was kinda hoping…'

'You hope away, lovey.' She drained her pinot, grinning with her fine eyebrows raised into arches.

'Another?' he asked.

'Could probably get away with one more, seein' as you offered so politely.'

Connor disappeared off to the bar, returning no more than two minutes later with the fresh beverages. Retaking his seat opposite the woman, she spoke to him in muted tones.

'I was kind of stalking, you know, in a roundabout sort of way.'

'Come again,' Connor said, nearly choking on a mouthful of ale.

'Work it out, ya daft sod! Erin's a lovely girl, but that's not the only reason I'm so keen to run her around.'

For weeks now Connor had been fighting a torturous battle with the demons in his own head. A multitude of dark scenarios had been playing out in spectral form like a twisted Jacob and Wilhelm Grimm fairy tale, with outlandish conclusions. Arguments were rife. He'd had one or two fallings out with Erin of recent, but in large he was determined to protect her innocent ears from the driving forces straining his brain with all the might of a compressed gas cylinder. What it was doing to his marriage though, the constant bust-ups with Jessie; they seemed forever to repudiate the other's views. It was not healthy, and not a common experience of their previously happy lives together.

The woman opposite wasn't stupid. She was smart, different from the rest. Attractive from the outside and intriguing to the core. He could be playful, act up and give her some old chat, but she could see right through the bravado.

'What's troubling you, Con?' she asked sympathetically.

He stalled, studying the contoured texture of the tabletop while Sheila waited patiently.

'It's Erin,' he said finally. 'She...' He looked around at the faces of the other patrons. 'I can't talk here. Too many people know me. Know Jessie.'

'Earwiggers,' Sheila said. 'Sod 'em.'

She fondled the handbag perched on the chair next to her. Fishing out a pen and a pocket notepad, she began to scribble something down. Ripping out a page, she returned both the pen and the pad to her bag.

'Another time,' she said, sliding the paper face-down across the surface of the table. Leaning forward, Sheila whispered discreetly, 'Somewhere more private.'

Downing the last of the pinot, she stood and said, 'Need a lift home?'

'No. Ta,' Connor replied looking up at her. 'It's not even nine yet, I'm staying for one or two more. Besides, the missus'll be staring out the window, grilling me over who's car I'm getting out of.'

'Well,' picking up her handbag, 'it's been fun. Hopefully I'll see you soon?'

Connor smiled and gave a single nod of the head for confirmation, leaving Sheila to swan elegantly out of the pub, her slender hips swaying seductively. Turning the leaf of paper over, he studied the scrawl. Below an S and above the concluding x was a mobile number.

FORTY-ONE

Prowling the cobblestoned jungle under blood orange artificial light, synthetic rubber clacking menacingly, the skulking slab of metal hunted vermin for sport. Its nocturnal eyes scrutinised side roads and scanned alleyways lit by counterfeit electrically powered Victorian lanterns. Shop windows revealed only its own lurching reflection and opposing storefronts, not even a fleeting shadow to hint at another lifeform to toy with.

The hour had turned midnight, though surely the intended target would still be out and about; that's just what they're like. Looking for trouble. Causing trouble of their own where there was none to be found.

The predator's side window slid down lethargically. Finally, voices. Young voices. Concealed in the gloomy entrance of a narrow alleyway, darkened human forms huddled and shuffled. One by one, faces revealed themselves in a demonic glow as a marijuana joint was passed from hand to hand.

The hunter slowed, studying the specimens. Nothing recognisable. Not the intended prey. Despondent, it moved on, a female hand reaching forward to fire up the demister. A clear night had brought with it a chill air, conjuring condensation on the inner sclera of the beast's single rectangular eye.

Leaving the streets, stomach empty of all but disappointment, the beast stopped at the red light on Trafalgar roundabout to wait frustratedly for no one at all to pass. That's when the brains behind the wheel spied them – two young figures heading up St. Clement's Hill. Both male. Both appetising.

'Hello. This is promising,' the female voice purred hungrily.

Lights changing from red to intermittent amber, intermittent amber to solid green, the throttle was squeezed, the clutch gently lifted. The driver headed for the second exit, all the while watching the backs of the youths, unsure of their identities from this angle, but growing increasingly hopeful.

Beside them now, the boys paid no mind to the passing vehicle, preoccupied as they were with a video on the small screen of a mobile phone – possibly someone falling to their death, or a gang attack on some hapless homeless person, but more likely vulgar pornography. A few yards beyond, the driver dabbed the centre pedal just enough to engage the brake lights with little detriment to the vehicle's momentum. In the rear-view she saw the young faces flash red.

'I had a dog, and his name was Bingo!'

Resisting attracting the boys' attention by using the public school junction not far ahead to perform an about-turn, she coaxed the vehicle further up the hill. Praying hard, she begged the Good Lord not to let the youngsters take the steps to their left, disappearing into the housing estate and taking this golden opportunity with them into the sprawl. Rounding the slight left-hander and slowing to a stop at the entrance to a quiet cul-de-sac, she performed a reverse turn and began her descent of the return journey.

At the side of the road, Ethan returned his mobile to his pocket, laughing as he saw the distant hedge turn from streetlight-orange to headlamp-yellow. 'Give you a fiver if you play chicken,' he said to his companion.

'You're grown up,' Coby returned. 'Anyway, it's too easy, they're so slow I could lie in the road and still 'ave time to roll out the way.'

'Go on then, big nuts.'

'Hmm,' Coby hesitated, 'maybe I'll just stand.'

'I'll give you twenty if you make them swerve out the way,' Ethan said with a challenging grin on his face.

Coby mulled it over. 'You're on,' he said, excitement brightening his face.

He headed into the road, stopping halfway across the oncoming lane. Keen to relive this moment for years to come, Ethan retrieved his phone from his pocket. Swiping at the camera icon, he hit the record button and trained the lens on his idiot mate, currently standing in the road and grinning like a basket case. The headlights were now fully in view, the car still travelling slowly some fifty or sixty yards away. He looked back to Ethan, his laughable expression strangely adorable.

Thirty yards.

Twenty-five.

A barrage of engine revs flared up, the headlights briefly dropping to the floor before jerking up. The oncoming vehicle had apparently dropped down a gear and was now rapidly increasing in speed.

'THEY'RE JUST FUCKING WITH YOU!' Coby heard Ethan roar from the side lines.

It'll swerve…

It'll swerve…

Blinding, glaring and instant, the vehicle's blocky front lamps sprang to full beam. Dazzled and aghast, the literal rabbit caught in the headlights, Coby's feet took root in the cracked bituminous ground. This vehicle had no intention of stopping, swerving, or even slowing.

'COBES, GET THE FU___'

The combination of angular metal buckling, audibly snapping leg bones, and skull and back thumping against glass, spreading a cobweb of lacerations throughout the windscreen, cut Ethan's words like he'd put a pistol in his mouth. Just as the aging live oak cannot withstand the Texan tornado, he witnessed Coby's roots tear violently from the earth's rugged surface, his friend's body whipped into the air like litter on a breeze. Dropping his phone to the floor, Ethan staggered on uncontrollable legs to where the broken body lay helpless in the road. Claret from his cracked skull sparkled in black rivulets on the dark asphalt. The night was silent; the car forgotten.

Crouching over his mate, lying mutilated because of a stupid dare – *his* stupid dare – Ethan's head buzzed with a tinnitus whine. Despair cancelling out all other sound, he failed to hear the padded approach of composed footsteps. He failed, too, to turn and see the wheel brace rising in an outstretched arch, catching in the streetlight's orange embrace like a mini lightsabre. The hiss as it cut forcefully through the air on its downward journey served only to amplify the consistent buzzing in his own consciousness.

FORTY-TWO

Streaming through the open kitchen window, cool autumn brightness spread celestial rays across the oak farmhouse table. Refreshing and promising, though the hope and positivity it offered bared no relevance to Tamsyn's diminishing mental health. Her hands trembled gently as they cradled her cup of tea. Steam performed pirouettes in the intense beams of light, yet the searing heat through thin porcelain went unnoticed as it sent sharp pins through her palms.

'Penny for 'em?'

Tamsyn looked up to see her mother enter the room, tying her robe. Not dressed yet, but hair and face looking immaculate as usual. *If you want to see what a girl will look like when they're older,* she mused, *just look at her mother. Bullshit!* 'Huh?'

'You're a million miles away, lovey,' Sheila answered. 'Better there, is it?'

'Where isn't it better,' Tamsyn mumbled, a statement not requiring a response.

Sheila looked upon her daughter and shook her head. 'We need to get you a fella.'

'Do me a favour,' frowned Tamsyn, 'I don't need a man, and no man in his right mind would want me anyway.'

'Find one who isn't in his right mind, then. Or get yourself a lass.'

'Are you off your head?' she said, screwing her face into a ball.

'Pot still hot?' Sheila gave no opportunity for an answer. 'Just saying. It's a different world from the one I grew up in. You should explore it while you've got the chance. I'd give it a go.'

'Stop, now!' Tamsyn winced. 'That's not an image I want in my head.'

'You know me, I like attention. Dunn bother me who's givin' it.'

'I think they call that a whore.'

'Don't be daft, I would'un charge for it,' Sheila smiled, pouring herself a brew.

'A slag then.'

'Who's a slag?' Talek's voice pitched in as he entered the kitchen.

'Ello, T-Man,' his gran called over her shoulder. 'Me, apparently.'

'Charming,' he sighed, taking the furthest seat from his mother.

Stirring her brew, Sheila placed the teaspoon down on the worktop. Lifting her cup, she turned, her eyes drawn through the window to one vacant space on the driveway. 'Uh, Tam Tam, where's Beige Beauty?'

Tamsyn spoke flatly, her tone impassive, 'Think it must've been stolen last night.'

'You 'avin' a giggle?' said Sheila, 'oo'd wanna nick that? No offense.'

'None taken.' Tamsyn never took her eyes from the steaming mug. 'You're the saddo who bought it for me.'

'Touché!' Sheila lowered her mug onto a placemat and placed her hands on Talek's shoulders. 'You're getting' muscly, lad. You workin' out?'

'No,' Talek blushed. 'I saw someone go in the church last night. It's happened before, as well.'

Tamsyn looked up for the first time during the conversation. 'Did you see what they looked like?'

'No.'

'Did you see them drive away?'

'No.'

'So, they may have stollen my car, and you didn't bother to pay attention?'

Talek lowered his gaze, deflated. 'No.'

'Oh, well thanks for your help, Sherlock,' said Tamsyn, mumbling as if an afterthought, 'pointless as it is.'

'Thass enough of that, young lady,' barked Sheila, stooping to kiss her grandson on the head. 'It *could* mean something, so at least he's keepin'em peeled. Have you phoned the rozzers?' She took a seat between the two opposing forces, hoping to sever the unhealthy bond between them.

'Not yet,' said Tamsyn, returning her attention to the tea she had little intention of drinking.

'Jesus in socks and sandals,' Sheila sighed. 'Why the bleddy hell not?'

'Just drop it, mum,' she moaned. 'They'll have nothing to go on, as usual, and wouldn't bother even if they did have. I'll do it when I can be arsed.'

Sheila looked her daughter over, bemused by the lack of urgency. 'Good idea, cos dragging yer feet over it won't look at *all* suspicious.'

'I'll just make out I didn't notice.'

'Right, Sonny Jim,' Sheila diverted her attention to Talek, 'looks like I'm doing the school run today. Wolf down some brekkie and get your tukus in the Mitsu.'

***

Stop-start, the four-by-four chugged in laborious convoy through Tresillian village. Rush hour was never an enjoyable experience heading towards Truro, from any direction, but this was ridiculous. No chance to even get above second gear, let alone push the pedal to the metal. Talek looked towards the gently flowing waters of the river, recalling with nausea and pity the day he and Erin sat looking at what was likely the outreached, pleading arm of a dead former fellow pupil. He was hoping to enjoy the privilege of riding shotgun for once, nevertheless he doubted whether he'd ever truly be able to enjoy this scenic stretch of road again.

A tacky jingle played on the radio.

'Did you hear that?' his gran asked, exasperated. '*More* music. Bleddy cheek. More flippin' adverts than anythin' else. If I 'ave to 'ear one more crappy rhyme about plastic bleedin' windows, I'll go Bodmin!'

Talek gave no answer as she flicked the radio off with a frustrated grunt.

They drew up alongside a large Audi showroom, Talek relieved at temporarily losing sight of the brown waters and muddy flats. Slowly, the winding death-channel crept back into his field of vision. Slower still, a bank of trees spared him of the view once more. As they exited the village, his gran gave another tired groan.

'I'm going to be late,' said Talek, his voice a disinterested drone.

'You and everyone else, laddie.'

Passing a bus shelter on his side of the carriageway, Talek saw she was right about that. A large number of children bearing the emblem of Clement Grove on their breast pocket stood awaiting their ride to school.

'Sod this for a game of soldiers,' his gran said, flicking the indicator lever with a determined digit. 'Time to hit the backroads.'

They dropped off the main road and down a short, steep slope. Over a quaint bridge and past a large cottage on their right, the road narrowed. Overhanging trees dismissed the morning sun. Around a sharp right-hander the hedges grew taller and more unkempt on the passenger side. A left-hander, and dullness deepened as hedges to both sides suddenly became more imposing. The twisting serpent whose back they travelled upon took another right, slighter this time. And then it was there, presented before him in all its unnerving glory: the mouth of Hell itself.

Dark, cavernous, ancient, taunting. Talek could smell its stale breath from here. Up until this point he had had the window slightly open. Rushing, panicking, he raised it, cancelling the world out with the invisible barrier.

Opening his mouth to protest, he said, 'Why did___'

'*SHHH,*' Sheila stopped him midflow. 'No talking under there,' she whispered, 'don't even breathe.'

'But Mum said___'

'Zip it! or the Devil will get ya.' She looked at Talek and put on a comical, evil laugh.

The Shogun rolled forward into the gloom. Instantaneously, the heavy aroma of grilled meat filled Talek's nostrils. Beads of sweat formed at every pore across his forehead and puffy, burning cheeks. Oven-like temperatures roasted his skin, prevented him from breathing.

Out into the tree-shaded daylight, and just like that, it was over. The heavy meat scent had thinned, leaving a mild barbeque aftertaste. The intense heat dispersed, displayed only in the beads of sweat that clung persistently to his clammy face, and dripping from his nose. His ability to breathe returned with a vengeance, his chest heaving acutely and painfully.

From the corner of her eye, Sheila noticed agitated movements in the seat next to her. Turning her head, her face contorted in horror at the sight of her grandson. 'What the blazes is wrong with you?'

'Didn't… didn't you feel that?' His voice trembled uncontrollably.

'Feel what?' she asked, confused and fearful. 'Tal?'

'And the smell!'

'What smell? All I got was damp, and teenaged boys' bedrooms. You should be used to that!' Sheila regretted the jest instantly. The boy's distress was unambiguous, oozing from every nervous movement.

'It was… *death*. We shouldn't be under there. *No one* should be under there.'

She reached across and put the palm of her hand on the back of his, wincing at its heat as he flinched at the iciness of her touch.

'Someone died under there,' said Talek, sobriety as clear as a foghorn on a desolate and foggy shoreline.

'Bless you're 'eart. You're being melodramatic, there's loads of stupid old stories of people dying there,' she said, lacking conviction, and knowing one of those tales to be all too true.

'I'm not making it up,' he pleaded, 'Erin read about it.'

'Did she now?' Sheila pulled a doubtful expression. 'You know, you can't believe everything you read. They're called *myths* for a reason.'

'The guy burned to death in his car,' persisted Talek. 'His name was Austin. And I feel what he went through.'

'Stop it! You're scaring yer granny.' Sheila demanded, fear overcoming every other emotion.

'No! That's not all…' He paused, waiting for an argument that did not appear to be coming from the pale and ghostly presence behind the wheel.

'…I can *hear* him screaming.'

FORTY-THREE

'For more on our main story from the Southwest, now, we cross live to our Cornwall Correspondent, Quint Molko, with details of a second tragedy in less than a month to strike the pupils of Clement Grove School, in Truro. Quint, we've heard that a teenaged boy was struck by a vehicle in the early hours of Friday morning; what more can you tell us?'

'Thank you, Amy. Well as you can see, I'm currently stood outside of the Royal Cornwall Hospital, where it has been announced this morning that the boy in question, now officially named as fourteen-year-old Coby Angove, sadly passed away in the Critical Care Unit during the early hours, as a result of the injuries he sustained from a road traffic collision sometime after midnight on Friday. The incident is being treated as a "hit-and-run", though we're being told there may be one witness to the collision that the police are keen to trace. A mobile phone, believed *not* to belong to the youth, was found at the scene. The phone is heavily damaged, however Devon and Cornwall Police are confident that their forensics team can access the files contained on the device, which will hopefully in turn shed some light on the events that transpired on that fateful night.'

'Now, Quint, are there any theories as to who the phone may belong to?'

'Yes, Amy. A police spokesperson has confirmed that *another* teenager, believed to be a friend of Coby Angove's, has subsequently been reported missing. The identity of the missing person has not yet been made public, but officials are gravely concerned about this person's own safety. Obviously, we'll bring you more on these breaking events as and when we can.'

'And of course, Quint, this follows another harrowing account we've covered previously, that of the suspected murder of fellow pupil, Jowan Collins. Can you bring us any updates on how that investigation is progressing?'

'Well, as you say, this is the second grievous occurrence to strike Clement Grove Secondary School in less than a month. It really is a distressing time for pupils, staff, the families, and *anyone* else connected with the school. All I can tell you at this time is that police are still appealing for information from the public regarding the whereabouts of Jowan's estranged father, one Matthew Rundle. Mr. Rundle remains unaccounted for and is, and I quote, "a person of significant interest". The public are being urged not to approach the man, who is considered "dangerous", and to contact the police immediately if they see or hear anything of him. A photograph of Mr. Rundle remains on our website, for the purposes of our viewers.'

'Quint, thank you. Quint Molko, there, live in Truro. And this is the photograph of Matthew Rundle, who has recently been freed after serving a life sentence, imposed upon him as a juvenile himself. Please *do* proceed with caution if you see him. Do not approach the man and, of course, get in touch with the officials if you have any information.'

Sheila picked up the remote and killed the power on the countertop's small flatscreen.

'Wowzers,' she said, casting a watchful eye at her daughter, 'what d'ya make of that, then?'

Tamsyn looked up from her crossword puzzle blankly. 'What should I make of it?'

'Don't play dumb with me, missy. You know who that boy was.'

'Course I do,' said Tamsyn. She looked back down and started scratching letters across the page. 'Just bad luck, I suppose... for him, at least.'

'Just bad luck?' Sheila shrugged her shoulders, shaking her head slowly. 'You told the Lizzie Lice about yer car yet?'

'*No*,' Tamsyn snarked, 'I'll get around to it.'

'Drekly, I s'pose?'

'There's no rush. It's not like I'm missing it.'

'Oh charmin', there's gratitude for you.'

Picking up her cup, Sheila drained the last of her lukewarm coffee, its bitter aftertaste complementing her expression. Her daughter showed no signs of picking up on the vibes, sat as she was, head down and nonchalantly glancing over the cryptic clues on the page. Frustrated, Sheila slammed her cup back onto the tabletop.

'What the fuck was that about?' Tamsyn asked, finally breaking from her puzzle to look her mum sharply in the eye.

'Don't use that language with me, madam. I'll wash yer mouth out with soap!' Sheila folded her arms onto the oak and leaned forward into an interrogative posture. 'Suppose it was your car that hit that poor lad. Have you thought about *that*?'

'There's nothing *poor* about him.'

'Granted, he was a little shit,' Sheila concurred, 'but he's dead all the same, and someone's gonna be up shit creek for it. I know the likelihood is it wasn't your car, but supposing it was, and you were too bone idle to report it missing? Some hit and runs are deliberate. Police start diggin', put two and two together, figure there's a vendetta…'

'There's no vendetta,' said Tamsyn defensively.

'Isn't there?' Sheila raised her eyebrows, tightening her mouth to a deep red fault line.

Tamsyn could feel the accusation burning into her brain, searching the deepest regions of her soul, fully expectant of stumbling upon some disturbingly dark answers. 'If you've got something to say, just say it!'

'No no,' Sheila chirped, leaning back in a less threatening demeanor, 'I'm sure nothing will come of it. I just hope you know what yer doing.'

'There's nothing to know. *If*, it was my car, they'll put it down to joyriders.'

'*If* you reported it stolen straight away, maybe. But now…'

Tamsyn let the comment slide without response, just an interfering old crow, not worth arguing with. Pushing her chair back loudly across the tiled floor, Tamsyn grabbed her magazine and swaggered out of the room, leaving a cold and toxic air in her wake as her mother eyed the back of her head, gravely.

FORTY-FOUR

Strolling into the restaurant, its eery quietness served up a post-apocalyptic flavour. A small number of middle-aged men sat sparsely throughout the vast dining space to the right: sales reps away from home, laptops before them or half-finished meals and partially drained pint glasses (each one breaking from their activities to cast the attractive newcomer lecherous glances); the occasional female, suited up, yet just as solitary as the men in the room, with laptops, or meals and partially drained glasses alike, only vino or short drinks. There was no sign of the lone male this cougar was greedily scanning the area for.

Moving forward, short heels clicking on the wooden floor, Sheila leaned, craning her neck to the bar area to her left.

Mm-hmm, there's my guy, she thought, a Cheshire cat grin stretching across her face.

Connor's own smile was cocksure as he spotted her stalking over: black lace blouse under an opened jacket, leather skirt coming to rest four inches above the knee, with a teasing slit running up one tight-clad (*or stockinged, with any luck*) thigh. Her heeled shoes accentuated her slim-but-firm calf muscles.

'This seat taken?' she said reaching the table.

'It is now,' Connor smirked. 'You didn't need to dress up on my account.'

Sheila looked him up and down: the frayed hems of old jeans just visible under the mahogany table, crinkled red and black checked shirt open down to the third button. Raising her head she sighed, 'Why not? You clearly made the effort.'

'Don't pretend you don't like a bit of rough.'

Enjoying the man's forwardness, she took the seat opposite, and made a fleeting visual observation of her surroundings. Nobody shared the smaller bar area with them. Beyond the large bay window, cool white lamps displayed a full carpark, the lack of available spaces the antithesis of the building's longing for life.

'So, why all the way out 'ere?' she asked.

'Figured no one would know me here. Must admit,' he said, lifting his ale, 'I didn't think you'd come.'

'It was an arbitrary decision,' said Sheila, toying with him.

'I've no idea what that means.'

'Ahh, poor little simpleton,' she joked. 'You not gonna get me a drink?'

'It's not just that no one would know me,' said Connor, taking her raised eyebrows as a cue to continue. 'No, I… I booked a room next door, in case you're… you know.'

'Up for it?' she said with an offended countenance. 'Bit presumptuous. What makes you think I'd be up for it?'

Connor looked down at his drink, inspecting the froth in the hope of finding an answer, any answer to diverge the conversation and spare his embarrassment. Why the hell did he come up with that ridiculous suggestion so early on?

The beer lay quiet, offering nothing. Thankfully, the woman opposite him was more responsive.

'Ply me with enough rioja and you may find out *exactly* what I'm up for.'

Leaning back, evidently pleased with the exchange, Connor clapped both hands on his knees, before standing and heading to the bar. 'Rioja it is!'

With the table to herself, Sheila grabbed her handbag and pulled out a small mirror. Checking her makeup, she gracefully added an extra layer of lippy. Her blood-red lips smiled back at her as she heard her target's voice in the background: 'Pint o' Doom, please, and a rioja… Large.'

Mission accomplished, she thought hungrily to herself.

'Why, thank you, sir,' she smiled, as Connor returned with the drinks. 'So, I gotta ask, where does wifey think you're spending the evening?'

'Playing cards with me brother.'

'And she won't expect you home from that?' Sheila questioned doubtfully.

'Nah,' he said, wiping foam from his top lip with the back of a hand. 'We usually don't finish 'til we pass out.'

'Won't his better half tell yours you weren't where you claimed to be?'

'No chance of that,' Connor smiled, 'she left 'im at Christmas.'

Casting a critical look over him, Sheila shook her head slowly. 'Is that really a smiling matter?'

'Defo, she's a bitch, and *way* too chummy with Jessie. Christ on a bike,' he blurted, noticing the hot older woman's empty wine glass, 'touch the sides, did it?'

'What's the problem?' Sheila gave a teasing grin. 'You wanna loosen me up you gotta put yer 'and in yer pocket.'

'Isn't it your round?'

'Don't be daft, lad, every round's your round tonight.' She gave Connor a smouldering, smoky-eyed glare, 'I think you'll find I'm worth every penny.'

***

An illuminated wall lamp to one side of the bed cast a network of shadows across the floor. Discarded items lay in scattered heaps throughout the lowly-lit area: Connor's frayed jeans and crumpled shirt, intertwined with Sheila's dark stockings and leather skirt. Laying forlorn over the back of the room's single acrylic chair was her lace shirt, ownerless of the body that had only seconds ago clambered off him. A pair of knickers lay at his side, the greenlight arching of her back as she lay earlier an enthralling invitation he hadn't experienced for a long while.

Above and around them the thick smell of exerted bodies hung in contrast to the low buzz of the room's air conditioning system.

Collapsing beside him, Sheila studied his heaving chest. Placing the palm of a hand on the well-formed muscle, she ran small circles in the short dark hair with her long nails.

'Jesus,' he breathed heavily, 'there's something to be said for experience.'

'Oy, cheeky bugger,' she whined, 'you callin' me old? Not exactly a spring chicken yourself. If you were, you'd be shaving this mop like other men do these days.'

'They're just boys, playing at being men. I'm one-hundred percent red-blooded *man meat*.'

'*Mmm*, can't argue with that,' Sheila cooed.

Letting the small talk fizzle out, the pair lay quietly, the whisper of their combined breathing and the hum from the wall vent taking over. Bodies passed the window in silhouette form through street lit curtains. A scuffling sound brought a bout of laughter from the passers-by, with a muffled *'dickhead'* aimed at one of the bar's drinkers who had evidently fallen over.

'Your Erin seems a nice girl,' Sheila said after a few moments. 'Gettin' on *very* well with my Talek. Think they might be courting.'

Connor lifted an arm across a plump pillow. The woman in turn raised her head, dropping it into the nook between his shoulder and chest.

'*Courting*?', he laughed. 'You get all defensive about your age, and then use lingo from the nineteen-twenties?'

Earning a playful slap for his jesting, he said, 'Yeah, she's a nice girl,' a drawn out pause, 'but she's not really...' He trailed off, holding something back.

'Not really what?' Sheila asked, lifting her head to meet his eyeline, surveying, coaxing.

'Nothing,' he said, after a moment's thought. 'It's nothing.'

'It don't sound like *nothing*,' said Sheila. She placed a gentle, persuasive kiss on his lips. 'You can tell me. I'm as good a listener as I am a fuckbuddy.'

'I *seriously* doubt *that*,' Connor sniggered, bringing a smile to the woman's face. 'Anyway, it's no biggie.'

'Hah, like something else I could mention.'

'Oof, you bitch!' he laughed aloud.

'Seriously, though,' she sobered, 'spill. I'm here for you now. I might not be when you wake up, but I am now.'

'She doesn't know,' he said, loosening up to his bed buddy's compassionate quality. 'Me, Jessie... our families, obviously they do. But not Erin.'

Sheila allowed him a moment to say what she was picking up on, in his own words – his own time.

'Erin's adopted,' Connor confessed, eventually.

'See,' she soothed, kissing him gently again, her lips hovering with prolonged tenderness, 'that wasn't so hard, was it?' Sheila resisted following her statement up with another derogatory inuendo.

'You don't think less of me?' he asked in a hushed voice. 'You know, for not producing one of my own?'

'*I* don't know your reasons,' she said, earnestly. 'Anyway, whatever they might be, I actually think *more* of you for it.'

'Really?'

'Yeah, it's a very magnanimous act, to take on someone else's child.'

Connor relaxed, feeling totally at ease with this new clandestine presence in his life.

'She was only a baby at the time,' he went on, a melancholic West Country drawl. 'Her mother abandoned her and left her for dead. Her own mother; a drugged-up alcoholic!'

'She's not her mother,' assured Sheila, 'just an incubator, an undeserving carrier.'

'She was on her own in her cot for a whole week, they reckon. Barely clinging to life.'

Sheila noticed a pool forming at the corner of Connor's eye, threatening to burst its banks.

Climbing on top of him she kissed him again, longer and deeper this time. 'Shhh, you don't need to say any more. Doctor prescribes some no holes barred pity-sex.'

'*No...* holes barred?' Connor burst in astonishment.

'Well,' she corrected herself, 'obviously *one* is, ya filthy pervert!'

FORTY-FIVE

The persistent rapping on the door was not going away, that much was clear. Since her son's prior disappearance, and the devastating revelation of his murder, all that Amber wanted to do was hide under a duvet on the sofa and cry.

Cry. Cry. Cry. And eventually, die.

The world outside had other ideas for her, it seemed, inundating her with unwanted attention, from unwanted well-wishers, with unwanted sympathies. Everything that wasn't going to bring Jowan back.

And as for *sympathy*. What the fuck could they possibly know about what she was going through? About what was best for *her*? The world outside was a putrid cesspit, full of plastic do-gooders thrusting their superfluous intentions upon her in a vain fool's attempt to make only themselves feel better – appear better to their equally abhorrent neighbours.

The pounding knuckles continued, a battering ram straight to Amber's central nervous system.

Enough was enough. '*FUCK OFF!*' she shouted from under the duvet.

RAP, RAP, RAP, came the response.

Amber gave in. Crawling from under her protective shield, she dropped her feet to the floor. Stretching forward, she clawed at the bucket – an ally that had not left her side since *that day* in mid-September. The day after the storm, and the first day of absolute darkness. The faithful bucket had taken anything she had to give it. This morning however, all she had to offer was a dry retching.

RAP, RAP, RAP.

'*Go fuck yourself,*' she whispered to the disordered room.

A shadow at the window. A violent knock on glass.

Rising on unsteady, sticklike legs, Amber staggered to the front door. Frigid air jabbed at her body with icicles of moisture as the wind pushed in. In the low yet still overwhelming light, the visitor's identity remained concealed to her bleary vision.

'Whoa, look at the state of you,' a vaguely familiar voice from yesteryear spoke, only deeper, more gruff than memory recalled.

Amber cast a look down at herself: stained fleece pyjamas under an old, ragged, open dressing gown; bare feet a corpse's pallor, with a map of blue veins, and red, hardened skin across her metatarsophalangeal joints (sometimes walking seemed too exertive, so crawling across the floor became the more attractive form of travel). The visitor studied the undesirable attire, raising his attention to her lowered head. The once vibrant ginger hair had prematurely drained to white in places, the areas of colour a ghost of the red flame he remembered, the blaze extinguished.

Looking up again, the haze clearing from her eyes, Amber recalled the face: older now, still good-looking, not that her contempt for the boy he had once been had ever allowed her to divulge that information.

'How did you find me?' she asked blankly.

'Nice to see you too,' said Kieran, 'or at least it would be if you made a tad more effort. Bit of makeup wouldn't go amiss, tighter… less clothing.'

'Cut the crap,' she barked.

'What?' he smiled. 'Just sayin', I've been surrounded by hairy asses a long time; would've been nice to see *your* milky cheeks for a change.'

Amber wasn't playing along.

'You not gonna invite me in?'

'No,' she replied.

'Fine, I'll invite myself in then.' He squeezed past her, arrogantly strolling into the living room.

Scoping around, he turned his nose up at the piles of clothing and sullied microwave meal-for-one containers that decorated the small space. A rainbow of crisp packets and chocolate wrappers, with not a single piece of fruit in sight. The room was murky, with no natural light, just the glare from the television and the grim morning striving to break though cheap curtains. Kieran wondered when they were last pulled open.

Taking a seat on the piled up duvet, he patted the sofa beside him. 'Wasn't exactly hard, you know,' he said, looking up at her from her nest of bedding. 'It's not like you haven't been in the news recently. Yeah, we get papers in the clink. And TV. Once I figured out the road, the first neighbour I knocked at was extremely accommodating. I'm just an old friend, worrying about an unfortunate mate.'

'Unfortunate?' Amber ignored his gesture, opting to sit on the floor in a clear patch of carpet below the window.

'Would you say *fortunate*?'

Amber scolded at him with distaste. 'You make me sick! What are you even doing here?'

'Looking for my kid sister.' Keiran eyed her expectantly.

'Well, I don't know her.'

'Oh, I think you do.' His face widened in a malevolent smile. 'LSA, aren't you?'

'*Was*, an LSA.' She rubbed absently at a dirty smear on the leg of her fleece bottoms.

'See,' he pulled a cigarette packet from his pocket, popped the lid, and slid a stick out, offering it forward. 'Suit yerself,' he said when she shook her head. 'See, one thing being inside has taught me is the value of connections. I know Billie was adopted by a Truro couple. I know they moved to Tresillian. And I know from the papers that you worked at Clement Grove, which would be her catchment school.'

She studied him, contemplating her next move. 'I still wouldn't know,' she lied. 'Adoptions are all kept secret.'

Leaning forward, the malicious smile never left his face. 'Yeah, on the Pupil Premium list. I know about that, too. Armed forces kids, vulnerable kids, fostered kids, adoptees… which LSA's have access to. *You* know every adopted girl in Year ten.' Kieran stood, stretching his legs and taking a deep, silent breath to display his size.

'You don't scare me,' Amber said, her words wavering a little. 'Nothing does. When everything's been taken from you, you have nothing left to lose.'

'You know what I've done. I spent years locked up because of you.'

'Because of *you*,' she braved.

'Look at us,' he took a drag from his smoke, exhaling a dirty cloud to the ceiling, 'playing the blame game. We're not kids anymore. And you don't know the half of what I'm capable of now.'

Strolling over to the fireplace, its artificial flame dormant, he eyed a mounted photo on the mantlepiece. A teenaged boy in a shirt and blazer smiled back at him, awkward, camera-shy. Picking it up with his free hand, he said with a smirk, 'This John?'

'Jowan. Put it back!'

'Bet he don't look like that anymore,' he sniggered. Raising the smouldering cigarette end and slowly easing it towards the printed face, he said, 'Let's make it more realistic.'

Amber shot up from the floor with unfathomable speed, snatching the photograph and pushing the unwanted guest away with surprising strength. He came back at her with brute force, sandwiching her body between the fireplace and his own rugged frame. The mantle dug painfully into her back.

'*Her name's Erin,*' Amber screamed in panic, 'Erin Samways. She lives opposite the Audi garage, not sure what number. She's the only adopted girl in Year Ten.' A tear rolled down her cheek at the condemning break in confidentiality against an innocent child.

To her surprise, a thumb with unimaginable tenderness stroked her face, wiping away the salty track.

'Thank you,' he said, conveying a flawless sincerity. 'And for what it's worth, I'm sorry for what Rundle's done to you; for what he might've done to your boy. I hope they catch the bastard and string him up.'

The demon from Amber's past leaned forward and placed a heartfelt kiss on her forehead. She closed her eyes, feeling his hand leave her face. When she opened them moments later, he was gone.

Alone again, cradling Jowan's photo to her chest, she sank to the floor and wept.

FORTY-SIX

As another dank and miserable night fell over Scoan's Cottage, Talek sat at his desk, basking in the homely rays of his tall lamp. He watched mesmerised as beads of moisture glistened in the glow, a strengthening wind plastering them against the outer face of the glass, sending them into a frenzied rave of movement. The Church of Saint Cohan lay hidden under a veil of impenetrable blackness, unwilling to share any of its potentially disturbing secrets. What had those elongated, empty eyes witnessed over the centuries? Who was the shadowy figure that only entered the cavernous ruin after nightfall? And to what purpose were their enigmatic visits? Talek knew that a number of old, derelict churches in the Cornish countryside had associated tales of active devil worship – groups seen or heard after dusk, symbols of red goat's heads on reverse pentagrams found on wooden doors or crumbling granite walls after daybreak, the red paint trickling like weeping wounds that never heal. He had seen no such symbols on the external walls of Saint Cohan's, however he'd had little opportunity to really study what awaited within.

On the cottage's lower level, in front of a roaring log fire, another blood was on the menu. Sheila filled a glass, plonked the Chianti bottle down onto the coffee table, and slung herself into the cushioned armchair, its fabric giving a welcoming *whoosh*.

'Want some fava beans with that?' Tamsyn mumbled sarcastically.

'Ooh, who died and left *you* a sense of humour?'

Tamsyn ignored the remark, opting instead to snatch up the remote and listlessly commence channel surfing.

Sheila leaned forward, picking up the glass and filling her mouth with the deep red liquid. 'Hmm…' she murmured, waving a hand, allowing herself time to swallow, '… I've got some news for you.'

'Something to do with where you were last night?' said Tamsyn, eyes not deviating away from the television.

'In a way, yes,' said Sheila.

Tamsyn turned her gaze on her mother, waiting momentarily. 'Well, come on then, out with it. Let me guess, you were out joyriding in my stolen car.'

'Alright, keep yer 'air on! Firstly, your car ain't *stolen* until you get off yer buns and report it; and secondly, where I was and who I was with is none of your bleddy business. But what I found out might interest you.'

Tamsyn sighed and leaned back, bored of her mother's habit of building an ultimately anti-climaxing drama.

'Talek's got a girlfriend,' she smiled smugly.

'What? That's not possible. He's never even had a friend, let alone a girlfriend,' snapped Tamsyn. 'Who told you that rubbish?'

'Oh, no one, I already knew that.'

'Since when?'

'Never you mind since when.' Sheila took another sip of Chianti. 'It may just tickle yer fancy to know who she is… or who I think she might be. What stock she's from.'

'Presuming you ever get around to telling me. For God's sake, woman, stop relishing in it and spit it out.'

'Her name's Erin,' she said with a smile, 'but supposing, just maybe, it used to be Billie?'

'Billie?' Tamsyn pondered, the penny taking an age to drop.

Sheila watched her daughter carefully, nodding slowly as recognition dawned on her gaunt face. 'The timing's right, the circumstances are right, and the information came from an extremely reliable source.'

'What source?' Tamsyn's interest piqued visibly at the news.

'Only the girl's adoptive favver!'

Tamsyn lowered her head, chewing the inside of her cheek in contemplation. Outside, a loud splatter of rain dashed against the windowpanes. The fire cracked. Sheila took another draught of her wine, eyes never leaving her daughter, burrowing into the ticking depths of her mind.

Lifting her head after a time, Tamsyn said, doubtful, 'I don't get it. Why would he admit that? To *you?*'

'Come on, Tammy,' Sheila smiled, 'I play the game. Men'll tell you anythin' when you drop yer kecks for 'em.'

Gross, thought Tamsyn. Washing the idea of her mother and another man from her mind, she pondered over her son's situation. *My boy… with the sibling of his dad's killer… It can't be…* The thought made her sick to the stomach. Anger burned furiously deep within her heavily beating heart. After allowing a silence to stagnate, she stood, wavering palpably in a storm of emotions. Refusing to vent her new-found rage in front of her mother, Tamsyn simply said, 'I'm going to bed.'

FORTY-SEVEN

The bell signalling the end of another school day clanged loudly. Louder still was the rush of sliding chairs and relieved pupils blurting their plans, or just nonsense jabber at the elation of a sniff at freedom. Talek calmy returned his textbooks and pencil case to his rucksack, remaining seated until the exodus became less of a gauntlet to run.

His mind had been away on other business all day. Erin had voiced her excitement at lunch regarding the prospect of another visit to Saint Cohan's, though Talek found it difficult to share in her spirit of adventure. *'It'll be fine,'* she had said, *'most dog people walk them the same time every day. We'll just sit back, watch, and wait for the old douchebag to piss off'.*

If that bloodthirsty hound barks at me again, he thought, *I'm likely to have a coronary, or worse still, crap my cacks.*

Pushing himself up, he made his way out of the classroom and to the building's main exit. Erin awaited him out front, leaning with one shoulder planted against the wall, a delicious smile on her mush. The wind was up, with droplets of Cornish mizzle being tossed like toy boats in the Bering Sea, and Erin's short, pleated skirt billowing to reveal long slender thighs up to a pair of tight navy blue PE shorts underneath, which Talek couldn't help but gawk at.

'Perv,' she said, smirking, spotting his hungry glare.

'I wasn't looking,' Talek said, embarrassment sending his face into an uncontrollable bouquet of red roses.

'Course not.' She pulled away from the wall and turned her back on him, lifting the hem of her skirt to reveal the back of her shorts. 'So, you won't be looking at this then?'

'Cute,' he laughed awkwardly, taking in the vista.

The pair headed off, laughing, rounding the corner to the bike sheds and car park.

'Ooh, your gran's picking you up. That's a treat for ya.' Erin waved at the smiling face in the driver's position.

'Yeah, for the foreseeable,' Talek muttered. 'Mum's car got nicked.'

'Holy shit!' Erin exclaimed.

'It's a blessing, really,' said Talek, 'she's so embarrassing.'

'Harsh… but probably true,' she conceded.

Ahead, the window of the Shogun rolled down. 'Lift?' Sheila called out.

'I'm fine, thank you,' said Erin, 'I've got my bike.'

The driver's door opened and Talek's gran stepped out. 'Not in this cruddy weather,' she said. 'Can't risk idiots like me on the road, struggling to see you. Get yer wheels and I'll sling'em in the back.'

For the duration of the journey, love's young dream sat together on the backseat, deep in conversation, voices lowered in conspiracy. Sheila cast the occasional glance with smiling eyes in the rear-view mirror, though the dodgy conditions commanded most of her attention.

Arriving at the girl's home, all three got out of the jeep, Talek insisting to his gran that he'd do the gentlemanly thing and retrieve the pushbike. A quick glance towards the large front window of the house was enough for Sheila to note that she was under observation. Behind the glass, Jessie stood motionless with folded arms. Sheila smiled and raised a greeting hand, receiving an uncaremonious nod of the head in return.

Teasy ol' troll, Sheila surmised, mild amusement lighting her face. *Bet ya don't know I rode yer 'ubby like a racing dunkey.*

'Thanks for the lift,' Erin said, breaking Sheila's reverie.

'No troubles, bubbles,' she smiled, 'be seein' you again soon.'

Talek gave Erin a brief wave, to which she responded by blowing a kiss, before the boy and his gran jumped back in the jeep. Engine firing into life, the bulky machine reversed back down the drive, waited for a gap in the passing traffic, and lurched away.

***

The bleak realm of Saint Cohan's whispered a thousand tortured voices. Mizzle gave way to dry, scented autumn air, yet the keen wind remained, rioting in the canopies above and howling through the church's open, stone-framed windows. Talek stood in concealment under the ruin's north face, deciphering the whispers, striving to differentiate each voice between that of the extant and that of the expired.

Time and tide had eaten away at his fascination of the churchyard and its possessions, the task at hand spreading a cancerous fear through his gut. Odorous rotting vegetation served to amplify the sickening feeling in his stomach.

'You're a bit exposed.' Erin's voice breaking out from behind caused him to start. 'The hound of the Baskervilles will be here any minute.'

Turning to face her, he said, 'It's been and gone, so your theory of walking them to a strict routine's pants.'

'You know,' Erin said, mildly offended, 'sometimes you can be a bit too honest.'

She leant forward, stooping to kiss him. 'Now,' she said, 'get me in that church.'

Walking around the west face, Talek performed his usual surveillance of Scoan's Cottage's windows. The coast was clear. Accepting in his own mind that any last minute protestations would fall on deaf ears, he took the lead and scaled the padlocked gate first. Erin followed, stumbling on the descent, her slinky frame coming to rest against his body. They drank in each other's warmth in a momentary huddle, before heading through the overgrown portal and into that other world, the outside world falling silent, as though cut off at the flick of a switch.

Here, the intestine of trees, vines and fallen stones was thicker than it first appeared, an internal jungle akin to the tropical biome at the Eden Project, although seriously in need of some of its heat and humidity. Standing side by side, they looked left, right, and left again. The soft padding of Erin's hand tickled against Talek's. Their fingers intertwined.

'I don't know where to start,' he said.

'Your guess is as good as mine,' she offered. 'There,' said Erin, motioning toward the tangle of flooring to their left, 'the ground's trampled.'

'Bloody hell,' he sniggered, 'd'you work for Scotland Yard, or something?'

'I flippin' should do,' said Erin. 'Look at the wall, down the bottom. What *is* that?'

At the junction where the uneven wall met the ground, an ornate, age-tainted grate of iron fronted a small, square opening in the structure. Tendrils of ivy climbed the surrounding brick and patchwork of plaster, hanging down over the shadowed opening like a protective nest of serpents.

'No idea,' admitted Talek, his round face contorted in contemplation.

'The ground,' she pointed, 'it's totally flattened, like someone's been kneeling at it.'

'Surely we haven't found what we came for already.'

'Only on way to find out,' encouraged Erin. 'Well? Get over there and get stuck in.'

'I'm not putting my hands in there,' Talek argued.

'You're gonna have to if you wanna find anything!'

'You do it then.'

'Chivalrous!' Erin mocked.

Dropping his shoulders, Talek gave in, treading carefully over to the nook, with Erin refusing to let go of his hand until they found themselves kneeling on the soft, soggy ground. Reaching forward, Erin edged the viny veil of ivy to one side. Behind it, the chamber lay open approximately a foot back into the stonework, matched by its width and heigh to form a perfect cube. The earth was brown, grainy, and level with nothing growing upon it, unlike every other square inch of flooring within the small church.

'Time to nut-up, little man,' she said softly.

'D'you really think this is what they come here to see?'

'Well,' Erin replied, taking a pensive breath, 'it's the best-kept spot in this place. Dig it up.'

Reaching back to the closest tree, she snapped off a branch. The dry limb cracked and reverberated loudly, like discharging a firearm in an auditorium. 'Here,' she said, offering the knuckled stick forward, 'use this.'

'I'm not digging it up,' Talek blurted in horror, 'what if it's a grave?'

'A grave,' she gesticulated, 'for what, a hamster? Look at the size of it.'

Talek shrugged. 'You never know.'

Erin only stared at him, eyebrows raised, until he took the stick. Motioning it forward, Talek started to score gentle lines in the earth. The light soil created a dusting of small dingy clouds, puffing up and falling slowly in the stagnated air.

'What are you, a fucking palaeontologist?' Erin sighed impatiently. 'Grab these and give me that.'

She took the stick, Talek taking over the task of holding back the vines. The relief on his face was palpable. Erin laughed quietly, the whispering sound returning from numerous walls and alcoves. With a stabbing hand she thrust the primitive tool into the ground, dragging out large spoils at a time.

'That's how it's done, little dude,' she said. 'I never asked,' she went on, 'what do you make of the Ethan Coby thing?'

'It's friggin' mental.' Talek paused for thought. 'Sounds totally wrong for me to look for the positives, but at least it's got Ryan and Oscar off my back.'

'It's not wrong,' Erin assured, deepening the hole with speed and ease, 'they've been at you for too long.'

Talek smiled sadly, fearful for his missing tormentor, ashamed by the gratification of being bully-free.

Looking back down at the girl's handywork, something not belonging to the earth, breaking through the surface, grabbed his attention. 'Whoa, slow down,' he said nervously. The item seemed to be of black fabric, dirt-stained and weathered.

Clearing away the loose debris, Erin dropped the stick and pulled a small, black velvet drawstring bag free from its confinements. Casting an apprehensive glance at Talek, she waited for the nod of authority and loosened a grubby bow tied as a seal. Kneeling to face him head-on, she turned her free hand palm-up and shook the bag over it, upended. Into her cupped palm fell a silver chain with a circular pendant attached.

Tentatively, Talek pinched the pendant between his thumb and index finger, turning it face-up in her hand. Revealed on its face, a man lumbered on, the burden of a child on his shoulder.

'SAINT CHRISTOPHER PROTECT US,' Erin read in a low mumble.

'Why would someone bury that here?' asked Talek. He waited for an answer that didn't appear to be coming.

Looking back into the nook, he scanned the rubble for anything that may help to unlock the puzzle. The void left by the velvet bag was now perfectly flat, still earthy in colour, but with a distinctive grain running across it in wavy parallel lines.

'There's something else,' he said.

'It's your turn,' Erin said solemnly.

Heaving his chest in an attempt to steady his nerves, Talek set to work with the discarded stick. The going was much harder than retrieving the pendant, the wooden surface taking up all but the entirety of the alcove. Digging down its front face, the item that now disclosed itself as a box sunk five inches deeper into the earth. A tarnished brass clasp secured the lid to the main body, the wares inside a secret seeking to evade discovery.

Striving to pull the box free, Talek toppled back as the clutching ground finally gave out. He repositioned himself, tentatively placing the box between Erin and himself.

'*You* wanna open it?' he asked the wide-eyed girl.

'There's still time for me to go off you, ya know!'

Steeling himself, Talek caught his finger under the brass clasp and pried it upwards. Grating in protest, the metal fixing obeyed reluctantly. Using both hands, fear coursing through his body like a low-voltage electrical current, he lifted the lid, hands shaking.

Crows cawed an ominous warning from the surrounding treetops. Wind whispered and echoed like the crying of wounded animals. In the churchyard, the dead lay in condemning silence. Neither Talek nor his counterpart made a sound. Staring fixedly into the box, the sight that greeted them stole any words their overwrought minds could think to say.

On a bed of burlap, curled in a disjointed foetal position, the infinitesimal bones of a human being rested. Its toppled skull, browning and not much larger than a cricket ball, stared up at the grey and equally lifeless sky through cavernous, eyeless sockets.

FORTY-EIGHT

Sergeant Rachel Levy poured herself a coffee – black, rich, and steaming, just what the doctor ordered after a late night catching up on a bounty of red tape paperwork. Taking a good sniff of the arabica aroma, she headed through to the buzzing hive of the station's conference room. She looked at her watch. In precisely two minutes and thirty... twenty-nine seconds, DI James McGann was due to address the *"crack team"* entrusted with investigating the Angove boy's hit and run, and the Scales' disappearance. The morning dew trickling down the grapevine carried word that "big news" was about to be delivered.

She took a seat next to Peters, a young constable placed under her wing for her nurturing and guidance, and to feed off her vast wealth of experience within the service.

'Big news, Boss,' he said, an excited countenance that you wouldn't ordinarily place with the death of a teenager.

'So everyone's saying,' Levy sighed. 'And wipe that grin off your face, constable, you're not at the bloody panto.'

'Feels like it around here, sometimes,' still grinning.

'Can't argue with that.'

'Didn't think to make me a coffee?'

'Mummy may do everything for you at home,' she said, raising one eyebrow, 'but in the grown-up world, *you* should be making *me* one. As your ranking officer, I've got to say I'm disappointed with your brown-nosing.'

Around them, papers shuffled on laps as other members of the team go up to speed with how the case was progressing. Others took the chance to squeeze in precious extra minutes to remedial projects they may have been working on, whilst awaiting McGann's imminent arrival. At the front of the room, a portable whiteboard stood offering little information: a closeup, grainy, colour photocopy of a school photograph featuring Coby Angove, with basic details scribbled below (name, age, date of birth, home address, date struck, time found, date and cause of death); plus, an even grainier, casual photo of the missing boy, Ethan Steven Scales.

Even Steven, Levy thought to herself, *parents can be so cruel.*

Scales' notes, printed in red and black ink, included similar corresponding information to the Angove boy's, though *date and cause of death* was replaced with *last known sighting*.

At the sound of a throat clearing hoarsely, mumbled conversations and shuffling papers petered out. Detective Inspector James McGann sauntered into the room, making his way to the board with a selection of images in one hand, bulging at one corner from the pre-applied tack on the back of each. His large gut of regular roast dinners, daily pasties, and pints of local ale preceded him, swaying from side to side with each laboured step. Without saying a word to address his subordinates, McGann turned and faced the board, sticking the A4-sized printouts up one after another.

Finally, he turned to face the expectant congregation.

'Okay,' he boomed proudly, placing both hands on his enormous belly, 'a breakthrough! The boffins have accessed and trawled through the mobile phone found at the site of our incident, and it's proven quite fruitful.' He scanned the room, making sure all eyes were on him. Satisfied that he had the attention of all in attendance, he continued. 'The phone belongs to our missing youth, Ethan Scales, placing him directly at the scene. Turns out somebody, presumably Scales himself, as he didn't feature in any of the footage, was recording the whole thing. Now, the video is blurry, his unsteady hand and bad light not helping there, but we've managed to salvage a few *very* useful freeze-frames.'

Thrusting his arm back, McGann stabbed a firm finger on one of the images. 'So, here it is. Nineteen eighty-four Volvo estate. Model: two-forty. Colour: beige. Luckily, the last image shows the licence plate quite clearly.'

Levy leaned forward, studying the shot meticulously, cupping her mug in both hands and hovering it just below her parted lips. Above was a blurred image of the vehicle's front end from sharp angle. A figure in the driver's seat loomed ghostlike in the grainy gloom.

'Registered to one Tamsyn Lean, of Scoan's Cottage in sleepy Merther.' McGann rubbed his stubbly chin, taking in the blank sea of faces. 'Just the other side of the Tresillian River, for those who don't know – *which seems to be most of you*,' he added under his breath.

Clearly disgruntled, McGann raised his voice. 'Need I remind you that the body of a child was found there only a few weeks ago?' The altering expressions informed the DI that the penny had finally dropped. 'No previous convictions. All we know about Miss Lean, is that she was the sole survivor of an arson attack back in the Y-two-K. Very likely unrelated, but at this stage we'd be foolish to rule anything out.'

McGann jabbed his plump finger at the windscreen shot. 'The quality is not great, I'm afraid, but what we can ascertain from this image is that the driver certainly appears female.' Breaking from scanning the room, he looked directly at Rachel. 'Sergeant Pepper, I want you over there now, and take your puppy with you.'

Constable Peters frowned at the reference, obviously regarding his lack-of-experience in the field. Levy patted his leg sympathetically.

'And don't fuck about drinking tea with the woman,' Detective Inspector McGann warned, 'we still have a missing boy on our hands, and as it happened right outside of our own station's front door… a total embarrassment… he *has* to be our number one priority now. No screwups. Just get her ass in here!'

***

Crossing the forecourt in a murky smog, Peters moaned, '*Puppy*? Cheeky tosser.'

'That's no way to speak about your superior,' Levy reprimanded.

'Don't tell me you don't feel the same,' Peters said, his voice struggling to overcome traffic noise from the busy A390. 'What was all that *"Sergeant Pepper"* crap about?'

Levy sighed, 'When I started here I had short hair. He said it made me look like a Beetle. Took and instant dislike to it; said he was more of a *Stones* man.'

'Nope. That means nothing to me,' he admitted freely.

'Ahh, God bless the youth of today,' she smiled. 'We're not taking that mobile advertisement,' she said, as Peters stopped at his car, 'we don't want to turn up in a squad car. And besides, I've witnessed your driving first-hand. We are not Luke and Bo.'

Great, thought Peters, scampering after the sergeant who had already built a lead, *another insult. Gonna be a delightful trip*.

A quarter of an hour later they were threading their way down a narrow country lane, thankful to the satnav for getting them this far, less thankful when it attempted to send them down a farmer's rutted private track. Both officers screwed their noses up as the sour reek of fresh cattle dung penetrated the Insignia's ventilation system before Levy could hit the recirculation button. The sergeant's scathing glance as Peter's had politely asked, *'you shit?'* informed the rookie that the time for joshing around was now over. It was time to get into character – allowing a humorous memory to brighten one's face was a definite no-no.

Levy pulled the gunmetal saloon up to a closed wooden gate at the side of an attractive, rustic stone cottage. White painted calligraphy on a slate plaque affixed to the adjacent wall stated that they had arrived at their destination. The robotic female voice through the satellite navigation system declared the same, only unhelpfully delayed.

Shutting off the engine, Levy pushed open her door and swung out a leg. Peters donned his peaked cap and followed suit, slowing to take in the idyllic countryside surroundings.

'It's Midsomer bloody Murders,' he smirked.

Levy shook her head in disapproval. 'Don't forget why we're here, young Thomas,' she reprimanded.

'Sorry boss,' said Peters, looking down and feeling foolish.

'Okay? Have we grown up enough to proceed?' Sergeant Levy asked him quietly as they arrived at a slatted wood front door. A small, eight by twelve inch window permitted little view of the cottage's interior.

'Yeah… Cool beans.'

Jesus Christ, Levy mused, *what am I working with here?*

She knocked on the glass panel, taken aback by how speedily the latch clicked, the door swinging inward.

'Yes?' a middle-aged woman quizzed, 'can I 'elp you?'

'Miss Lean?' Sergeant Levy returned.

'Mrs.'

'Registered owner of an eighty-four Volvo estate?'

'No,' the woman said calmly. 'That's my daughter… Tamsyn.' Mrs Lean turned her head to the darkened cottage. '*TAMMY! TAMSYN, THE OL' BILL ARE 'ERE TO SEE YA!*'

The woman turned back to the officers. 'So, you found it, then?'

Levy and Peters exchanged confused glances.

'Sorry,' said Levy, 'found what?'

'The bleddy car,' Sheila said, making no effort to hide her exasperation. 'The Volvo you just mentioned.' Her tone had turned insultingly sarcastic.

'We weren't aware…'

'It's okay, mum,' said the daughter as she arrived at the door, though looking at the pair together, Levy would hazard a guess at them being sisters, and the daughter being the older of the two siblings at that. 'I still haven't reported it.'

'Ah, well,' her mother said, 'that's you in the shit.'

'Miss Lean?' Sergeant Levy turned her attention to the newcomer.

'Yes.'

'Can I just confirm that *you* are the owner of an eighty-four Volvo Estate?'

'I am, yes,' said Tamsyn.

'And you say the car is___'

'Yes,' Tamsyn sighed in frustration. 'It was on the drive last Thursday night, gone Friday morning.'

Levy looked to Peters, hoping to see that he had made the same mental note of the corresponding dates. His vacant eyes denied he was riding the same train of thought.

Turning back to Tamsyn, Sergeant Levy pressed, 'And you didn't report this?'

'Didn't see the point,' the haggard looking woman replied insolently.

Wow, Rachel Levy mused, astounded. 'Miss Lean, we have evidence connecting your vehicle to a major incident that happened on St. Clement's Hill in the early hours of Friday the third of October. We need to ask you some questions.'

'Sure,' said Tamsyn, seemingly unperturbed, 'come in.'

'I'm afraid it's more serious than that, Miss Lean,' replied Levy. 'We're going to need you to accompany us to the station.'

'*What?*' Tamsyn gaped, finally realising the gravity of the situation, 'am I under arrest?'

'Regrettably, I feel you've left us little choice,' Levy said sombrely, nodding a silent command to her colleague.

Stepping forward, Peters took the bewildered woman by the arm.

'Tamsyn Lean,' Levy continued, 'I'm arresting you on suspicion of causing death by dangerous driving, and in connection with the disappearance of a missing person. You do not have to say anything, but it may harm your defence if you do not mention when questioned something which you later rely on in court. Anything you do say may be given in evidence.'

FORTY-NINE

Staring blankly at the screen of his laptop, the digits blurring as if viewed through a pair of out of focus binoculars, Talek's mind turned one dismal corner after another, searching for answers that he wouldn't find until this laborious task was over, and the homework police's checks were complete. Despite knowing that little light would likely be shed on the subject of his mother's whereabouts – as per Gran's Rules – he had lost all interest in the maths work, an area all previous teachers of his would agree he thrived in.

Beyond the bedroom window, daylight had been consumed by night, the outside world swallowed up along with Talek's powers of concentration. The standing lamp remained unilluminated, a piercing white light from the screen his only means of guidance.

Pull your finger out, jackass. Just five questions.

Breathing deep, he cracked on, picking up the pen next to him to jot down his methods. At the realisation that he could no longer see the markings in his workbook clearly, he raised himself up on fatigued legs, pins and needles kicking in instantly at the movement, and waddled his way to the lamp.

He headed for the door, opening it as silently as he could manage, and put one ear to the gap. No sound from downstairs. Redoubling his efforts, he resumed his draining battle with the task at hand.

Thirty minutes later, Talek stood in the lounge, watching over his gran's shoulder as she surveyed the work. Eagle-eyed, the woman meticulously examined each and every question, ensuring the boy had worked to the ability she knew he was capable of. Finally satisfied, Sheila slid the laptop across the coffee table. Leaning back in the recliner, she crossed her legs and intertwined her fingers over her slight midsection, looking every bit the contemplative therapist.

'Sit down, sonny Jim,' she said.

Her soothing tone did little to settle Talek's feelings of apprehension, but he obeyed the order and took his place on the sofa, waiting nervously.

'Now,' she managed eventually, shuffling uncomfortably before leaning forward once more, 'I'm sure it'll all come to nothing…'

'But?'

'Your mum's at the police station.' Sheila watched as her grandson's eyebrows raised in disbelief. 'That lad at your school… who was hit by the car?'

Talek nodded an understanding.

'Well, it was your mum's car.'

Looking down, Talek absently picked at the cuticles on his fingers – a sure sign that he was deeply concerned. 'She didn't…'

'What?' Sheila blurted. 'No, Tal. She'd never do that. But the police think she did.'

'Why would they think that?' His eyes darted to hers, pleading. 'The car was stolen.'

'She never reported it,' she said. 'They've got evidence. It was *her* car, and they reckon it was a woman driving it. Gorblimey I need a glass of wine; be a little love and fetch me the bottle on the sideboard, and the biggest glass you can find. *Not* a pint glass!'

'In a minute,' he said abruptly.

Sighing as if talking to herself, Sheila said, 'I should've just reported it meself. But that would've caused bleddy hellup with yer muvver. You know what she's like.'

'Do I?' he asked.

Pushing himself slowly from the sofa, Talek made his way to the sideboard. He swung open a natural oak door and pulled out a large Bordeaux glass. Plucking up the bottle, he returned and placed the two items on the table before her. Sheila poured herself a drink, necking half the glass in one fell swoop, before wiping her mouth with the back of a hand.

'The night the car went missing,' Talek spoke, retaking his seat, 'it was the night I saw someone go in the church. I know mum brushed over it, but do *you* think they could've taken it?'

Beyond the living room window, a gentle breeze carried the low hum of an engine. Talek got up and faced up to the leaded pane, only to see a set of white lights pass by on its way to Koth Sans Farm, the dead end of their dead road.

'Wouldn't be any better if they did,' Sheila's voice came from the depths of the room.

'What's that supposed to mean?' Talek quizzed, turning his back on the disappointment outside.

'The person you see,' she said after taking another draught of Dutch courage, 'It's yer mum. She's been going in there for years, ever since…' Sheila trailed off.

'Ever since what?' Talek pressed.

'Never mind. Just a long time, that's all.'

Fishing in his trouser pocket, Talek pulled out an object, letting it drop and dangle from a finger. It was dull, aged, and failed to catch in the light, but Sheila could clearly see its metallic make-up.

'What's that?' she asked sternly.

'Saint Christopher,' he answered, raising it to eye level, captivated by its gently swaying motion.

'Who got you one of those?'

'No one.' His plain expression matched that of a blank page, only without the metaphoric connotations of a world's-your-oyster, endless possibilities hopefulness. 'Found it. In the church.'

'Put it back,' said Sheila, sharply.

'Why? What do you know about it?' Talek spoke without removing his fixated eyes from the pendant. 'Did mum burry it there?'

Sheila looked to the bottle thoughtfully. 'She might've done.'

Getting up from her chair, she crossed to the sofa, sitting down and patting the vacant cushion at her side. 'Come on,' she said, 'sit with old granny.'

Talek stepped away from the window. Placing the pendant on the coffee table, he took a seat as he was bid. Sheila stared fixedly at the Saint Christopher, knowing full well where it came from, and suddenly wishing she had never left her daughter alone with the corpse that torturous fourteen years ago.

Cautiously lowering a comforting hand to Talek's leg, she said, 'The pendant… it was your dad's.'

Talek's eyes widened in surprise.

'At least, I assume it was,' she said. 'He was supposed to be sent home wearing it. For the funeral.'

Narratives regarding his father were never recited aloud. All he knew was that the man died in some sort of accident before Talek was born. The subject was taboo, brushed over by the woman next to him, and, on the very odd occasion he'd asked his mother, she had all but refused to accept the man's existence.

'Your mum asked for some time alone with him,' she trudged on, 'say her goodbyes and what 'ave you. I shouldn't've agreed, not with the state she was in. But what could I do?'

A tear rolled down the woman's face. Talek's own eyes welled as she picked up her glass with a trembling hand.

'You look just like him, you know. He'd 'ave been so proud of you, turning into the fine young man you are with no real male influences in yer life. What with him gone, and my William, too, both before you made yer way into the world.'

'What was he like?' Talek ventured.

'Didn't really get the chance to know 'im that well,' she smiled, 'but he seemed nice enough, bit of a loveable rogue.'

Sheila spotted the surprise in her grandson's countenance at the admission and grinned. 'My Tammy was a different person then. Fun. Youthful. Beautiful. It broke her up when it happened. Destroyed her. Now I feel I don't know her at all. She's someone else now.'

A tear of Talek's own fell. Wiping it with a thumb, he sobbed, 'You think she did it, don't you? Coby, I mean.'

Looking him soberly in the eyes, Sheila took both his hands in hers. 'I pray to God that she didn't. But she was so reluctant to tell someone about the car, so… Might've just been her pig-headedness, but, truth is, son, I dunno what she's capable of anymore. *"Karma will find a way of dealing with them"*, those were 'er words.'

'There were bones,' said Talek, pained.

Shelia gawked at the boy, eyes suddenly wide with concern.

'A baby,' Talek filled in the blanks, 'buried with the Saint Christopher.'

Feeling a sickly churning in her stomach, Sheila pushed herself up from the sofa. It was her turn to seek comfort of the consuming darkness beyond the window. Deep in mental reflection, she studied her likeness in the darkened glass. Whether a trick of the light, or through the weight of entombed memories and disturbing new revelations, the face looking solemnly back at her appeared old for the first time in its life.

'She was right,' Sheila whispered to herself.

'Right about what?'

'When she was carrying you,' she said, wiping moisture from her cheeks, 'she fell down some stairs. Told me she'd 'ad a miscarriage. I didn't believe 'er; I could see you were still growing away inside of 'er. But she was adamant, said she'd seen the proof.' Sheila turned back to the horrified face on the sofa. 'Came as a total shock to 'er when you popped out, I can tell ya. I guess she was telling the truth.'

'So,' Talek managed to squeeze out, 'who's the baby in the church?'

'I'm guessing that would've been your brother or sister. Your twin, Tal.'

Leaning forward, Talek began to inhale large gulps of air. His head swam sickeningly, the thought of digging up his own sibling bringing a crippling nausea to his stomach. Just a simple interrogation regarding the whereabouts of his mother had thrown him like a skiff into a storm. Rushing to his rescue through turbulent waters, Sheila threw herself down, grabbing both of his hands.

'Whatever happens, love, we've got each other. Whatever your ma did or didn't do, you've got to know that she's not herself. And she's well within reason to go a bit mad, what with having to secretly bury her own child, and your dad being burned alive___'

'*BURNED ALIVE?*' Talek shrieked, the seastorm intensifying with a life-threatening upsurge.

Sheila covered her face in dismay, cursing herself for breaking such tragic news so heedlessly. 'Yes, son. In his car. Your mum was in it, too. He saved her life. Your daddy died a hero.'

Talek lowered his head, striving to process this inconceivable fable. 'Devil's Arch,' he mumbled.

'What?' Sheila said in astonishment, 'how did you___'

'That's why she wouldn't let me go there.' Head still down, bewildered. 'That's why I feel like I do under there. The man I can hear screaming, it's him, it's, my…'

'Talek,' said Sheila, frightened, 'how do you know all this?'

'I told you before. Erin looked it up,' he said, voice distant, 'after my first… episode, or whatever it was.'

'Course you did. That shouldn't have slipped me mind. I'm sorry,' soothed Sheila, guiding a stubborn hand to smooth his back. 'I dearly like that girl, you know, but she's far too nosy for 'er own good. Some things are better left alone.'

'I asked her to look,' he said. 'It's my fault.'

'None of this is your fault,' she sighed, taking her distraught grandson in her arms and rocking him gently. 'Or Erin's. It's good that she's lookin' out for you. Keep hold of that one, Tally, you've got a real gem there.'

Kissing his tight curls, they cried the remainder of the evening out, two individuals with a conjoined broken heart.

FIFTY

Opting to travel in rambunctious, body odour-rich luxury for today, Erin's stop was reached. Jumping from the school bus, she broke into an erratic sprint as soon as her hard-soled shoes hit the pavement. The decaying light and heavy thunderclouds provided the lion's share of her motivation. Reaching home, she crashed through the front door, shouting a rushed *'Hi'* to her mother as she bounded up the stairs. Once again, Talek had failed to show for school, with apparently either no reason, or no wish to provide her with one. Worrying of another cruel drama or calamitous incident to have befallen the unfortunate soul, Erin had taken the chance during an IT lesson – her own phone battery being predictably and frustratingly flat – to jump on her personal email and ping over a host of questions. No answer came before the bell rang to kick her and the masses out of class.

Storming into her bedroom, she took in the state of the bed. Tidily made, duvet smoothed out impeccably, no charger.

'*MUM!*' she shouted over her shoulder. '*WHERE'S MY CHARGER?*'

'*WHAT?*'

'*MY PHONE CHARGER!*'

'*IN YOUR DESK DRAWER. YOU LEFT IT ON YOUR BED, SWITCHED ON AGAIN,*' Jessie yelled back. '*YOU'LL BURN THE BLOODY HOUSE DOWN ONE DAY!*'

Erin headed to the desk, muttering under her breath, 'Burn the fucking house down. Are you for real, woman?'

Retrieving the charger from the top drawer, she shoved its points into the wall socket, flicked the switch, and plugged the USB into her mobile's charger port. Allowing a few seconds for the juice to flow, she pressed firmly on the ON button. Waves across the screen, back and forth over and over, seeming to take forever to boot up. As the home screen eventually appeared (an image that always prompted her to smile: her first grave rubbing set as the background), no new notification boxes revealed themselves. No shrill ping to second that emotion. Nadda.

Tapping on the Gmail icon, just in case the device was on a go-slow, no unread messages welcomed her.

'Fuck it!'

Spinning, she bolted from the room, descending the stairs two at a time.

'I'm going out!'

'Where?' came Jessie's exasperated voice from the kitchen. The only reply that echoed through the hall was a loud *slam* of the front door as it rattled the frame.

Running around the side of the house, Erin backed her pushbike out of the shed, swung it a one-eighty, and jumped on. The first drops of rain, few and far between, yet as fat as garden peas, began to fall from the blackening sky. At the bottom of the descending driveway, she swerved onto the pavement, almost crashing into a gang of younger children taking up the whole path on their stunt scooters. Derogatory names and obscenities streamed after her like a vicious, chasing tornado, as the kids were scattered in every direction like skittles. Beating on the pedals as hard as she could manage, Erin paid no mind to the shouts, or turn to see the raised fingers.

'Fuckin' sla___'

Before Arty could utter the final letter, he felt a strong hand grasp his raised wrist. His mates gasped in horror, skulking back, wanting nothing to do with this unknown newcomer who'd manifested from thin air. Arty turned to see a broad chest towering over him, pectoral muscles stretching the fabric of a tight grey T-shirt. Arty's arm seared under the vice-like grip, the skin twisting in a Chinese burn.

'*Man*,' he struggled, 'get the fu... *argh*!'

'Watch your fucking mouth, you little shit,' the man hissed. 'That girl. You know her?'

'Yeah,' Arty winced, 'everyone knows her. She's a freak!'

The burning intensified, like he was being lathered with molten steel.

'What's her name?' The man's teeth grinded together, accentuating his protruding chin.

The rain upped its game, falling in fatter drops, more numerous than before. Arty was thankful for this, at least, as he stood silent, the liquid helping hide his tears in front of his crew.

'Name!' the man reasserted, applying yet more pressure on the spindly wrist.

'*Argh!* Erin,' the boy squealed. 'Her name's Erin!'

Agonising heat spread throughout his arm as the man freed it from his crippling grip. Striking white finger marks glowed in the red raw surrounding flesh.

'I need your scooter,' the guy said.

'What? No *wa*___' Arty choked on the words as the hand returned, only this time clasping around his throat. The other hand scooped down, cupping his balls. As easy as if his body was nothing more than a bag of skin filled with helium, he felt himself being hoisted from the ground.

'It wasn't a request,' the man said.

Faster than Arty could say *get your hands off my nuts*, he became aware that he was soaring through the saturated air. They say your whole life passes before your eyes when you dance with death. Arty soon realised that garden walls do much the same. Landing in a heap on the grassy ground of beyond the blockwork, the youngster laid crumpled and crying as his friends fled the scene.

Grabbing the child's scooter and swinging it in the intended direction, Kieran thanked the good public for their favourable unwillingness to intervene. Looking preposterously oversized as he planted one foot on the deck, he peered through the rain. By this time, heavy drops fell in line like strands of drying spaghetti. In the distance, it was dismaying to see the girl had built up a healthy lead on him. *His* girl. His sister, Billie. Fourteen years had passed since he had last laid eyes on her, but in truth he did not need that little gobshite to confirm her name. Kieran had recognised the facial features that they shared as soon as she came down the drive: the delicate cheekbones, the narrow chin, piercing crystal-blue eyes. Her raven veil was in bold contrast to his fair hair, but as he'd watched from under the bank of trees across the flowing A390 moments before, he could see that her origin was unmistakable.

Holding the bars of the scooter firmly, Kieran kicked at the ground with one foot, beginning the chase through the saturated street with a steely determination.

Arriving at the end of the village, drained of breath, and soaked to the bone, the old dog could see the speeding hare cross the Tresillian River, disappearing around a right-hander. Making it to the junction himself, his blurred vision was met by a narrow country lane. The girl on the bike was nowhere to be seen, nonetheless the ascending road gave Kieran an invigorating confidence; she would not get far before he'd have her in his sights once more.

Once his target was reacquired, the ex-con redoubled his efforts to keep his younger sister locked on. As she pressed on, Kieran's strength waned, his head dizzying, a stitch developing in his side, the remaining miles to trek to the youngster's destination unknown.

What's she up to all the way out here? The middle of buttfuck nowhere!

Taking another right turn, he followed down a long, winding descent, spotting the girl finally bring her bike to rest at the entryway of a chocolate box cottage. An aging slate roof overhung a traditional stone façade. Georgian windows peered out across endless fields and meadows. A bulky four-by-four took up half the drive. Coming to a stop by dragging one foot along the gritty road, aiming for stealth but fearing he created the exact opposite, Kieran pulled over and took refuge behind a low stone wall, green with a squalor of wild plants and weeds. Gravestones entwined with ivy and lichen paved the way to a grotesque church, its colossal frame devoured by nature. Ducking down, he watched as his baby sister dismounted, leaning her ride against a hedge. Pushing the heavy gate open, Billie headed for the picturesque dwelling's front door.

***

'Ello, love,' Sheila said after opening the door, surprised by the sight of the young visitor.

'Hi,' Erin replied nervously. 'Is Talek in? He's not answering my emails; I was worried about him.'

'Hasn't the news travelled down through the school's gossipmongers yet?'

Erin shook her head, suddenly looking even more nervous than when the door first crept sluggishly open.

'Crikey!' Sheila exclaimed, 'thought they'd be all over that. You'd best stop makin' me doorstep untidy and come in.'

Stepping anxiously through, Erin was led to a cosy, yet Talekless living room. Relief surged from her core as the woman called her grandson's name, followed by creaking footsteps through the beamed ceiling.

'Sit down, darlin', I'll get you a drink. Lemonade? Squash? Gin?'

'Lemonade would be great, please,' Erin answered with an edgy smile.

Sheila exited to the kitchen as Talek appeared through a door in the back wall. Hurrying over to him, Erin threw her arms around him, embracing him whilst unifying her head with his.

'Whoa, chill out,' said Talek, forcing an easy tone, 'it's not like I'm dying or anything.'

Erin relaxed her grip. 'How am I supposed to know that, when you don't answer your messages?'

'Oh, sugar. Sorry, I haven't checked them today.'

'So,' she said, flustered but calming gradually, 'what's this *news* your gran said about?'

'Oy, missy,' Sheila cut in as she returned with two glasses, 'thought I told you to sit. Go on, park your buns!'

Erin did as instructed, after taking a glass from Sheila's outstretched hand. 'Thank you.'

Taking the other glass, Talek placed himself next to Erin on the sofa.

Sheila took a seat in an armchair to the side and eyed the girl with a forlorn smile. 'I just assumed you'd heard what happened, seein' as 'ow you were brave enough to come to the door this time.'

'No, nothing.' A nervous tension was beginning to work its way into her system once more. She took a sip of her lemonade to wet her parched mouth.

'Mum's been arrested,' Talek cut in.

'What!' Erin exclaimed. 'When? Why?'

Sheila took the reins again. 'That little demon child from your school. The one who's rotting in Hell, where he belongs…' She waited for a surprised acknowledgement from the girl. 'Turns out it was her car that run 'im down.'

Erin tried in vain to process the information. 'But surely they don't think *she* had anything to do with it, do they? She wouldn't.'

'Know her well, do you?' Sheila quizzed, unfairly.

Erin took another swig, diverting her attention to the bare coffee table.

'No,' resumed Sheila. 'I would've thought the same as you, once. But now… I dunno. The car's missing, and she dunt seem to give a rodent's rectum about it.'

'Tal,' said Erin after a moment of quiet reflection, 'I'm so sorry. You okay?'

'He'll be fine,' Sheila answered on his behalf. 'As long as he's got us two. We can count on you, can't we? He needs your companionship, now more than ever.'

'Course,' said Erin, 'always.'

'Good,' Sheila smiled empathically, 'I knew you were a goodun.'

Sitting in awkward silence, the deepening grey sky filled the room with an impending doom. Erin's head swished as this implausible story whipped up a storm in her mind.

'You gonna stay fer tea?' Sheila asked eventually.

'I'd best get back,' answered Erin, 'I'll already be in enough trouble being out on my bike in this.' She motioned to the conditions outside.

'Nonsense,' assured Sheila, 'you won't be on that thing. I'll whip us up somethin' to eat, then run you home.'

It was gone seven by the time Sheila hauled the bike into the back of the Shogun. Erin's belly was full of roast chicken, steamed vegetables, and perfect roast potatoes, crispy on the outside, light and fluffy on the inside. Her head continued to spiral in a whirlpool of shock and horror, with a sudden tiredness affecting her eyes and joints.

'Righty-ho,' Sheila said to the young couple, 'I'll turn me back while you two say yer bu-byes. Dunt need to see that at my age.'

'But,' Talek protested, 'I'm coming with you.'

'No you aint,' Sheila overruled, 'someone needs to be 'ere in case they decide to let yer mother go. Anyway, me and this gorgeous girlie of yours need to talk about you behind yer back, not to yer face.'

Seeing his obvious disappointment, Erin gave him a hug and kissed his frowning lips. 'See you at school tomorrow?'

'Yeah, I'll be back.'

'Alright, Arnie. Don't forget the leather jacket and shades.'

They both giggled. Sheila pulled the gate back, climbed in the driver's seat and reached over, popping the passenger open. Talek gave a still wave as Erin hiked herself up into the vehicle. A fresh bout of chuckles hit him as she blew him a kiss. His gran shook her head, smiling, before acting out the same hand-to-mouth gesture. The glow of retreating headlights cast him in a falling darkness, the night's cloak working from his hair downwards as the jeep reversed cautiously from the driveway.

FIFTY-ONE

Crouching low in a deep-walled opening to the churchyard, Kieran cowered out of the main beam's periphery. He watched on as red taillights evanesced into the winding country lanes, contemplating his next move. He had seen Erin enter the vehicle, seen her kiss this boy before that, whoever he was. He had also observed how the boy did not get in the four-by-four himself.

There was no way to catch up with whoever was ferrying his sister around. The next phase of his ad lib plan had to be to pay the lad a visit; find out who he is, and what his intentions are.

To hell with his intentions, Kieran decided.

He had waited in the shadows long enough, and there was no room for distractions. Either the kid would have to be compliant or face the consequences. Compliance would certainly make things easier... for both of them. The consequences? Unpredictable.

Standing straight, doubtful of any other individual spotting him lurking in the dark, Kieran stepped out into the lane and headed for the cottage. The gate to the driveway hung open. Silently, he moved onto the property and peered through the first of three front-facing windows along the ground floor. His eyes were met with an ill-lit living space, just one tall lamp from another era providing the main source of illumination, and embers glowing weakly from an open fireplace. On a coffee table before an empty armchair and an empty sofa sat a pair of drinking glasses, both as deserted as the furniture. The television screen was blank, and paintings of vintage farm machinery and steam trains adorned the walls, walls of which the lower portion were dark tongue and groove wood cladding, the upper surfaces cream and gold damask wallpaper. Kieran half expected to see the token set of three nostalgic wooden mallards soaring across the wall. To the right of the rear wall, a door stood ajar. Crisp light leaked through, but nothing moved in the cramped space beyond.

Making his way to the second window, he was met with the same room; nothing altered, nothing new to note. Passing the front door, Kieran reached the third window, smaller than the other two, yet still a huge upgrade on the Fairmantle Street terraced house in which he grew up. The room beyond was in complete darkness, though cupping his hand to his brow and pressing up against the chill, rain-wettened glass, he could vaguely make out the outlines of a traditional farmhouse kitchen.

No fruit to be picked, he headed back to the front door, placing his hand on the ironmongery and applying a light pressure. Not expecting a positive response, it came as a pleasant surprise when the door clicked open, scraping with a shush over a brush welcome mat.

Welcome indeed, he thought, stepping surreptitiously onto its coarse hairs, refraining from wiping his grimy feet. Stopping to listen attentively, other than the low buzz of electrical appliances from the kitchen, and the distant ticking of a clock somewhere in the shadows, the house was silent. Other than the lingering scent of a roast dinner (making his mouth water and his stomach yearn for some good, old-fashioned home cooking), nothing gave away the presence of any soul in occupancy. Kieran was no genius, though thankfully you didn't need to be Poirot to determine that the kid was home alone and would be found upstairs. From what Kieran could ascertain so far from his reconnaissance mission, there was no other place he *could* be.

Taking great pains not to make his own presence known, the uninvited guest stepped slowly and silently into the living room. He stopped halfway to the door at the back of the room. Still nothing could be heard from above. Returning to his stalking, Kieran exited the living room to find himself stood at the bottom of well-lit staircase. Placing one foot on the first step, the old wooden boards under plush carpet sounded out a pained, protesting moan. Panicked, he withdrew his foot sharply, listening hard for any telltale sounds from the aging cottage.

Fucking old houses, he cursed both himself and the building.

Leaning forward he bent low, probing at the second step with the flat of a hand. Judging this one to be firm enough to keep its mouth shut, Kieran raised a foot high and skipped the first step. He pulled himself up by a single wooden banister, never taking his eye from where the staircase rounded a corner further on. Continuing his ascent, a new sound broke the repetitive quietude.

Music.

Jackpot! The kid was here, and as the devil's luck would have it, he had just given away his precise location.

Rounding the corner, the landing loomed just three more steps away. Kieran crept to the top, ready to assess the unfamiliar lay of the land. To the right a single slatted door stood closed. To the left there was a short passageway, leading to three more doors, all of matching aesthetics to the one on the right. Two were also closed tight, one angled inward by five or six inches. Light poured onto the room's carpet from the landing's overhead, and though the rest of the room seemed dull in comparison, it was evident that there was some other form of illumination within. What was also evident, as Kieran rocked up from the last stair, was that this was the room from which some shitty boy band could be heard rattling their tripe from tinny speakers.

He may've kissed my sister, but he's gotta be gay to listen to that shite. He smiled at the thought, his little sister going out with a closet dick-licker. *Not for long, though, softlad.*

A man with this intruder's violent experience needed no weapon to take this little maggot out right now if push came to shove, but the sight of something being wielded purposefully was always a persuasive accompaniment. There was little on offer at the top of the stairs, but looking to the landing's only windowsill, Kieran saw just such an aid: a large travertine vase of dried flowers. Working as quietly as possible, he grabbed the stone in one hand, busying the other to remove the flowers. Placing them gently on the carpet presented its own challenges, keeping their incessant rustling to a minimum a struggle. Mission accomplished, he puffed his chest out and raised his muscular shoulders, enlarging himself to his full and threatening potential before creeping to the open door.

Through the gap he could see what in all appearances looked like a teenaged boy's bedroom, just with certain elements from a bygone time. A laptop sat on a weathered desk. The screen displayed the shitty boy band, prancing around on stage, each with a microphone in hand, yet none of them having the talent to play an actual instrument. An ornate floor lamp provided to rest of the room's haunting light. To the right hand wall, the bottom corner of a single bed could be seen. Kieran's grasp on the neck of the bulky vase tightened as he pictured the boy laying unsuspecting upon it, an opened copy of *Gay Times* beside him, todger in hand.

He nudged the door, hoping to allow just enough of a gap to squeeze his head through without alerting the boy of his arrival. The man cringed as the door's bottom edge shushed across the carpet; someone needed to plane that fucker. Listening, his ass tightening up like a drumskin, no movement came from within. Kieran had gotten away with that one.

Sliding his head through the gap once more, he saw that the bed was empty of all but its bedding: no boy splayed out playing with himself, yet there was a visible indent running along the duvet's centre. He *was* here, and something had alerted him to another presence in the old house.

He entered the room, stepping gingerly despite not having any real care if he was heard at this point. From the darkness under the bed, his trainers and the hems of his jeans were visible. They edged closer. There were only two hiding places in the kid's bedroom: under the bed, and in the wardrobe; what was Kieran to do?

He looked to the wardrobe. It was small, but manageable for someone of the youngster's stature. If he was in there, he wasn't going anywhere.

There's no Narnia to escape to, little buddy.

Getting down slowly to his knees, the interloper put a cheek to the carpet and flung the overhanging bedclothes skywards.

Fuck!

Nothing. Empty as a celibate's carnal promise. No pile of dirty clothes, or rotting food, or piss filled bottles, crispy socks… none of the things that any *normal* teenaged lad would have under their bed. The darkened space was absolute in its abandonment.

Preparing to raise himself from the floor, Kieran thought about the room's only other hideaway. 'I know you're in there, kid,' he said calmly. 'I'll go easy on you if you get out of there before I___'

Cutting off his words with a shotgun suddenness, the clatter of a door flying open and striking a solid object came from somewhere outside of the bedroom, somewhere leading off the landing. *How the fuck?*

Erratic footsteps bounded down the stairway; the little prick must have been holed up in another room. Angry with himself for not checking behind the closed doors along the way, Kieran sprang to his feet, losing his balance in the rush and crashing backwards against the wall. A bolt of pain charged through his neck as the base of his skull connected with the hard surface. Dazed, he rubbed at the agonising spot and surged on unsteady legs towards the landing.

Panicked and racing through the lower level, Talek grabbed at a Maglite lying on the antique telephone table in the hallway, before bursting through the front door. Scrambling to the gate, the heavy barrier hung handily open, as if an advocate for his survival. He weighed his options: to the left, Koth Sans Farm, with its host of scrubland and pastures, and a warren of outbuildings to aid his flight to freedom; to his right, Saint Cohan's Church, its dark corners and starving eyes anxiously awaiting some unsuspecting victim to silently swallow whole.

One false step from an intruder tonight on the creaky bottom stair had acted as the first step towards saving his life, affording him the opportunity to stealthily (yet speedily) vacate the bedroom. Petrified, he'd waited it out in the bathroom across the landing for the opportune moment to flee the scene. That act had gone without a hitch, however one false step for *him* now, over the cracked lips of that old relic in the dark, would prove more catastrophic than the intruder's misfortune. Talek could easily find himself with a broken ankle, or a dislocated knee. Game over, no extra lives, no two-hundred quid for passing "*go*".

Hastily, he took the left turn. The paved road continued for some fifty yards. Talek knew that there was no respite beyond the farm; nowhere he could lose the pursuer and outrun him. The moonlight would surely betray his position in the vast open fields. His only hope was to find somewhere in the mishmash of aging byres and barns to hide. And hide *good*.

Ahead of him lay a broad, open structure. Great, girthy beams of wood held the roof up at its face.

Originally meant for a squadron of machinery, the space now lay vacant, forlorn and crying out for a tractor, or ploughing equipment… any damn thing to create a shield or a screen for the startled prey. To the right hand side of the large opening a set of rickety double doors barred access to a storage barn. His body slammed against them painfully – not that the boy had a chance to notice. Breathless and frenzied, Talek grabbed at the bolt and shook hard. It was no use; the way was padlocked and impenetrable.

Resuming his flight at a canter, Talek passed the front of the building and followed its footprint around to one side. He ran a hand along a damp uneven mixture of stone and mortar, steadying himself as the bottoms of his jeans tangled and snagged in brambles. Just ahead, the light from the moon awarded him with the sight of a second set of doors. Nettles and brambles crawled up the rotting wooden fronts, yet to the boy's relief he could see that one door stood askew, angling marginally inwards, an invitation to what? Liberation? Incarceration? Either way, it was his only hope.

Squeezing through the gap, Talek's flaring nostrils were met with a cloying smell of damp, must, age and earth. A weighty scent of rotting carcasses tainted the already unbearable air: *rats*. He tried to push the image of piled up rodent bodies from his mind, their fur matted, flesh maggot eaten, tine-like bones breaking through decaying openings, hard leathery tales untouched by the decomposition process and frightfully lifelike. He heaved the door to with his back, his T-shirt cold against the frost-like layer of sweat on his skin. All lunar light was shut out. The building was windowless. All manner of things could be eaten up in this all-encompassing darkness. He would have to turn on the Maglite, but he was confident that once he could find something to shore up the door, no rays would escape to the outside world.

Scanning the cavernous space with the concentrated, bright beam, the perfect item lay conveniently placed just two yards from the door; God was evidently smiling down on the innocent youth tonight. Talek had no idea what the bulky piece of machinery was, though a large and narrow, age-stained steel wheel to each side, and a wooden beam protruding from the front, suggested that in another life this might have been dragged across the fields by steadfast, hardy horses. A covered box – which may have stored seeds or some such in its heyday – stretched between the two wheels, its panelled body perforated by the digestive systems of generations worth of woodworms and grubs. A series of heavy-duty springs ran parallel to each other from top to tail, linking a metal framework, and just as feasted upon by the elements as the wheels.

Talek made his way to the end of the connecting beam. It lifted easily from the earthen floor, yet moving the lump of wood and seized metal was another thing altogether. With the greatest of efforts, and after narrowly falling short of writing it off as a hopeless mission, the machinery finally gave. Letting out a grating squeal in tune with Talek's own whines of exertion, slow and strained the old workhorse rolled back, eventually coming to rest against the inward opening doors. The entryway was effectively barred.

Nonetheless, this hulk of an insurance policy was not enough. Talek wanted to be as far from those doors as he possibly could be when the inevitable cracking of footsteps in the outer thickets approached. He trained the torch beam on other areas of the barn. Along the wall to his left, half-height wooden panels created separate stools. Each section housed nothing other than dead space.

His lack of knowledge regarding the unknown pursuer's whereabouts was crippling. Talek had to find some way of gaining a view of outside, yet the absence of windows made this desire highly improbable. Sketching a map of the building's geography in his head, he knew that if he strode forward and eventually to the right, he'd meet the pair of doors he had run in to previously. The padlock would keep him safe, as no stalker would ever presume the boy had a key to fit; it wasn't even *his* farm, and whoever it was giving chase would soon realise that the cottage and the farm were not linked. And just maybe, with enough of praying – if God really was looking out for him – there would be enough of a crack in the old slats of wood to peer through. The doors looked right out over the approaching road. At least then he would know if the intruder made the correct decision regarding which direction to pursue. If Talek didn't see a figure on the road soon enough, he'd find somewhere closer to home to conceal himself and await the welcomed sight of his gran's headlights.

Gotta be worth a try, he determined, *just don't forget to turn your friggin' torch off when you get there!*

Traipsing cautiously forward into unknown depths, Talek constantly diverted the focus of the Maglite between what lay ahead and what lay at his feet. Tripping over and making a clatter would be a complete div move.

Strands of straw and clumps of dry, cracked earth littered his path. The odd discarded tool deceitfully attempted to topple him: a leaf rake lying in his path, which, unlike the garden rake in many cartoons, would not fling up and hit the boy square in the face, but would make a considerable racket if he got himself tangled up in it; a hand scythe, *that could come in handy*.

What was he thinking? A devout pacifist – and more importantly, a chickenshit – Talek could not use a weapon on another living soul any more than he could call them a derogatory name to their face. All set to kick the scythe from view, lest it could be used *against* him, he stopped and considered the noise it would create. *Best leave that* right *there.*

Ahead, another wooden partition rose, a good metre higher than the stalls he'd passed. A black hole of an opening could just be seen angled off the recesses to the right side. Stopping, Talek struggled to steady his breathing, along with the sudden surge of his heart, pumping against his ribs like a pedal to the skin of a bass drum. *He could be behind there…*

Irrational thinking to the max. The guy could not have gotten through the locked door, and he certainly could not have entered the same way as Talek did – this unknown person would have had to have passed him to get there. Plus, there was the heavy machinery barricading the way. He pushed the thought away. If Talek wanted to gain a view of the road, he would have to man up and pass the latest stall. Literally anything could be lurking in the darkened hide, but the likelihood was there'd be nothing, an empty, uninteresting chamber, just like all the others he had seen. These doubts were merely his overactive imagination striving to adjust to an unprecedented situation.

Bravery reinstalled – at least to an extent to propel him forward, if not to shine the torch into the watchful alcove – he took several studious steps. Using his built-in navigation system, Talek inched closer on what he was confident was the correct path. To his right, angular shadows rose in an irregular network of patterns, before the beam of his torch hit on something that kicked its glowing ray away at a right angle. Dark limbs rose from the shadows, arms reaching up ready to pounce. Panicked, he stumbled backwards. Severe pain shot through his spine as his backside slammed against the packed floor. The torch spilled from his grip. Growing menacingly in size, the limbs that caused such hysteria flashed from side to side in its frantic, rolling light. Talek shielded his face with both arms, awaiting a brutal, life-extinguishing attack, fear washing the pain he was already experiencing from the forefront of his consciousness.

Nothing happened.

The rolling torch came to a stop, along with its ominous scratching sound that had sent an invasion of goosebumps across his skin. No one pounced. No one kicked him while he was down. Imagination – or more realistically, terror – getting the better of him, the prey had simply fallen victim to his own feet getting tangled up and tripping him.

Raising himself to sitting, the ache returning in a brutal aftershock, Talek let out a low whine. Even the simple act of reaching for the torch proved enough of a challenge. Training the light on his imaginary assailant, all that revealed itself from the shadowy realm was a pile of old furniture, coated in year-upon-year of dust, cobwebs, dead insects, and gangly arachnids. Drawer units; a dresser; chairs stacked atop one another, their shapely turned-wood legs reaching skywards.

Dipshit.

An embarrassed laugh wheezed from his lungs, lungs that still felt airless from the wind-expelling fall. Shaking his head, regardless of what kind of attention his little mishap may have attracted, he smiled foolishly. Attempting to gain whatever self-control he could be win back, Talek rested his wrists upon his knees, the adjustment causing the beam to play off a flat, metallic object. Taking a moment, he gazed at the cause of beams diversion. At the base of the furniture stack sat a mahogany-framed mirror, the same dust and matted webbing blighting its once perfect reflectiveness. Talek studied his tarnished doppelganger in the mirror, wondering what the kid looking back at him had ever done wrong to be faced with this trauma. All his life he'd kept to himself, no intentions to ever harm or offend anyone; yet here he was, sat in a rundown old barn, hiding for the sole purpose of survival… survival from an unknown would-be assailant with equally unknown motives.

What the…

His breathing stopped, his stomach suddenly churning violently. Talek squinted, studiously eyeing the previously unnoticed object in the stall over his reflection's shoulder; the same stall that sat at his very own back in the somatic world. He wanted to turn and look back. Maybe it was a trick of the mind. But this was no trick; Talek knew that much. The object over his mirror image's shoulder was one he had known his entire life. It was one he could recognise in a heartbeat, and one he would never forget.

FIFTY-TWO

Standing rooted to the cracked ground, the pain through Talek's core forgotten, the vile aroma impregnated within the frame of the old barn faded out of existence. With his heart palpitating and body convulsing, his lower limbs fought to stay upright as they weakened in fright. Looking back at him, two dull, rectangular glass eyes goaded, daring the familiar youngster to come closer. Within the tenebrous expanse between the two headlamps, the front grill vaulted inwards, fractured and fragmented through impact. The brand's synonymous oblique chrome trim spanning the grill from corner to corner had been contorted into a *v*, like snapping jaws of an old videogame character.

Oh, Pacman! Talek thought. *I know what you've been eating.* Lifting his gaze, the youngster turned his attention the bonnet – now concave, whereas it used to be marginally convex. Higher still, a shattered windscreen. The main site of impact was unmistakeable, dead in the shield's centre. Steeling himself to accept the dull-eyed light's invitation, Talek stepped forward in slow, short, reluctant strides. Flashing the Maglite across the screen, he trained it on the area where the cracks were at their most abundant, splintering outwards from an epicentre as weblike as the barn's unwanted furniture. Blackened flakes of dried liquid, *blood*, he winced, adhered in scattered, monochrome droplets to the glass. Tacky dark hair sprouted from a deep fissure.

That was the kicker. Talek whirled around, arching his back away from the vehicle. Urging, he lost possession of the roast dinner he had consumed earlier that evening, when life came crumbling down around him, and Erin stood selflessly by him, patiently restoring the broken fragments. Crouching, he placed a hand upon each knee.

His breath rasping, the rancid aroma of butyric acid filled his nose and mouth, making him heave all over again.

Involuntarily, his breathing stopped, his respiratory system stunned into inaction as a sound rose from somewhere to the rear of the vehicle. A shuffle. He was not alone. Somehow the assailant had entered the barn without previously drawing attention to themselves. Talek thumbed the button at the base of his torch, concealing himself in instant darkness. As quietly as he could implore his every movement to be in the near silent cavern, he crouched by his mother's carelessly concealed Volvo.

Shuffle.

Whoever had followed him could surely not have gotten to this part of the old farm building. The vehicle was enclosed on three sides by thick, wooden partition walls. No one could have made it this far without his knowing about it. Convincing himself that this was fact, not some falsely reassuring fantasy, Talek braved clicking the torch back to life. Straightening up, he traced the surroundings over the car. *If he is here, at least I can blind the bastard before I leg it.*

No human form revealed itself in the beam of light.

Shuffle.

To his left. And close; too close.

Shining the light on the windows of his mother's car, he checked the driver's first. Seat empty. Keys in the ignition. *She left in a hurry*, he realised. *Of course she did; she had just mowed Coby down*. Rear door: nothing remarkable, nothing out of the ordinary.

Shuffle. And a… a moan? *What the…?*

The long, hearse-like side window of the estate car was next. Sucking in a deep breath, lungs aching as they attempted to draw any courage that may be floating in the air around, Talek placed his torch to the glass. The boot area was piled with blankets. At the centre, a misshaped bundle writhed and squirmed.

Fuck. Fuck. Oh fuck.

The *F*-word sounded grotesque coming from himself, despite the fact it remained unspoken aloud.

Regardless of the fear of the unknow coursing through his veins, whatever was fighting for freedom under those old blankets needed his help. Reaching for a handle at his side, he pulled the door open, its aging hinges letting out an agonising wail.

Man up, you got this.

He gripped the Maglite between his teeth, arched his back, and crawled into the backseat. Leaning over and using both hands, Talek set to work on flinging the numerous blankets to the rear of the boot, until the struggling bundle lay exposed in the glow.

'*Ethan!*'

His nemesis lay in a foetal position at the centre of the estate's flat bed, hands bound behind his back, the wound rope leading down to tied feet. His mouth was gagged, his eyes blindfolded. Talek was not stupid; this captive was a boy who never camouflaged over the fact that he would happily kill him. Starting with the gag and blindfold, he would seek assurances before removing the rest of the bonds: the ones restraining those lethal hands.

'You!' Ethan wheezed as he turned his head, the glaring beam forcing salt liquid from his darkness-acclimatised eyes. Talek's face was concealed by the brightness shining from his mouth, yet his small, black hands were totally unmistakeable. 'Get me the fuck out of here!'

'I… I'm here to help you,' Talek implored. 'Don't kill me.'

'I'm not gonna fuckin' kill you, twat! Just untie me.'

Talek thought hard, flustered and panicked. He couldn't just leave the kid here. Untying him was the only viable option. *To hell with the consequences.* He set to work loosening the bonds, feet first. After a struggle with the knots, he eventually freed Ethan's hands. Ethan crawl-flopped over the back of the seat, strengthless and exhausted by his time in cramped confinement. The two boys stumbled awkwardly from the vehicle, both falling drained and starved of oxygen against the car's body. Neither spoke nor moved for several strained minutes.

Finally, Ethan managed to break the monotonous sound of heavy breathing. 'Coby?'

Frowning and welling up, Talek looked at the boy's scuffed and grazed face. Ethan had clearly been through all manner of hell. Talek shook his head slowly in response.

'What the fuck?' Ethan whimpered, to himself more than anything else. 'I need a drink. My mouth's dryer than a camel's cunt in a sandstorm.'

Talek turned his head, eyeing the boy sympathetically. 'We'll get you some at my house. But we can't go yet... someone's after me.'

'Well shit,' Ethan actually managed a snigger, a defiant, incongruous sound if ever Talek had heard one, 'you make friends everywhere you go, don't you.'

Talek gave a toneless, airy laugh, 'Seems that way.'

'How far is your house? And where the fuck even are we?'

'Couple hundred yards,' Talek resumed his whisper. 'We're in one of the barns on next door's farm. We need to be real quiet though. Just 'til I'm sure.'

Ethan lowered his chin to his chest. Through clenched teeth he said, 'That fuckin' psycho woman ain't there, is she?'

Talek's emotional connection to his mother took control. In defensive mode, he sighed, 'She's not a *psychopath*, she's just... I dunno... Mum's like, cursed or something.'

Turning his head sharply, Ethan stared.

Unsettled by the look, Talek said, 'What? What is it?'

Ethan's expression was grave. 'Dude, it wasn't your *mum* that did this.'

FIFTY-THREE

The night remained cloudy, though the earlier rains had cleared out of town, leaving a melancholy peacefulness in their wake. The roads were decidedly devoid of traffic as Tresillian village lay draped in a veil of serenity. In spite of the absence of other road users, the Shogun rolled lazily along. Purring like a kitten, it stuck resolutely to the thirty miles per hour speed limit, the driver on her best behaviour. Time was not exactly on her side, but there was no sense in unwittingly attracting unwanted attention.

Looking across to the sleeping passenger, that insultingly youthful face and flawless skin dipping in and out of the passing streetlights' lustrous orange hue, Sheila allowed herself a smile before returning her focus back to the way ahead.

Heading deeper into the dozing village, the older woman spotted the girl's home through the glass of her driver's door. Light shone from the living room window. Within those walls, the girl's adoptive parents would be watching rubbish on television, bittered by each other's company, and both secretly pondering over the return of her precious cargo. Despite their joint concern over the late hour, they would likely be unwilling to spark up a conversation with regards to their daughter's whereabouts, for fear of it breaking into yet another slanging match.

Entertained and warmed by the image, along with the schemes in her Machiavellian mind, Sheila allowed herself another contented smile. Holding her hand aloft and adopting Queen Elizabeth II's iconic signature wave, she kept the four-wheel drive's course direct along the main drag, passing the family's driveway, still sticking religiously to that speed limit.

'*Oops*,' she snickered.

FIFTY-FOUR

The news crept through the corridors of his mind like the beast of a bad dream, the kind of nightmare where you wake sweaty and shaking only to find it was no hallucination at all. The beast... his gran, was very much real. Living and breathing and of the same land as himself.

His *gran*... Impossible! She wouldn't leave his mum, her own daughter, to take the rap... she *couldn't*. Things like that just don't happen.

'I know what I saw,' said Ethan, reading Talek's thoughts. His voice was low and eerily comforting.

'And she hit you... left Coby for dead? It doesn't make sense.' Try as he might, Talek could not process the version of events his lifelong tormenter had fed him. It had to be a ruse, yet to what purpose, Talek could not fathom.

Ethan turned his face away, revealing a hideously swollen gash on the back of his head. His blonde hair was a matted mess of tacky, flaking copper. 'Pretty damning,' he said.

'How can you be sure? I mean, if you were knocked out.'

'She's been here since. And I saw her through the windscreen, before she... you know.' Ethan put his hands to his face, rubbing his burning eyes. 'Your mum's a freak, everyone knows that, but your gran's a fucking headcase.'

'I think I'm gonna puke,' said Talek.

'Join the club. You're just lucky you've got something in you to puke.'

'Hasn't she fed you?'

'Gave me somethin' a couple days ago,' groaned Ethan, arms lowering to cradle his aching gut. 'Only brought me water yesterday. Other than that, I think she'd happily let me starve to death.'

Talek shot to the woman's defence, 'She's not a mur___' He stopped short of completing the word. *If Ethan's telling the truth, that's* exactly *what she is.*

'Oh shit,' Talek continued, mortified by fact that the thought that had only just entered his head, 'Erin. She's with her now.'

'She's safe,' said Ethan, 'Erin's never done anything to you.'

'You think that's why my gran did this? That's crazy. All you lot did was pick on me a bit.'

Ethan cast a look that said Talek was stupid. 'And why else do you think she'd do it?'

Talek couldn't conjure up an answer. The thought that his inability to get the bullies off his back could have started all of this; that *he* was inadvertently responsible for Coby's death, nauseated him deeply.

'Well,' said Ethan, 'no one can say you didn't get your own back. I deserved a kick-in, but Coby? That's fucked up, big time.' He struggled to his feet, letting out a shallow whine of discomfort. 'Come on. We haven't heard a sound, the coast has gotta be clear by now.'

As he said the words, a thunderous clash obliterated the stagnant air, ricocheting from the bare internal walls and age-weakened ceiling. The boys stared at each other, shocked and wide-eyed as another crash followed Ethan's kiss of death statement. Accompanying this latest booming impact, a splitting, splintering of wood rang out like firecrackers in a tin bucket.

'What the fu___' started Ethan, words silenced as a heavy wooden panel slammed to the floor not far away.

'Get down!' Talek hissed.

Throwing himself to the dirty floor between the partition wall and the old Volvo, Ethan crawled over, seeking refuge with the kid he'd bullied for an untold number of years. From the crash site, something clambered over metal in a series of clangs and scrapes, before thudding to the ground.

Feet?

Yelping at the pain in his ribs as the other boy thrust an elbow into him, Talek screwed his face up and looked at his abuser.

'The light. Fucking dipshit!' Ethan warned in a harsh whisper.

Shit, thought Talek, fumbling frantically at the Maglite, shaky hands prolonging the power killing process.

Too slow. Footsteps approached from beyond the half wall. Not daring to move a muscle, both boys held their breath until their lungs burned. Reaching the stall wall, the footsteps ceased. Seconds passed in total silence, turning into minutes. One. Two.

What the hell's he doing? Talek wondered. Surely the pursuer hadn't turned and left without making another sound? Talek supposed it *was* a possibility. I mean, the youngster who feared just about everything in life had practically shat himself during the explosion at the site of his barricade. *And* at the purposeful strides in their direction. With the current state his mind was in, he could have missed absolutely anything: a marching band passing through; a Spitfire flypast; a visit from a Hollywood A-lister.

Against their backs, the metal panels of the Volvo chilled them to the core. The compact earth began to numb their backsides. Soon enough, one of them would have to do something; they couldn't just sit here with their thumbs up their asses for eternity... or could they?

With no chance of his breathing recovering its normal rhythm any time soon, Talek put a trembling hand to the dust, pushing himself up and standing as soundlessly as possible. Darkness surrounded him. Gaining a visual of his surroundings proved hopeless.

Instead, he tried to block off all other senses and shift the powers of perception to his ears.

Nothing. Regardless of how diligent his efforts were, they appeared to be alone once more.

Sitting back down, again every care taken to remain undetected, he looked to where he could sense Ethan's presence and whispered, 'He didn't see us. I think he's gone.' Feeling for the button at the base of the Maglite, he took a gulp of foul tasting Dutch courage from the air. Letting it out again in a long, fluid motion, Talek thumbed at the rubber pad.

'Nope, still 'ere, girls,' came a man's voice from above.

Floored by fear, the two youths darted a synchronising glance upwards, towards the gruff new voice. The stranger's face appeared demonic as he casually lit a cigarette, the devilish orange glow greying as he blew a cloud of smoke down upon them.

'Please don't kill us,' whimpered Talek, his throat only capable of projecting a high, feminine note.

'I'm not gonna kill you.' The figure spoke with a creepy casualness, like old friends just shooting the shit about football, or girls or whatever, over a friendly pint. 'At least, I don't *intend* to kill you. I mean, there's no guarantees, either way. But whether I do or not is completely down to you butt-stuffers.'

Protesting, Ethan piped up, 'We're not___'

'Chill, Roxette,' the man said, the reference going way over Ethan's blonde upright hair, 'I know you ain't. I saw your boyfriend here kissing my kid sister.'

Talek contemplated the man's words. They made no sense, and as intimidated as he felt, setting him straight was possibly the only way out of this predicament. 'Erin doesn't *have* a brother.'

The older boy looked down at him from over the partition, drawing on his cigarette. 'Erin might not have, little man…' *Not you as well. What the fuck?* Talek thought, '… but Billie does.'

Billie? 'Who the hell's Billie?' said Talek, now convinced that they were in the company of a lunatic. 'You're off your friggin' head, man!'

'Keep talkin' like that, sweetcheeks, and I *will* have to kill you. Both of you. Them's the rules.' Another puff, again blowing the smoke down at the pair. 'Seems you don't know yer girlfriend very well.'

The man straightened to his full terrifying stature and nonchalantly strolled around to the opening of the stall. Both boys tensed up as he came into full view, their bodies tightening, turning to stone. The threatening figure bowed marginally, raised his right hand to put the smoke between his set lips, removed it with his left. Extending his now free right to Talek, the boy flinched back, before spotting the flat, vertical-palmed gesture. Taken aback, Talek's mind caught in a conundrum: take the hand and be ripped from the floor and slaughtered; or ignore the hand and be kicked to death on the spot.

The big dude nodded to the hand, refusing to withdraw the offer.

Ethan nudged his plaything in the side. 'Do it, tosser.'

Swallowing hard, Talek reached forwards and took the hand. It was firm, callused, and gigantic compared to his own teenaged build.

'Kieran,' said the intruder.

What the frig is he playing at? 'T… Talek.'

'Well, T…T…T…Talek,' he mimicked, 'what the fuck? What sort of name is that?'

'Dunno.' Talek looked to his feet, embarrassed. 'Never really asked.'

'Well, whatever,' said Kieran. 'Now, kiddo, here's what's gonna happen. I need to see my sister. She was a baby when I…' he chose his words carefully, '… went away for a while. Probably doesn't even know I exist.' The boy seemed to be listening intently, albeit with a countenance that suggested a forthcoming argument. 'And that's where you come in.'

'I___'

'Shut it!' Kieran snapped. His venomous tone appeared to have the desired effect. 'You're safe, for now. But tomorrow you're gonna break the news to her…'

Kieran spotted the other boy raise his hand, like the dopey twat thought he was in a classroom or something, and not a shitty old barn with a very real threat stood before him. 'Need to go to the toilet?' Kieran teased. 'Put your fuckin' hand down and tie a knot in it.' Turning his attention back to the black kid with the weird name, he said, 'Then you can bring me in. After that we'll just take it from there. She'll think I'm a nonce if I try to get to her alone.'

Concerned for the welfare of the girl he was very possibly in love with, Talek ventured, 'What if I don't?'

Smirking, Kieran squatted, bringing his pale eyes level with the boy's dark orbs. 'You *know* what happens if you don't.' The smirk still on his hard mouth, Kieran extended his index and middle fingers, and ran their tips slowly across his throat. 'Clear, little boy?'

Downgraded from little man, *brilliant.*

Breaking the tension between the two, the other boy started to wave frantically, demanding more urgency than just raising his hand had managed to transmit.

'What is it, sideshow?' Kieran said, annoyance seeping out stronger with each word.

Ethan coughed. Speaking weakly, he warned, 'You don't wanna wait for tomorrow.'

'What?' Kieran's face contorted in confusion. 'Fuck ya talkin' about?'

'You can't wait,' the boy repeated. Nodding at Talek, he said, 'She's with his gran. The woman's a murdering schizo!'

FIFTY-FIVE

Leaving the sanctuary of the streetlights, Sheila's slipped the Shogun off the main drag, down into the dip at the Pencalenick end of the deathly quiet back lane. Being a seldom travelled artery of old Cornish backways, interruptions at this time of night would range from next to nothing, to non-existent. Just what the doctor ordered. She chuckled at the algae-stained National Speed Limit sign; *Sixty? Good luck with that, Council dipshits*. Crossing a narrow bridge over the Trevella Stream, the sound of babbling water – water that would feed the voluminous body of Tresillian River a quarter of a mile away, where the smirking woman had not long since left a young, lifeless package for nature to absorb, and interfering old Mother Nature to spoil the party and uncover – murmured placidly. The tranquil gurgles drifted with soothing fluidity through her open window. She breathed in the aroma of soggy riverbanks and fallen leaves; a nostalgic, thought provoking scent if ever there was one.

Beyond the low-walled bridge, Coachman's Cottage rested peacefully within its surroundings of swaying, chattering trees. Welcoming yellow light leaked from its ground-level windows and tall glass panes of the picturesque entrance hall. Arch-topped cast iron gates stood firmly closed, the cottage's residents cooped up comfortably within its cosy interior. They would have no reason to venture out on roads patrolled by the spirits of earthbound highwaymen and long-dead horses tonight.

Erin remained soundly asleep in the passenger seat, a helpful ingredient added to her lemonade back at Scoan's Cottage acting with its intended affect. Reaching across, Sheila ran a gentle finger down the girl's pale cheek. She didn't stir.

'Not long now, lovey,' Sheila cooed.

Bearing around to the right, the road closed in on the vehicle as it began its sharp incline. Sheila dropped down a gear as the ascent started to tell on the engine. Releasing the clutch, she attempted to keep the revs, and therefore the rattle of the motor, low. Following the winding blacktop around a sharp left, then a slight right, Devil's Arch lit up with a hellfire toxicity in the four-by-four's full beam. She stopped at the entrance, taking in the decaying stone structure in all its satanic beauty. Its mouth hung open, blackened and beckoning.

Gently dabbing the accelerator again, she rolled the beast gently forward. Breaking all the ancient rules on talking and breathing underneath the centuries-old horror story, Sheila spoke quietly. 'Hello, Austin. I've brought a pressie for ya.'

Breaching the short, sombre tunnel, moist, sooty walls transfigured to glistening emerald moss at her window. Continuing onwards, she left the Arch to dwell in its morbid misery behind her. Still no movement from the passenger seat at her side. Sheila refocused on the way ahead, reaching the end of the sharpest climb and pulling into a passing place. Here, she shut off the power, pushed the door open and climbed out, stretching her legs, her back – limbering up for the most strenuous aspect of her oddly invigorating mission. The air was cold, a crisp bite setting upon her face in the settling mist. Waves of whitened air bathed in moonlight swam past her eyes, swept along by a keen easterly breeze. Apart from that cool blow working its way through the foliage, no other sound disrupted the country night's serenity. The pair were entirely alone.

Sheila crossed the road, where a steel framework gate barred access to a dusty track, running perpendicular to the road along an open field. Confident that the girl was still in a state of unconsciousness, the calculating woman donned a pair of leather gloves, setting to work at a loosely tied length of rope looped between the steel and a chunky wooden gatepost. The knot freed, offering minimal resistance, allowing Sheila to push the gate inwards. Lifting it over tufts of long grass to ensure it would not swing shut, the woman looked left, right, and left again, just like the Green Cross Code Man used to preach. The way was clear, no distant engine noises, no headlights rising above hedgerows for the entire distance in either direction.

'Good to go,' she said, her voice low as she approached the Shogun.

Sparking the engine into life, Sheila made a sharp turn, crossing the road and heading onto the rutted track. Ahead and to the right of this bumpy lane sat copse of trees, beyond those, a private house. She doubted that her headlights would penetrate the dense body of trunks and undergrowth so as to draw attention from the property owners, and the lofty canopies were certainly tall enough for the beams to fail to peer over the tops. Nevertheless, it was always better to be safe than sorry. There would be a lot of sorry people after tonight, but *she* would not be one of them. She leaned from her open window, howling mockingly at the moon, purely to assuage her own amusement. A World War II searchlight in the sky, the lunar gargantuan currently provided more than enough illumination to navigate by – as long as these clouds continued to break. Killing the headlights, the vehicle stumbled along in pale anthracite stealth.

As towering evergreens and autumn-stripped sycamores loomed close enough to permeate the jeep's interior with fresh, woodland smells, Sheila steered off the track, cutting along the grass at their base. The vehicle bumped languidly across the turf. Her precious cargo rocked gently to and fro in the front seat, but did not wake, or even moan in semiconscious protest.

Reaching the far end of the copse, Sheila was met by the field's eastern border: a patchy growth of shrubs and brambles, and a confusion of stubbly, viny limbs. This was all good. She'd been here before, knew the lay of the land, knew of the gritty footpath passing just metres beyond the growth. The footpath that led across the jagged stone roof of Devils Arch, where on this night the girl with demon blood flowing through her rancid veins will draw her last breath.

The thought escaped her body in a satisfied sigh. Her grandson will no longer be subjected to the evil vermin connected with his father's violent demise. The two men that were once vicious thugs as boys would *both* know how it feels to have someone taken from them.

Climbing down from the driver's seat with her lips curled in a sneer, Sheila made her way to the boot. Opening it out, she grabbed a rucksack from the back floor, along with an old blanket, and eased the tail shut as quietly as she could manage. She arrived at the passenger door and spread the blanket along the dew-glistened grass. Laying the bag at her feet, she opened it up, removing a drawstring sack in the process before opening up the passenger side. The girl never flickered her eyelids as the woman tilted her sleeping head forward and slipped the sack over her silky raven hair, drawing its toggle up tight around the scrawny neck.

So far, so good. Shame the same can't be said for the rest of it, but it'll be worth the effort.

Grabbing the girl by both shoulders, Sheila leaned her forward, reposition her hands under Erin's armpits. Pulling the girl free from the jeep, she lowered her carefully onto the blanket.

Yer as light as a feather. Skinny bitch. 'Just goin' for a little walk,' she said, a casual tone like they were just a couple of old friends, heading for some idyllic coffeehouse.

Rezipping the bag, she hoisted it onto her shoulders and grabbed two corners of the blanket. Dragging the drugged body along the uneven ground was challenging. The footpath was sure to make for a more manageable terrain, its fine grainy surface nature's rolling road. Pulling the burdened material through the undergrowth proved backbreaking work, with thorns and brambles clawing and tearing at the fabric. Thinking ahead, Sheila would have to burn the blanket when this was through, scrub the back of the jeep of any loose fibres. Once through, sapped of energy yet determined to endeavour, Sheila's theory of the gritty pathway turned out to be an accurate one. In actual fact, with the narrow track sloping downwards all the way, the task transpired to be a much simpler, less arduous undertaking than the sprightly grandmother had anticipated. *Bony-assed bitch shot along like a rat up a drainpipe!*

Now, after taking five to catch her breath and restore some of her sapped strength, Sheila set to work, gathering the appropriate item from her rucksack and preparing it accordingly. She stopped what she was doing momentarily, looking over at the form slumped against the wall atop Devil's Arch. How the mite hadn't awakened yet, the experienced kidnapper did not know. Sheila must have used way too much of that shit. How didn't the girl notice the unsavoury tang? *Unless it's tasteless.* Sheila wouldn't know; you don't fuck around with illegitimate sedatives from untrustworthy sources yourself. That sort of kamikaze conduct could very well get you dead.

'Sorry, flower,' she laughed, 'but you didn't expect me to try a bit first, did ya?'

No answer. Of course not.

'Come on, chick, don't be shy. It's *under* the Arch you're not supposed to talk; not over it. Bleddy kids these days!'

Clutching the mortiferous accessory she had been working on – a crafter exercising her expertise, pursuing her malevolent interests – in one hand, Sheila pushed herself to standing and secured the finished article to the wooden safety fencing. Affixed to the low stone wall, the fencing spanned the length of the ancient bridge; the perfect modern addition that would serve her vigilante mission admirably. The light breeze picked up with renewed purpose. Whining through the gaping mouth of the bleak underpass, it cried a morose entreaty to the lady above. The Arch was apparently hungry for souls to join Austin and who-knows-how-many others; more spirits to cradle in its dark, stinking, eternal womb. It would bear new life, or rather new death, tonight.

Singing in chorus with the whipping wind, another whine introduced itself into the deepening night. Down at Sheila's side, the bundle propped against the rugged wall began to writhe restlessly.

FIFTY-SIX

'You're in the front, little guy,' Kieran ordered. 'You think I'm gonna trust you two cock-knockers behind me, you're thicker than you look.'

He jumped in the driver's seat. Turning the key, he was relieved to hear the engine roar into life at the first attempt. Skirting around the front, his legs producing lengthy shadows on the inner wall, Talek pulled the passenger door open and slid in. Despite the abominable fear flowing through is body, he couldn't help but feel privileged to be allowed up front – even if the instruction was unnecessarily barked at him.

Ethan stood panting at the offside rear door, emotions raw and a debilitating panic attack brewing deep in his chest. The thought of stepping back into the vehicle that had until recently imprisoned him came with overwhelming angst.

Pulling down the window, Kieran snapped, 'Get in, shit for brains! And buckle the fuck up. I've never driven before.'

'Maybe this isn't such a good idea,' Talek said meekly as the other kid mustered the courage to get in the back.

'Shut your face and grow a pair,' growled Kieran, 'D'you wanna help your girlfriend or not?'

Put firmly in his place, and remaining silent, Talek gave an apologetic nod.

'Relax,' said Keiran, his cunning smile diabolical, 'I've seen this done enough. Should be a piece of piss.'

He shoved the stick into position, gearbox crunching as he battled with the aging clutch.

God, Talek silently conversed with the Lord, *if you're listening, please remember I've never done anything bad*.

Ahead and to the left, the Volvo's headlights presented a set of double doors. These doors, the man behind the wheel assumed, were the ones he'd spotted first from outside, bolted shut and padlocked. He slugged forward out of the stall, straightening up at the doors' inner face. 'Ready, ladies?'

Talek shook his head nervously and forced his eyes shut. Gravity sucking him forcefully back into the seat, the vehicle's front end lifted under forceful acceleration. With a deafening crash, the wooden doors exploded into the night, a million splinters flying erratically, a swarming solider beetle invasion devastating the heathland.

'*WHOOO!*' the driver hollered wildly, and unexpectedly enough for Talek to near shit his pants. 'Let's do that again.'

The boy riding shotgun certainly did not want to do it again, yet in the back of the car Ethan sat with a smile on his face. He was beginning to look up to this deranged newcomer; could see a lot of himself in him. Summoning the courage to open his eyes, Talek saw his house fly past in a blur. *He left the bloody door open.* Kicking himself, he felt ashamed of thinking like such an old biddy when there were far more pressing matters at hand.

Deeper into the Merther back lanes, unsettling nausea blossomed in the boy's gut. Being mainly used to his mother's slow, composed driving, this new helter-skelter rally style, with a driver who openly admitted to never having done it before, was petrifying. Grey trunks in the gloom flew past on either side, like the woodlands had come to life and were fleeing from whatever unknown fate awaited him on the other side. His head spinning, Talek lunged forward sharply, partly to block out the charging army of trees, but mainly to puke in the footwell.

Kieran laughed at the kid's predicament, as Talek's thoughts turned to his mother. He felt suddenly appalled. His mum was sat in a prison cell, or an interrogation room, going through absolute hell over a murder and kidnapping she did not commit… Her own mother, throwing her under the bus and leaving it to wheelspin madly on her face, screaming insanely as flesh tore from bone.

'Get yer head up, pussyflaps,' Kieran demanded. 'Keep your eye out for that bitch's car!'

Scared into action, the boy did just that. She could pass at any moment… or not at all. Talek could not determine which would be worse.

Either way, just thinking about it was enough to induce a complete mental breakdown. Surly she wouldn't do anything to Erin; she liked her, didn't she?

You keep telling yourself that, little man. He was doing it himself now, so long had the mocking term been driven into him. But Talek knew he was wrong about the woman he'd looked up to his entire life; the woman who acted as grandmother, *and* mother, when his real mum wasn't up to the job.

She's capable of anything.

With the relief one feels when they wake from their worst nightmare yet, right at the moment the malicious adversary was about to strike the fatal blow, the back lanes were over. Turning left onto the main road from the Probus bypass to Tresillian, the unlikely trio in the Volvo had not seen a single other vehicle on their journey. That all changed now. Pulling out behind a clapped out old van, a discotheque of headlights streamed towards them on the other side of the carriageway. Kieran accelerated, hanging mere feet from the van's twisted rear bumper, weaving from side to side ready to pounce upon any gap in the oncoming traffic with room enough to burn past.

'Can you hang back a bit,' Talek shouted over the straining engine, 'I can't see what's coming.'

'Then look harder!' Kieran called back, pulling out before swerving back in line once more.

He edged the wheel over again. Enough time? Maybe. Kieran decided he'd take that chance. Flooring the throttle, he swung over to the opposite lane. In a moment of terror, Talek covered his eyes and whimpered as twin lights appeared from around a slight bend in the road. The oncoming vehicle was approaching so rapidly, Talek was assured that the suicidal maniac behind the wheel of his mother's car was not the only one with a blatant disregard for the village's speed limit. A horn flared up ahead. Feeling the Volvo swerve violently, Talek listened blind as a screech of rubber on asphalt was followed by an unbearable crunching of metal, his body thrust painfully against the grip of his seatbelt as two moving vehicles collided.

I'm dead, he had time to think before a sudden change in direction slammed his body to the passenger door. Claret trickled warmly down his cheek as his head struck the glass. Near to vomiting yet again, he felt his body being continually hurled, a loan coin shaken in a kiddie's piggy bank. *Heads you win, tales you lose.*

A deranged whoo-hoo and a shoving hand from the passenger seat informed the adolescent that he was not dead.

'*GET THE FUCK OFF ME!*' the driver bellowed.

The old Volvo persevering, Talek spun his gaze to the passenger door mirror. Displayed in miniature, the van that had been hampering their desperate journey now sat idle behind, angled against a wall and mounted upon the pavement. Both headlights were out, its front end severely smashed in. Body parts hung from the rear of the Volvo, twisted and flapping. Somehow, a head-on collision with the speeding motorist had been miraculously avoided. Taking a moment to catch his breath, settling his nerves seemingly beyond his capabilities for the time being, Talek heard Ethan laughing hysterically from the backseat.

'More fun than your mate, here,' said Kieran, eyeing the boy in the rear-view mirror. 'We'll 'ave to go for a beer when this is over. Why are you friends with this nerd, anyway?'

'I'm not,' Ethan chuckled immaturely, 'I hate the prick!'

Hurt after daring to think the bitter enemies had made a breakthrough tonight, partially buried the hatchet Talek said, 'Just slow down, we don't wanna miss Erin's drive.'

'Billie's drive,' Kieran corrected.

'Whatever,' said Talek, only daring to voice it under his breath.

Pulling the car to the side of the road and bringing it to a halt, whilst keeping the motor running, Kieran stared across the A390. Looking in the same direction, Talek took in two vehicles. Neither were his gran's four-wheel drive.

'Shit,' said Talek, 'she's not there.'

'We may have missed the ol' fucker on her way back,' added Ethan, unhelpfully.

'Go knock,' Kieran said, not taking his eyes from the cars on the driveway. 'Maybe she already dropped Billie off.'

'I can't,' Talek argued, irked at the man's continual use of the unfamiliar name. 'If she's not there, they'll think she's at my house. Then we're no further forward.'

'You, in the back.' Kieran craned his head around, looking between the headrests. 'You go. Pretend you're a mate of hers.'

'What?' asked Ethan in surprise, 'I hardly know___'

'Go and I'll set you up with her,' the big lad smiled. 'Dunno what she's doin' with this tit anyway.'

Talek intervened. 'She won't be intere___'

'Button it, needle dick,' snapped Kieran.

Ahead, black trees and hedges adopted an electric blue hue. Distant sirens could be heard, closing in rapidly. Seconds later a pair of squad cars darted past, beacons blinding and engines furious.

Kieran turned his full attention to the kid in the back. 'Go, now! Gotta get a wriggle on; those fuckers'll be turning back for us as soon as the dippit in the van blabs.'

Ethan sprang from the back of the car, battling pain and fatigue as he crossed the road and hit the driveway. Talek watched on, a mixture of panic and pity tightening his chest and devouring his brain: panic for Erin and what may have befallen her; and pity for Ethan. The attempted sprint was a seriously dampened down version of the one that used to have him running away like the scared pussy he was. The kid's lack of food and hydration had clearly taken a damning toll.

As Kieran peered attentively for any sign of the cops' return in the driver's wingmirror, Talek saw Connor open the front door. Ethan looked small and insignificant in the man's shadow. Talek's heart sank as Connor shook his head and raised his hands in a *no idea* gesture.

Running back with an exerted hobble, Ethan avoided the oncoming traffic and jumped in the back. 'She ain't there.'

'Bollocks!' exclaimed Kieran. 'Now what?'

'I don't know,' Talek mumbled in response, rubbing his burning eyes as his head started to pound.

'Well, she's *your* gran,' said Kieran, his tone brutal and his face set, 'where does she normally take people to kill them?'

'She's not going to do that!'

'Really believe that do you?' Kieran was becoming more aggressive as the seconds passed, causing Talek to dawdle in distress. 'Fuck this shit, we gotta get outta here.'

Pushing the stick into first gear and paying his side mirror a cautionary glance, Kieran hit the gas pedal and shot back onto the main carriageway. Taking the first offered opportunity to leave the main road that exited the village, slung the Volvo down a steep left-hander. The enforced decision only served to heighten Talek's distress. They were now on yet another claustrophobia-inducing backroad. It was one that he'd come to know only too well in recent weeks: the road where the father he never got to meet took his dying breath.

FIFTY-SEVEN

'Hello, treasure,' smiled Sheila. She had removed the sack from the girl's head, and now crouched before her feeling immense gratification at the look of dumbstruck bewilderment on her hostage's face. 'What's the matter? Cat got yer tongue?'

'Wha… what's going on?' Erin finally managed, head dazed and groggy.

'Well, I would've thought that was obvious,' said Sheila, her tone gently mocking, 'but I suppose you've still got the drugs in yer system, making you a bit… well, dopey.'

Erin's brain swam in her head like a lackadaisical jellyfish suspended in saltwater, its bobbing dictated by the movement of the tides. '*Drugs?*' she slurred, screwing her face up and scrutinising the woman. The wear and tear of age was visible in the moonlight. Her advanced years displayed themselves for the first time, transforming the pleasant, carefree woman Erin thought she knew into some sinister witch she did not recognise.

'Don't judge me, young lady. I couldn't bleddy well get you 'ere if you were awake.' Sheila placed a hand on the girl's outstretched leg. 'It was a necessity. Nothing personal.'

A cold wind licked Erin's face, bringing with it the scent of decaying leaves, and… something else; something ancient and inhospitable.

'How is *this* not personal?' she quizzed, her eyes scanning the gloom in an attempt to place the unrecognisable location. 'And what kind of hell is this place?' Her narrow fingers clawed at a rough, moist floor. Concentrating her will on her arms, she tried to push herself up. Nothing happened, her vitality apparently on vacation, unwilling to return to her disinterested limbs.

'Oh, this isn't hell, li'l darlin',' Sheila smirked grotesquely. 'This is just the gateway. And don't try to move, your bony sub-size six ass is gonna be quite useless for a smidge longer yet.'

The woman raised her gaze, surveying the open sky overhead and the surrounding treetops. Her features reflected like aging chinaware in the moon's glow. 'But here,' the old woman's attention returned to the stricken girl, 'let me tell you about *here*.'

Sheila paused, keeping the unseen thread between the two sets of eyes intact. Deep in thought? To add suspense? Only she would know her reasoning. 'I would've had a son in law by now. Strappin' young lad. Fine lookin', black, sculpted. Could quite've gone for a piece of that, myself; you know what I mean? Oh, you may look surprised,' Sheila added, noticing the girl's sceptical expression. 'My Tammy was a beautiful young woman back then. Not the shadow of a human being you see now, the walking corpse. No, her verve left this mortal coil the night her fella was taken from her… by *your* bastard brother.'

Erin's mind boggled. If she'd not have been so petrified, she might have laughed in the old woman's lunatic face. Instead, she said meekly, 'You're mental. I don't have a brother. I'm an only child.'

'Oh, you dear, sweet, innocent thing.' Mocking again. 'Your parents have been lying to you your whole life,' Sheila tutted disapprovingly. 'Or should I say, *supposed* parents. Keeping you in the dark, hiding you from the truth about what you *really* are. What poisoned blood runs through your veins.'

Head still reeling, Erin grappled with the unpalatable tale she was being force-fed. 'It's you whose the liar,' she managed to spit back.

The woman laughed, a wicked, disturbing cackle. 'Nay, lass, it's *you* who's mental. I wasn't even fishing for information, just after a good shag, that's all, the night your *dad*,' she raised two fingers from each hand, signing inverted commas as she said the word, 'took me to bed in a sordid hotel room.'

A tear rolled down Erin's cold-bitten cheek in pained comprehension.

'That's right, sweetie,' Sheila went on. 'Couldn't wait to rip me clothes off, the randy bugger. He went at me like a sex-starved honey badger.' She looked up, satisfaction at the memory written on her moonlit skin. 'Anyway, when we were done, lying there naked in each other's exhausted arms, he just… blabbed. Opened up like a pair o' floodgates. You're desperate for me to tell you what 'e said, I can tell.'

The mention of floodgates was apropos, Erin's own defences breached by an uncontrollable surging tide of emotions.

The sound carried by the night air, an engine revved strenuously. Somewhere close by a clutch was being ridden to within an inch of its life. Sheila crouched low, placing a hand to the girl's head, forcing her below the top of the low wall. Headlights beamed over Devil's Arch, the engine calming as a vehicle negotiated the deceptively tight underbelly of the old bridge below.

Lifting her head above the bony scute-like stones, Sheila watched a pair of taillights disappear up the black and twisted back lane, its tired engine petering into insignificance. Satisfied that they were alone with the Devil and the darkness once more, Sheila continued, 'So, here it is. Your mum… the *real* one, that is, is or was, I dunno which, a drug addict. Yer dad, a waste of space alcoholic. You're a crack baby,' she said, pulling a ridiculing frown. 'Probably explains why you're so pale and emaciated. According to the imposter posing as yer favver, they left you for dead when yer brother was caught. Arrested for killing *my* potential son in law, and leaving my daughter to listen to his dying screams. Underneath this very earth, your bastard brother and his bastard mate poured petrol over their car; sparked a light; and ran off laughing like a couple of hyenas as the flames engulfed an innocent, loving young couple.'

Shock and incapacity dictating her actions, Erin soaked up the devasting news. Fearing the personal consequences of what these kids – kids she had never known – had done, she said, 'So what are you gonna do to me? With me, I mean.'

'Well, isn't that obvious?' replied Sheila. 'Me, my Tammy, my Tal, have had to live with that loss. Fourteen years! That's all the little shits got. Juveniles. Life sentences my arse. *Justice*, they call it. The judicial system's bollocks, but luckily I'm 'ere to put it right, impose my own sentence. Judge, jury… and executioner.'

Sickened to her stomach, Erin filled her lungs, her head spiralling all the harder over the excess oxygen. 'But, if he *is* my brother, I don't know him, and I had nothing to do with any of it.'

Laughing evilly, Sheila said, 'Well, that's just rotten luck. You know he's just been released?'

The girl cowering before her, tears glistening and cheeks burning with colour, stared blankly back.

'And the other one, just before him. I wanted them both to suffer loss like we have. The loss of a loved one. The lasting ruin the aftermath brings. The first one was an easy decision, and an even easier target. Rundle. You may have heard the name on the news recently.'

Sheila looked to Erin for confirmation. The youngster lowered her head. Nauseated, she mumbled through a veil of fallen silky hair, 'Yes.'

'Well, I had no idea who his family was. I had to do me 'omework.' she said softly, 'But I knew he had a son.'

'Jowan,' whispered Erin.

'Bingo!' Sheila raised her eyebrows in silent admiration of the girl's ability to think straight under such overwhelming adversity.

'You didn't.'

'Hmm?' Sheila queried, her demeanour blasé. 'Oh yes, I did. It was simple. I was parked down the road from school, just an out of touch old fogey trying to get to grips with my new phone. He was smart... well, not smart enough, maybe. I wound down me window, pleading pathetically, and he just jumped in.' She sniggered, turning her face to the rugged floor and shaking her head. 'Asked me what I wanted to do, and started tapping away. You know, it's amazing, I totally have this fast-paced new world of technology to thank. Technology got him in the car, and technology prevented anyone else from noticing. So many school kids walking past. Hundreds. Every one of them glued to their bleddy mobile phones. Including that tiny, ever-so-helpful lad, only he was glued to mine.'

Erin looked up in disgust before scoping left to right and back again for any means of escape from this crazy woman, this crazy situation.

'I pulled a fencing wire from down beside me seat without him even noticing.' She was enjoying reliving the moment; Erin could see it in her calculating eyes. 'Flung it 'round his neck. Pulled tight. The kids walking past were like flippin' zombies. Didn't 'ave a clue what was goin' on.' Sheila pondered for a moment, the seconds dragging like hours. 'I'll never forget seeing his chest expand and contract for the last time, his face, round and purple. He looked like a plump blueberry, ripe for pickin'.'

'You're sick,' Erin wheezed, shuddering at the apparent delight her boyfriend's gran took from reliving the macabre events.

'No, honey,' said Sheila, a sad smile bringing shadows to her eyes, 'your brother's sick. And his li'l friend. Fourteen years I had to wait for that Rundle kid to be released. I had to coincide the boy's disappearance with *him* getting out. Timing was critical. He was always gonna be the prime suspect once he was back out darkening the streets.'

Erin shivered, the chill air, the mist, the shock, it was all too much. Voice trembling, she ventured, 'So, what does this all have to do with me? I don't know the guy you're claiming is my brother, and he doesn't know me.'

'But sweetheart, he does. He was much older than you. You're all he has left in the world.' Sheila replaced her hand on Erin's leg. The strong-willed girl mustered the fortitude to retract it. 'Your druggy, alcy parents are untraceable. And they didn't want anything to do with either of you anyway. Trust me, he remembers you.'

'What about your grandson? He's never had what we've got. He'll never forgive you for this.'

'Ooh,' teased Sheila, 'it's true love, my heart bleeds. But your real family's blood runs through you, crack baby, you could *never* be good enough for my tallywhacker.'

Plucking up an insurmountable amount of courage, Erin challenged, 'I don't think you've got it in you.'

'Underestimating me could be your biggest mistake yet.' The crazy woman was laughing again. 'You think I stopped at *Jowan*?'

Erin's stomach cramped. *Surely there's not more.*

'Those two lads that were pickin' on *my* boy?'

This was too much. Erin couldn't respond, didn't dare to ask the question. Sheila nodded, as if reading the stricken girl's thoughts, her countenance a demon puppet's sadistic smile.

'You let your own daughter take the rap for that,' she challenged. 'What the fuck is wrong with you?'

'Duplicity is one of my many strengths,' replied Sheila. 'Anyway, that's not my daughter. Not anymore. She passed away the night her Austin burned. All that's left of that girl is the shell she once thrived in. *I*, am all my Talek needs, not his mother, and certainly not *you*.'

A whipping wind stirred, singing hauntingly through the arch beneath their chilled bodies.

'You hear that?' Sheila asked. 'Austin's calling for you.'

Nearing hysteria, Erin forced her eyes to follow the woman's movements. Her lethal hand reached out to one side, returning with a length of rope. One end was fastened around a wooden railing. The other was circular, knotted to form a noose.

Throat constricting, hampering her speech, Erin strained to say, 'You're the Antichrist.'

'Don't be absurd,' Sheila said through gritted teeth, amusement giving way to anger for the first time in the long exchange, 'the Antichrist wouldn't protect my boy like *I* do.'

***

Offering a silent prayer for the man whom he now knew to be his father, Talek wiped a layer of sweat from his forehead as the trio emerged from under Devil's Arch. The burning sensation had reduced drastically on this visit. Through praying, or just a forewarned knowledge of the devastating impact that creepy old archway had on him, he neither knew nor cared. Able to breathe easily again, Talek was thankful, whatever the reason behind this positive progression.

'There's someone up there.' Ethan's voice came low and uneasy from the back of the car. Turning to take another look at the freaky little bridge, like something straight from the set of one of those old Hammer

Horrors his mum used to pass out in front of, a head rising over the stone, cast a devilish red by the taillights, commanded his attention.

'Sure you're not just seeing things, kid?' said Kieran.

'Definitely not,' the boy responded. 'It looked like a woman, but it was hard to tell.'

'Right,' said Kieran, a tight-lipped urgency seeping through, 'how the fuck do we get up there?'

'I don't know,' Ethan answered, flustered.

'I do,' Talek said apprehensively. 'There, that field on the right with the open gate.'

Pressing hard on the brake pedal, Kieran swung the steering wheel and guided the Volvo through the opening.

'Cut across the grass,' said Talek, 'that way.' He stretched out his arm, pointing beyond a sea of grey-green grass.

'Okay, dickweed!' snapped Kieran. 'Just get yer fucking hand out me face.'

Rocking and bouncing as they edged along lumpy turf and scrub, the lurching Volvo's headlights picked out a stationary vehicle in the top corner, ominous below the backdrop of guarding trees.

Talek sighed, his emotions ready to induce more vomiting. 'Shit… it's her.'

Pulling up beside the jeep, Kieran killed the engine. 'Get out,' he said calmly.

'Maybe I should go on my own,' said Talek, unfastening his seatbelt.

'Fuck that.' Kieran kept that same calmness in the no-nonsense rebuke.

'Maybe I can talk her down,' the kid pleaded, 'she'll listen to me. You'll just end up___'

'What?' Kieran turned his head, staring the youngster down. 'You think I'm gonna kill her or something?'

'Aren't you?'

'That all depends on her.'

Pushing the door open, Talek climbed out. Bending to peer back in, he said, 'Just give me a chance.'

Kieran heaved in a deep intake of cool air and rubbed his face of the frustration.

'The clock's ticking,' prompted Talek.

'I'm good 'ere,' Ethan chipped in. Ignored by the other two, his job was apparently – and thankfully – done.

'Fine,' conceded Kieran, 'go talk to her, but I'll be right fucking behind you. I'm not letting you out of my sight, and if the moment comes…'

Talek didn't need the big man to express exactly what comes next.

***

'What… what are you doing?' Erin's body convulsed, the words coming out shaky and stricken.

'Hark!' Sheila demanded. Softening her tone, she said, 'You'll make this so much easier for yerself if you button it and play along nicely.' She lifted the noose to the girl's face. 'Just pop this on a mo, my little lovely.'

Beneath the two figures, one crouching awkwardly, one slumped uncomfortably, Devil's Arch continued to howl. The sound emanating from below seemed hungry and incredibly animalistic, a Barghest begging for a soul to squeeze. Sheila lowered the noose into position, holding the rope tight in one hand as she slid the hangman's knot closer to Erin's neck with the other.

'Stop blubbering, there's a good girl,' said Sheila. 'You should be enjoying this, bein' all gothy like you are.

Morbidity should come with the territory.' Rising to a standing position, Sheila arched her back, massaging the small with both hands. 'Get up!'

'I ca… I can't move.' Erin's heart palpitated, beating an erratic drum solo. Her head swam, caught between ordering her body to do something, *anything*, or considering if this whole ordeal would be easier to bear if she could sink back into unconsciousness.

'Oh for goodness' sake, useless mare,' Sheila complained, 'you really gonna make this old bird do all the dunkey work? Your job's simple. All you have to do is *cease* to *be*. But *nooo*, you have to go and be a pain in the ass about it. No pun intended.'

She bent forward, sliding a hand under each of Erin's armpits. Straining and groaning, she heaved the girl up and slid her backside onto the narrow tip of the wall. Jagged stones cut agonisingly into Erin's flesh, the fence's beams hard on her back the only thing preventing her from falling to her death.

Again, Sheila straightened and dug her fingers into the base of her spine. 'Halfway there, cherub,' she panted. 'Gawd blimey, tell you're Cornish, you even die dreckly.'

Erin drooped her head, her emotions at breaking point. She looked along the short length of rope hanging limp beneath her chin. Its opposite end clung to one fencepost, wrapped multiple times and secured with a series of knots. There was no way out. Even if her strength did return, it'd take forever to work through those bonds. Stubbornly, her head wanted to fight. Her body, nevertheless, seemed incapable of even the most mundane of actions, indifferent to the life or death conflict that presented itself on this haunting, harrowing night.

Growling, Sheila gyrated, a dog wringing itself speedily after an unwanted bath, limbering her body for the next mammoth task. 'Ready for round two, little miss lazybones?'

Bowing, she guided the girl's slight frame to her shoulder. Pushing herself up, the exertion from taking the weight of them both pronounced itself in a fit of huffs and puffs. By the time the crazy old sociopath was done, Erin found herself sat upon the top railing of the fence. It bowed and shifted sickeningly under her load. At this elevated point the wind blew keener, pressing her to work her core to the best of her depleted ability.

'How's yer balance?' Sheila teased.

'Just get on with it,' said Erin, hoping to convey a nonchalant apathy. 'But be prepared for Talek to hate your guts for the rest of your life.'

Sheila let out a bemused laugh. 'Ahh, bless. You really think e's gonna know? This is nothin' more than just another teen suicide. It's all the rage for your generation; no one will bat and eyelid. I dropped you outside of your place, you seemed fine. That was the last I saw of you.'

'He's not stupid,' sneered Erin.

'No, far from it,' Sheila concurred. 'But he'll believe anything I tell him. Always has. Even believed his own *mother* was capable of murder. Like she's got the gall to do anything like that.' She said the last line as if speaking to herself. 'And that's not about to change now. In fact, if anything it'll bring us closer together. His mum gone, his girlfriend immutably gone. And I'll be the one who's there to guide him through the heartache. His rock. The *bridge* in his storm, you might say.' Sheila gave a little chuckle at her own witty reference. 'Now,' her face turned grave, her mouth set, eyes gleaming with demonic determination, 'any last requests before you atone for the misdemeanour of that brother of yours?'

'GRAN!' The woman's scornful gaze shot sharply in the direction of the intrusive call. Talek stepped to the edge of the bridge. 'What the hell are you doing?'

'Tal, sweetie,' Sheila grovelled, 'this isn't wha___'

'Really?' A palpable nervousness encroached on the boy's attempt of bravery. 'That's good, 'cause from where I'm standing it looks like you're trying to kill my girlfriend.'

Sheila made to step forward. Noticing a movement in her peripheral, she stayed herself. Snapping at the girl perched on the fence, she warned, 'Don't move!' Keeping her immobilising stare on her grandson, she said, 'You don't know her. What her family's done.'

Erin interrupted, pleading, 'Don't listen to her, Talek, she's lost the plot.'

'Shut it, you!' Sheila scolded.

'Why don't you just let her down,' said Talek, hoping to strike reason but with little confidence, 'then we can all talk about whatever this is together.'

'It's too late for her,' said Sheila, raising a hand to the figure hunched on the wooden railing. Relief flooded through Erin's core once she understood the woman was simply pointing a finger. 'Only God can redeem her now, and He'll get to pass His judgment soon enough.'

'Gran,' said Talek, his voice low and empathic, 'I know you must have your reasons, but you're scaring her. And me.'

'That girl's evil, son, you don't know what she's capable of.' Colour began to flush through Sheila's face as anger boiled from within. 'If it wasn't for her putrid kin, *you'd* still have a favver.'

'Erin's right, Gran. You've lost it.' Talek's barely audible words were whipped up and carried away by the mid-autumn wind. 'I might not know *everything* about her, but it's enough to know I'm in love with her.'

In stark contradiction to the macabre plight, and this heinous place, intensified in the dead of night, Erin's lips curled in a smile. Her tears still streamed, only now they flowed with a large dose of happiness in their salty track. Everything was going to be okay. Her favourite person on the face of the Earth was here to save her, to whisk he from the brink of death and hold her, while the rest of existence faded into obscurity.

'Jesus Christ!' Sheila laughed, wicked and scornful. 'Have you heard yerself? Love, he says,' laughing harder and placing an am-dram hand on her chest. 'You're a *child*. You have no idea about love. I'm your mother. Mine is the only love you need.'

'You are NOT my MOTHER!' Talek raised his voice in rage and disbelief. 'My *mum* is sat in a police cell because of what *you* did!'

'You're the one who's "lost it",' Sheila said, taking a determined step towards him. 'Stay there, bitch,' she snapped, noticing another cautious movement at the fence from the corner of her eye. Keeping her focus on her grandson, she said, 'My Tammy's crazier than a shithouse rat. She's where she belongs.'

'Except she's not, is she?' Talek calmed his voice, composing, calculating. 'She's where *you* belong. I found Ethan. Still alive, no thanks to you.'

'Well,' said Sheila, attempting to portray sincerity, 'obviously that's good news, but where you think *I* come into it, I have no idea.'

'He told me everything.' Taking a step back, he kept his eyes on the woman he would never call *'Gran'* again, awaiting her next move with bated breath.

'Really?' she smiled wickedly. '*Everything*? Did he tell you that your precious girlfriend's own brother killed your dad? Burned him alive right under our feet. Your dad's the only reason your *mother* made it out alive.' The word "mother" came out with a venomous sting.

Erin's brother? Talek heeded, suddenly mindful of the man waiting in the wings. A murderer standing before his face, a murderer concealed in shadow at his back. How the hell was this going to end anything other than badly?

'I understand, my little angel,' soothed Sheila, 'this is hard to take in. But once it's done, it's done for good. You and me, Tal, you and me versus the world. No one will ever hurt you again. Not while I'm around.'

Sheila held out a hand. Talek took a trepid step forward, ignoring the offered hand for the present.

'You and me?'

'Yes,' she smiled sweetly. 'You and me. That girl is the spawn of Satan. We can end this together.'

Another slow step forward. He took the hand.

Erin's guts twisted violently, sickness brewing at the scene developing before her. 'Talek… don't…'

'Don't listen to her,' said Sheila, eyeing him in earnest, 'don't let that Devil's tongue warp your mind. She'll deceive you. This has to end, and it has to end *here*. One push, baby. One little push, and it's over. It'll be quick. She deserves to suffer, but this way she'll be spared of that.'

He nodded slowly at the old woman as her face glimmered gravely in the moon's dull glow. Sheila understood its meaning. Finally, the boy accepted the inevitable. Turning, she led him closer to the fence. Erin's blotchy, reddened face pleaded to him, reaching out, begging silently for this madness to stop.

Sheila's words came with a damnatory finality, 'Rest in peace, fallen angel.'

Lifting one cobralike arm, palm outwards ready to strike, a violent jolt shot through Sheila's vulnerable ribs. The clammy hand that held hers released as she spun, her flailing arm landing a blow on the girl's chest. Losing her footing, Sheila crashed to the floor. Talek watched in nauseating horror as Erin toppled backwards, disappearing behind the walls of Devil's Arch as she plummeted, screaming out a dreadful, harrowing howl.

'NO!' Talek yelled, his hopes and dreams evaporating before his very eyes, swallowed by this noxious hellhole.

Scrunching along the dirt track, heavy footsteps pounded rapidly toward the timeworn bridge. Too panicked to think of anything other than Erin, Talek blanked them out. Lunging at the fence, the moss-slippery wood bowing at the point of impact, he looked down, scared half to death at what he knew in his traumatised mind he would find: Erin's body swinging listlessly, face blue, and head at a sickeningly crooked angle.

What he saw was unfathomable. Erin's body swayed above the slick road, yet her upturned face and desperate staring eyes bored into his. The rope around her neck was slack, her hands clasped desperately to a piece of rock jutting from the top edge of the bridge.

From behind came a booming voice, *'WHAT THE FUCK'VE YOU DONE? STUPID BITCH!'*

The altercation taking place held no importance to him. That evil woman had caused this. She was on her own to deal with the consequences. *You made your bed...*

'Hold on,' he said to the dismayed face hovering below him, 'we got this.'

Collapsing to his knees, Talek set to work on the series of knots that held the rope firmly fixed to the makeshift gallows. The schizophrenic old bat had done a good job. Erin's neck would have snapped without the coarse material even threatening to spoil the party. The scuffling and grunting continued audibly over his shoulder. Sure, that Kieran guy was big, and no doubt the bookies would price him at odds-on, but evidently the woman was putting on a much better show than anyone would have expected, wowing the crowds as she had done all throughout her fraudulent life.

Attempting, and succeeding, to convince himself he couldn't care less, Talek continued to work at the knots. Pinching here, pulling there, resorting to biting when the slightest movement of cord seemed impossible. *She's still your gran*, a voice niggled at the back of his mind. *Family is family*. He pushed it away. The woman who had been so good to him during his existance had given up that right when she stood by as his mother was arrested; stood by while she was carted away like a frightened lamb on its first and final trip to the slaughterhouse.

The final knot gave. Pulling fast, unwinding, unwrapping, he let the rope fall. It hung from Erin's neck like the lead of an absconding dog.

'Let go,' he said, 'you'll be okay.'

'I can't,' she cried, her hair a raven veil as she lowered her head, searching for a floor that escaped her perception in the darkness.

'It's not very high. Just stay straight. It might hurt, but at least you'll land feet first. And watch your head.'

'Worried I might damage my beautiful face?' she joked, managing a laugh as out of place as a nun at an Ann Summers party.

'It'll still be the best face I've ever seen.'

Looking up at him Erin managed a smile, edgy and understandably so given the gravity of the situation, but beautiful in its defiance of the surroundings. Turning sincere, her fingers finally losing their grip on the slick stone, she said, 'I want you to tell me that when this is all over.'

'I will.'

She let go, dropping dismayingly from sight.

Shooting his head through the railings, Talek saw her lying in a heap in the middle of the road. 'You okay?'

'Brilliant,' she groaned. 'Absolutely bloody brilliant. Just forgot to land on my feet.'

Dragging herself wearily up, she craned her neck to take in the scene at the grizzly bridge's pinnacle. '*TALEK, LOOK OUT!*' she screamed, shrill and ear-splitting.

Deprived of time to react, Talek felt clawing hands on his back. Fabric cut into his fleshy neck as whoever it was pulled at his T-shirt. Spinning around against his will, he came face to face with the raging woman.

'What have you done, you stupid, *stupid* little boy?' Sheila snarled. Her breath heated his face, its bitter odour steaming in the cold air. 'She needs to pay. They *all* need to pay.'

How the hell had she gotten the better of the time-served brute? The crazy old woman clearly had the ferocity and guile of a Nile crocodile. Shifting her grasp, she gripped the front of Talek's shirt with one talon, wrapping the other around his throat.

'*USELESS!*' she roared, slamming his head back against the railing, '*JUST AS USELESS AS YER FUCKING MOTHER!*' *Slam.* '*I WAS DOING THIS FOR YOU!*' *Slam.* '*ALL FOR YOU, YOU UNGRATEFUL LITTLE SHIT!*'

A white world flashed through his mind as the back of his head struck the wood over and over.

Sheila leaned her face closer. Talek could taste the reek of brandy that oozed from her mouth. Lowering her voice, she snarled, 'And this is what I get for my troubles, huh? You try to get yer own grandmother killed.'

'I never___'

Slam.

'*LIAR!*' she bellowed.

Slam.

'*LIAR!*'

A deathly crack rang out, the force driven through his head splitting the weakened wooden rail in two. Posts *clunked* in echoes as they plummeted to the hard tongue of the archway. His safety barrier destroyed, Talek found his torso suspended in thin air. Even after the rush of events, fear never prevented him from realising he would land on his head when his lower back and legs joined the rest of him. His skull would split on the asphalt, his brains staining the dark surface a broth of red and grey. The end of the road at the end of the game.

It is a strange thing, the images that involuntarily run through our minds the moment before death takes us. Below his overhanging body a girl screamed a series of words, inaudible, inconsequential. Taking him back to a time where he considered the inscription engraved onto his own headstone, Talek envisaged the memorial once more: JUST ONE friend. Rest alone, sad little man.

With his vision clouding, the claws clamped around his throat constricting his windpipe and starving him of oxygen, he tried to smile. Drained of the last of his strength, the smile remained beneath the surface, unbeknown to anyone other than himself.

As the world around him faded into a myriad of undefined shapes and colours, he felt his body slump to the floor, the firm ground as icy as the touch of a hand from the grave. Straining his eyes upwards, struggling to grasp what was going on around him, a spectral figure passed overhead. Loose clothing fluttered and flailed about the apparition. As quickly as the unidentifiable vision appeared, it vanished.

Another scream rang out from below. *Below? I didn't go over.*

Arriving at his side a tall, hulking figure leaned over the wall atop Devil's Arch. With the miniscule amount of strength Talek had left, he rolled onto his knees. Leaning his head over the low wall, he gazed down. Kieran stood beside him, his breathing rapid, battling exhaustion.

With a mouth stuffed with silence, Talek stared open-mouthed. At the Arch's gruesome maw stood his girlfriend, the lower portion of her face buried behind trembling hands. Her blue eyes had blackened in the shadow of the demonic tunnel. At her feet, his gran lay on her side, partially swallowed by the jaws of Devil's Arch. Looking down at the creator of this bloodthirsty vendetta, the fight spent, her body broken and bent, the young boy fought not to heave again. Blood the colour of tar trickled from her upturned ear, following the contours of her prominent cheekbone, and disappearing at the corner of her mouth; the metallic haemoglobin flavour of thwarted revenge.

FIFTY-EIGHT

'To Cornwall, and a major development now in the cases of the deaths of two teenagers in Truro. Originally the subjects of two separate investigations, the cases of murdered, Jowan Collins, and fatal "hit and run" victim, Coby Angove, have been drawn together in a dramatic turn of events. The body of Jowan Collins was discovered in a river near Truro on the eighteenth of September. Devon and Cornwall Police launched an extensive search to ascertain the whereabouts of the boy's estranged father in connection with his disappearance, though new information suggests that he is no longer a suspect. The second young male, Coby Angove, was struck by a car on St. Clement's Hill on the night of October third, and later passed away as a result of his injuries. A third child – a friend of Angove's – who went missing on the night of the tragic collision, has been found safe and well, and is recovering at home with his family after the ordeal.

'A fifty-six-year-old woman is now under police guard at The Royal Cornwall Hospital after apparently sustaining a traumatic brain injury. The woman – who has yet to be named – is suspected of being responsible for both fatalities, and of the third youngster's disappearance. Local police have confirmed that the new information came to light in the aftermath of an altercation including a small number of people at Pencalenick, Truro, that took place last night. It was here that the woman sustained___'

Fetching up the remote, Talek silenced the television. Erin placed a comforting hand on his arm, dismayed to see him flinch away under her touch. Could he ever trust anyone again? Ever not be on constant guard?

'Sorry,' she said, 'I didn't mean to startle you.'

'It's not your fault,' Talek sighed, 'I just wasn't expecting it.'

There was a lengthy pause. Pulling her feet up onto the sofa, Erin nuzzled her head into the crook of his shoulder. Despite her taking a shower, the silken hair that usually carried Talek away to lazy summer days chilling in wildflower meadows – or perhaps more accurately, chilling in solemn churchyards – now harboured in its glassy black waters an undertow of Devil's Arch's stale, lurid breath. He rubbed his chin over the smooth strands, hoping to kick up its previous energising floral vitality.

'You must be missing your mum,' Erin spoke gently into the cotton fabric of his shirt.

'Yeah, a bit,' he said, 'but it's all good while I've got you with me.'

'You've got me for as long as you need me. I'm kinda hoping that's forever.'

Erin couldn't see his smile from where her eyes rested, but she could sense that it was there. After all the hardship they had been through – hardship nobody deserved, but especially people as young as themselves – she smiled too. Sitting quietly for a time, they took in the sounds of nature drifting through the open lounge window. Breeze tickled at leaves in the garden hedge, songbirds trilled and chattered. The road gave no sounds to spoil the couple's reverie. Inside, all was still. The clock ticked gently. No telltale stair creaked to warn of an intruder. For the first time ever, everything was perfect.

Erin was the first to break the perfect serenity, though her soothing tones blended in with fluidity. 'What time's she due home?' she asked, gliding one hand across his flat belly.

Talek let out a nervous yet contented breath, 'She's getting out about three. There's just some paperwork to finish up, apparently, before they let her go.'

'Nice to know they couldn't do that without her there,' she said sarcastically, 'seeing as how they dragged her in and kept her there when she'd done nothing wrong.

And she's sure she doesn't want my dad to pick her up? He doesn't mind.' Despite finding out some deeply upsetting home truths about who Connor is to her, and the terrible thing he had done behind Jessie's back, he would always be "dad" to her; nothing was going to break that unshakeable bond.

'Nah, she's good,' he said, placing his hand over hers and relaxing back into the plump cushions. 'She said she wants to get the bus. Probably killing time, scared to see me.'

'And when that drops her at Tresillian? It's not exactly door-to-door service in the sticks.'

'That's *her* problem.'

Erin chuckled. 'What a charmer you are.'

Soaking up each other's warmth in the peaceful, otherwise empty farmhouse, they continued to enjoy the tranquillity and privacy they were awarded, the world currently just made for two. It would only be for a short while longer, nonetheless a small portion of their conjoined hearts wished they could make this occasion last forever.

Just as their guard was let down in a moment of bliss, a gut-wrenching scream broke the tranquillity. Both teens laughed uneasily as the distant pheasant's rough cry split the air around them, bringing back fond memories of one of their earliest private interactions together, as they staked out the glorious relic sleeping in its cloak of emerald ivy next door.

Settling back down, Talek sparked a new topic of conversation, something that had been feasting on his mind like an unwavering brain-eating amoeba. 'How are your folks taking it? Your dad I mean, particularly, seeing as he's the one who told my… her about you being, you know.'

'Adopted? It's okay, you can say it. Just don't even think about calling me Billie! But yeah,' she sighed, 'I don't think he'll ever forgive himself for that. As for the way he told her, I don't think he's let that one slip to mum yet.' She shuddered against him. 'Hopefully he never does. That's probably the only way they'll ever make it through this.'

'And your brother?'

'Kieran? He's the new bloody hero.' Erin's body adjusted slightly as Talek noticeably tensed against her. 'Not like that. Not with me; you'll always hold that title as far as I'm concerned. It's just Dad. It's like he's treating him like the son he never had or something. Even had him stay over last night... *Hey, Kier, wanna stay for tea? Wanna stop over*, blah, blah, blah!'

'Seriously?' Talek sat up and turned his baffled face towards her. 'Why the hell's he being like that?'

'I dunno,' said Erin, conveying empathy in an attempt to reassure the recently acquainted, yet most important person in her life. 'I'm wondering if he's worried, you know, like if he lets Kieran out of his sight I might just run off with him. According to Kieran, that's what he wanted all along; rescue me from the life I had the shit luck to be born into. God knows what it was like for him, growing up with *her*.'

'And would you? Run off with him, I mean.'

'Not a chance!' She eyed him sincerely, straightening herself and cupping a flushed cheek in each hand. 'I'll tolerate him for their sakes, but for now that's as far as I can go. He may be the only person who cared about me when I was a baby, but there's a lot of troubled water still flowing under *that* bridge.'

'I can never forgive him,' Talek said. The seriousness in his tone hit like a physical blow to her stomach, though she wholeheartedly understood his position. 'He took my dad away. My whole shitty existence has been shaped by him.'

'I know,' she soothed, placing her lips gently upon his. Breaking after several heavenly seconds, she said, 'I wouldn't *ever* expect you to, and I'll never forgive him either.'

'Really?'

'Really!'

She instigated another kiss, praying that one day her boyfriend would have the confidence to kiss her unprompted.

'Your life's been filled with one tragedy after another,' said Erin, 'I know that. But I also know that from here on, it's going to be *sooo* much better, especially if you keep me around.'

She waited for what seemed an eternity for an answer, fearing that it may never come as he sat staring purposefully into her eyes, her mind, her soul.

Finally, at the point she could not hold her breath in suspense for a second longer, Talek spoke. 'Do you think… people as young as us…'

An engine whined softly outside as his mind toyed with the right words. Switching his focus to the window, unlit blue beacons from two police vehicles passed the front wall. They didn't stop. *On the way to the farm*, he assumed, to begin scouring every inch of the barn where his mother's Volvo was found with the hapless, bruised and terrorised Ethan curled up and tied up in the boot.

'Never mind,' he sighed, 'It's stupid.'

'I wouldn't expect anything else from you,' grinned Erin. 'Come on. Try me.'

'It's embarrassing!'

'Get over it, big man,' she said, laughing now, 'haven't we been through too much for coyness?'

Thinking it over, their short lives together playing out in a slideshow of flashbacks through his mind, he decided she was probably right. Also, '*Big* man?'

'Yeah, you're *Big* Man now.'

He smiled, absorbing the ego-inflating promotion to adulthood. 'Thanks. You know, it sounds stupid, but you always did make me feel much taller than I am... even though you tower over me.'

She smiled, clutching his hand tightly as her eyes welled.

'What I was gonna say, Talek resumed, 'is, does anyone who gets together at are age actually... make it? You know, stay together. Forever?'

Wrapping her arms around him, Erin squeezed, caressing him in an inescapable bearhug. 'They do,' she whispered, 'and we will, too. As long as I've got you, and you've got me, we don't need *anyone* else.'

She pulled back, allowing herself to tread water blissfully in the deep brown pools of his eyes. This time, the big man moved first. They kissed again, deeper, slower, open-mouthed.

Looking at him contentedly as their lips parted, she issued an instruction. 'Go on, big guy, choose a crappy DVD to watch. I'm gonna go up and get your duvet, then I'll see what booze that batshit old woman left for us. The next few hours are ours to do whatever the bloody hell we like.'

FIFTY-NINE

ABSOLUTION

The foyer was dreary and dispiriting, its clinical pale green walls and grey linoleum flooring soulless, impersonal. Sitting on a metal bench affixed to both the wall and floor – presumably for safety reasons, no way to hoist it up and thrust it at some smug officer's vexatious physiognomy. Its thin layer of blue cushioning did little to stop the ache as Tamsyn's bony bum cheeks cut in.

'Thanks, Spence,' the front counter officer said, taking a clear bag of belongings from a young man who vanished into the office behind as quickly as he'd materialised. 'Miss Lean,' the front of house attendant spoke without looking over. 'Your personal effects.'

Rising to her feet slowly, allowing the feeling to return to her glutes and the backs of her thighs, she strolled listlessly to the desk.

'Sign here.' He tapped an impatient finger on a document lying on the counter.

Taking a pen the officer slid across the desktop as though he would need to disinfect his hands if they made any contact with hers, Tamsyn checked the bag. The clothing she wore at the time of her arrest; her handbag, with a purse containing a small amount of cash that she had to assume was still inside; forms of identification… shoelaces (like she was going to hang herself with those). She scrawled by the scratched '*x*' and dropped the pen to the countertop.

'Okay,' he sighed, 'you're free to go.'

'Don't I get a lift?'

'Sorry, mam, not a service we offer. Train station's out front, or there's a bus stop on the main street.'

Tamsyn grabbed the bag. 'You drag me in here, when I'd done nothing wrong, might I add, and now I have to find my own way home?'

'That's right.' He raised a hand to the main exit, 'Have a nice day.'

Huffing, Tamsyn turned to the exit, fighting a tear, hiding her fragility. She would not give this jumped up ignoramus the satisfaction of witnessing her pain.

Outside the skies were grey, the pavements and roads dotted with few pedestrians and motors. Newquay in mid-October was not the buzzing hive of activity its summer counterpart became every year: tourists engulfing every square inch of the pavements, traffic at a standstill, and bar fronts a boisterous brawl of bare-chested young drinkers with dodgy T-shirt suntans, shorts and shades, blurting out their approval to the passing short skirts and indecorous bikini tops. Reaching the junction of Station Parade and Cliff Road, Tamsyn stopped and gazed at a run of shop windows to her right. *CAR PARTS & ACCESSORIES*, the bold signage on the glass proclaimed. Tamsyn rounded the corner, locating the entrance and heading in.

Inside was a treasure trove for the petrolhead. In general, Tamsyn had no interest in cars. The majority of the miscellany of items she glanced over were meaningless and confusing. But she couldn't help but think that Austin would have loved it here, gushing over all the shiny items, and stereos, steering wheels, pedals, whatever the hell *that* thing was in front of her. Totally in his element. He would have bored her to tears for hours in here, and she would have cherished every second of it.

But that was a long time ago. Another life. Another lost and previous version of herself.

Spotting a display of small semi-open-fronted bins, Tamsyn headed over. Jubilee clips; no. Bulbs; no. Dust caps; don't think so, somehow. More clips, their purpose unknown.

Aha, she thought, *about time*. Grabbing a pack of the longest she could find, she made a beeline for the till.

All paid up and hitting the stale town air again, Tamsyn crossed the road. Her concentration focused solely on her mission, she never bothered to check for oncoming vehicles. It didn't matter; God clearly intended for her to continue through her miserable life for as long as possible, a parasite depleting the world of valuable oxygen, with nothing left to offer in return. Safely across to the other side, she reached her next stop: a factory shop that should cater for the rest of her needs. After visiting the kitchen section, the stationery section, and the back to school clothing and accessories area, she coughed up. Placing her supplies in a rucksack she had just purchased along with them, she slung it over one shoulder and cleared out.

A fine mizzle had descended over the melancholy streets and buildings of the summer town by the time Tamsyn made it to the nearest bus stop. Sweating through humidity, the air pressure played on her nerves, a tension headache spreading from her temples, crushing her brain, clouding her vision. As a person who devoutly avoided this location on any normal occasion, Tamsyn could not even hazard a guess as to where she may find a pharmacy.

No bother. She would just wait until she got to Truro. That was home, with the familiar streets on which she had grown up and knew like the back of her hand. Until then, the pain was no worse than anything she had already been forced to endure.

A double-decker bus rolled towards her. Slowing up, the brakes gave an airy hiss as the stinky diesel drew to a stop.

'Single to Truro, please,' she said as she climbed aboard, rifling through the loose change in her purse.

Handing over the cash, she took the ticket spat out by a machine at the driver's side and headed to one of the vacant seats on the lower deck. Fortuitously, the often crammed public transport service was as dead as the town Tamsyn was leaving behind. Peace and quiet would not wash her skin of the frightful experiences bestowed upon her by her mother, but it may help the pain in her head. As the bus trundled through quaint villages and lush open countryside, made mournful by a callous, heavy sky, she pondered over just how the woman who carried her for nine months, brought her into the world and nurtured her into adulthood, could with vicious intent set about bringing such an odious final chapter to her already blighted life. Her own kin. Her mother's contaminated blood coursing through her system.

What poison had the deranged, doting grandmother managed to fill Talek's head with while the boy's mother rotted in incarceration? The thought filled Tamsyn with dread. How appalling the eventual reunion was sure to be.

Maybe she was wrong. Maybe learning about his gran's ruthless actions would make it easier. So many maybes. Maybe not finding out would be the simplest solution. *I mean, what kind of mother am I anyway? I couldn't even protect him from his own family.*

That could change… maybe. *Maybe, maybe, bloody maybe!*

Tamsyn tried to soak in the beauty of her home county, all the while its serenity dissolving as Chopin's Funeral March played on repeat in her head – the music she would have to face whilst attempting to repair the damage caused by the incomprehensible actions of a venomous serpent, hunting through the stricken nest of Scoan's Cottage. Austin had left what Tamsyn believed to be an unfillable void, but in the aftermath, Sheila had now proved her wrong. The twisted witch had successfully managed to fill that void with shit. Shit piled upon shit, piled upon shit.

Grinding to a halt, the automatic doors of the double-decker flapped open stutteringly. The few remaining travellers clambered through the isle, disembarking at Truro's main station. Tamsyn followed lethargically, the last to vacate the vehicle. She took in a breath of oppressive city air. Fish and chips, pasties, and pungent yeasty odours from the ale house, mingled with diesel fumes as busses sat idling. The cocktail of odours left a bitter taste. Seagulls yelped loudly from the piazza, begging for castoffs from alfresco diners and fighting over the scraps. The damp mist that Tamsyn had breathed in earlier had not made it as far as her hometown, and through thick, muggy air she walked to her intended destination, the ache in her head growing into a crushing thud. Luckily, the nearby convenience store would supply what her brain demanded.

Whether unready or unwilling to face her son – the jury still out on how to convey what she needed him to understand – she walked on, allowing her feet to do the talking. Wandering semiconsciously, she headed down New Bridge Street, taking a right into an alleyway leading to the river walk. On a slabbed pathway, Tamsyn strolled lazily through the gardens of Garras Wharf, turning her face to the floor as a group of the city's homeless population goofed about drinking beer from large, gold cans, laughing in raised voices. By and large they lacked interest in the passer-by, paying her no mind. Nevertheless, Tamsyn's tight frame slumped in relief as she made it past the small crowd and disappeared down a set of steps leading to the subway.

Climbing another set of steps, this time on the opposite side of the Morlaix Avenue carriageway, Tamsyn stopped to lean against a cool metal railing. She stared aimlessly into murky waters of Truro River below, the nondescript brown reflecting her mood. Grumbling morosely, her stomach demanded food. Despite its greedy exigencies, even the slightest hint of an appetite remained absent. She had turned down breakfast at the police station (or as she had derisively began to refer to it, the Hotel California), unable to comprehend being looked after and catered for by the same establishment that held her against her will. She was done with the law; she had checked out later than she'd liked, but she did manage to leave. From now on, the fuzz could go fuck themselves.

Finally renewed of the strength to go on, Tamsyn hit the pavement, following the route to Trafalgar Roundabout. Arriving moments later at the foot of St. Clement's Hill, she turned a blind eye to the ugly, concrete mass of the city's police station. Beginning the slow ascent, focusing on the cracked tar at her feet, her shoe struck a steel object. A black metal leg rose to a sign of vibrant reflective blue. In the foreground of the blue blanket, a mottled silvery-white inscription compelled Tamsyn to bolt for the rising tangle of weeds and brambles at her side, heaving up fetid gas from her empty stomach.

POLICE ACCIDENT.

Her legs weakened, knees faltering and forcing her to grab at the hedge to keep from falling. Thorny brambles pierced the soft padding of her palm, the resulting pain both harsh and sweet. A passing car slowed, the passenger window rolling down for the driver to call across and offer their assistance. With her back to the road, Tamsyn waved a dismissive hand. The car pulled away, leaving her on her own once more, just as she had hoped would be the case.

Gaining a touch of self-control and washing the image of the sickening bold print from her mind as a searing shower cleanses the body of the grimy rigours of life, she urged herself to stand upright. Leaving the warning sign to dwindle away behind her, banishing it to her past, Tamsyn continued her climb. City buildings, including its dominant cathedral with its ornate stone carvings, grew smaller each time she glanced over her shoulder, fading to resemble nothing more than a scale model. With each and every step, the growing distance worked toward the gratifying conclusion of removing her from society.

After a tiresome uphill slog, the ground levelled. Tamsyn's taut calf muscles were finally awarded the reprieve they had been crying out for in burning wails. She passed the rugby club, blanking its open, empty field as she considered the next establishment on her route. A deep dread filled her head at the thought of the numerous, scattered buildings of her son's school, soon to encroach on her eyeline. Would he be there today? Probably not. The young man would likely be at home, awaiting her return. Whether he waited eagerly or nervously, the tortured woman could not predict. Doubtlessly, he'd be confused about how to greet his mother, of how to start a conversation that no dependent young person should ever have to face.

You can't do this, teased the devil on one shoulder. *One day at a time*, encouraged the less convincing opposing angelic force.

Tamsyn checked her watch. Any time now kids would breach those exits like a charging army. Facing the floor, she redoubled her efforts, determined to be beyond the many watching windows of Clement Grove Secondary before the exodus. Passing at a brisk pace, Tamsyn did not so much as glance at the premises as she trekked towards the adjoining back lane, nigh on fifteen years after her last expedition on its beguiling turf.

Precisely a quarter of an hour later, she was there. Unwelcoming, repulsive in its ancient splendour, Devil's

Arch yawned under a mishmash of rock and mortar. Intrados of black and grey stonework hung suspended in the air, the abhorrent teeth of some unspeakable prehistoric beast waiting to chomp down on any unsuspecting prey. Tamsyn stood at its lip, listening for Austin, hearing a low moan travel through its fetid throat: A haunting wind? The tortured cry of its numerous victims? Tamsyn could not say for sure.

Turning to her side, she swung the loose bag strap over her unburdened shoulder and plunged her hands into the vegetation clinging to a towering hedge at the Arch's opening like some cult hero's loyal band of groupies. Once again, Tamsyn savoured the bittersweet bite of thorns. She kicked the toe of one shoe at the growth, establishing a firm foothold, before pushing herself from the asphalt with the other. It was a struggle, and a joyous one at that. Within a couple of minutes Tamsyn conquered the summit of her age-old adversary.

Removing the rucksack, the victor of this most recent battle sank onto gravelly ground. Resting her back against cool, supportive rock, she opened her bag and rummaged through its contents, removing a freshly purchased A4 notepad and ballpoint pen. A foreboding silence struck under the sky of menacingly hovering thunderheads. Despite the array of surrounding trees, bracken, and tangled foliage, a haven for wildlife to thrive in, there came no sound other than the wind, and whatever sullen conversation Devil's Arch had to offer. No rodents scurried. No crows cried their raucous prophecies. No songbirds countered with a reassuring melody.

Tamsyn's mind ran through everything she needed to say to her son. Things that may prove easier to convey on paper, rather than from her own tormented tongue spewing them out and fumbling over the correct words as she endeavoured to avoid eye contact with the impeccant child. Tapping the pen against her top lip in deliberation, low revving engine noises drifted up from the depths of the road. One. Two. Three cars, all coming from the direction of Truro: parents who had collected their children from school and now took the shortcut home to Tresillian, Ladock, Probus, and other outlying villages and hamlets serviced by the busier A390 (though as to why anyone would voluntarily opt to take this diabolical rat run, Tamsyn could not wrap her head around).

As the first of the engines echoed under the old bridge, the stone vibrating gently through her body, Tamsyn leaned her head back against the biting stone and closed her eyes. Austin's words from so long ago, *Then you'll know not to talk when we go under there,* replayed in her head. His grinning face, how he eyed her through the gloom, plotting, teasing. She wondered if the children in the cars below had been raised on the same cautionary tales of Devil's Arch as her own generation, and countless generations before. Were they silently casting coaxing glances at their fellow passengers, or holding their breath, anxiously awaiting unhindered daylight to spare them of Satan's death grip?

Further handfuls of commuters had passed through the Arch's bowels as Tamsyn sat lost in reflection, the end of her pen chewed and still no words forming on the lined pages on her lap. Overhead, rustling leaves had transformed from deep browns and reds into black, batlike shadows, swooshing, dancing, falling into the abyss. Aluminium clouds deepened to steels, to charcoals, and eventually to an indeterminable blanket of bituminous pitch. Senses attuning to the deepening gloom, her auditory perception heightened, and she soaked in the sounds of the evening. Jittery wings fluttered as crows made themselves comfortable for the night in lofty nests, their dark beaks still silent. In the black hole below, saliva dripped from the calloused roof of the demon's mouth, hitting the floor in reverberating pitter-patters. Drifting upwards on a current of humid air, Austin's voice serenaded her with words of encouragement, orchestrating aspects of the profound correspondence his former lover was yet to pen.

Fishing through her rucksack again, Tamsyn felt the cold steel barrel of a torch. She pulled it free, diving back in to search for the pack of batteries she had picked up at the same time. She had little idea that these were a necessary purchase on her visit to the factory shop – just one of those things on the counter to help part compulsive spenders of a few extra pennies at the till… *while you're here, can we interest you in…* – but now, thanks to her dithering, she was pleased that she'd snatched them up. Navigating with her fingers, rather than her temporarily blinded eyes, Tamsyn unscrewed the torches base, slid a plastic cartridge from within, and inserted three triple *A* batteries. After reassembling the pieces, she clicked it into life. Its sudden brilliance on the white paper assaulted her darkness-acclimatised retinas. Clicking the button twice more, the harsh light dimmed to a bearable glow. Tamsyn clamped the cylindrical body between her teeth, readied her pen once more, and listened intently to the voice below. Austin would help her assemble his previous ramblings into the coherent sentences she'd struggled to grasp in her anxious disposition.

An hour passed with the rapidity of a dreamless sleep. No vehicles had traversed the gateway to hell for an indeterminate length of time. Late evening dew glistened on the bordering stone walls at the torch beam's peripheral. Tamsyn's clothing grew heavy with moisture from the humid twilight air.

Tearing out the completed pages of untidy script – a catalogue of her deepest, most regretful thoughts – she folded along their centre and placed them into her rucksack, along with her pad and pen. Slowly, solemnly, she stood and stretched, the lifeblood returning to her lower limbs in dull, aching throbs. Hitching the bag onto her back, Tamsyn took the few short steps to the hedge from which she had gained access to the Arch's monstrous head. Grabbing at the fence's top railing for support, she noticed for the first time the horrific, telltale break at its centre. Nauseousness suddenly returning, she turned her back on the splintered wood, focusing instead on the road below before scrabbling down through the vines and brambly tendrils.

Upon reaching terra firma, she steeled herself to face Devil's Arch. On one side of the gaping maw, what was left of Tamsyn Lean… on the other side, several miles distant, home, family. Her shoes scrunched on road debris as she shuffled from one foot to the other, eyeing the bloodthirsty tunnel in all its terrifying splendour.

'I'm not afraid of you,' she said, her timid tones failing to project the defiance she was aspiring to achieve.

The Arch stared back impassively, whispering sweet nothings on the through-flowing breeze.

Stepping forward, fearful yet determined, Tamsyn thumbed the torch back to life. She scanned the walls to either side. Blacks and browns, greys and greens met her gaze, the irregular, crumbling stone slick with damp. The roof carried the same uneven blend of shapes, colours, and moisture, like she was stepping into an old copper mine in a bygone century. Water particles accumulated above, swelling until they could hold on no longer. Cool and slimy they fell, in her hair, on her shoulders, another burden to carry. Others patted heavily at her feet. Underneath the vaulted ceiling the plummeting drops sounded more like a spitting log fire than splattering liquid. Tamsyn thought this was apt, like the antagonistic Arch was teasing her about one fateful night in previous chapter that she'd played the hardest part in: the part of the survivor.

Stopping at the point she judged to be where she sat soon after the turn of the new millennium, Tamsyn took a swallow of the cavern's unsavoury breath. Removing her bag, her fingers searched for the wall. Running their tips down its slippery surface, she pressed her back against stone, sliding down its niggling rises and falls.

Recalling Austin's words, the childlike playfulness of his smile, Tamsyn closed her eyes, embracing the past for just a few precious moments, absorbing it through her skin like a hot oil massage. She sensed her lover's presence as if he were flesh and bone resurrected, placing his hand on hers, assuring her with soothing, liquid tones – *everything will be okay*. Her heart thumped triumphantly, blood surging to her brain intoxicatingly as his warm skin caressed hers – thriving, mortal skin, not the expected icy, postmortal touch from beyond the grave.

She opened her eyes and reached for her rucksack. Pulling out the letter to her son, she directed the torch beam to the scribbled text. Blotches had smudged the letters in places, forming inky blots of varying sizes, the smaller from evening dew, the larger from her own tears. Breathing deeply again, pungent, stale air sinking to the bottom of her lungs, she began to read the note back. It had to be right. Had to be sincere and fitting.

Dear Talek,

I would dearly have liked to have the strength to say these things to your face, and in a perfect world, I would have. But few know better than you and I that this world is not perfect. If I had sat before you, I fear I would lack the courage to look into your beautiful eyes and tell you everything you need to know, the truths you deserve to hear. And to apologise for all the unspeakable things I have brought upon your short life.

I need to start at the beginning, which is the night your father was taken from me. His name was Austin, and he was the most wonderful man I'd ever met. I was deeply in love with him. The future would have been so different had the evil world we live in not seen fit to rob me of him. His parting gift to me, was you, though I spent the rest of my life in denial. Looking into your face, all I could see was Austin, every feature you possess in a mini replica. I existed in two separate worlds: one where I wrapped you in cotton wool, protecting you from the monsters outside; and one where I saw you as a cruel reminder of all that I had lost.

I was wrong to think the latter, I know that. But nothing I can ever do will get those years back. Nothing can make up for the way I treated you, the toxic mixture of devotion and despise. I was broken. You are everything to me, all I have left, and I hope one day you can find it in yourself to forgive me.

I have spent too many years hiding things from you. Terrible things. I tried all manner of ways to justify this to myself, convincing myself that it was for your own good. I realise now that it was all from a selfish need to close the door on the past, in a way that could only serve me. So here it is, another admission I should have made long ago.

When I was pregnant with you, I suffered a miscarriage. I believed, and in all honesty hoped, that that would be the end of it; that God was sparing me of a duty I didn't believe I could perform in my state. I never considered at the time that I might be carrying twins – another cruel twist of fate I had to endure. I lost a daughter, and you a sister. I was going to name her Delilah. Instead, I buried her tiny body in an unmarked grave within Saint Cohan's Church. She rests in a small alcove at the wall to the left. It was me you saw at night. Maybe now that it's not a secret, you could visit her, too. I'm sure she would like that. To have her brother looking out for her, to read her stories.

For many years I have put on a religious front. The truth is, I stopped believing a long time ago. If there was a God, he would have taken you, too. You could have spent the rest of eternity with Delilah, looked after her better than I ever could, and you both would have been spared of being raised by a broken mother who gave up on everything. Yet when I look at you now, at the fine human being you've grown into, I know you were meant to be. You are a true blessing to anyone you choose to share your life with.

Which brings me to another confession. Your father's parents. I guess, after losing the will to contact them when they flew your dad back to the Dominican Republic — where they originally moved over from — I just never got around to telling them they had a grandson. On the top shelf of my wardrobe there's a shoebox. In it, you'll find their address. Use this information for whatever means you like, though I'm certain they'd be overjoyed to hear from you, to learn of their son's existence continuing through you. The box also contains photos of your daddy. I'm sure you'll see why I sometimes found it so hard to look at you, though now seeing you would be the greatest feeling of all.

Yes, I could have told you about the shoebox to your face, but I guess by now you know why I didn't.

I am a terrible person for holding these things from you. A terrible mother, and one that didn't deserve the infant I was gifted. I owed it to you to tell you sooner about your father, your twin sister, of how you came to be. In this Godless world I can never get that time back. For either of us. Your grandmother is evil, and between us we have destroyed your childhood. But not your future! I'm so pleased that you found Erin. Her bloodline does not determine who she is today, and I know you're strong enough not to let it get in the way of tomorrow. I wholeheartedly hope she'll be your rock, like your father was mine, but you don't need my mother, or me, to turn your fortunes around.

Just know that, despite the dismissive actions I have unfairly thrown your way over the years, Mummy loves you very much. Be brave and lead the best life you can. You're a wonderful young man, too precious for this planet, but promise me you'll see it out. Have kids, grow old, and be happy.

Mum
xx

Refolding her sentimental truths, Tamsyn rested the note on her lap. From her rucksack she pulled out a roll of green plastic food bags, the cable ties from the motor store, two boxes of paracetamol tablets, and a bottle of still water. She ripped the first bag from the roll and flared it out in the gloomy air, its echo passing out from the Arch and into the night. Picking up the torch and training the beam around and above, she searched for Austin. All that greeted her were the narrow grotesque walls and ceiling that had helped confine him, bringing about his tragic demise.

Popping the entire contents of one blister pack into a shaking palm, she whispered, 'This is for you, my love.'

She scooped the pills into her mouth, almost choking on the excessive amount, and swallowed them with half a bottle of water. The same process was carried out with the second pack.

Not planning on a half job – this was no cry for help – Tamsyn threaded a handful of the cable ties together forming a lethal python, a constrictor in need of something to wrap its muscular huntress' body around. She lifted the bloated plastic bag. Sliding it down over her hair, her face, she pulled it in at her neck. Wrapping the chain of ties around its downturned opening, Tamsyn zipped them tight, ensuring that she left no room for air or error.

The oxygen level reduced. Breathing became laborious. The overdose of pain killers dizzied her head and fogged her perception. Condensation built on the inner face of the shrinking plastic, banishing the outside world and all its ills in an ethereal mist.

As the darkened archway consumed the last earthly breaths of its latest sacrificial offering, Tamsyn felt a smile forming on her lips; her first genuinely contented smile in her recent memory.

In the stillness of the Pencalenick back lane, the condemning, cavernous maw of Devil's Arch smiled with her.

THE END

Acknowledgements

Firstly, I would like to thank my readers; without you, what would be the point? Although I get serious joy from realising just what dastardly deeds my characters are capable of, knowing that I'm not the only one who wants to follow them to the bitter end is huge, so thank you all.

My thanks are also extended to my wife and children – the ones who have to put up with my ever changing mood on a daily (or often in the blinking of an eye) basis, from being so high I radge about like a macaque on crack, to being *that guy* that screams obscenities and punches his own head, rather than leaving fist-shaped cavities in our plasterboard walls.

And my family, the ones who keep asking *'When's yer new book gonna be ready?'*... There are too many to name individually, but Muvver and favver, you're the biggest culprits, and I have to tell you guys, that really helps to keep me going!

I'm must also thank my Auntie Susie, for warping my mind with such horrific films and books when I was just a yonker. P.S. I "borrowed" *IT* from you years ago, and I don't think I ever gave it back.

And lastly, to my English lecturer, Becky. Always to Becky, for the self-belief you instilled in me, and the way you delivered the power of the written word and made each lesson something to cherish. The world lost some of its sparkle when you were cruelly taken from us too early. The next one's for you.

Yeghes da! poblow.

About the Author

Kevin Knuckey (or Knuckey Fried Chicken, Jake the Peg, Knuckle Sandwich, Five-Knuckle Shuffle – take your pick) was born in Cornwall and raised on gory horror films and savage novels from an inappropriately tender age, *Horror Express* and *Salem's Lot* being particularly esteemed movie introductions for a yonker. The first book he read cover-to-cover: *The Jungle Book* (Disney's illustrated rendition). The second: Stephen King's *The Shining*.

Inspired whilst working as a primary school teaching assistant, he began to plot his first children's book, though after pulling himself aside and having a serious chat with himself, Kevin decided the targeted market was not ready for an old folk's home that processed its residents and served them through the sinister owner's freshest business venture, Old Biddy's Burgers.

Experiencing the physical deterioration that comes with Hereditary motor and sensory neuropathy, however (don't be fooled by the hereditary part, this Kernewek kid's a true anomaly), Kevin has streamlined his attention, remaining true(ish) to the genre he was born into and thrives in, for an age-appropriate audience. Keeping the unforgiving Cornish coast and bleak countryside at the heart of his writing, Kevin's debut novel – the psychological thriller *Hell's Mouth* (2022) – sees him utilise his twisted nature and unsettling interest in the macabre, whilst his characters act out all of their darkest fantasies within the mind-bending and brutal realms of human capability.

Printed in Great Britain
by Amazon